PROPERTY OF

THAT, EXCEPTING IN RARE CASES, YOU MIGHT AS WELL SEND TO THE FOUNDLING HOSPITAL AND BORROW A BABY AS TO BORROW A BOOK WITH THE IDEA OF ITS BEING ANY GREAT SATISFACTION. WE LIKE A BABY IN OUR CRADLE, BUT PREFER THAT ONE WHICH BELONGS TO THE HOUSEHOLD. WE LIKE A BOOK, BUT WANT TO FEEL IT IS OURS. WE NEVER YET GOT ANY ADVANTAGE FROM A BORROWED BOOK. WE HOPE THOSE NEVER REAPED ANY PROFIT FROM THE BOOKS THEY BORROWED FROM US, BUT NEVER RETURNED.—

      *   ❖   *

DON'T WORRY YOUR FRIENDS BY BORROWING THIS BOOK. BUY ONE.

    *   *   *

FOR · SALE · BY · ALL · BOOK · DEALERS
OR BY MAIL ON RECEIPT OF PRICE
BY PUBLISHER.

PESCHEL PRESS ~ P.O. BOX 132 ~ HERSHEY, PA 17033 ~ EMAIL: BPESCHEL@GMAIL.COM ~ WWW.PESCHELPRESS.COM

D1566950

The
Complete,
Annotated
Whose Body?

THE
COMPLETE,
ANNOTATED
WHOSE BODY?

DOROTHY L. SAYERS

NOTES AND ANNOTATIONS
BILL PESCHEL

PESCHEL PRESS ~ HERSHEY, PA.

Cover design by Bill Peschel.

Cover art: Modified from "The Anatomy Lesson of Dr. Joan Deyman" by Rembrandt.

www.peschelpress.com

ISBN-13: 978-1-950347-00-1

ISBN-10: 1-950347-00-1

Third edition: June 2019

TO TERESA,

MY ACUSHLA

NOTES TO THE READER

"The Complete, Annotated Whose Body?" contains features the reader should be aware of.

Footnotes: The footnotes come from the two authors. Sayers' four footnotes are included in the body of the text. The footnotes are supplied by Bill Peschel and serve several functions:

Word definitions: To figure out what words to define, several people of various ages read "Whose Body?" and marked the words they did not understand. They noted cultural and literary references, words understandable to British readers but not Americans (jumper, motor-lorry, finding her range) and words that might seem obvious to some readers, but not to others. What color is primrose? What's claret? What is a Niagara? The annotator went through the suggestions and tried to define the truly rare or unusual words without overloading the text.

Interpretations: Explanations are provided of certain subjects for readers who are unfamiliar with, for example, the subtleties of England's social classes, the inquest system, and pounds and pence.

Biblical quotations: All excerpts are drawn from the King James Version.

Essays: In the back of the book are essays about various aspects of the novel, Lord Peter and Dorothy L. Sayers. They are not necessary to understand the story, but they can help deepen your enjoyment of the novel.

About this edition: This edition was transcribed by John Mark Ockerbloom and Mary Mark Ockerbloom from the first edition published in the U.S. by Boni and Liveright in 1923. The text can be found at http://digital.library.upenn.edu/women/sayers/body/whose-body.html. The U.S. copyright for this edition expired in 1951, when copyright was not renewed as required in the 28th year. Since this book was first published in the U.S., the copyright is not eligible for GATT restoration. Sayers made changes to the novel in subsequent editions, and some of them have been included.

And now, a personal request.

If you like this book: Tell your friends about it, or post a review on your social networking sites or the website where you bought this book. Word of mouth can spur sales, help me support my family and encourage me to spend more time writing! Thank you.

Bill Peschel

CONTENTS

(Note: The chapter headings were added by the editor to aid the reader.)

1. Lord Peter's flat   2. Hyde Park   3. Green Park
4. Buckingham Palace   5. St. James Park   6. Piccadilly Circus
7. Harley Street   8. Goodge Street   9. Great Ormond
    10. St. Pancras Station   11. Scotland Yard (in 1922)

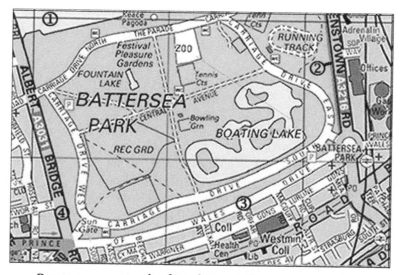

Battersea area, south of Lord Peter's flat
1. River Thames   2. Queenstown Road
3. Prince of Wales Road   4. Albert Bridge Road

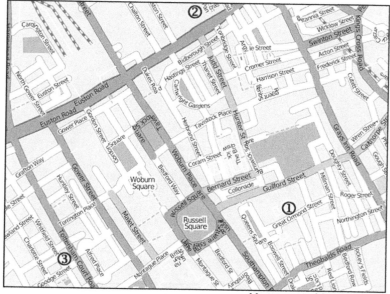

Map courtesy of OpenStreetMap

1. Great Ormond Street, where Police-Inspector Parker lives
2. St. Pancras Station, where Mr. Thipps checked his bag
3. Goodge Street, where Mr. Thipps ended up after the raid

To M. J.[1]

Dear Jim:
This book is your fault. If it had not
been for your brutal insistence, Lord
Peter would never have staggered
through to the end of this enquiry.
Pray consider that he thanks you with
his accustomed suavity.

Yours ever,
D.L.S.

---

[1] .J. Muriel "Jim Jaeger, a longtime friend of Sayers who encouraged her to write
the novel.

CHAPTER I

O H, DAMN!" SAID LORD PETER Wimsey at Piccadilly Circus.[1] "Hi, driver!"

The taxi man, irritated at receiving this appeal while negotiating the intricacies of turning into Lower Regent Street across the route of a 19 'bus, a 38-B[2] and a bicycle, bent an unwilling ear.

"I've left the catalogue[3] behind," said Lord Peter deprecatingly, "uncommonly careless of me. D'you mind puttin' back to where we came from?"

"To the Savile Club,[4] sir?

---

[1] A major road junction in London's West End where Piccadilly Road intersects with Regent and Glasshouse streets, Shaftesbury Avenue and Leicester (pronounced Lester) Square. The American equivalent would be Times Square in New York City. The word circus is derived from the Latin word meaning "circle."

[2] The names of two London bus routes. The 'bus is a shortened form of the word omnibus. See the essay "Omnibus: One Vehicle's Journey Through Linguistics."

[3] Lord Peter is heading to an auction of rare books. High-end auction houses issue catalogues describing their offerings in detail.

[4] A club for gentlemen, not to be confused with today's "gentlemen's clubs" which are strip clubs with a fig leaf of respectability. Clubs such as the Savile, Boodle's (founded in 1762) and White's (founded in 1693) were once part of a grand tradition in which upper-class gentlemen would gather to dine, drink, network and, occasionally, die in the smoking room (see "The Unpleasantness at the Bellona Club"). During the 20th century, many clubs were forced to merge or close as the number of wealthy men able to support such establishments declined.

The Savile Club was established in 1868 at Trafalgar Square. Its membership consists of a mix of professionals such as scientists, doctors and

"No—110 Piccadilly[5]—just beyond—thank you."

"Thought you was in a hurry," said the man, overcome with a sense of injury.

"I'm afraid it's an awkward place to turn in," said Lord Peter, answering the thought rather than the words. His long, amiable face looked as if it had generated spontaneously from his top hat, as white maggots breed from Gorgonzola.[6]

The taxi, under the severe eye of a policeman, revolved by slow jerks, with a noise like the grinding of teeth.

The block of new, perfect and expensive flats[7] in which Lord Peter dwelt upon the second floor, stood directly opposite the Green Park,[8] in a spot for many years occupied by the skeleton of a frustrate commercial enterprise. As Lord Peter let himself in he heard his man's voice in the library, uplifted in that throttled

---

lawyers, and artists such as actors, composers and writers. Between 1882 and 1927, it was located at 107 Piccadilly, almost next door to Lord Peter's flat, hence the cab driver's confusion. It is now at 69 Brook Street in Mayfair.

[5] Sayers housed Lord Peter on a busy street in one of the best neighborhoods in central London. A short stroll west of his home is Hyde Park. Across the street is Green Park, bounded on its south side by Buckingham Palace, and to its east the government seat at Whitehall and the Thames. Lord Peter also lives a short cab ride west of the nightlife district in the West End.

[6] Some cheeses, including a type of gorgonzola, can be made with the help of small white worms, the "maggots" in Sayers' description. For example, a Sardinian sheep milk cheese called casu marzu is fermented by introducing the eggs of the cheese fly. The eggs hatch and the larvae eat the cheese and break down its fats in the digestive system. Of course, you have to eat the cheese while the maggots are still alive. Eating it with decaying maggots would be gross.

This is the first description we get of Lord Peter, and it's not an attractive one. Sayers sets him apart from the popular fictional detectives of her time, such as Sherlock Holmes, who debuted in 1887, and Agatha Christie's Hercule Poirot (1920). He's less heroic and more comical, almost kin to P.G. Wodehouse's Bertie Wooster, who first appeared in 1917. Certainly, Sherlock Holmes would *never* burble about finding a body in the bath.

[7] An apartment on a single floor of a building. Derived either from the Scots *flet*, meaning the inner part of the house, or the Old English word for a floor or dwelling.

[8] A 47-acre park in London consisting of wooded meadows and paths. It is one of eight Royal Parks owned and run by the Crown, including Hyde, St. James' and Greenwich Park. Some were former hunting grounds and many have bandstands and open-air stages where regular free concerts and plays are held.

stridency[9] peculiar to well-trained persons using the telephone.

"I believe that's his lordship just coming in again—if your Grace would kindly hold the line a moment."

"What is it, Bunter?"

"Her Grace has just called up from Denver,[10] my lord. I was just saying your lordship had gone to the sale when I heard your lordship's latchkey."[11]

"Thanks," said Lord Peter; "and you might find me my catalogue, would you? I think I must have left it in my bedroom, or on the desk."

He sat down to the telephone with an air of leisurely courtesy, as though it were an acquaintance dropped in for a chat.

"Hullo, Mother—that you?"

"Oh, there you are, dear," replied the voice of the Dowager Duchess.[12] "I was afraid I'd just missed you."

"Well, you had, as a matter of fact. I'd just started off to Brocklebury's sale to pick up a book or two, but I had to come back for the catalogue. What's up?"

"Such a quaint thing," said the Duchess. "I thought I'd tell you. You know little Mr. Thipps?"

"Thipps?" said Lord Peter. "Thipps? Oh, yes, the little architect man who's doing the church roof. Yes. What about him?"

"Mrs. Throgmorton's just been in, in quite a state of mind."

"Sorry, Mother, I can't hear. Mrs. Who?"

"Throgmorton—Throgmorton—the vicar's wife."

"Oh, Throgmorton, yes?"

"Mr. Thipps rang them up this morning. It was his day to come down, you know."

"Yes?"

"He rang them up to say he couldn't. He was so upset, poor little man. He'd found a dead body in his bath."

---

[9] *Throttled.* Strangled or choked. *Stridency.* A harsh, shrill or discordant sound.

[10] A village in the county of Norfolk, a coastal area northeast of London. Duke's Denver, Lord Peter's family seat, is located several miles east of the village.

[11] A key used to open a lock on an outside door.

[12] A *dowager* is a woman who possesses a dower, or life interest in her deceased husband's property. A *duchess* is the wife of a duke. The current Duke of Denver is Lord Peter's eldest brother, Gerald.

"Sorry, Mother, I can't hear; found what, where?"

"A dead body, dear, in his bath."

"What?—no, no, we haven't finished. Please don't cut us off. Hullo! Hullo! Is that you, Mother? Hullo!—Mother!—Oh, yes—sorry, the girl was trying to cut us off.[13] What sort of body?"

"A dead man, dear, with nothing on but a pair of pince-nez.[14] Mrs. Throgmorton positively blushed when she was telling me. I'm afraid people do get a little narrow-minded in country vicarages."[15]

"Well, it sounds a bit unusual. Was it anybody he knew?"

"No, dear, I don't think so, but, of course, he couldn't give her many details. She said he sounded quite distracted. He's such a respectable little man—and having the police in the house and so on, really worried him."

"Poor little Thipps! Uncommonly awkward for him. Let's see, he lives in Battersea,[16] doesn't he?"

"Yes, dear; 59 Queen Caroline Mansions; opposite the Park.[17] That big block just around the corner from the Hospital. I thought

---

[13] Phone calls were timed so that you could talk for three minutes before incurring an additional charge. Since an operator, who connects callers by plugging wires into a board, might be monitoring several conversations at the same time, mix-ups could cause calls to be prematurely terminated.

[14] A pair of glasses consisting of two lenses connected by a metal bridge, sometimes with a string attached that is looped around the neck or a vest button. The word is derived from the French *pincer*, to pinch, and *nez*, nose.

[15] A vicar is the title given to a parish priest. In the Anglican Church, England is divided into parishes and grouped into dioceses, each overseen by a bishop. Depending on who appointed him and how he is paid, the priest of the parish could be called a rector, vicar, curate (a sort of assistant to the parish priest) or even a perpetual curate (who acts as a parish priest but over a small parish). The vicarage, therefore, is the home of the vicar. It doesn't mean that a rector lives in a rectorage. He lives in a rectory.

[16] A district on the south side of the Thames, near the center of the city.

[17] *Battersea Park.* A 200-acre green space opened in 1858 that's home to a children's zoo and the London Peace Pagoda. It is bounded on the north by the River Thames, the east by Queenstown Road, the south by Prince of Wales Drive, and the west by Albert Bridge Road.

Queen Caroline Mansions. On Prince of Wales Drive are buildings with names such as Park Mansions, Primrose Mansions and Prince of Wales Drive Mansions, that are rented as apartments. Queen Caroline Mansions doesn't exist, but it could fit in very nicely among them.

perhaps you'd like to run round and see him and ask if there's anything we can do. I always thought him a nice little man."

"Oh, quite," said Lord Peter, grinning at the telephone. The Duchess was always of the greatest assistance to his hobby of criminal investigation, though she never alluded to it, and maintained a polite fiction of its non-existence.

"What time did it happen, Mother?"

"I think he found it early this morning, but, of course, he didn't think of telling the Throgmortons just at first. She came up to me just before lunch—so tiresome, I had to ask her to stay. Fortunately, I was alone. I don't mind being bored myself, but I hate having my guests bored."

"Poor old Mother! Well, thanks awfully for tellin' me. I think I'll send Bunter to the sale and toddle round to Battersea now an' try and console the poor little beast. So-long."

"Good-bye, dear."

"Bunter!"

"Yes, my lord."

"Her Grace tells me that a respectable Battersea architect has discovered a dead man in his bath."

"Indeed, my lord? That's very gratifying."

"Very, Bunter. Your choice of words is unerring. I wish Eton and Balliol[18] had done as much for me. Have you found the catalogue?"

"Here it is, my lord."

"Thanks. I am going to Battersea at once. I want you to attend the sale for me. Don't lose time—I don't want to miss the Folio Dante[19] nor the de Voragine—here you are—see? 'Golden

---

[18] *Eton College* is an independent school — that is, not funded by the state — for boys ages 13 to 18 and attended mostly by sons of the English upper and upper-middle classes. It is located near Windsor, in Berkshire, about 20 miles west of London. *Balliol* is a college, founded in 1263 and one of 38 that form the University of Oxford, itself founded in the 10th century. Sayers' son, Anthony Fleming, went to Balliol.

[19] [Sayers' footnote] This is the first Florence edition, 1481, by Niccolo di Lorenzo. Lord Peter's collection of printed Dantes is worth inspection. It includes, besides the famous Aldine 8vo. of 1502, the Naples folio of 1477—"edizione rarissima," according to Colomb. This copy has no history, and Mr.

Legend'—Wynkyn de Worde, 1493[20]—got that?—and, I say, make a special effort for the Caxton folio of the 'Four Sons of Aymon'— it's the 1489 folio and unique. Look! I've marked the lots I want, and put my outside offer against each. Do your best for me. I shall be back to dinner."

"Very good, my lord."

"Take my cab and tell him to hurry. He may for you; he doesn't like me very much. Can I," said Lord Peter, looking at himself in the eighteenth-century mirror over the mantelpiece, "can I have the heart to fluster the flustered Thipps further—that's very difficult to say quickly—by appearing in a top-hat and frock-coat?[21] I think not. Ten to one he will overlook my trousers and

---

Parker's private belief is that its present owner conveyed it away by stealth from somewhere or other. Lord Peter's own account is that he "picked it up in a little place in the hills," when making a walking-tour through Italy.

[20] Lord Peter collects incunabulum: books, pamphlets and other material created before 1501 when the printing press came into use. Here is what he wanted Bunter to bid on:

Folio Dante. A reference to the 1481 edition of the works of Dante Alighieri (c.1265-1321) containing his "Divine Comedy" that describes his journeys through Hell, Purgatory and Paradise. Books are categorized according to the size of their pages, and a *folio* is one of the largest, with each page about 8¼ inches by 13 inches. During the last decade of her life, Sayers worked on translating the "Comedy," completing "Hell" and "Purgatory" and most of "Paradise."

de Voragine — "Golden Legend" — Wynkyn de Worde, 1493. A collection of the lives of the saints compiled by Jacobus de Voragine (c.1230-1298), the archbishop of Genoa. Although called "Legenda Sanctorum" (Readings of the Saints), it was also known as "Legenda Aurea" (Golden Legend) because it was thought worth its weight in gold. It was a popular work in medieval times, and after the invention of the printing press, versions were published in every major European language.

Wynkyn de Worde (d. 1534) was an English printer who worked with printer William Caxton (ca. 1415-1422-ca.1492) and was one of the first to produce books for the public rather than for noble patrons.

Four Sons of Aymon. A medieval French romance telling of Charlemagne's struggles with the four chivalrous noblemen of the title. Although it dates from the late 12th century, the version Lord Peter wanted was the first English edition, printed in 1489 by William Caxton.

[21] A man's knee-length coat. It was commonly cut tight at the waist and could be single- or double-breasted.

mistake me for the undertaker.[22] A grey suit, I fancy, neat but not gaudy, with a hat to tone, suits my other self better. Exit the amateur of first editions; new motif introduced by solo bassoon; enter Sherlock Holmes, disguised as a walking gentleman. There goes Bunter. Invaluable fellow—never offers to do his job when you've told him to do somethin' else. Hope he doesn't miss the 'Four Sons of Aymon.' Still, there is another copy of that—in the Vatican.[23] It might become available, you never know—if the Church of Rome went to pot or Switzerland invaded Italy— whereas a strange corpse doesn't turn up in a suburban bathroom more than once in a lifetime—at least, I should think not—at any rate, the number of times it's happened, with a pince-nez, might be counted on the fingers of one hand, I imagine. Dear me! it's a dreadful mistake to ride two hobbies at once."[24]

He had drifted across the passage into his bedroom, and was changing with a rapidity one might not have expected from a man of his mannerisms. He selected a dark-green tie to match his socks and tied it accurately without hesitation or the slightest compression of his lips; substituted a pair of brown shoes for his black ones, slipped a monocle[25] into a breast pocket, and took up a beautiful Malacca[26] walking-stick with a heavy silver knob.

"That's all, I think," he murmured to himself. "Stay—I may as well have you—you may come in useful—one never knows." He added a flat silver matchbox to his equipment, glanced at his watch, and seeing that it was already a quarter to three, ran briskly

---

[22] A word dating from the 15th century for mortician or funeral director.
[23] [Sayers' footnote] Lord Peter's wits were wool-gathering. The book is in the possession of Earl Spencer. The Brocklebury copy is incomplete, the five last signatures being altogether missing, but is unique in possessing the colophon.
[24] A reference to a hobby horse, a toy consisting of a stuffed horse's head mounted on a stick, sometimes with a small wheel attached at the base. Understandably, trying to ride two of them at once can lead to confusion.
[25] A lens encircled by a wire to which a string is attached. A monocle could be worn to correct eyesight, as a magnifying glass, or, particularly among the upper classes, because it was stylish to wear.
[26] A variety of rattan or palm plant, named for a town in western Malaysia. Unlike most palm plants, Malacca has a solid stem, making it ideal for use as a cane.

downstairs, and, hailing a taxi, was carried to Battersea Park.[27]

Mr. Alfred Thipps was a small, nervous man, whose flaxen hair was beginning to abandon the unequal struggle with destiny. One might say that his only really marked feature was a large bruise over the left eyebrow, which gave him a faintly dissipated air incongruous with the rest of his appearance. Almost in the same breath with his first greeting, he made a self-conscious apology for it, murmuring something about having run against the dining-room door in the dark. He was touched almost to tears by Lord Peter's thoughtfulness and condescension in calling.[28]

"I'm sure it's most kind of your lordship," he repeated for the dozenth time, rapidly blinking his weak little eyelids. "I appreciate it very deeply, very deeply, indeed, and so would Mother, only she's so deaf, I don't like to trouble you with making her understand. It's been very hard all day," he added, "with the policemen in the house and all this commotion. It's what Mother and me have never been used to, always living very retired,[29] and it's most distressing to a man of regular habits,[30] my lord, and reely, I'm almost thankful Mother doesn't understand, for I'm sure it would worry her terribly if she was to know about it. She was upset at first, but she's made up some idea of her own about it now, and I'm sure it's all for the best."

The old lady who sat knitting by the fire nodded grimly in response to a look from her son.

---

[27] A 200-acre green space opened in 1858 that's home to a children's zoo, a lake for boating, and the London Peace Pagoda. It also contains several gardens — including one devoted to sub-tropical plants — lodges, shelters and war memorials.

[28] Why should Mr. Thipps be grateful for Lord Peter's behavior? A less-known definition of condescension in Merriam-Webster is the "voluntary descent from one's rank or dignity in relations with an inferior." In England's class system, how you act toward a person depends on whether they rank higher or lower than you. A sprig of the nobility ranks above a common architect. Lord Peter is not obliged to take notice of Mr. Thipps, so the fact that he not only willingly does so, but calls at Mr. Thipps' home to help, is cause for gratitude.

[29] Secluded.

[30] Mr. Thipps meant living according to an unvarying schedule: getting up at the same time every morning, going to bed at the same time each night, attending church, and not carousing or getting into trouble. In short, not doing anything that would cause the neighbors to gossip about you.

"I always said as you ought to complain about that bath, Alfred," she said suddenly, in the high, piping voice peculiar to the deaf, "and it's to be 'oped the landlord'll see about it now; not but what I think you might have managed without having the police in, but there! you always were one to make a fuss about a little thing, from chicken-pox up."

"There now," said Mr. Thipps apologetically, "you see how it is. Not but what it's just as well she's settled on that, because she understands we've locked up the bathroom and don't try to go in there. But it's been a terrible shock to me, sir—my lord, I should say, but there! my nerves are all to pieces. Such a thing has never 'appened—happened to me in all my born days. Such a state I was in this morning—I didn't know if I was on my head or my heels— I reely didn't, and my heart not being too strong, I hardly knew how to get out of that horrid room and telephone for the police. It's affected me, sir, it's affected me, it reely has—I couldn't touch a bit of breakfast, nor lunch neither, and what with telephoning and putting off clients and interviewing people all morning, I've hardly known what to do with myself?"

"I'm sure it must have been uncommonly distressin'," said Lord Peter, sympathetically, "especially comin' like that before breakfast. Hate anything tiresome happenin' before breakfast. Takes a man at such a confounded disadvantage, what?"

"That's just it, that's just it," said Mr. Thipps, eagerly, "when I saw that dreadful thing lying there in my bath, mother-naked,[31] too, except for a pair of eyeglasses, I assure you, my lord, it regularly turned my stomach, if you'll excuse the expression. I'm not very strong, sir, and I get that sinking feeling sometimes in the morning, and what with one thing and another I 'ad—had to send the girl for a stiff brandy or I don't know what mightn't have happened. I felt so queer, though I'm anything but partial to spirits as a rule. Still, I make it a rule never to be without brandy in the house, in case of emergency, you know?"

"Very wise of you," said Lord Peter, cheerfully, "you're a very far-seein' man, Mr. Thipps. Wonderful what a little nip'll do

---

[31] As naked as the day you were born.

in case of need, and the less you're used to it the more good it does you. Hope your girl is a sensible young woman, what? Nuisance to have women faintin' and shriekin' all over the place."

"Oh, Gladys is a good girl," said Mr. Thipps, "very reasonable indeed. She was shocked, of course, that's very understandable. I was shocked myself, and it wouldn't be proper in a young woman not to be shocked under the circumstances, but she is really a helpful, energetic girl in a crisis, if you understand me. I consider myself very fortunate these days to have got a good, decent girl to do for me and Mother, even though she is a bit careless and forgetful about little things, but that's only natural. She was very sorry indeed about having left the bathroom window open, she reely was, and though I was angry at first, seeing what's come of it, it wasn't anything to speak of, not in the ordinary way, as you might say. Girls will forget things, you know, my lord, and reely she was so distressed I didn't like to say too much to her. All I said was, 'It might have been burglars,' I said, 'remember that, next time you leave a window open all night; this time it was a dead man,' I said, 'and that's unpleasant enough, but next time it might be burglars,' I said, 'and all of us murdered in our beds.' But the police-inspector[32]—Inspector Sugg, they called him, from the Yard—he was very sharp with her, poor girl. Quite frightened her, and made her think he suspected her of something, though what good a body could be to her, poor girl, I can't imagine, and so I told the inspector. He was quite rude to me, my lord—I may say I didn't like his manner at all. 'If you've got anything definite to accuse Gladys or me of, Inspector,' I said to him, 'bring it forward, that's what you have to do,' I said, 'but I've yet to learn that you're paid to be rude to a gentleman in his own 'ouse—house.' Reely," said Mr. Thipps, growing quite pink on the top of his head, "he regularly roused me, regularly roused me, my lord, and I'm a mild man as a rule."

"Sugg all over," said Lord Peter, "I know him. When he don't know what else to say, he's rude, Stands to reason you and the girl wouldn't go collectin' bodies. Who'd want to saddle himself with a body? Difficulty's usually to get rid of 'em. Have you got rid of

---

[32] A supervisory rank, above sergeant but below chief inspector. They're called inspectors today.

this one yet, by the way?"

"It's still in the bathroom," said Mr. Thipps. "Inspector Sugg said nothing was to be touched till his men came in to move it. I'm expecting them at any time. If it would interest your lordship to have a look at it—"

"Thanks awfully," said Lord Peter, "I'd like to very much, if I'm not puttin' you out."

"Not at all," said Mr. Thipps. His manner as he led the way along the passage convinced Lord Peter of two things—first, that, gruesome as his exhibit was, he rejoiced in the importance it reflected upon himself and his flat, and secondly, that Inspector Sugg had forbidden him to exhibit it to anyone. The latter supposition was confirmed by the action of Mr. Thipps, who stopped to fetch the doorkey from his bedroom, saying that the police had the other, but that he made it a rule to have two keys to every door, in case of accident.[33]

The bathroom was in no way remarkable. It was long and narrow, the window being exactly over the head of the bath. The panes were of frosted glass; the frame wide enough to admit a man's body. Lord Peter stepped rapidly across to it, opened it and looked out.

The flat was the top one of the building and situated about the middle of the block. The bathroom window looked out upon the backyards of the flats, which were occupied by various small outbuildings, coal-holes,[34] garages, and the like. Beyond these were the back gardens of a parallel line of houses. On the right rose the extensive edifice of St. Luke's Hospital, Battersea, with its grounds, and, connected with it by a covered way, the residence of the famous surgeon, Sir Julian Freke, who directed the surgical side of the great new hospital, and was, in addition, known in Harley Street[35] as a distinguished neurologist with a highly

---

[33] Indicating that Mr. Thipps is a very cautious, careful man.
[34] A hatch in the sidewalk used to access an underground coal bunker. Delivery men would lift the hatch (which otherwise would be latched down from inside) and pass down sacks of coal which the homeowner or servant would store. This made delivery convenient and kept dusty workmen out of the house.
[35] A street in the City of Westminster in London, known as a home for doctors and medical organizations since the 1800s.

individual point of view.

This information was poured into Lord Peter's ear at considerable length by Mr. Thipps, who seemed to feel that the neighbourhood of anybody so distinguished shed a kind of halo of glory over Queen Caroline Mansions.

"We had him round here himself this morning," he said, "about this horrid business. Inspector Sugg thought one of the young medical gentlemen at the hospital might have brought the corpse round for a joke, as you might say, they always having bodies in the dissecting-room. So Inspector Sugg went round to see Sir Julian this morning to ask if there was a body missing. He was very kind, was Sir Julian, very kind indeed, though he was at work when they got there, in the dissecting-room. He looked up the books to see that all the bodies were accounted for, and then very obligingly came round here to look at this"—he indicated the bath—"and said he was afraid he couldn't help us—there was no corpse missing from the hospital, and this one didn't answer to the description of any they'd had."

"Nor to the description of any of the patients, I hope," suggested Lord Peter casually.

At this grisly hint Mr. Thipps turned pale.

"I didn't hear Inspector Sugg enquire," he said, with some agitation. "What a very horrid thing that would be—God bless my soul, my lord, I never thought of it."

"Well, if they had missed a patient they'd probably have discovered it by now," said Lord Peter. "Let's have a look at this one."

He screwed his monocle[36] into his eye, adding: "I see you're troubled here with the soot blowing in.[37] Beastly nuisance, ain't it?

---

[36] A monocle custom-made for the wearer is easy to keep in place. When it is not, or, in this case, when Sayers wanted to emphasize Lord Peter using his lens as a magnifying glass, he worked his monocle so that it fit snugly.

[37] In the 1920s, London's more than 7 million inhabitants made it the most populous city in the world. That also meant hundreds of thousands of chimneys burning coal for fuel and depositing soot that caused serious health problems. The Great Smog of 1952, when weather conditions wrapped London in a thick blanket of smog for four days, reportedly caused at least 4,000 premature deaths — later

I get it, too—spoils all my books, you know. Here, don't you trouble, if you don't care about lookin' at it."

He took from Mr. Thipps's hesitating hand the sheet which had been flung over the bath, and turned it back.

The body which lay in the bath was that of a tall, stout man of about fifty. The hair, which was thick and black and naturally curly, had been cut and parted by a master hand, and exuded a faint violet perfume, perfectly recognizable in the close air of the bathroom. The features were thick, fleshy and strongly marked, with prominent dark eyes, and a long nose curving down to a heavy chin. The clean-shaven lips were full and sensual, and the dropped jaw showed teeth stained with tobacco. On the dead face the handsome pair of gold pince-nez mocked death with grotesque elegance; the fine gold chain curved over the naked breast. The legs lay stiffly stretched out side by side; the arms reposed close to the body; the fingers were flexed naturally. Lord Peter lifted one arm, and looked at the hand with a little frown.

"Bit of a dandy,[38] your visitor, what?" he murmured. "Parma violet[39] and manicure." He bent again, slipping his hand beneath the head. The absurd eyeglasses slipped off, clattering into the bath, and the noise put the last touch to Mr. Thipps's growing nervousness.

"If you'll excuse me," he murmured, "it makes me feel quite faint, it reely does."

He slipped outside, and he had no sooner done so than Lord Peter, lifting the body quickly and cautiously, turned it over and inspected it with his head on one side, bringing his monocle into play with the air of the late Joseph Chamberlain[40] approving a rare orchid. He then laid the head over his arm, and bringing out the silver matchbox from his pocket, slipped it into the open mouth.

---

studies suggest as many as 12,000 — and led to the Clean Air Act of 1956 which banned the use of coal for domestic use in cities.

[38] Someone who pays exaggerated attention to his personal appearance. Possibly a shortened version of "jack-a-dandy" from the 1780s.

[39] A perfume made with a member of the violet family.

[40] British businessman and politician (1836-1914) who, while he never made prime minister, was one of the most influential statesmen of the 19th and 20th centuries. He favored sporting an orchid in his buttonhole, and his collection was renowned.

Then making the noise usually written "Tut-tut," he laid the body down, picked up the mysterious pince-nez, looked at it, put it on his nose and looked through it, made the same noise again, readjusted the pince-nez upon the nose of the corpse, so as to leave no traces of interference for the irritation of Inspector Sugg; rearranged the body; returned to the window and, leaning out, reached upwards and sideways with his walking-stick, which he had somewhat incongruously brought along with him. Nothing appearing to come of these investigations, he withdrew his head, closed the window, and rejoined Mr. Thipps in the passage.

Mr. Thipps, touched by this sympathetic interest in the younger son of a duke, took the liberty, on their return to the sitting-room, of offering him a cup of tea. Lord Peter, who had strolled over to the window and was admiring the outlook on Battersea Park, was about to accept, when an ambulance came into view at the end of Prince of Wales Road.[41] Its appearance reminded Lord Peter of an important engagement, and with a hurried "By Jove!" he took his leave of Mr. Thipps.

"My mother sent kind regards and all that," he said, shaking hands fervently; "hopes you'll soon be down at Denver[42] again. Good-bye, Mrs. Thipps," he bawled kindly[43] into the ear of the old lady. "Oh, no, my dear sir, please don't trouble to come down."

He was none too soon. As he stepped out of the door and turned towards the station,[44] the ambulance drew up from the other direction, and Inspector Sugg emerged from it, with two constables. The Inspector spoke to the officer on duty at the Mansions, and turned a suspicious gaze on Lord Peter's retreating back.

"Dear old Sugg," said that nobleman, fondly, "dear, dear old bird! How he does hate me, to be sure."

---

[41] Prince of Wales Drive, which runs along the south edge of Battersea Park, was previously known as Prince of Wales Road.
[42] A reference to the home of his brother, the Duke of Denver.
[43] Cry out loudly.
[44] Battersea Park railway station at the southeast corner of the park. To return home, Lord Peter would catch a train to Victoria Station, a major railway terminus south of Buckingham Palace, and either catch a cab or walk up Grosvenor Place along the west side of Buckingham Palace's gardens.

CHAPTER II

EXCELLENT, BUNTER," SAID LORD PETER, sinking with a sigh into a luxurious armchair. "I couldn't have done better myself. The thought of the Dante makes my mouth water—and the 'Four Sons of Aymon.' And you've saved me £60—that's glorious. What shall we spend it on, Bunter? Think of it—all ours, to do as we like with, for as Harold Skimpole so rightly observes, £60 saved is £60 gained,[1] and I'd reckoned on spending it all. It's your saving, Bunter, and properly speaking, your £60. What do we want? Anything in your department? Would you like anything altered in the flat?"

"Well, my lord, as your lordship is so good"—the man-servant paused, about to pour an old brandy into a liqueur glass.[2]

---

[1] The villain from Charles Dickens' "Bleak House," believed to be based on the critic and essayist Leigh Hunt (1784-1859). At first, Skimpole seems like a genial, childish fellow, but he is revealed as a monstrous parasite, sponging off people by acting like a child naïve about money and the ways of the world. However, Skimpole says nothing close to Lord Peter's quote. He could have been thinking of Richard Carstone, who was as feckless about money as Skimpole was about debt. Consider this scene, when Carstone is returned the money he had given the bailiff to pay off Skimpole's debt. Instead of seeing it as money recovered, Carstone thinks of it as five pounds earned and should be spent:

"Let me see!" he would say. "I saved five pounds out of the brickmaker's affair; so, if I have a good rattle to London and back in a post-chaise, and put that down at four pounds, I shall have saved one. And it's a very good thing to save one, let me tell you; a penny saved, is a penny got!"

[2] A small glass used to serve liqueur such as brandy, typically after dinner.

"Well, out with it, my Bunter, you imperturbable[3] old hypocrite. It's no good talking as if you were announcing dinner—you're spilling the brandy. The voice is Jacob's voice, but the hands are the hands of Esau.[4] What does that blessed darkroom of yours want now?"

"There's a Double Anastigmat[5] with a set of supplementary lenses, my lord," said Bunter, with a note almost of religious fervour. "If it was a case of forgery now—or footprints—I could enlarge them right up on the plate.[6] Or the wide-angled lens would be useful. It's as though the camera had eyes at the back of its head, my lord. Look—I've got it here."

He pulled a catalogue from his pocket, and submitted it, quivering, to his employer's gaze.

Lord Peter perused the description slowly, the corners of his long mouth lifted into a faint smile.

"It's Greek to me,"[7] he said, "and £50 seems a ridiculous price for a few bits of glass. I suppose, Bunter, you'd say £750 was a bit

---

[3] A person who is extremely calm, impassive and steady, even in stressful situations.

[4] A reference to Genesis 27:22, in which Jacob steals the birthright of his first-born twin brother, Esau, from their father, the patriarch Isaac. Old, blind and wanting to pass his authority to Esau, Isaac sends him to hunt for meat, with which he would use to bless Esau. While Esau was gone, his mother, Rebekah dressed Jacob in his brother's clothes, laid goatskins on his arms to simulate Esau's hairiness, and sent him in with meat. Isaac, feeling the goatskins, says, 'The voice is the voice of Jacob, yet the hands are the hands of Esau,' " but blesses Jacob anyway.

[5] A lens that corrects a defect in the optical system that creates a blurred image. A double anastigmat refers to the use of two lenses working together.

[6] Early cameras recorded images onto chemically treated glass plates. Bunter's suggestion would make it easy to produce detailed photos of crime-scene evidence.

[7] A common expression that was probably in use before Shakespeare dropped it into "Julius Caesar." In Act I, Scene 2, Casca was asked if Cicero gave a speech at a festival in which Caesar was offered a crown:

CASCA: Ay, he spoke Greek.

CASSIUS: To what effect?

CASCA: Nay, an I tell you that, I'll ne'er look you i' the face again: but those that understood him smiled at one another and shook their heads; but, for mine own part, it was Greek to me.

out of the way for a dirty old book in a dead language, wouldn't you?"[8]

"It wouldn't be my place to say so, my lord."

"No, Bunter, I pay you £200 a year to keep your thoughts to yourself. Tell me, Bunter, in these democratic days, don't you think that's unfair?"

"No, my lord."

"You don't. D'you mind telling me frankly why you don't think it unfair?"

"Frankly, my lord, your lordship is paid a nobleman's income to take Lady Worthington in to dinner and refrain from exercising your lordship's undoubted powers of repartee."[9]

Lord Peter considered this.

"That's your idea, is it, Bunter? Noblesse oblige—for a consideration.[10] I daresay you're right. Then you're better off than I am, because I'd have to behave myself to Lady Worthington if I hadn't a penny. Bunter, if I sacked you here and now, would you tell me what you think of me?"

"No, my lord."

"You'd have a perfect right to, my Bunter, and if I sacked you on top of drinking the kind of coffee you make, I'd deserve everything you could say of me. You're a demon for coffee, Bunter—I don't want to know how you do it, because I believe it to be witchcraft, and I don't want to burn eternally. You can buy your cross-eyed lens."

"Thank you, my lord."

---

[8] Some of Lord Peter's recent purchases at auction were written in Latin.

[9] Not a real person, but there is Lady Worthington in "Won by Waiting" (1879), the first novel by Edna Lyall (a pseudonym for Ada Ellen Bayly). Bayly (1857-1903) was a popular novelist whose support for political causes, including women's emancipation, were reflected in her works. Except for the name, there doesn't seem to be a connection between "Whose Body?" and Lyall's Lady Worthington, who is portrayed as graceful, young and generous, but whose strong dislikes "was perhaps the reason why she was often not so much appreciated as she ought to have been."

[10] Honorable, generous and responsible behavior demanded from those of high rank or birth. From the French for "obligations of the nobility," the phrase has been traced back to 1837.

"Have you finished in the dining-room?"

"Not quite, my lord."

"Well, come back when you have. I have many things to tell you. Hullo! who's that?"

The doorbell had rung sharply.

"Unless it's anybody interestin' I'm not at home."[11]

"Very good, my lord."

Lord Peter's library was one of the most delightful bachelor rooms[12] in London. Its scheme was black and primrose;[13] its walls were lined with rare editions, and its chairs and Chesterfield sofa suggested the embraces of the houris.[14] In one corner stood a black baby grand, a wood fire leaped on a wide old-fashioned hearth, and the Sèvres vases[15] on the chimneypiece were filled with ruddy and gold chrysanthemums. To the eyes of the young man who was ushered in from the raw November fog it seemed not only rare and unattainable, but friendly and familiar, like a colourful and gilded paradise in a mediæval painting.

"Mr. Parker, my lord."

Lord Peter jumped up with genuine eagerness.

"My dear man, I'm delighted to see you. What a beastly foggy night, ain't it? Bunter, some more of that admirable coffee and another glass and the cigars. Parker, I hope you're full of crime—nothing less than arson or murder will do for us to-night. 'On such a night as this—'[16] Bunter and I were just sitting down to carouse.

---

[11] A polite lie made possible only when you have a servant running interference for you.

[12] An apartment consisting of a sitting room, bedroom and a bath, sometimes with a kitchenette, ideal for a bachelor, but not for a respectable woman who would either be living with her family or husband.

[13] Although the flower by that name comes in a multitude of shades, the color is yellow with a hint of black to it.

[14] A masculine-looking sofa, usually rectangular, made of rich, polished leather and held in place with rows of studs. It is typically associated with English clubs. *Houris:* In Islam, the beautiful women who reside in paradise.

[15] A vase named for the commune — an administrative district that's the equivalent of a village — known for manufacturing porcelain since 1756. It is located in the southwestern suburbs of Paris.

[16] *On such a night as this:* Lord Peter is quoting from the meeting between Lorenzo and Jessica in Act V of Shakespeare's "The Merchant of Venice."

I've got a Dante, and a Caxton folio that is practically unique, at Sir Ralph Brocklebury's sale. Bunter, who did the bargaining, is going to have a lens which does all kinds of wonderful things with its eyes shut, and

> We both have got a body in a bath,
> We both have got a body in a bath—
> For in spite of all temptations
> To go in for cheap sensations
> We insist upon a body in a bath—[17]

Nothing less will do for us, Parker. It's mine at present, but we're going shares in it. Property of the firm. Won't you join us? You really must put something in the jack-pot. Perhaps you have a body. Oh, do have a body. Every body welcome.

Comparing themselves to history's great lovers, Lorenzo begins by bringing up, "in such a night as this":

> "When the sweet wind did gently kiss the trees,
> And they did make no noise, in such a night,
> Troilus methinks mounted the Troyan walls,
> And sigh'd his soul toward the Grecian tents,
> Where Cressid lay that night."

Cressida ends up betraying Troilus by falling in love with the Greek hero Diomedes. Jessica in turn praises Thisby, who dies as a result of her love for Pyramus. The couple's joke becomes apparent as they continue to bring up ill-fated lovers as examples of their passion for each other.

Likewise, Lord Peter sees the humor in eagerly anticipating hearing a tale of "arson and murder" from Inspector Parker.

[17] *body in the bath.* Lord Peter is improvising. "For in spite of all temptations / to go in for cheap sensations" is from "HMS Pinafore" by Gilbert & Sullivan. When a common sailor is caught by the captain of the Pinafore in the act of running off with his daughter, the crew defends his act because he is an Englishman:

> "For in spite of all temptations
> To belong to other nations
> He remains an Englishman,
> He remains an E-e-e-e-e-englishman!"

THE COMPLETE, ANNOTATED WHOSE BODY?

Gin a body meet a body
    Hauled before the beak,
Gin a body jolly well knows who murdered a body and that
old Sugg is on the wrong tack,
    Need a body speak?[18]

Not a bit of it. He tips a glassy wink to yours truly and yours
truly reads the truth."

"Ah," said Parker, "I knew you'd been round to Queen Caroline
Mansions. So've I, and met Sugg, and he told me he'd seen you.
He was cross, too. Unwarrantable interference, he calls it."

"I knew he would," said Lord Peter, "I love taking a rise out of

---

[18] Lord Peter is improvising from "Comin' Through the Rye" by Robert Burns
(1759-1796). *Beak* is a judge in the Cockney dialect, and while magistrate John
Fielding (1721-1780) was called "the blind beak of Bow Street," it is not certain
if he inspired the phrase.

    O Jenny's a' weet [wet], poor body,
    Jenny's seldom dry:
    She draigl't [dragged] a' her petticoatie [petticoats],
    Comin thro' the rye!

    Comin thro' the rye, poor body,
    Comin thro' the rye,
    She draigl't a' her petticoatie,
    Comin thro' the rye!

    Gin [Should] a body meet a body
    Comin thro' the rye,
    Gin a body kiss a body,
    Need a body cry?

    Gin a body meet a body
    Comin thro' the glen,
    Gin a body kiss a body,
    Need the warld ken [world care]?

    Gin a body meet a body
    Comin thro' the grain,
    Gin a body kiss a body,
    The thing's a body's ain [own]

dear old Sugg, he's always so rude. I see by the Star[19] that he has excelled himself by taking the girl, Gladys What's-her-name, into custody. Sugg of the evening, beautiful Sugg![20] But what were you doing there?"

"To tell you the truth," said Parker, "I went round to see if the Semitic-looking[21] stranger in Mr. Thipps's bath was by any extraordinary chance Sir Reuben Levy. But he isn't."

"Sir Reuben Levy? Wait a minute, I saw something about that. I know! A headline: 'Mysterious disappearance of famous

---

[19] An evening newspaper founded in London in 1888. Its circulation grew rapidly as a result of its coverage of the Jack the Ripper case, and it is suspected that its reporters wrote the "Dear Boss" letter which gave the Whitechapel murderer his name.

[20] Lord Peter is parodying a parody. The original was a popular song called "Star of the Evening," which was converted by Lewis Carroll in "Alice in Wonderland" to "Soup of the Evening":

> Beautiful Soup, so rich and green,
> Waiting in a hot tureen!
> Who for such dainties would not stoop?
> Soup of the evening, beautiful soup!
> Soup of the evening, beautiful soup!
> Beau - ootiful soo - oop!
> Beau - ootiful soo - oop!
> Soo - oop of the e - e - evening,
> Beautiful, beautiful soup!
>
> Beautiful soup! Who cares for fish,
> Game, or any other dish?
> Who would not give all else for two
> Pennyworth only of beautiful soup?
> Pennyworth only of beautiful soup?
> Beau - ootiful soo - oop!
> Beau - ootiful soo - oop!
> Soo - oop of the e - e - evening,
> Beautiful, beautiful soup!

[21] Jewish looking. The word is derived from Shem, one of the three sons of Noah, and was originally applied to the family of languages of Middle Eastern origin, including the ancient and modern forms of Arabic, Hebrew and Aramaic. It was first applied to Jews as "anti-Semitic" in 1879 by the German journalist Wilhelm Marr in his pamphlet "The Victory of Germandom over Jewry."

financier.' What's it all about? I didn't read it carefully."

"Well, it's a bit odd, though I daresay it's nothing really—old chap may have cleared for some reason best known to himself. It only happened this morning, and nobody would have thought anything about it, only it happened to be the day on which he had arranged to attend a most important financial meeting and do some deal involving millions—I haven't got all the details. But I know he's got enemies who'd just as soon the deal didn't come off, so when I got wind of this fellow in the bath, I buzzed round to have a look at him. It didn't seem likely, of course, but unlikelier things do happen in our profession. The funny thing is, old Sugg has got bitten with the idea it is him, and is wildly telegraphing to Lady Levy to come and identify him. But as a matter of fact, the man in the bath is no more Sir Reuben than Adolf Beck, poor devil, was John Smith.[22] Oddly enough, though, he would be really extraordinarily like Sir Reuben if he had a beard, and as Lady Levy is abroad with the family, somebody may say it's him, and Sugg will build up a lovely theory, like the Tower of Babel,[23] and destined so to perish."

"You're certain of your facts, I suppose."

"Positive. Sugg, of course, says he doesn't take account of fancy religions—"

"Sugg's a beautiful, braying ass," said Lord Peter. "He's like a detective in a novel. Well, I don't know anything about Levy, but I've seen the body, and I should say the idea was preposterous upon the face of it. What do you think of the brandy?"

---

[22] A notorious trial in the 1890s, Beck was mistakenly identified and convicted as the man who defrauded numerous women. Three years later, he was convicted again for a similar crime, only the real criminal was captured and Beck was pardoned. Beck's ordeal pointed out the weakness of witness identification in criminal cases and led to the creation of a court of appeals. See the essay "Adolf Beck: Seeing Is Not Believing."
[23] A story from Genesis about the origin of the world's many languages. In Chapter 11, when "the whole earth was of one language, and of one speech," a city and tower was built on the plain of Shinar "whose top may reach unto heaven; and let us make a name, lest we be scattered abroad upon the face of the whole earth." The Lord chose to "confound their language, that they may not understand one another's speech" and "scatter them abroad upon the face of all the earth."

"Unbelievable, Wimsey—sort of thing makes one believe in heaven. But I want your yarn."

"D'you mind if Bunter hears it, too? Invaluable man, Bunter—amazin' fellow with a camera. And the odd thing is, he's always on the spot when I want my bath or my boots. I don't know when he develops things—I believe he does 'em in his sleep. Bunter!"

"Yes, my lord."

"Stop fiddling about in there, and get yourself the proper things to drink and join the merry throng."

"Certainly, my lord."

"Mr. Parker has a new trick: The Vanishing Financier. Absolutely no deception. Hey, presto, pass! and where is he? Will some gentleman from the audience kindly step upon the platform and inspect the cabinet? Thank you, sir. The quickness of the 'and deceives the heye.'"[24]

"I'm afraid mine isn't much of a story," said Parker. "It's just one of those simple things that offer no handle. Sir Reuben Levy dined last night with three friends at the Ritz. After dinner the friends went to the theatre. He refused to go with them on account of an appointment. I haven't yet been able to trace the appointment, but anyhow, he returned home to his house—9 Park Lane[25]—at twelve o'clock."

"Who saw him?"

"The cook, who had just gone up to bed, saw him on the doorstep and heard him let himself in. He walked upstairs, leaving

---

[24] The complete phrase, typical of a magician's stage patter is "the quickness of the hand deceives the eye." Lord Peter adds a Cockney accent for humorous effect. The Encyclopaedia Britannica of 1911 notes that the magician's motto is inaccurate because the success of a trick depends more on misdirecting the audience rather than speed.

[25] A major north-south road in central London that forms the eastern boundary of Hyde Park, around the corner from Lord Peter's flat at 110 Piccadilly. At this time, it was the home of a considerable number of mansions and had been since it was mentioned in William Makepeace Thackeray's "Vanity Fair" (1848). Sherlockians will recall that in "The Adventure of the Empty House," Col. Sebastian Moran shot the Honourable Ronald Adair "with an expanding bullet from an air-gun" through the open window of his home at No. 427 Park Lane. How he managed to do it without being seen while standing in the middle of Hyde Park has been the subject of much debate among Sherlockians.

his greatcoat on the hall peg and his umbrella in the stand—you remember how it rained last night. He undressed and went to bed. Next morning he wasn't there. That's all," said Parker abruptly, with a wave of the hand.

"It isn't all, it isn't all. Daddy, go on, that's not half a story," pleaded Lord Peter.

"But it is all. When his man came to call him he wasn't there. The bed had been slept in. His pyjamas and all his clothes were there, the only odd thing being that they were thrown rather untidily on the ottoman at the foot of the bed, instead of being neatly folded on a chair, as is Sir Reuben's custom—looking as though he had been rather agitated or unwell. No clean clothes were missing, no suit, no boots—nothing. The boots he had worn were in his dressing-room as usual. He had washed and cleaned his teeth and done all the usual things. The housemaid was down cleaning the hall at half-past six, and can swear that nobody came in or out after that. So one is forced to suppose that a respectable middle-aged Hebrew financier either went mad between twelve and six a. m. and walked quietly out of the house in his birthday suit on a November night, or else was spirited away like the lady in the 'Ingoldsby Legends,' body and bones, leaving only a heap of crumpled clothes behind him."[26]

"Was the front door bolted?"

"That's the sort of question you would ask, straight off; it took me an hour to think of it. No; contrary to custom, there was only the Yale lock on the door.[27] On the other hand, some of the maids

---

[26] A collection of myths, legends and ghost stories, supposedly written by Thomas Ingoldsby of Tappington Manor, actually a pen-name of cleric, humorous poet and novelist Richard Harris Barham (1788-1845). The reference is from a comic poem "The Blasphemer's Warning: A Lay of St. Romwold." During his wedding feast, a knight eats a spoonful of Charlotte Russe — a dessert of Bavarian cream and ladyfingers — which inflames his "sad raging tooth." The pain inspires an outburst of cursing, which causes his bride to vanish, leaving her clothes behind.

[27] A company associated with the pin tumbler lock, which uses a key with an edge milled to various heights. Inserting the key into the lock raises a series of pins to different heights. Each pin, which holds the cylinder in place, is cut into two pieces, so only the correctly sized key would allow the cylinder to be rotated and the lock to be unlocked.

had been given leave to go to the theatre, and Sir Reuben may quite conceivably have left the door open under the impression they had not come in. Such a thing has happened before."

"And that's really all?"

"Really all. Except for one very trifling circumstance."

"I love trifling circumstances," said Lord Peter, with childish delight; "so many men have been hanged by trifling circumstances. What was it?"

"Sir Reuben and Lady Levy, who are a most devoted couple, always share the same room.[28] Lady Levy, as I said before, is in Mentone[29] at the moment for her health. In her absence, Sir Reuben sleeps in the double bed as usual, and invariably on his own side—the outside—of the bed. Last night he put the two pillows together and slept in the middle, or, if anything, rather closer to the wall than otherwise. The housemaid, who is a most intelligent girl, noticed this when she went up to make the bed, and, with really admirable detective instinct, refused to touch the bed or let anybody else touch it, though it wasn't till later that they actually sent for the police."

"Was nobody in the house but Sir Reuben and the servants?"

"No; Lady Levy was away with her daughter and her maid. The valet, cook, parlourmaid, housemaid and kitchenmaid[30] were the

---

[28] Upper-class couples tended to favor separate bedrooms for various reasons. A couple might prefer different hours for waking and sleeping; it allowed room for the man's valet and the wife's lady's maid to perform their duties; and, if worse came to worse, couples in arranged marriages that didn't take could lead separate lives. In the case of the Levys, sharing a bed could be taken as a sign of affection and compatibility, or that they're hopelessly middle-class.

[29] A commune — an administrative district that's the equivalent of a village — on France's southern coast near the border with Italy. It is called Menton in France, Mentone in Italy.

[30] Positions within the strict hierarchy of the servant class. The *valet* was the male servant who attended his employer. Generally, he was responsible for the care of the master's clothes and appearance, but depending on the household, he could also act as a personal assistant and run all sorts of errands.

The *parlourmaid* was responsible for maintaining the house's public rooms, such as the sitting, drawing and dining rooms. The *housemaid* was a general-purpose worker. The *kitchenmaid*, of course, assisted the cook. The between

only people in the house, and naturally wasted an hour or two squawking and gossiping. I got there about ten."

"What have you been doing since?"

"Trying to get on the track of Sir Reuben's appointment last night, since, with the exception of the cook, his 'appointer' was the last person who saw him before his disappearance. There may be some quite simple explanation, though I'm dashed if I can think of one for the moment. Hang it all, a man doesn't come in and go to bed and walk away again 'mid nodings on'[31] in the middle of the night."

"He may have been disguised."

"I thought of that—in fact, it seems the only possible explanation. But it's deuced[32] odd, Wimsey. An important city man, on the eve of an important transaction, without a word of warning to anybody, slips off in the middle of the night, disguised down to his skin, leaving behind his watch, purse, cheque-book, and—most mysterious and important of all—his spectacles, without which he can't see a step, as he is extremely short-sighted. He—"

"That is important," interrupted Wimsey. "You are sure he didn't take a second pair?"

"His man vouches for it that he had only two pairs, one of which was found on his dressing-table, and the other in the drawer where it is always kept."

Lord Peter whistled.

"You've got me there, Parker. Even if he'd gone out to commit

---

maid, by the way, worked wherever she was needed, the scullery maid helped in the kitchen, and the chamber maid cleaned the bedrooms.

The parlourmaid, housemaid and kitchenmaid tended to be as young as 19, and ranked above the between maid and scullery maid and below the cook, lady's maid (as the woman who tended Lady Levy would be called) and the housekeeper (who supervised the maids).

[31] "With nothing on," spoken in a mock-German dialect. A reference to "De Maiden Mid Nodings On," a story burlesquing Teutonic legends by Charles Godfrey Leland (1824-1903), an American humorist and folklorist who wrote comic stories told in dialect.

[32] A euphemism for devilish. Probably associated with cards or dice, where scoring a two is called deuce (from the Old French dues, "two") and considered unlucky.

suicide he'd have taken those."

"So you'd think—or the suicide would have happened the first time he started to cross the road. However, I didn't overlook the possibility. I've got particulars of all to-day's street accidents, and I can lay my hand on my heart and say that none of them is Sir Reuben. Besides, he took his latchkey with him, which looks as though he'd meant to come back."

"Have you seen the men he dined with?"

"I found two of them at the club. They said that he seemed in the best of health and spirits, spoke of looking forward to joining Lady Levy later on—perhaps at Christmas—and referred with great satisfaction to this morning's business transaction, in which one of them—a man called Anderson of Wyndham's[33]—was himself concerned."

"Then up till about nine o'clock, anyhow, he had no apparent intention or expectation of disappearing."

"None—unless he was a most consummate actor. Whatever happened to change his mind must have happened either at the mysterious appointment which he kept after dinner, or while he was in bed between midnight and 5:30 a. m."

"Well, Bunter," said Lord Peter, "what do you make of it?"

"Not in my department, my lord. Except that it is odd that a gentleman who was too flurried or unwell to fold his clothes as usual should remember to clean his teeth and put his boots out. Those are two things that quite frequently get overlooked, my lord."

"If you mean anything personal, Bunter," said Lord Peter, "I can only say that I think the speech an unworthy one. It's a sweet little problem, Parker mine. Look here, I don't want to butt in, but I should dearly love to see that bedroom to-morrow. 'Tis not that I mistrust thee, dear, but I should uncommonly like to see it. Say me not nay—take another drop of brandy and a Villar Villar, but say

---

[33] Anderson's identity is qualified further by his club. Windham — its correct spelling — was founded in 1828 and located for most of its existence at 13 St. James's Square. It merged with the Marlborough and Orleans club in 1945 to form the Marlborough-Windham Club and was moved to 52 Pall Mall. It closed in 1953.

not, say not nay!"[34]

"Of course you can come and see it—you'll probably find lots of things I've overlooked," said the other, equally, accepting the proffered hospitality.

"Parker, acushla,[35] you're an honor to Scotland Yard. I look at you, and Sugg appears a myth, a fable, an idiot-boy, spawned in a moonlight hour by some fantastic poet's brain. Sugg is too perfect to be possible. What does he make of the body, by the way?"

"Sugg says," replied Parker, with precision, "that the body died from a blow on the back of the neck. The doctor told him that. He says it's been dead a day or two. The doctor told him that, too. He says it's the body of a well-to-do Hebrew of about fifty. Anybody could have told him that. He says it's ridiculous to suppose it came in through the window without anybody knowing anything about it. He says it probably walked in through the front door and was murdered by the household. He's arrested the girl because she's short and frail-looking and quite unequal to downing a tall and sturdy Semite with a poker. He'd arrest Thipps, only Thipps was away in Manchester all yesterday and the day before and didn't come back till late last night—in fact, he wanted to arrest him till I reminded him that if the body had been a day or two dead, little Thipps couldn't have done him in at 10:30 last night. But he'll arrest him to-morrow as an accessory—and the old lady with the knitting, too, I shouldn't wonder."

---

[34] *Villar Villar.* A brand of cigar imported in Lord Peter's time from Cuba. *Say me not nay.* From "Duke Magnus and the Mermaid," a folk song from Scandinavia. It begins:

> Duke Magnus looked out through the castle window,
> How the stream ran so rapidly;
> And there he saw how upon the stream sat
> A woman most fair and lovelie,
>
> Duke Magnus, Duke Magnus, plight thee to me,
> I pray you still so freely;
> Say me not nay, but yes, yes!

[35] A term of endearment, from the Irish meaning "O pulse of my heart."

"Well, I'm glad the little man has so much of an alibi,"[36] said Lord Peter, "though if you're only gluing your faith to cadaveric lividity, rigidity, and all the other quiddities,[37] you must be prepared to have some sceptical beast of a prosecuting counsel walk slap-bang through the medical evidence. Remember Impey Biggs defending in that Chelsea tea-shop affair? Six bloomin' medicos contradictin' each other in the box, an' old Impey elocutin' abnormal cases from Glaister and Dixon Mann[38] till the eyes of the jury reeled in their heads! 'Are you prepared to swear, Dr. Thingumtight, that the onset of rigor mortis indicates the hour of death without the possibility of error?' 'So far as my experience goes, in the majority of cases,' says the doctor, all stiff. 'Ah!' says Biggs, 'but this is a Court of Justice, Doctor, not a Parliamentary election. We can't get on without a minority report.[39] The law, Dr. Thingumtight, respects the rights of the minority, alive or dead.' Some ass laughs, and old Biggs sticks his chest out and gets impressive. 'Gentlemen, this is no laughing matter. My client—an upright and honourable gentleman—is being tried for his life—for his life, gentlemen—and it is the business of the prosecution to show his guilt—if they can—without a shadow of doubt. Now, Dr. Thingumtight, I ask you again, can you solemnly swear, without the least shadow of doubt—probable, possible shadow of doubt— that this unhappy woman met her death neither sooner nor later

---

[36] A statement identifying where a person, usually a suspect in a crime, was when it was committed. From the Latin meaning "somewhere else."

[37] A reference to the stages of decomposition the body, or *cadaver*, undergoes after death. Examining the state of the body can provide clues to how and when the person died. *Lividity* refers to the settling of blood in the portions of the body closest to the ground, causing the skin to turn a purplish-red. *Rigidity,* also called rigor mortis, refers to the stiffening of the muscles that begins about three hours after death and can last up to three days. Other *quiddities* — meaning the essence or inherent nature of an object — can include pallor mortis (the paleness in light-skinned bodies immediately after death), algor mortis (the reduction in body temperature) and the state of decomposition.

[38] The authors of two standard reference works. *Dr. John Glaister* (1856-1932) wrote "A Textbook of Medical Jurisprudence, Toxicology and Public Health." *Dr. J. Dixon Mann* (1840-1912) wrote "Forensic Medicine and Toxicology."

[39] A dissenting opinion issued from a faction on a committee investigating a particular issue.

than Thursday evening? A probable opinion? Gentlemen, we are not Jesuits, we are straightforward Englishmen.[40] You cannot ask a British-born jury to convict any man on the authority of a probable opinion.' Hum of applause."

"Biggs's man was guilty all the same," said Parker.

"Of course he was. But he was acquitted all the same, an' what you've just said is libel." Wimsey walked over to the bookshelf and took down a volume of Medical Jurisprudence.[41] "'Rigor mortis—can only be stated in a very general way—many factors determine the result.' Cautious brute. 'On the average, however, stiffening will have begun—neck and jaw—5 to 6 hours after death'—m'm—'in all likelihood have passed off in the bulk of cases by the end of 36 hours. Under certain circumstances, however, it may appear unusually early, or be retarded unusually long!' Helpful, ain't it, Parker? 'Brown-Séquard[42] states ... 3½ minutes after death.... In certain cases not until lapse of 16 hours after death ... present as long as 21 days thereafter.' Lord! 'Modifying factors—age—muscular state—or febrile diseases—or where temperature of environment is high'—and so on and so on—any bloomin' thing. Never mind. You can run the argument for what it's worth to Sugg. He won't know any better." He tossed the book away. "Come back to facts. What did you make of the body?"

"Well," said the detective, "not very much—I was puzzled—frankly. I should say he had been a rich man, but self-made, and that his good fortune had come to him fairly recently."

---

[40] A Roman Catholic religious order, known formally as the Society of Jesus. Founded in 1534 to strive "for the propagation and defense of the faith and progress of souls in Christian life and doctrine," according to its founding document, the Jesuits emphasize learning and intellectual research. Impey here is playing the anti-intellectual card, implying that a jury of stout, plain-speaking Englishmen isn't like the Popish hair-splitting Jesuits.

[41] A book by Alfred Swaine Taylor (1806-1880), a toxicologist and the father of British forensic medicine. Its full title is "The Principles and Practice of Medical Jurisprudence."

[42] Charles-Édouard Brown-Séquard (1817-1894), a French doctor known for his groundbreaking research on the nervous system and the presence and effects of hormones in the blood.

"Ah, you noticed the calluses on the hands—I thought you wouldn't miss that."

"Both his feet were badly blistered—he had been wearing tight shoes."

"Walking a long way in them, too," said Lord Peter, "to get such blisters as that. Didn't that strike you as odd, in a person evidently well off?"

"Well, I don't know. The blisters were two or three days old. He might have got stuck in the suburbs one night, perhaps—last train gone and no taxi—and had to walk home."

"Possibly."

"There were some little red marks all over his back and one leg I couldn't quite account for."

"I saw them."

"What did you make of them?"

"I'll tell you afterwards. Go on."

"He was very long-sighted—oddly long-sighted for a man in the prime of life; the glasses were like a very old man's. By the way, they had a very beautiful and remarkable chain of flat links chased with a pattern. It struck me he might be traced through it."

"I've just put an advertisement in the Times[43] about it," said Lord Peter. "Go on."

"He had had the glasses some time—they had been mended twice."

"Beautiful, Parker, beautiful. Did you realize the importance of that?"

"Not specially, I'm afraid—why?"

"Never mind—go on."

"He was probably a sullen, ill-tempered man—his nails were filed down to the quick as though he habitually bit them, and his fingers were bitten as well. He smoked quantities of cigarettes without a holder. He was particular about his personal appearance."

"Did you examine the room at all? I didn't get a chance."

---

[43] A daily newspaper founded in 1785. It is the original Times, its name appropriated by newspapers around the world, including "The New York Times" and the "Los Angeles Times."

"I couldn't find much in the way of footprints. Sugg & Co. had tramped all over the place, to say nothing of little Thipps and the maid, but I noticed a very indefinite patch just behind the head of the bath, as though something damp might have stood there. You could hardly call it a print."

"It rained hard all last night, of course."

"Yes; did you notice that the soot on the window-sill was vaguely marked?"

"I did," said Wimsey, "and I examined it hard with this little fellow, but I could make nothing of it except that something or other had rested on the sill." He drew out his monocle and handed it to Parker.

"My word, that's a powerful lens."

"It is," said Wimsey, "and jolly useful when you want to take a good squint at somethin' and look like a bally fool all the time. Only it don't do to wear it permanently—if people see you full-face they say, 'Dear me! how weak the sight of that eye must be!' Still, it's useful."

"Sugg and I explored the ground at the back of the building," went on Parker, "but there wasn't a trace."

"That's interestin'. Did you try the roof?"

"No."

"We'll go over it to-morrow. The gutter's only a couple of feet off the top of the window. I measured it with my stick—the gentleman-scout's vade-mecum,[44] I call it—it's marked off in inches. Uncommonly handy companion at times. There's a sword inside and a compass in the head. Got it made specially. Anything more?"

"Afraid not. Let's hear your version, Wimsey."

"Well, I think you've got most of the points. There are just one or two little contradictions. For instance, here's a man wears expensive gold-rimmed pince-nez and has had them long enough to be mended twice. Yet his teeth are not merely discoloured, but

---

[44] From the Latin for "go with me," a *vademecum* is a useful book that one carries around. In "The Unpleasantness at the Bellona Club" and "Unnatural Death," Lord Peter muses about writing "The Murderer's Vade-Mecum, or 101 Ways of Causing Sudden Death."

badly decayed and look as if he'd never cleaned them in his life. There are four molars missing on one side and three on the other and one front tooth broken right across. He's a man careful of his personal appearance, as witness his hair and his hands. What do you say to that?"

"Oh, these self-made men of low origin don't think much about teeth, and are terrified of dentists."

"True; but one of the molars has a broken edge so rough that it had made a sore place on the tongue. Nothing's more painful. D'you mean to tell me a man would put up with that if he could afford to get the tooth filed?"

"Well, people are queer. I've known servants endure agonies rather than step over a dentist's doormat. How did you see that, Wimsey?"

"Had a look inside; electric torch,"[45] said Lord Peter. "Handy little gadget. Looks like a matchbox. Well—I daresay it's all right, but I just draw your attention to it. Second point: Gentleman with hair smellin' of Parma violet and manicured hands and all the rest of it, never washes the inside of his ears. Full of wax. Nasty."

"You've got me there, Wimsey; I never noticed it. Still—old bad habits die hard."

"Right oh! Put it down at that. Third point: Gentleman with the manicure and the brilliantine and all the rest of it suffers from fleas."

"By Jove, you're right! Flea-bites. It never occurred to me."

"No doubt about it, old son. The marks were faint and old, but unmistakable."

"Of course, now you mention it. Still, that might happen to anybody. I loosed a whopper in the best hotel in Lincoln the week

---

[45] A flashlight, invented by Conrad Hubert (1855-1928), a Russian inventor and businessman who changed his name from Akiba Horowitz after arriving in America. He founded the American Electrical Novelty and Manufacturing Co. and sold a flashlight promoted as "Ever Ready." In 1905, Hubert renamed his company American Ever Ready. The Ever Ready name was applied to his batteries, now called Eveready, and the company is now called Energizer Holdings Inc.

before last. I hope it bit the next occupier!"[46]

"Oh, all these things might happen to anybody—separately. Fourth point: Gentleman who uses Parma violet for his hair, etc., etc., washes his body in strong carbolic soap—so strong that the smell hangs about twenty-four hours later."

"Carbolic to get rid of the fleas."

"I will say for you, Parker, you've an answer for everything. Fifth point: Carefully got-up gentleman, with manicured, though masticated, finger-nails, has filthy black toe-nails which look as if they hadn't been cut for years."

"All of a piece with habits as indicated."

"Yes, I know, but such habits! Now, sixth and last point: This gentleman with the intermittently gentlemanly habits arrives in the middle of a pouring wet night, and apparently through the window, when he has already been twenty-four hours dead, and lies down quietly in Mr. Thipps's bath, unseasonably dressed in a pair of pince-nez. Not a hair on his head is ruffled—the hair has been cut so recently that there are quite a number of little short hairs stuck on his neck and the sides of the bath—and he has shaved so recently that there is a line of dried soap on his cheek—"

"Wimsey!"

"Wait a minute—and dried soap in his mouth."

Bunter got up and appeared suddenly at the detective's elbow, the respectful man-servant all over.

"A little more brandy, sir?" he murmured.

"Wimsey," said Parker, "you are making me feel cold all over." He emptied his glass—stared at it as though he were surprised to find it empty. set it down, got up, walked across to the bookcase, turned round, stood with his back against it and said:

"Look here, Wimsey—you've been reading detective stories, you're talking nonsense."

---

[46] The presence of fleas, bedbugs and other insects has disturbed the sleep of travelers since Roman times. In "The Law of Hotel Life" (1879), Robert Vashon Rogers tells an anecdote about a man signing the register at a hotel and seeing a bedbug crawl out of a crack and march across the page: "I've been bled by St. Joe fleas, bitten by Kansas City spiders, and interviewed by Fort Scot graybacks, but I'll be hanged if I ever was in a place before where the bedbugs looked over the hotel register to find out where your room was."

"No, I ain't," said Lord Peter, sleepily, "uncommon good incident for a detective story, though, what? Bunter, we'll write one, and you shall illustrate it with photographs."

"Soap in his—Rubbish!" said Parker. "It was something else—some discoloration—"

"No," said Lord Peter, "there were hairs as well. Bristly ones. He had a beard."

He took his watch from his pocket, and drew out a couple of longish, stiff hairs, which he had imprisoned between the inner and the outer case.

Parker turned them over once or twice in his fingers, looked at them close to the light, examined them with a lens, handed them to the impassible Bunter, and said:

"Do you mean to tell me, Wimsey, that any man alive would"—he laughed harshly—"shave off his beard with his mouth open, and then go and get killed with his mouth full of hairs? You're mad."

"I don't tell you so," said Wimsey. "You policemen are all alike—only one idea in your skulls. Blest[47] if I can make out why you're ever appointed. He was shaved after he was dead. Pretty, ain't it? Uncommonly jolly little job for the barber, what? Here, sit down, man, and don't be an ass, stumpin' about the room like that. Worse things happen in war.[48] This is only a blinkin' old shillin' shocker.[49] But I'll tell you what, Parker, we're up against a criminal—the criminal—the real artist and blighter with imagination—real, artistic, finished stuff. I'm enjoyin' this, Parker."

---

[47] Blessed.

[48] A variation on the old expression "worse things happen at sea," suggesting that your problems might not seem so bad compared with the uncertainties of living near and sailing on the ocean. The phrase was possibly inspired by the Great Storm of 1703, when a hurricane struck England's South Coast and killed between 8,000 and 15,000 people.

[49] A popular novel with a heavy emphasis on crime and violence that sold for a shilling. Also called a penny dreadful or a dime novel. Sample titles include "The Life and Horrid Adventures of the Celebrated Dr. Faustus," "Captive of the Banditti," and "The Lunatic and His Turkey: A Tale of Witchcraft." Lord Peter's pleasure in the mystery will prove ironic.

CHAPTER III

ORD PETER FINISHED A SCARLATTI sonata, and sat looking thoughtfully at his own hands. The fingers were long and muscular, with wide, flat joints and square tips. When he was playing, his rather hard grey eyes softened, and his long, indeterminate mouth hardened in compensation. At no other time had he any pretensions to good looks, and at all times he was spoilt by a long, narrow chin, and a long, receding forehead, accentuated by the brushed-back sleekness of his tow-coloured hair. Labour papers, softening down the chin, caricatured him as a typical aristocrat.[1]

"That's a wonderful instrument," said Parker.

"It ain't so bad," said Lord Peter, "but Scarlatti wants a harpsichord.[2] Piano's too modern—all thrills and overtones. No good for our job, Parker. Have you come to any conclusion?"

"The man in the bath," said Parker, methodically, "was not a well-off man careful of his personal appearance. He was a labouring man, unemployed, but who had only recently lost his employment. He had been tramping about looking for a job when he met with his end. Somebody killed him and washed him and

---

[1] Newspapers aligned with the Labour Party, which advocates government control of key industries and the economy, the redistribution of wealth, publicly funded health care and education and increased rights for workers. In 1924, the first Labour government was formed under Ramsay MacDonald with help from the Liberal Party. It lasted nine months before collapsing.

[2] Domenico Scarlatti (1685-1757) was an Italian composer best known for his 555 keyboard sonatas. He wrote mostly for the harpsichord or the pianoforte, an early forerunner of the piano, hence, Lord Peter's observation that "Scarlatti wants a harpsichord."

scented him and shaved him in order to disguise him, and put him into Thipps's bath without leaving a trace. Conclusion: the murderer was a powerful man, since he killed him with a single blow on the neck, a man of cool head and masterly intellect, since he did all that ghastly business without leaving a mark, a man of wealth and refinement, since he had all the apparatus of an elegant toilet handy, and a man of bizarre, and almost perverted imagination, as is shown in the two horrible touches of putting the body in the bath and of adorning it with a pair of pince-nez."

"He is a poet of crime," said Wimsey. "By the way, your difficulty about the pince-nez is cleared up. Obviously, the pince-nez never belonged to the body."

"That only makes a fresh puzzle. One can't suppose the murderer left them in that obliging manner as a clue to his own identity."

"We can hardly suppose that; I'm afraid this man possessed what most criminals lack—a sense of humour."

"Rather macabre humour."

"True. But a man who can afford to be humourous at all in such circumstances is a terrible fellow. I wonder what he did with the body between the murder and depositing it chez[3] Thipps. Then there are more questions. How did he get it there? And why? Was it brought in at the door, as Sugg of our heart suggests? or through the window, as we think, on the not very adequate testimony of a smudge on the window-sill? Had the murderer accomplices? Is little Thipps really in it, or the girl? It don't do to put the notion out of court merely because Sugg inclines to it. Even idiots occasionally speak the truth accidentally. If not, why was Thipps selected for such an abominable practical joke? Has anybody got a grudge against Thipps? Who are the people in the other flats? We must find out that. Does Thipps play the piano at midnight over their heads or damage the reputation of the staircase by bringing home dubiously respectable ladies? Are there unsuccessful architects thirsting for his blood? Damn it all, Parker, there must be a motive somewhere. Can't have a crime without a motive, you know."

---

[3] French word for home, from the Latin *casa* for cottage.

"A madman—" suggested Parker, doubtfully.

"With a deuced lot of method in his madness. He hasn't made a mistake—not one, unless leaving hairs in the corpse's mouth can be called a mistake. Well, anyhow, it's not Levy—you're right there. I say, old thing, neither your man nor mine has left much clue to go upon, has he? And there don't seem to be any motives knockin' about, either. And we seem to be two suits of clothes short in last night's work. Sir Reuben makes tracks without so much as a fig-leaf,[4] and a mysterious individual turns up with a pince-nez, which is quite useless for purposes of decency. Dash it all! If only I had some good excuse for takin' up this body case officially—"

The telephone bell rang. The silent Bunter, whom the other two had almost forgotten, padded across to it.

"It's an elderly lady, my lord," he said, "I think she's deaf—I can't make her hear anything, but she's asking for your lordship."

Lord Peter seized the receiver, and yelled into it a "Hullo!" that might have cracked the vulcanite.[5] He listened for some minutes with an incredulous smile, which gradually broadened into a grin of delight. At length he screamed, "All right! all right!" several times, and rang off.

"By Jove!" he announced, beaming, "sportin' old bird! It's old Mrs. Thipps. Deaf as a post. Never used the 'phone before. But determined. Perfect Napoleon. The incomparable Sugg has made a discovery and arrested little Thipps. Old lady abandoned in the flat. Thipps's last shriek to her, 'Tell Lord Peter Wimsey.' Old girl undaunted. Wrestles with telephone book. Wakes up the people at the exchange.[6] Won't take no for an answer (not bein' able to hear

---

[4] A reference to the story of Adam and Eve, who, after eating the fruit from the Tree of Knowledge, "knew that they were naked, and they sewed fig leaves together, and made themselves aprons." Beginning about 1530, carved, cast or painted fig leaves were used to cover the genitals on artworks.

[5] A hardened rubber compound that weathers to a dull, dark-grey finish. The name is derived from vulcanization, the chemical process that converts rubber into more durable materials by adding sulfur or other curatives. Produced by the Goodyear Vulcanite Company, the compound was unstable and could break easily, and it was superseded by Bakelite, an early plastic.

[6] The telephone exchange, where operators connected phone calls.

it), gets through, says, 'Will I do what I can?' Says she would feel safe in the hands of a real gentleman. Oh, Parker, Parker! I could kiss her, I reely could, as Thipps says. I'll write to her instead—no, hang it, Parker, we'll go round. Bunter, get your infernal machine and the magnesium.[7] I say, we'll all go into partnership—pool the two cases and work 'em out together. You shall see my body to-night, Parker, and I'll look for your wandering Jew[8] to-morrow. I feel so happy, I shall explode. O Sugg, Sugg, how art thou suggified![9] Bunter, my shoes. I say, Parker, I suppose yours are rubber-soled. Not? Tut, tut, you mustn't go out like that. We'll lend you a pair. Gloves? Here. My stick, my torch, the lampblack, the forceps, knife, pill-boxes—all complete?"

"Certainly, my lord."

"Oh, Bunter, don't look so offended. I mean no harm. I believe in you, I trust you—what money have I got? That'll do. I knew a man once, Parker, who let a world-famous poisoner slip through his fingers, because the machine on the Underground[10] took nothing but

---

[7] A reference to Bunter's camera. To provide enough light to take a picture, powdered magnesium was poured onto a metal dish and ignited, using sparks from a flint wheel to create a flash. While effective, it was difficult to synchronize with the shutter and the open flame could cause a fire. It wasn't until the late 1920s that the flashbulb came into popular use.

[8] A Jewish character from medieval Christian folklore who taunted Jesus and was cursed to wander the earth until the Second Coming. Possibly inspired by Jesus' words in Matthew 16:28: "Verily I say unto you, there be some standing here, which shall not taste of death, till they see the Son of Man coming in his kingdom." The "Flores Historiarum" (Flowers of History) in the 1220s recorded the story of a visit to England by an Armenian archbishop. The bishop reported meeting a Jewish shoemaker named Cartaphilus who, as Jesus rested while carrying his cross to his crucifixion, hit him and said, "Go on quicker, Jesus! Go on quicker! Why dost Thou loiter?" Understandably irritated, Jesus replied, "I shall stand and rest, but thou shall go on till the last day."

[9] From "Romeo and Juliet," Act II, Scene 4, in which Mercutio creates a pun on the first part of Romeo's name, equating it with fish eggs:
BENVOLIO: Here comes Romeo, here comes Romeo.
MERCUTIO: Without his roe, like a dried herring: flesh, flesh, how art thou fishified!

[10] The London subway system, also known as the Tube. Founded in 1863, it's the world's first subway and the longest. Despite the name, more than half the line runs aboveground. In the pre-decimal currency of the time, 240 pennies made up 1 pound.

pennies. There was a queue at the booking office and the man at the barrier stopped him, and while they were arguing about accepting a five-pound-note (which was all he had) for a twopenny ride to Baker Street, the criminal had sprung into a Circle train,[11] and was next heard of in Constantinople, disguised as an elderly Church of England clergyman touring with his niece. Are we all ready? Go!"

They stepped out, Bunter carefully switching off the lights behind them.

As they emerged into the gloom and gleam of Piccadilly,[12] Wimsey stopped short with a little exclamation.

"Wait a second," he said, "I've thought of something. If Sugg's there he'll make trouble. I must short-circuit him."

He ran back, and the other two men employed the few minutes of his absence in capturing a taxi.

Inspector Sugg and a subordinate Cerberus[13] were on guard at 59, Queen Caroline Mansions, and showed no disposition to admit

---

[11] The Underground is broken down into routes, each with its own name. The Circle route opened in 1884 and loops around the center of London north of the Thames, with connections to the railroad stations at Victoria, King's Cross, Paddington and Liverpool Street.

[12] *Gloom and gleam.* The romantic London fog, through which one can imagine Jack the Ripper or Sherlock Holmes (or Lord Peter) striding, was in reality a foul mixture of water vapor, smoke and soot, fed by the pervasive use of coal for heat and power. The fog weakened lungs and caused fatal traffic collisions. R. Russell in "London Fogs" (1880) described it as "brown, reddish-yellow, or greenish, darkens more than a white fog, has a smoky, or sulphurous smell, is often somewhat dryer than a country fog, and produces, when thick, a choking sensation. Instead of diminishing while the sun rises higher, it often increases in density, and some of the most lowering London fogs occur about midday or late in the afternoon. Sometimes the brown masses rise and interpose a thick curtain at a considerable elevation between earth and sky. A white cloth spread out on the ground rapidly turns dirty, and particles of soot attach themselves to every exposed object." By the 1920s, when traffic lights and electric billboards were installed, the lights of Piccadilly Circus must have gleamed under a thick blanket of English industrial fog.

[13] The three-headed hound in Greek and Roman mythology that guarded the gates of Hades.

unofficial enquirers. Parker, indeed, they could not easily turn away, but Lord Peter found himself confronted with a surly manner and what Lord Beaconsfield described as a masterly inactivity.[14] It was in vain that Lord Peter pleaded that he had been retained by Mrs. Thipps on behalf of her son.

"Retained!" said Inspector Sugg, with a snort, "she'll be retained if she doesn't look out. Shouldn't wonder if she wasn't in it herself, only she's so deaf, she's no good for anything at all."

"Look here, Inspector," said Lord Peter, "what's the use of bein' so bally[15] obstructive? You'd much better let me in—you know I'll get there in the end. Dash it all, it's not as if I was takin' the bread out of your children's mouths. Nobody paid me for finding Lord Attenbury's emeralds for you."[16]

"It's my duty to keep out the public," said Inspector Sugg, morosely, "and it's going to stay out."

"I never said anything about your keeping out of the public,"[17] said Lord Peter, easily, sitting down on the staircase to thrash the matter out comfortably, "though I've no doubt pussyfoot's a good

---

[14] A description of Britain's policy toward its colonies which, in essence, allowed them to rule themselves so long as they didn't cause trouble. Prime Minister Benjamin Disraeli, the 1st Earl of Beaconsfield (1804-1881), abandoned this policy to counter Russia's desire to expand into Afghanistan. The phrase was coined by Sir James Mackintosh (1765-1832), a Scottish politician who had observed that the House of Commons, which "faithful to their system, remained in a wise and masterly inactivity."

[15] A substitute curse word, replacing "bloody" which as a reference to Christ would be considered crude and blasphemous.

[16] Lord Peter's first case, and the subject of the third post-Sayers novel by Jill Paton Walsh, published in 2010.

[17] Lord Peter was making a joke by deliberately misunderstanding Sugg's "keep out the public" as "keep out of *the* public" (e.g., the pub). *Pussyfoot.* Lord Peter is referring to William E. "Pussyfoot" Johnson, an American prohibitionist. As a U.S. special agent in the Indian Territory (and when it became a state, Oklahoma), he earned his nickname for his cat-like raids on gambling saloons, bars and brothels, earning more than 4,400 convictions during his three years in the service. He toured the U.S. and Europe extensively on behalf of the Anti-Saloon League. During his 1919 temperance campaign in Britain, medical students caught him and paraded him through London on a stretcher before police rescued him, but not before he lost the sight in an eye from a flying object. Abstinence advocates became known as "pussyfooters."

thing, on principle, if not exaggerated. The golden mean, Sugg, as Aristotle says, keeps you from bein' a golden ass.[18] Ever been a golden ass,[19] Sugg? I have. It would take a whole rose-garden to cure me, Sugg—

"You are my garden of beautiful roses,
My own rose, my one rose, that's you!"[20]

"I'm not going to stay any longer talking to you," said the harassed Sugg, "it's bad enough—hullo, drat that telephone. Here, Cawthorn, go and see what it is, if that old catamaran[21] will let you into the room. Shutting herself up there and screaming," said the Inspector, "it's enough to make a man give up crime and take to hedging and ditching."[22]

The constable came back:

"It's from the Yard, sir,"[23] he said, coughing apologetically,

---

[18] In considering how one should live, the Greek philosopher Aristotle (384 BC–322 BC) concluded that within each virtue there is a golden mean (mean, by the way, is defined in this instance as the middle point between extremes) that we should follow. For example, courage is a virtue, but too much of it leads to recklessness, and too little of it to cowardice. Other virtues, and their extremes, include gentleness (irascibility/dispiritedness); truthfulness (exaggeration/self-depreciation); wittiness (buffoonery/boorishness); and generosity (wastefulness/stinginess).

[19] A reference to "Metamorphoses," also known as "The Golden Ass," a bawdy novel by Apuleius (c.125–c.180). *A whole rose-garden to cure me.* When the narrator, Lucius, gets transformed into an ass, he returns to human form by eating a crown of roses held by a priest of Isis.

[20] From "The Garden of Roses," a popular song sung by Harry Macdonough and the Haydn Quartet in 1910. Macdonough (1871-1931) was a prolific Canadian singer who recorded hundreds of songs for Edison Records and the Victor Talking Machine Company and later became a record company executive.

[21] A disagreeable old woman. The word was commonly used during the late 18th and 19th centuries.

[22] A traditional method of building a fence around a farm using cut branches intertwined into a waist-high barrier. Traditionally, a tenth of the farm's hedges would be done each year, creating a renewal cycle of 10 years. Hedging can be performed with skill and artistry. Competitions are held, and there are even regional styles of hedge-laying.

[23] Scotland Yard. The headquarters of London's Metropolitan Police. Although the original location was at 4 Whitehall Place, its rear entrance opened onto Great

"the Chief says every facility is to be given to Lord Peter Wimsey, sir. Um!" He stood apart noncommittally, glazing his eyes.

"Five aces," said Lord Peter, cheerfully. "The Chief's a dear friend of my mother's. No go, Sugg, it's no good buckin' you've got a full house. I'm goin' to make it a bit fuller."[24]

He walked in with his followers.

The body had been removed a few hours previously, and when the bathroom and the whole flat had been explored by the naked eye and the camera of the competent Bunter, it became evident that the real problem of the household was old Mrs. Thipps. Her son and servant had both been removed, and it appeared that they had no friends in town, beyond a few business acquaintances of Thipps's, whose very addresses the old lady did not know. The other flats in the building were occupied respectively by a family of seven, at present departed to winter abroad, an elderly Indian colonel of ferocious manners, who lived alone with an Indian man-servant,[25] and a highly respectable family on the third floor, whom the disturbance over their heads had outraged to the last degree. The husband, indeed, when appealed to by Lord Peter, showed a little human weakness, but Mrs. Appledore, appearing suddenly in a warm dressing-gown, extricated him from the difficulties into which he was carelessly wandering.

"I am sorry," she said, "I'm afraid we can't interfere in any way. This is a very unpleasant business, Mr.—I'm afraid I didn't catch your name, and we have always found it better not to be

---

Scotland Yard, hence the name. During moves to larger facilities in 1890 and 1967, the headquarters building was renamed New Scotland Yard. The head of the service is known as the commissioner and classified as "chief police officer," known colloquially as "the chief."

[24] Lord Peter is indulging in a poker reference. Although the best hand is a royal flush (ace, king, queen, jack and 10), Lord Peter tops that with five aces, which in a game using one deck would provoke accusations of cheating. Lord Peter seems to be implying that he pulled an ace out of his sleeve by relying on his friendship with the chief of Scotland Yard to get around Sugg. A full house is a five-card hand consisting of three of a kind and two of a kind, which allows him to make a pun about his joining the investigation to make the house "a bit fuller."

[25] A valet or personal assistant, responsible for running the household and performing whatever tasks his master desired.

mixed up with the police.[26] Of course, if the Thippses are innocent, and I am sure I hope they are, it is very unfortunate for them, but I must say that the circumstances seem to me most suspicious, and to Theophilus too, and I should not like to have it said that we had assisted murderers. We might even be supposed to be accessories. Of course you are young, Mr.—"

"This is Lord Peter Wimsey, my dear," said Theophilus mildly.

She was unimpressed.

"Ah, yes," she said, "I believe you are distantly related to my late cousin, the Bishop of Carisbrooke. Poor man! He was always being taken in by impostors; he died without ever learning any better. I imagine you take after him, Lord Peter."

"I doubt it," said Lord Peter. "So far as I know he is only a connection, though it's a wise child that knows its own father.[27] I congratulate you, dear lady, on takin' after the other side of the family. You'll forgive my buttin' in upon you like this in the middle of the night, though, as you say, it's all in the family, and I'm sure I'm very much obliged to you, and for permittin' me to admire that awfully fetchin' thing you've got on. Now, don't you worry, Mr. Appledore. I'm thinkin' the best thing I can do is to trundle the old lady down to my mother and take her out of your way, otherwise you might be findin' your Christian feelin's gettin' the better of you some fine day, and there's nothin' like Christian feelin's for upsettin' a man's domestic comfort. Good-night, sir—good-night, dear lady—it's simply rippin' of you to let me drop in like this."

"Well!" said Mrs. Appledore, as the door closed behind him.

And—

"I thank the goodness and the grace
That on my birth have smiled,"[28]

---

[26] Reputation and social standing plays a great role in the English class system. As Mrs. Appledore explains, it simply wouldn't do to be mixed up in police business and thought of as helping a murderer.

[27] A proverb that's quoted in "The Merchant of Venice." In Act II, Scene 2, Launcelot Gobbo, Shylock's servant, meets his blind father, who doesn't recognize him. Launcelot tells him "if you had your eyes, you might fail of the knowing me: it is a wise father that knows his own child."

[28] From the poem "The Thankful Child."

said Lord Peter, "and taught me to be bestially impertinent when I choose. Cat!"[29]

Two a. m. saw Lord Peter Wimsey arrive in a friend's car at the Dower House[30], Denver Castle, in company with a deaf and aged lady and an antique portmanteau.[31]

"It's very nice to see you, dear," said the Dowager Duchess, placidly. She was a small, plump woman, with perfectly white hair and exquisite hands. In feature she was as unlike her second son as she was like him in character; her black eyes twinkled cheerfully, and her manners and movements were marked with a neat and

---

I thank the goodness and the grace
Which on my birth have smiled,
And made me in my early days
A happy free-born child.

I was not born a little slave
To labor in the sun,
And wish that I were in the grave,
And all my labor done.

My God, I thank thee, who hast planned
A better lot for me,
And placed me in this happy land,
Where I may hear of Thee.

A version of this poem appeared in "The Slave's Friend," a tract published for children in 1836 by the American Anti-Slavery Society.

[29] This is a deliberate slight and one source of Lord Peter's uncharacteristically bitchy reaction. Under the English class system, you are not related to anyone below your rank; they are related to you. Mrs. Appledore was implying that the late bishop outranked Lord Peter, which he certainly did not. *Carisbrooke* is a village on the Isle of Wight and the home of St. Mary's Church, which dates to the 14th century.

[30] A home on an estate where the widow of the late owner lives. If her husband dies and the heir is unmarried, she is customarily allowed to stay in the main house until he is married.

[31] A suitcase.

rapid decision. She wore a charming wrap from Liberty's,[32] and sat watching Lord Peter eat cold beef and cheese as though his arrival in such incongruous circumstances and company were the most ordinary event possible, which with him, indeed, it was.

"Have you got the old lady to bed?" asked Lord Peter.

"Oh, yes, dear. Such a striking old person, isn't she? And very courageous. She tells me she has never been in a motor-car before. But she thinks you a very nice lad, dear—that careful of her, you remind her of her own son. Poor little Mr. Thipps—whatever made your friend the inspector think he could have murdered anybody?"

"My friend the inspector—no, no more, thank you, Mother—is determined to prove that the intrusive person in Thipps's bath is Sir Reuben Levy, who disappeared mysteriously from his house last night. His line of reasoning is: We've lost a middle-aged gentleman without any clothes on in Park Lane; we've found a middle-aged gentleman without any clothes on in Battersea. Therefore they're one and the same person, Q.E.D.,[33] and put little Thipps in quod."[34]

"You're very elliptical, dear," said the Duchess, mildly. "Why should Mr. Thipps be arrested even if they are the same?"

"Sugg must arrest somebody," said Lord Peter, "but there is one odd little bit of evidence come out which goes a long way to support Sugg's theory, only that I know it to be no go by the evidence of my own eyes. Last night at about 9:15 a young woman was strollin' up the Battersea Park Road for purposes best known to herself,[35] when she saw a gentleman in a fur coat and top-hat saunterin' along under an umbrella, lookin' at the names of all the

---

[32] A department store founded by Arthur Liberty in 1875. Drawing on its connections with designers in the Arts and Crafts and Art Nouveau movements, the store became known for its stylish clothing. It is still in business.

[33] *Quod erat demonstrandum*, a Latin phrase which means "what was to be demonstrated." Traditionally used at the end of a mathematical proof or philosophical argument to indicate that the theory has been proved.

[34] Slang for prison, possibly derived from quadrangle, the enclosure where prisoners took exercise, used as early as 1700.

[35] Lord Peter is implying that she is a prostitute. Her behavior with the gentleman and her reluctance to be explicit to Sugg and offending his "very pure, high-minded ideals" confirms it.

streets. He looked a bit out of place, so, not bein' a shy girl, you
see, she walked up to him, and said, 'Good-evening.' 'Can you tell
me, please,' says the mysterious stranger, 'whether this street leads
into Prince of Wales Road?' She said it did, and further asked him
in a jocular manner what he was doing with himself and all the rest
of it, only she wasn't altogether so explicit about that part of the
conversation, because she was unburdenin' her heart to Sugg,
d'you see, and he's paid by a grateful country to have very pure,
high-minded ideals, what? Anyway, the old boy said he couldn't
attend to her just then as he had an appointment. 'I've got to go
and see a man, my dear,' was how she said he put it, and he
walked on up Alexandra Avenue towards Prince of Wales Road.
She was starin' after him, still rather surprised, when she was
joined by a friend of hers, who said, 'It's no good wasting your
time with him—that's Levy—I knew him when I lived in the West
End,[36] and the girls used to call him Pea-green Incorruptible'[37]—
friend's name suppressed, owing to implications of story, but girl
vouches for what was said. She thought no more about it till the
milkman brought news this morning of the excitement at Queen
Caroline Mansions; then she went round, though not likin' the
police as a rule, and asked the man there whether the dead
gentleman had a beard and glasses. Told he had glasses but no
beard, she incautiously said: 'Oh, then, it isn't him,' and the man
said, 'Isn't who?' and collared her. That's her story. Sugg's
delighted, of course, and quodded Thipps on the strength of it."

"Dear me," said the Duchess, "I hope the poor girl won't get
into trouble."

"Shouldn't think so," said Lord Peter. "Thipps is the one that's

---

[36] An area of central London that includes Soho and parts of Mayfair and
Chinatown. Near the royal seat of power at Westminster, it was favored by the
elite, not only because it was upwind of the smoke from the city, but for the
entertainment it offers.

[37] A reference to Maximilien Robespierre (1758-1794), a leading revolutionary
who helped institute the Reign of Terror during the French Revolution and was
eventually executed under it. His supporters named him "the incorruptible" in
praise of his virtue. The sea-green modifier was added by Thomas Carlyle (1795-
1881) in "The French Revolution," his monumental three-volume history as a
reference to Robespierre's sallow complexion.

going to get it in the neck.[38] Besides, he's done a silly thing. I got that out of Sugg, too, though he was sittin' tight on the information. Seems Thipps got into a confusion about the train he took back from Manchester.[39] Said first he got home at 10:30. Then they pumped Gladys Horrocks, who let out he wasn't back till after 11:45. Then Thipps, bein' asked to explain the discrepancy, stammers and bungles and says, first that he missed the train. Then Sugg makes enquiries at St. Pancras[40] and discovers that he left a bag in the cloakroom[41] there at ten. Thipps, again asked to explain, stammers worse an' says he walked about for a few hours—met a friend—can't say who—didn't meet a friend—can't say what he did with his time—can't explain why he didn't go back for his bag—can't say what time he did get in—can't explain how he got a bruise on his forehead. In fact, can't explain himself at all. Gladys Horrocks interrogated again. Says, this time, Thipps came in at 10:30. Then admits she didn't hear him come in. Can't say why she didn't hear him come in. Can't say why she said first of all that she did hear him. Bursts into tears. Contradicts herself. Everybody's suspicion roused. Quod 'em both."

"As you put it, dear," said the Duchess, "it all sounds very confusing, and not quite respectable. Poor little Mr. Thipps would be terribly upset by anything that wasn't respectable."

"I wonder what he did with himself," said Lord Peter

---

[38] The punishment for murder in England until 1965 was death by hanging. Since "get it" meant to be caught and/or punished, it's only a short step to imply that Mr. Thipps might pay the ultimate price if convicted of murder.

[39] A city about 180 miles northwest of London. A major manufacturing center during the Industrial Revolution, *Manchester* processed at least 65% of the world's cotton before the First World War.

[40] A major railway station in central London. Considering that it is north of the Thames — even north of Lord Peter's home — it's understandable that Inspector Sugg would want to know why Mr. Thipps was checking his bag in a cloakroom so far from his respectable flat across the river. Pancras, by the way, was a Roman who was beheaded around 304 at age 14 during the persecution of the Christians under Diocletian. Some of his relics were taken to England, where a number of churches were dedicated to him, including St. Pancras Old Church in London.

[41] A manned room at a railway station where luggage or parcels can be stored temporarily. This allowed passengers to spend the day in town to conduct their business without dragging along unwieldy baggage.

thoughtfully. "I really don't think he was committing a murder. Besides, I believe the fellow has been dead a day or two, though it don't do to build too much on doctors' evidence. It's an entertainin' little problem."

"Very curious, dear. But so sad about poor Sir Reuben. I must write a few lines to Lady Levy; I used to know her quite well, you know, dear, down in Hampshire,[42] when she was a girl. Christine Ford, she was then, and I remember so well the dreadful trouble there was about her marrying a Jew. That was before he made his money, of course, in that oil business out in America. The family wanted her to marry Julian Freke, who did so well afterwards and was connected with the family, but she fell in love with this Mr. Levy and eloped with him. He was very handsome, then, you know, dear, in a foreign-looking way, but he hadn't any means, and the Fords didn't like his religion. Of course we're all Jews nowadays[43] and they wouldn't have minded so much if he'd pretended to be something else, like that Mr. Simons we met at Mrs. Porchester's, who always tells everybody that he got his nose in Italy at the Renaissance, and claims to be descended somehow or other from La Bella Simonetta[44]—so foolish, you know, dear—as if anybody believed it; and I'm sure some Jews are very good people, and personally I'd much rather they believed something,[45] though of course it must be very inconvenient, what with not working on Saturdays and circumcising the poor little babies and

---

[42] A coastal county southwest of London.

[43] In the aftermath of World War I, financially pressed aristocratic families were either going into business or marrying into families of industrialists. Entering the House of Lords were "soap and pickles lords" — as Sayers called them in "Clouds of Witness" — who used their money to rise into the aristocracy. The Dowager Duchess is implying that everyone, even the aristocracy, is grubbing for money.

[44] Simonetta Vespucci (c.1453-1476) was the wife of Italian nobleman Marco Vespucci of Florence and reputed to be the mistress of Giuliano de Medici, the brother of Lorenzo the Magnificent, the Renaissance ruler of Florence. She was considered to be the greatest beauty of her age and immortalized in portraits, paintings and poems.

[45] The Dowager Duchess might be referring to the commonly held belief that Jews do not believe in a heaven. This is, at its kindest, a simplification, as their beliefs in the afterlife range from recognizing the existence of an eternal soul and nothing else, to Jewish mysticism recognizing no less than seven heavens.

everything depending on the new moon[46] and that funny kind of meat they have with such a slang-sounding name, and never being able to have bacon for breakfast. Still, there it was, and it was much better for the girl to marry him if she was really fond of him, though I believe young Freke was really devoted to her, and they're still great friends. Not that there was ever a real engagement, only a sort of understanding with her father, but he's never married, you know, and lives all by himself in that big house next to the hospital, though he's very rich and distinguished now, and I know ever so many people have tried to get hold of him—there was Lady Mainwaring wanted him for that eldest girl of hers, though I remember saying at the time it was no use expecting a surgeon to be taken in by a figure that was all padding—they have so many opportunities of judging, you know, dear."

"Lady Levy seems to have had the knack of makin' people devoted to her," said Peter. "Look at the pea-green incorruptible Levy."

"That's quite true, dear; she was a most delightful girl, and they say her daughter is just like her. I rather lost sight of them when she married, and you know your father didn't care much about business people, but I know everybody always said they were a model couple. In fact it was a proverb that Sir Reuben was as well loved at home as he was hated abroad.[47] I don't mean in foreign countries, you know, dear—just the proverbial way of putting things—like 'a saint abroad and a devil at home'—only the other way on, reminding one of the Pilgrim's Progress."[48]

---

[46] The months in the Jewish calendar are calculated based on the appearance of the new moon, which allows for variations in the dates of some holidays. For example, Rosh Hashanah can fall between Sept. 5 and Oct. 5.

[47] This is an inversion of the Christian proverb about those who portray themselves as Christian outside the home while acting otherwise inside.

[48] A novel by English preacher John Bunyan (1628-1688). It is written as an allegory, in which symbolic figures are cast into human form (for example, by representing death as the Grim Reaper). "Pilgrim's Progress" portrays the spiritual quest of Christian, representing humanity, and his journey to Heaven atop Mount Zion. The Dowager is referring to a passage in Chapter 12, when Christian is speaking to Faithful about their new travel companion, Talkative:

"Remember the proverb, 'They say and do not,' [Matthew 23:3] but 'the Kingdom of God is not in word, but in power.' [1 Corinthians, 4:20] He talketh of

"Yes," said Peter, "I daresay the old man made one or two enemies."

"Dozens, dear—such a dreadful place, the City, isn't it? Everybody Ishmaels together[49]—though I don't suppose Sir Reuben would like to be called that, would he? Doesn't it mean illegitimate, or not a proper Jew, anyway? I always did get confused with those Old Testament characters."

Lord Peter laughed and yawned.

"I think I'll turn in for an hour or two," he said. "I must be back in town at eight—Parker's coming to breakfast."

The Duchess looked at the clock, which marked five minutes to three.

"I'll send up your breakfast at half past six, dear," she said. "I hope you'll find everything all right. I told them just to slip a hot-water bottle in; those linen sheets are so chilly; you can put it out if it's in your way."[50]

---

prayer, of repentance, of faith, and of the new birth; but he knows only to talk of them. I have been in his family, and have observed him both at home and abroad; and I know what I say of him is the truth. His house is as empty of religion as the white of an egg is of savour. There is there neither prayer nor sign of repentance for sin… Thus say the common people that know him: A saint abroad and a devil at home. His poor family finds it so, he is such a churl, such a railer at, and so unreasonable with his servants, that they neither know how to do for or speak to him. Men that have any dealings with him say, it is better to deal with a Turk than with him; … For my part, I am of the opinion that he has, by his wicked life, caused many to stumble and fall; and will be, if God prevent not, the ruin of many more."

So the Duchess, in her roundabout way, is praising Sir Reuben, despite her late husband's attitude toward businessmen.

[49] Another variation on the Dowager Duchess' "we're all Jews nowadays" remark. Ishmael is considered a prophet by Islam and credited with rebuilding the Kaaba in Mecca with Abraham's help. In Judaism, he is seen as a wicked through repentant man in Judaism. He was the eldest son of Abraham and Hagar, herself a maidservant given to Abraham as a surrogate by his wife, Sarah. When Sarah became pregnant with Isaac, Hagar was expelled from the tribe with her son, although comforted by God's promise to Abraham that He would "make Ishmael into a nation."

[50] *Hot water bottle.* A rubber bladder filled with hot water, used when getting into bed was a chilly experience in the days before central heating. Before the invention of rubber, a metal container containing hot coals was used, at the risk of scorching the sheets. *Linen.* A fine textile made from the fibers of the flax plant. Linen is particularly valued in hot weather for its coolness, but, as the Duchess notes, it can be uncomfortable in winter.

CHAPTER IV

"SO THERE IT IS, PARKER," said Lord Peter, pushing his coffee-cup aside and lighting his after-breakfast pipe; "you may find it leads you to something, though it don't seem to get me any further with my bathroom problem. Did you do anything more at that after I left?"

"No; but I've been on the roof this morning."

"The deuce[1] you have—what an energetic devil you are! I say, Parker, I think this co-operative scheme is an uncommonly good one. It's much easier to work on someone else's job than one's own—gives one that delightful feelin' of interferin' and bossin' about, combined with the glorious sensation that another fellow is takin' all one's own work off one's hands. You scratch my back and I'll scratch yours, what? Did you find anything?"

"Not very much. I looked for any footmarks of course, but naturally, with all this rain, there wasn't a sign. Of course, if this were a detective story, there'd have been a convenient shower exactly an hour before the crime and a beautiful set of marks which could only have come there between two and three in the morning, but this being real life in a London November, you might as well expect footprints in Niagara.[2] I searched the roofs right along—and came to the jolly conclusion that any person in any blessed flat in the blessed row might have done it. All the staircases open on to the roof and the leads are quite flat; you can

---

[1] Devil.
[2] Niagara Falls, located on the U.S.-Canadian border outside Buffalo, N.Y.

walk along as easy as along Shaftesbury Avenue.³ Still, I've got some evidence that the body did walk along there."

"What's that?"

Parker brought out his pocketbook and extracted a few shreds of material, which he laid before his friend.

"One was caught in the gutter just above Thipps's bathroom window, another in a crack of the stone parapet just over it, and the rest came from the chimney-stack behind, where they had caught in an iron stanchion.⁴ What do you make of them?"

Lord Peter scrutinized them very carefully through his lens.

"Interesting," he said, "damned interesting. Have you developed those plates, Bunter?" he added, as that discreet assistant came in with the post.

"Yes, my lord."

"Caught anything?"

"I don't know whether to call it anything or not, my lord," said Bunter, dubiously. "I'll bring the prints in."

"Do," said Wimsey. "Hallo! here's our advertisement about the gold chain in the Times—very nice it looks: 'Write, 'phone or call 110, Piccadilly.'⁵ Perhaps it would have been safer to put a box number, though I always think that the franker you are with people, the more you're likely to deceive 'em; so unused is the modern world to the open hand and the guileless heart, what?"

"But you don't think the fellow who left that chain on the body is going to give himself away by coming here and enquiring about it?"

"I don't, fathead," said Lord Peter, with the easy politeness of the real aristocracy, "that's why I've tried to get hold of the jeweler who originally sold the chain. See?" He pointed to the paragraph.

³ A major street in central London, running from Piccadilly Circus to New Oxford Street. Named for Anthony Ashley-Cooper, the 7th Earl of Shaftesbury (1801-1885), a social reformer who attempted to improve life for the poor in housing, hospitals and factories.

⁴ *Parapet.* A low wall lining the edge of a roof. *Chimney-stack.* A chimney, usually containing more than one flue, typically found in apartment buildings or large houses. *Stanchion.* An upright bar or post.

⁵ Before the introduction of phone numbers, operators connected calls using addresses.

"It's not an old chain—hardly worn at all. Oh, thanks, Bunter. Now, see here, Parker, these are the fingermarks[6] you noticed yesterday on the window-sash and on the far edge of the bath. I'd overlooked them; I give you full credit for the discovery, I crawl, I grovel, my name is Watson, and you need not say what you were just going to say, because I admit it all. Now we shall—Hullo, hullo, hullo!"

The three men stared at the photographs.

"The criminal," said Lord Peter, bitterly, "climbed over the roofs in the wet and not unnaturally got soot on his fingers. He arranged the body in the bath, and wiped away all traces of himself except two, which he obligingly left to show us how to do our job. We learn from a smudge on the floor that he wore india rubber boots,[7] and from this admirable set of fingerprints on the edge of the bath that he had the usual number of fingers and wore rubber gloves. That's the kind of man he is. Take the fool away, gentlemen."

He put the prints aside, and returned to an examination of the shreds of material in his hand. Suddenly he whistled softly.

"Do you make anything of these, Parker?"

"They seemed to me to be ravellings of some coarse cotton stuff—a sheet, perhaps, or an improvised rope."

"Yes," said Lord Peter—"yes. It may be a mistake—it may be our mistake. I wonder. Tell me, d'you think these tiny threads are long enough and strong enough to hang a man?"

He was silent, his long eyes narrowing into slits behind the smoke of his pipe.

"What do you suggest doing this morning?" asked Parker.

"Well," said Lord Peter, "it seems to me it's about time I took a hand in your job. Let's go round to Park Lane and see what larks Sir Reuben Levy was up to in bed last night."

---

[6] Fingerprints. The use of fingerprints to identify criminals had been in use in England since 1900.
[7] Natural rubber, derived from latex tapped from rubber plants much like maple syrup. British planters introduced commercial cultivation of rubber in India by 1902.

"And now, Mrs. Pemming, if you would be so kind as give me a blanket," said Mr. Bunter, coming down into the kitchen, "and permit of me hanging a sheet across the lower part of this window, and drawing the screen across here, so—so as to shut off any reflections, if you understand me, we'll get to work."

Sir Reuben Levy's cook, with her eye upon Mr. Bunter's gentlemanly and well-tailored appearance, hastened to produce what was necessary. Her visitor placed on the table a basket, containing a water-bottle, a silver-backed hairbrush, a pair of boots, a small roll of linoleum, and the "Letters of a Self-made Merchant to His Son,"[8] bound in polished morocco.[9] He drew an umbrella from beneath his arm and added it to the collection. He then advanced a ponderous photographic machine and set it up in the neighbourhood of the kitchen range; then, spreading a newspaper over the fair, scrubbed surface of the table, he began to roll up his sleeves and insinuate himself into a pair of surgical

---

[8] A self-help book published in 1902 by George Horace Lorimer (1867-1937), consisting of letters from a Chicago pork packer, John Graham, to his son, Pierrepont "Piggy" Graham, as he enters Harvard. The letters were full of aphorisms and advice:

* About business: "I can't hand out any ready-made success to you. It would do you no good, and it would do the house harm. There is plenty of room at the top here, but there is no elevator in the building."

* Generosity: "The meanest man alive is the one who is generous with money that he has not had to sweat for, and the boy who is a good fellow at someone else's expense would not work up into first-class fertilizer."

* Women: "Marriages may be made in heaven, but most engagements are made in the back parlor with the gas so low that a fellow doesn't really get a square look at what he's taking."

Socialist author Upton Sinclair (1878-1968) called "Letters" "a work of commercial depravity." We know that Sayers owned the sequel, "Old Gorgon Graham: More Letters From a Self-Made Merchant to His Son," so she probably had a copy of this volume as well.

[9] Goatskin that's been dyed red on the grain side and then tanned to bring out its characteristic bird's-eye pattern. Originally imported from Morocco. In the Bob Hope-Bing Crosby movie "The Road to Morocco," they sing that "like Webster's Dictionary / we're Morocco bound."

gloves. Sir Reuben Levy's valet,[10] entering at the moment and finding him thus engaged, put aside the kitchenmaid, who was staring from a front-row position, and inspected the apparatus critically. Mr. Bunter nodded brightly to him, and uncorked a small bottle of grey powder.[11]

"Odd sort of fish,[12] your employer, isn't he?" said the valet, carelessly.

"Very singular, indeed," said Mr. Bunter. "Now, my dear," he added, ingratiatingly, to the parlourmaid, "I wonder if you'd just pour a little of this grey powder over the edge of the bottle while I'm holding it—and the same with this boot—here, at the top— thank you, Miss—what is your name? Price? Oh, but you've got another name besides Price, haven't you? Mabel, eh? That's a name I'm uncommonly partial to—that's very nicely done, you've a steady hand, Miss Mabel—see that? That's the fingermarks— three there, and two here, and smudged over in both places. No, don't you touch 'em, my dear, or you'll rub the bloom off. We'll stand 'em up here till they're ready to have their portraits taken. Now then, let's take the hairbrush next. Perhaps, Mrs. Pemming, you'd like to lift him up very carefully by the bristles."

"By the bristles, Mr. Bunter?"

"If you please, Mrs. Pemming—and lay him here. Now, Miss Mabel, another little exhibition of your skill, if you please. No— we'll try lampblack[13] this time. Perfect. Couldn't have done it better myself. Ah! there's a beautiful set. No smudges this time. That'll interest his lordship. Now the little book—no, I'll pick that up myself—with these gloves, you see, and by the edges—I'm a

---

[10] A gentleman's male servant. Generally responsible for caring for the master's clothes and appearance, he could also act as a personal assistant and run errands.

[11] A powder used to identify and lift fingerprints, generally made of zinc stearate or lead. Powders come in a variety of colors and can be magnetized for use on metal surfaces. Some powders are more suitable for certain materials, plus it helps if the color contrasts well against the object being tested, so the examiner can see the print clearly.

[12] Slang for a peculiar fellow.

[13] Fine soot left over when organic compounds are not completely burned. In powder form, it is combined with rosin and Fuller's earth and used to raise fingerprints off surfaces.

careful criminal, Mrs. Pemming, I don't want to leave any traces. Dust the cover all over, Miss Mabel; now this side—that's the way to do it. Lots of prints and no smudges. All according to plan. Oh, please, Mr. Graves, you mustn't touch it—it's as much as my place is worth to have it touched."

"D'you have to do much of this sort of thing?" enquired Mr. Graves, from a superior standpoint.

"Any amount," replied Mr. Bunter, with a groan calculated to appeal to Mr. Graves's heart and unlock his confidence. "If you'd kindly hold one end of this bit of linoleum, Mrs. Pemming, I'll hold up this end while Miss Mabel operates. Yes, Mr. Graves, it's a hard life, valeting by day and developing by night—morning tea at any time from 6:30 to 11, and criminal investigation at all hours. It's wonderful, the ideas these rich men with nothing to do get into their heads."

"I wonder you stand it," said Mr. Graves. "Now there's none of that here. A quiet, orderly, domestic life, Mr. Bunter, has much to be said for it. Meals at regular hours; decent, respectable families to dinner—none of your painted women—and no valeting at night, there's much to be said for it. I don't hold with Hebrews as a rule, Mr. Bunter, and of course I understand that you may find it to your advantage to be in a titled family, but there's less thought of that these days, and I will say, for a self-made man, no one could call Sir Reuben vulgar, and my lady at any rate is county—Miss Ford, she was, one of the Hampshire Fords,[14] and both of them always most considerate."

"I agree with you, Mr. Graves—his lordship and me have never held with being narrow-minded—why, yes, my dear, of course it's a footmark, this is the washstand linoleum.[15] A good Jew can be a good man,[16] that's what I've always said. And regular hours and

---

[14] When gossiping about a person, it can help to identify what part of England their family comes from, especially when dealing with common names.
Hampshire is a county on England's southern coast and the home of Jane Austen, Charles Dickens and the British army, navy and air force.
[15] A covering used to protect a wooden floor from water stains.
[16] One important consideration in Judaism is the determination of what constitutes a "good Jew." Is it by rigorously observing the rituals? By living according to the Torah (known in Christianity as the first five books of the Old Testament:

considerate habits have a great deal to recommend them. Very simple in his tastes, now, Sir Reuben, isn't he? for such a rich man, I mean."

"Very simple indeed," said the cook, "the meals he and her ladyship have when they're by themselves with Miss Rachel—well, there now—if it wasn't for the dinners, which is always good when there's company, I'd be wastin' my talents and education here, if you understand me, Mr. Bunter."

Mr. Bunter added the handle of the umbrella to his collection, and began to pin a sheet across the window, aided by the housemaid.

"Admirable," said he. "Now, if I might have this blanket on the table and another on a towel-horse[17] or something of that kind by way of a background—you're very kind, Mrs. Pemming.... Ah! I wish his lordship never wanted valeting at night. Many's the time I've sat up till three and four, and up again to call him early to go off Sherlocking at the other end of the country. And the mud he gets on his clothes and his boots!"

"I'm sure it's a shame, Mr. Bunter," said Mrs. Pemming, warmly. "Low, I calls it. In my opinion, police-work ain't no fit occupation for a gentleman, let alone a lordship."

"Everything made so difficult, too," said Mr. Bunter, nobly sacrificing his employer's character and his own feelings in a good cause; "boots chucked into a corner, clothes hung up on the floor, as they say—"

"That's often the case with these men as are born with a silver spoon in their mouths,"[18] said Mr. Graves. "Now, Sir Reuben, he's never lost his good old-fashioned habits. Clothes folded up neat, boots put out in his dressing-room, so as a man could get them in the morning, everything made easy."

Genesis, Exodus, Leviticus, Numbers and Deuteronomy)? What if you don't observe Jewish law or attend services, but live ethically? A common prejudice against Jews is that they favor their religion over the community, and while Sayers herself might have believed it — see her wartime letter in the essay "English Anti-Semitism" — Bunter, it seems, does not.

[17] A rack consisting of several bars from which towels are draped. Bunter is setting up a neutral background to photograph Sir Reuben's possessions.

[18] To be born rich. Graves is drawing a comparison between Lord Peter, born to wealth and therefore filled with bad habits, and Sir Reuben, a self-made man who never forgot where he came from.

"He forgot them the night before last, though."

"The clothes, not the boots. Always thoughtful for others, is Sir Reuben. Ah! I hope nothing's happened to him."

"Indeed, no, poor gentleman," chimed in the cook, "and as for what they're sayin', that he'd 'ave gone out surrepshous-like[19] to do something he didn't ought, well, I'd never believe it of him, Mr. Bunter not if I was to take my dying oath upon it."

"Ah!" said Mr. Bunter, adjusting his arc-lamps[20] and connecting them with the nearest electric light, "and that's more than most of us could say of them as pays us."

"Five foot ten," said Lord Peter, "and not an inch more." He peered dubiously at the depression in the bed clothes, and measured it a second time with the gentleman-scout's vade-mecum. Parker entered this particular in a neat pocketbook.

"I suppose," he said, "a six-foot-two man might leave a five-foot-ten depression if he curled himself up."

"Have you any Scotch blood in you, Parker?" enquired his colleague, bitterly.

"Not that I know of," replied Parker. "Why?"

"Because of all the cautious, ungenerous, deliberate and cold-blooded devils I know," said Lord Peter, "you are the most cautious, ungenerous, deliberate and cold-blooded. Here am I, sweating my brains out to introduce a really sensational incident into your dull and disreputable little police investigation, and you refuse to show a single spark of enthusiasm."

"Well, it's no good jumping at conclusions."

"Jump? You don't even crawl distantly within sight of a conclusion. I believe if you caught the cat with her head in the cream-jug[21] you'd say it was conceivable that the jug was empty

---

[19] Another use of the Cockney accent for humorous effect.
[20] A type of lamp that produces light from two electrodes in a gas-filled bulb. A fluorescent tube operates on the same principle.
[21] A small pot that holds cream, usually for tea.

when she got there."

"Well, it would be conceivable, wouldn't it?"

"Curse you," said Lord Peter. He screwed his monocle into his eye, and bent over the pillow, breathing hard and tightly through his nose.

"Here, give me the tweezers," he said presently. "good heavens, man, don't blow like that, you might be a whale." He nipped up an almost invisible object from the linen.

"What is it?" asked Parker.

"It's a hair," said Wimsey grimly, his hard eyes growing harder. "Let's go and look at Levy's hats, shall we? And you might just ring for that fellow with the churchyard name, do you mind?"

Mr. Graves, when summoned, found Lord Peter Wimsey squatting on the floor of the dressing-room before a row of hats arranged upside-down before him.

"Here you are," said that nobleman cheerfully, "now, Graves, this is a guessin' competition—a sort of three-hat trick,[22] to mix metaphors. Here are nine hats, including three top-hats.[23] Do you identify all these hats as belonging to Sir Reuben Levy? You do? Very good. Now I have three guesses as to which hat he wore the night he disappeared, and if I guess right, I win; if I don't, you win. See? Ready? Go. I suppose you know the answer yourself, by the way."

"Do I understand your lordship to be asking which hat Sir Reuben wore when he went out on Monday night, your lordship?"

"No, you don't understand a bit," said Lord Peter. "I'm asking if you know—don't tell me, I'm going to guess."

"I do know, your lordship," said Mr. Graves, reprovingly.

"Well," said Lord Peter, "as he was dinin' at the Ritz[24] he wore a topper. Here are three toppers. In three guesses I'd be bound to hit the right one, wouldn't I? That don't seem very sportin'. I'll

---

[22] Lord Peter is referring to the three-shell game, in which a dry pea is put under one of three walnut shells. The shells are moved about, and the bettor has to guess which shell the pea is under. In dishonest hands, the shell game is a "short-con" used to swindle the marks.

[23] A tall, flat-crowned black hat usually worn with formal wear.

[24] A hotel at 150 Piccadilly, down the street from Lord Peter's residence, opened in 1906 by Swiss hotelier Cesar Ritz.

take one guess. It was this one."

He indicated the hat next the window.

"Am I right, Graves—have I got the prize?"

"That is the hat in question, my lord," said Mr. Graves, without excitement.

"Thanks," said Lord Peter, "that's all I wanted to know. Ask Bunter to step up, would you?"

Mr. Bunter stepped up with an aggrieved[25] air, and his usually smooth hair ruffled by the focussing cloth.[26]

"Oh, there you are, Bunter," said Lord Peter; "look here—"

"Here I am, my lord," said Mr. Bunter, with respectful reproach, "but if you'll excuse me saying so, downstairs is where I ought to be, with all those young women about—they'll be fingering the evidence,[27] my lord."

"I cry you mercy,"[28] said Lord Peter, "but I've quarrelled

---

[25] Feeling troubled or distressed.

[26] A large piece of cloth attached to the back of a camera that uses chemically-treated glass plates instead of film. The operator ducks underneath it and frames the subject by looking through the lens. When he is ready to take the picture, he slides the glass plate into place and opens the shutter. The cloth makes the process easier by blocking unwanted light.

[27] That is, handling the object and possibly smudging fingerprints.

[28] A common phrase in Shakespeare's. It is also a line from a sonnet by John Keats written to his lover, Fanny Brawne, the year after they were betrothed. He died of tuberculosis in Italy before they could marry, and she stayed in mourning for him for six years. The sonnet runs:

> I cry your mercy — pity — love! — ay, love!
>   Merciful love that tantalises not
> One-thoughted, never-wandering, guileless love,
>   Unmask'd, and being seen — without a blot!
> O! let me have thee whole, — all — all — be mine!
>   That shape, that fairness, that sweet minor zest
> Of love, your kiss, — those hands, those eyes divine,
>   That warm, white, lucent, million-pleasured breast, —
> Yourself — your soul — in pity give me all,
>   Withhold no atom's atom or I die,
> Or living on, perhaps, your wretched thrall,
>   Forget, in the mist of idle misery,
> Life's purposes, — the palate of my mind
> Losing its gust, and my ambition blind!

hopelessly with Mr. Parker and distracted the estimable Graves, and I want you to tell me what finger-prints you have found. I shan't be happy till I get it, so don't be harsh with me, Bunter."

"Well, my lord, your lordship understands I haven't photographed them yet, but I won't deny that their appearance is interesting, my lord. The little book off the night table, my lord, has only the marks of one set of fingers—there's a little scar on the right thumb which makes them easy recognized. The hairbrush, too, my lord, has only the same set of marks. The umbrella, the toothglass[29] and the boots all have two sets: the hand with the scarred thumb, which I take to be Sir Reuben's, my lord, and a set of smudges superimposed upon them, if I may put it that way, my lord, which may or may not be the same hand in rubber gloves. I could tell you better when I've got the photographs made, to measure them, my lord. The linoleum in front of the washstand is very gratifying indeed, my lord, if you will excuse my mentioning it. Besides the marks of Sir Reuben's boots which your lordship pointed out, there's the print of a man's naked foot—a much smaller one, my lord, not much more than a ten-inch sock,[30] I should say if you asked me."

Lord Peter's face became irradiated with almost a dim, religious light.[31]

---

[29] A glass kept on a bathroom sink used for rinsing the mouth as well as to hold the toothbrush. Toothbrush holders were not common at the time. The first U.S. patent for one was filed in 1922.

[30] In the days before polyesters and other stretchable fabrics, socks were made out of cotton, wool or other natural materials that did not stretch as far and had to be sized.

[31] From "Il Penseroso" ("The Contemplative Man"), a poem by John Milton (1608-1674) in which, near the end, the speaker hopes for a glimpse of heaven:

> "And storied windows richly dight [adorned]
> Casting a dim, religious light.
> There let the pealing Organ blow,
> To the full voiced Quire [choir] below,
> In Service high, and Anthems clear,
> As may with sweetness, through mine ear . . .
> Dissolve me into ecstasies,

"A mistake," he breathed, "a mistake, a little one, but he can't afford it. When was the linoleum washed last, Bunter?"

"Monday morning, my lord. The housemaid did it and remembered to mention it. Only remark she's made yet, and it's to the point. The other domestics—"[32]

His features expressed disdain.

What did I say, Parker? Five-foot-ten and not an inch longer. And he didn't dare to use the hairbrush. Beautiful. But he had to risk the top-hat. Gentleman can't walk home in the rain late at night without a hat, you know, Parker. Look! what do you make of it? Two sets of finger-prints on everything but the book and the brush, two sets of feet on the linoleum, and two kinds of hair in the hat!"

He lifted the top-hat to the light, and extracted the evidence with tweezers.

"Think of it, Parker—to remember the hairbrush and forget the hat—to remember his fingers all the time, and to make that one careless step on the telltale linoleum. Here they are, you see, black hair and tan hair—black hair in the bowler and the panama,[33] and black and tan in last night's topper.[34] And then, just to make certain that we're on the right track, just one little auburn hair on the pillow, on this pillow, Parker, which isn't quite in the right place. It almost brings tears to my eyes."

"Do you mean to say—" said the detective, slowly.

"I mean to say," said Lord Peter, "that it was not Sir Reuben Levy whom the cook saw last night on the doorstep. I say that it was another man, perhaps a couple of inches shorter, who came here in Levy's clothes and let himself in with Levy's latchkey. Oh, he was a bold, cunning devil, Parker. He had on Levy's boots, and every stitch of Levy's clothing down to the skin. He had rubber gloves on his hands which he never took off, and he did everything

---

And bring all Heaven before mine eye."

This gives you some idea of what came over Lord Peter, inspired by the sight of a 10-inch sock.

[32] The other servants.

[33] A brimmed hat made from straw, ideal for summer wear.

[34] Slang for top hat

he could to make us think that Levy slept here last night. He took his chances, and won. He walked upstairs, he undressed, he even washed and cleaned his teeth, though he didn't use the hairbrush for fear of leaving red hairs in it. He had to guess what Levy did with boots and clothes; one guess was wrong and the other right, as it happened. The bed must look as if it had been slept in, so he gets in, and lies there in his victim's very pyjamas. Then, in the morning sometime, probably in the deadest hour between two and three, he gets up, dresses himself in his own clothes that he has brought with him in a bag, and creeps downstairs. If anybody wakes, he is lost, but he is a bold man, and he takes his chance. He knows that people do not wake as a rule—and they don't wake. He opens the street door which he left on the latch when he came in— he listens for the stray passer-by or the policeman on his beat. He slips out. He pulls the door quietly to with the latchkey. He walks brisky away in rubber-soled shoes—he's the kind of criminal who isn't complete without rubber-soled shoes. In a few minutes he is at Hyde Park Corner.[35] After that—"

He paused, and added:

"He did all that, and unless he had nothing at stake, he had everything at stake. Either Sir Reuben Levy has been spirited away for some silly practical joke, or the man with the auburn hair has the guilt of murder upon his soul."

"Dear me!" ejaculated[36] the detective, "you're very dramatic about it."

Lord Peter passed his hand rather wearily over his hair.

"My true friend," he murmured, in a voice surcharged with emotion, "you recall me to the nursery rhymes of my youth—the sacred duty of flippancy:

'There was an old man of Whitehaven
Who danced a quadrille with a raven,

---

[35] The southeast corner of Hyde Park, a few steps down Piccadilly from Lord Peter's residence. This reinforces the assumption that Sir Reuben's home is close by.

[36] A common dialog tag of the time, used to indicate an impetuous response. Now that the meaning of the word has shifted, it has become a source of merriment, especially if used in a romance (e.g., "'I love you!' he ejaculated cockily.")

But they said: It's absurd
To encourage that bird—
So they smashed that old man of Whitehaven.'[37]

That's the correct attitude, Parker. Here's a poor old buffer spirited away—such a joke—and I don't believe he'd hurt a fly himself—that makes it funnier. D'you know, Parker, I don't care frightfully about this case after all."

"Which, this or yours?"

"Both. I say, Parker, shall we go quietly home and have lunch and go to the Coliseum?"[38]

"You can if you like," replied the detective; "but you forget I do this for my bread and butter."

"And I haven't even that excuse," said Lord Peter; "well, what's the next move? What would you do in my case?"

"I'd do some good, hard grind," said Parker. "I'd distrust every bit of work Sugg ever did, and I'd get the family history of every tenant of every flat in Queen Caroline Mansions. I'd examine all their boxrooms and rooftraps,[39] and I would inveigle[40] them into conversations and suddenly bring in the words 'body' and 'pince-nez,' and see if they wriggled, like those modern psycho-what's-his-names."

"You would, would you?" said Lord Peter with a grin. "Well, we've exchanged cases, you know, so just you toddle off and do it.

---

[37] A poem by Edward Lear (1812-1888), poet, artist and illustrator, from his "Book of Nonsense" (1846).

[38] Although he is addressing Parker, Peter seems to be talking more to himself, since it makes no sense for him to invite Parker home for lunch when, as we shall see, he has an invitation to dine with Freddy Arbuthnot. Instead, once the thrill of detecting has worn off, Lord Peter understands that a man has vanished, his family grieves for him, and the instigator has "has the guilt of murder upon his soul." The fallout from this realization will have consequences for Lord Peter's mental well-being.

The *London Coliseum* is a theatre on St. Martin's Lane. Also known as the Coliseum Theatre, it is now the home of the English National Opera.

[39] A *box room* is used to store boxes, trunks and other items. *Roof traps* are hatches that allow access to the roof from inside the house.

[40] To acquire by ingenuity or flattery.

I'm going to have a jolly time at Wyndham's."[41]

Parker made a grimace.

"Well," he said, "I don't suppose you'd ever do it, so I'd better. You'll never become a professional till you learn to do a little work, Wimsey. How about lunch?"

"I'm invited out," said Lord Peter, magnificently. "I'll run round and change at the club. Can't feed with Freddy Arbuthnot in these bags;[42] Bunter!"

"Yes, my lord."

"Pack up if you're ready, and come round and wash my face and hands for me at the club."

"Work here for another two hours, my lord. Can't do with less than thirty minutes' exposure. The current's none too strong."

"You see how I'm bullied by my own man, Parker? Well, I must bear it, I suppose. Ta-ta!"

He whistled his way downstairs.

The conscientious Mr. Parker, with a groan, settled down to a systematic search through Sir Reuben Levy's papers, with the assistance of a plate of ham sandwiches and a bottle of Bass.[43]

Lord Peter and the Honourable[44] Freddy Arbuthnot, looking together like an advertisement for gents' trouserings, strolled into the dining-room at Wyndham's.

"Haven't seen you for an age," said the Honourable Freddy, "what have you been doin' with yourself?"

"Oh, foolin' about," said Lord Peter, languidly.

---

[41] A club for gentlemen. Windham, its correct spelling, was founded in 1828 and located for most of its existence at 13 St. James's Square. It merged with the Marlborough and Orleans club in 1945 to form the Marlborough-Windham Club and was moved to 52 Pall Mall. It closed in 1953.

[42] Trousers.

[43] A brand of beer, established in 1777 in Burton upon Trent, Staffordshire, by William Bass.

[44] A title used by the son of a baron or viscount — the two lower ranks in the five-step English noble hierarchy — or the younger son of an earl, marquess or duke. As the youngest son of the late Duke of Denver, Wimsey is referred to as Lord Peter.

"Thick or clear, sir?"[45] enquired the waiter of the Honourable Freddy.

"Which'll you have, Wimsey?" said that gentleman, transferring the burden of selection to his guest, "they're both equally poisonous."

"Well, clear's less trouble to lick out of the spoon," said Lord Peter.

"Clear," said the Honourable Freddy.

"Consommé Polonais,"[46] agreed the waiter. "Very nice, sir."

Conversation languished[47] until the Honourable Freddy found a bone in the filleted sole, and sent for the head waiter to explain its presence. When this matter had been adjusted Lord Peter found energy to say:

"Sorry to hear about your gov'nor, old man."

"Yes, poor old buffer," said the Honourable Freddy; "they say he can't last long now. What? Oh! the Montrachet '08. There's nothing fit to drink in this place," he added gloomily.[48]

After this deliberate insult to a noble vintage there was a further pause, till Lord Peter said: "'How's 'Change?"[49]

"Rotten," said the Honourable Freddy.

He helped himself gloomily to salmis of game.[50]

"Can I do anything?" asked Lord Peter.

---

[45] The two divisions of soup. Clear soups are generally bouillon or consommé. Thick soups use thickening agents such as vegetable purees, cream, rice, flour or grains.

[46] An older edition of the "Larousse Gastronomique" cookbook describes it as soup in the Polish style, with chopped hard-boiled egg and noisette butter (lightly browned with lemon juice) added.

[47] Dispirited, feeble or weak.

[48] *Montrachet* is a dry white wine made from Chardonnay grapes in the Burgundy region of France. It is considered an excellent wine, so Freddy's comment that "there's nothing fit to drink in this place" is more a reflection of his morose state of mind rather than a comment on the club's cellars.

[49] The London Stock Exchange in London's financial district.

[50] Cooked pieces of birds — partridges, grouse or quails, for example — arranged on a plate with gravy (made from the bones, trimmings, skin and general odds and ends) poured over it. Another version calls for the game to be cooked most of the way through in the oven, then cut into joints, placed in a buttered sauté dish with mushrooms and sliced truffles, cooked over hot water for a half hour, and served on bread with gravy.

"Oh, no, thanks—very decent of you, but it'll pan out all right in time."

"This isn't a bad salmis," said Lord Peter.

"I've eaten worse," admitted his friend.

"What about those Argentines?"[51] enquired Lord Peter. "Here, waiter, there's a bit of cork in my glass."

"Cork?" cried the Honourable Freddy, with something approaching animation; "you'll hear about this, waiter. It's an amazing thing a fellow who's paid to do the job can't manage to take a cork out of a bottle. What you say? Argentines? Gone all to hell. Old Levy bunkin' off[52] like that's knocked the bottom out of the market."

"You don't say so," said Lord Peter; "what d'you suppose has happened to the old man?"

"Cursed if I know," said the Honourable Freddy; "knocked on the head by the bears, I should think."

"P'r'aps he's gone off on his own," suggested Lord Peter. "Double life, you know. Giddy old blighters, some of these City men."

"Oh, no," said the Honourable Freddy, faintly roused; "no, hang it all, Wimsey, I wouldn't care to say that. He's a decent old domestic bird, and his daughter's a charmin' girl. Besides, he's straight enough—he'd do you down fast enough, but he wouldn't let you down. Old Anderson is badly cut up about it."

"Who's Anderson?"

"Chap with property out there. He belongs here. He was goin' to meet Levy on Tuesday. He's afraid those railway people will get in now, and then it'll be all U.P."[53]

"Who's runnin' the railway people over here?" enquired Lord Peter.

"Yankee blighter, John P. Milligan. He's got an option, or says

---

[51] Before World War I, with the help of European banks, Argentina had become a rising economic powerhouse similar to Japan in the 1980s, although on a smaller scale. For more information, see the essay "Argentine Banks: High Times On The Pampas."

[52] To leave in haste.

[53] Not an abbreviation, but a way of showing emphasis by spelling out the letters.

he has. You can't trust these brutes."

"Can't Anderson hold on?"

"Anderson isn't Levy. Hasn't got the shekels.[54] Besides, he's only one. Levy covers the ground—he could boycott[55] Milligan's beastly railway if he liked. That's where he's got the pull, you see."

"B'lieve I met the Milligan man somewhere," said Lord Peter, thoughtfully; "ain't he a hulking brute with black hair and a beard?"

"You're thinkin' of somebody else," said the Honourable Freddy. "Milligan don't stand any higher than I do, unless you call five-feet-ten hulking—and he's bald, anyway."

Lord Peter considered this over the Gorgonzola.[56] Then he said: "Didn't know Levy had a charmin' daughter."

"Oh, yes," said the Honourable Freddy, with an elaborate detachment. "Met her and Mamma last year abroad. That's how I got to know the old man. He's been very decent. Let me into this Argentine business on the ground floor, don't you know?"

"Well," said Lord Peter, "you might do worse. Money's money, ain't it? And Lady Levy is quite a redeemin' point. At least, my mother knew her people."

"Oh, she's all right," said the Honourable Freddy, "and the old man's nothing to be ashamed of nowadays. He's self-made, of course, but he don't pretend to be anything else. No side.[57] Toddles off to business on a 96 'bus[58] every morning. 'Can't make up my

---

[54] An ancient unit of currency or weight. Although associated with Jews, a number of ancient peoples used shekels as currency, including Phoenicians, Moabites and Edomites. It is now the currency of Israel. Freddy's use of the word for Jewish currency instead of, say, pounds, could reflect an Englishman's attitude toward the Jewish presence in the banking industry.

[55] The particulars of this business deal aren't clear because Sayers is more interested in the mystery of Sir Reuben's death, so only enough details are needed to bring in Milligan as a suspect and supply a motive.

[56] The cheese course usually occurs near the end of the meal, after the main course but before the dessert, in the belief that it aids digestion.

[57] No boastfulness or arrogance.

[58] The Route 96 omnibus is indicative of Sir Reuben's lower-middle-class background. For more information, see the essay "Omnibus: One Vehicle's Journey Through Linguistics."

mind to taxis, my boy,' he says. 'I had to look at every halfpenny[59] when I was a young man, and I can't get out of the way of it now.' Though, if he's takin' his family out, nothing's too good. Rachel—that's the girl—always laughs at the old man's little economies."

"I suppose they've sent for Lady Levy," said Lord Peter.

"I suppose so," agreed the other. "I'd better pop round and express sympathy or somethin', what? Wouldn't look well not to, d'you think? But it's deuced awkward. What am I to say?"

"I don't think it matters much what you say," said Lord Peter, helpfully. "I should ask if you can do anything."

"Thanks," said the lover, "I will. Energetic young man. Count on me. Always at your service. Ring me up any time of the day or night.[60] That's the line to take, don't you think?"

"That's the idea," said Lord Peter.

Mr. John P. Milligan, the London representative of the great Milligan railroad and shipping company, was dictating code cables[61] to his secretary in an office in Lombard Street,[62] when a

---

[59] Before the United Kingdom shifted to a decimal form of currency in 1971, with 100 pence equaling 1 pound, it used a complex system that was as rich in tradition as it was baffling to the outsider. Basically, 20 shillings made up 1 pound, and 12 pennies (or pence) made up 1 shilling. Hence, 240 pennies, or 480 half-pennies, made up 1 pound. Complicating the system was the existence of special coins, including guineas (1 pound plus 1 shilling), crowns (5 shillings), half-crowns (2½ shillings), florins (2 shillings), farthings (one-fourth of a penny) and mites (one-eighth of a penny).

[60] Telephone him. Before electronic chirps or snatches of popular songs summoned you to your smartphone, a bell inside the phone rang to indicate an incoming call.

[61] A *cable* is a telegram sent through an electric cable, as opposed to a telegraph line. Messages were charged by the word, which encouraged the use of codes that could combine several words into one. For more information, see the essay "Commercials Codes: Secrecy On The Cheap."

[62] A street in the London's financial district where money has congregated in one form or another since King Edward I (1239-1307) granted land there to goldsmiths emigrating from northern Italy. It became the home of insurance giant

card was brought up to him, bearing the simple legend:

LORD PETER WIMSEY

MARLBOROUGH CLUB[63]

Mr. Milligan was annoyed at the interruption, but, like many of his nation, if he had a weak point, it was the British aristocracy. He postponed for a few minutes the elimination from the map of a modest but promising farm, and directed that the visitor should be shown up.

"Good-afternoon," said that nobleman, ambling genially in, "it's most uncommonly good of you to let me come round wastin' your time like this. I'll try not to be too long about it, though I'm not awfully good at comin' to the point. My brother never would let me stand for the county,[64] y'know—said I wandered on so nobody'd know what I was talkin' about."

"Pleased to meet you, Lord Wimsey," said Mr. Milligan. "Won't you take a seat?"

"Thanks," said Lord Peter, "but I'm not a peer,[65] you know—that's my brother Denver. My name's Peter. It's a silly name, I always think, so old-world and full of homely virtue and that sort of thing, but my godfathers and godmothers in my baptism are responsible for that, I suppose, officially—which is rather hard on them, you know, as they didn't actually choose it. But we always have a Peter, after the third duke, who betrayed five kings somewhere about the Wars of the

---

Lloyd's of London when Lloyd's Coffee House moved there in 1691 and was the home of most of the nation's banks until the 1980s.

[63] Founded on 1868 by the Prince of Wales — later Edward VII (1841-1910) — and established at 52 Pall Mall. In 1945, the club merged with the Orleans and Windham clubs to form the Marlborough-Windham Club, but declining membership forced it to close in 1953.

[64] Run for Parliament representing Norfolk. In the House of Commons, there are currently eight seats representing different areas of the county. Duke's Denver is in the South West Norfolk constituency.

[65] A peer is a subset of the aristocracy who holds the title of duke, marquess, earl, viscount or baron. Peers could sit in the House of Lords until 1999, when an act was passed reducing its membership from 1,330 to 669.

Roses,[66] though come to think of it, it ain't anything to be proud of. Still, one has to make the best of it."

Mr. Milligan, thus ingeniously placed at that disadvantage which attends ignorance,[67] manœuvred for position, and offered his interrupter a Corona Corona.

"Thanks, awfully," said Lord Peter, "though you really mustn't tempt me to stay here barblin' all afternoon. By Jove, Mr. Milligan, if you offer people such comfortable chairs and cigars like these, I wonder they don't come an' live in your office." He added mentally: "I wish to goodness I could get those long-toed boots off you. How's a man to know the size of your feet? And a head like a potato. It's enough to make one swear."

"Say now, Lord Peter," said Mr. Milligan, "can I do anything for you?"

"Well, d'you know," said Lord Peter, "I'm wonderin' if you would. It's damned cheek to ask you, but fact is, it's my mother, you know. Wonderful woman, but don't realize what it means, demands on the time of a busy man like you. We don't understand hustle over here, you know, Mr. Milligan."

"Now don't you mention that," said Mr. Milligan; "I'd be surely charmed to do anything to oblige the Duchess."

He felt a momentary qualm as to whether a duke's mother were also a duchess, but breathed more freely as Lord Peter went on:

"Thanks—that's uncommonly good of you. Well, now, it's like this. My mother—most energetic, self-sacrificin' woman, don't

---

[66] A series of civil wars from 1455 to 1485 between two branches of the Plantagenet family for the throne of England. They were the houses of Lancaster, whose symbol was the red rose, and York, the white. During this tumultuous period, England was ruled by five kings: Henry VI (Lancaster), Edward IV (York), Edward V (York), Richard III (York) and the eventual winner, Henry Tudor, of Lancastrian ancestry who married the daughter of the Yorkish king to reunite the houses as Henry VII (1457-1509). His son became the notorious Henry VIII, he of the six wives, who ruled England for 23 years. The fact that the third duke successfully betrayed everyone might not speak much for his loyalty, but a lot for his survival skills.

[67] Unaware or unwilling to admit his ignorance of the subtleties of the English peerage, Milligan decides not to pursue the matter and changes the conversation with the offer of a cigar. A Corona Corona, also called a Double Corona, is not a brand, but a cigar size, in this case about 7½ inches long.

you see, is thinkin' of gettin' up a sort of a charity bazaar[68] down at Denver this winter, in aid of the church-roof, y'know. Very sad case, Mr. Milligan—fine old antique—early English windows and decorated angel roof,[69] and all that—all tumblin' to pieces, rain pourin' in and so on—vicar catchin' rheumatism[70] at early service, owin' to the draught[71] blowin' in over the altar—you know the sort of thing. They've got a man down startin' on it—little beggar called Thipps—lives with an aged mother in Battersea—vulgar little beast, but quite good on angel roofs and things, I'm told."

At this point, Lord Peter watched his interlocutor[72] narrowly, but finding that this rigmarole[73] produced in him no reaction more startling than polite interest tinged with faint bewilderment,[74] he abandoned this line of investigation, and proceeded:

"I say, I beg your pardon, frightfully—I'm afraid I'm bein' beastly long-winded. Fact is, my mother is gettin' up this bazaar, and she thought it'd be all awfully interestin' side-show to have some lectures—sort of little talks, y'know—by eminent business men of all nations. 'How I did it' kind of touch, y'know—'A Drop of Oil with a Kerosene King'—'Cash Conscience and Cocoa' and so on.[75] It would interest people down there no end. You see, all

---

[68] A fundraiser in which games of chance are offered and food is sold.

[69] An architectural feature, usually found in medieval and later timber-roof structures, in which the ends of ceiling beams are decorated with carved angels. Most commonly found in East Anglia, the region northeast of London which includes Norfolk.

[70] A general disorder of the joints and connective tissue, encompassing various forms of arthritis, rheumatic fever and heart disease, lupus or back pain. Although wet weather is commonly believed to cause rheumatic pain, one study finds a firmer connection with changes in barometric pressure.

[71] A draft.

[72] An old word from the 1500s meaning a person participating in a conversation.

[73] Confusing or meaningless talk.

[74] Lord Peter mentions Thipps to see Milligan's reaction to the unexpected surfacing of his name.

[75] Although Sayers had not yet begun her advertising work at S.H. Benson's, she already had the knack for writing these titles that could have come out of any magazine aimed at the middle class hoping to better themselves through self-improvement.

my mother's friends will be there, and we've none of us any money—not what you'd call money, I mean—I expect our incomes wouldn't pay your telephone calls, would they?—but we like awfully to hear about the people who can make money. Gives us a sort of uplifted feelin', don't you know. Well, anyway, I mean, my mother'd be frightfully pleased and grateful to you, Mr. Milligan, if you'd come down and give us a few words as a representative American. It needn't take more than ten minutes or so, y'know, because the local people can't understand much beyond shootin' and huntin', and my mother's crowd can't keep their minds on anythin' more than ten minutes together, but we'd really appreciate it very much if you'd come and stay a day or two and just give us a little breezy word on the almighty dollar."

"Why, yes," said Mr. Milligan, "I'd like to, Lord Peter. It's kind of the Duchess to suggest it. It's a very sad thing when these fine old antiques begin to wear out. I'll come with great pleasure. And perhaps you'd be kind enough to accept a little donation to the Restoration Fund."

This unexpected development nearly brought Lord Peter up all standing. To pump, by means of an ingenious lie, a hospitable gentleman whom you are inclined to suspect of a peculiarly malicious murder, and to accept from him in the course of the proceedings a large cheque for a charitable object, has something about it unpalatable to any but the hardened Secret Service[76] agent. Lord Peter temporized.

"That's awfully decent of you," he said. "I'm sure they'd be no end grateful. But you'd better not give it to me, you know. I might spend it, or lose it. I'm not very reliable, I'm afraid. The vicar's the right person—the Rev. Constantine Throgmorton, St. John-before-

---

In later printings, Sayers altered the titles of the talks. Originally, they were "A Drop of Oil with Mr. Rockefeller" and "Cash and Conscience" by Cadbury's Cocoa.

[76] A member of the Secret Service Bureau, founded in 1909 to counter threats from other nations, particularly Germany. When World War I started, the agency was split into Military Intelligence, Section 5 (MI5), and the Secret Intelligence Service (MI6).

the-Latin-Gate Vicarage,[77] Duke's Denver, if you like to send it there."

"I will," said Mr. Milligan. "Will you write it out now for a thousand pounds, Scoot, in case it slips my mind later?"

The secretary, a sandy-haired young man with a long chin and no eyebrows, silently did as he was requested. Lord Peter looked from the bald head of Mr. Milligan to the red head of the secretary, hardened his heart and tried again.

"Well, I'm no end grateful to you, Mr. Milligan, and so'll my mother be when I tell her. I'll let you know the date of the bazaar— it's not quite settled yet, and I've got to see some other business men, don't you know. I thought of askin' Lord Northcliffe to represent English newspapers, you know, and a friend of mine promises me a leadin' German—very interestin' if there ain't too much feelin' against it down in the country,[78] and I'd better get Rothschild, I suppose, to do the Hebrew point of view. I thought of askin' Levy, y'know, only he's floated off in this inconvenient way."

"Yes," said Mr. Milligan, "that's a very curious thing, though I don't mind saying, Lord Peter, that it's a convenience to me. He had a cinch[79] on my railroad combine, but I'd nothing against him personally, and if he turns up after I've brought off a little deal I've got on, I'll be happy to give him the right hand of welcome."

A vision passed through Lord Peter's mind of Sir Reuben kept somewhere in custody till a financial crisis was over. This was exceedingly possible, and far more agreeable than his earlier

---

[77] The address is the name of a Roman Catholic feast day which, until 1960, was held on May 5. According to tradition, the apostle John was arrested and brought to Rome where the Emperor Domitian (ruled 81-96 AD) ordered that he be thrown into a vat of boiling oil near Rome's Latin gate. But, according to "Lives of the Saints," "the seething oil was changed in his regard into an invigorating bath, and the Saint came out more refreshed than when he had entered the caldron."

[78] Considering World War I ended a few years before, it's understandable that there would be a concern that a German would not be welcome at a village fundraiser.

[79] A tight grip.

conjecture;[80] it also agreed better with the impression he was forming of Mr. Milligan.

"Well, it's a rum go,"[81] said Lord Peter, "but I daresay he had his reasons. Much better not enquire into people's reasons, y'know, what? Specially as a police friend of mine who's connected with the case says the old johnnie dyed his hair before he went."

Out of the tail of his eye, Lord Peter saw the red-headed secretary add up five columns of figures simultaneously and jot down the answer.

"Dyed his hair, did he?" said Mr. Milligan.

"Dyed it red," said Lord Peter. The secretary looked up. "Odd thing is," continued Wimsey, "they can't lay hands on the bottle. Somethin' fishy there, don't you think, what?"

The secretary's interest seemed to have evaporated. He inserted a fresh sheet into his loose-leaf ledger, and carried forward a row of digits from the preceding page.

"I daresay there's nothin' in it," said Lord Peter, rising to go. "Well, it's uncommonly good of you to be bothered with me like this, Mr. Milligan, my mother'll be no end pleased. She'll write you about the date."

"I'm charmed," said Mr. Milligan, "very pleased to have met you."

Mr. Scoot rose silently to open the door, uncoiling as he did so a portentous[82] length of thin leg, hitherto hidden by the desk. With a mental sigh Lord Peter estimated him at six-foot-four.

"It's a pity I can't put Scoot's head on Milligan's shoulders," said Lord Peter, emerging into the swirl of the city, "and what will my mother say?"[83]

---

[80] A theory based on the evidence; in this case, that Sir Reuben was dead.

[81] An odd or surprising event. In use since at least the 19th century, when it appeared in Dickens' "Pickwick Papers." The meaning of rum as a modifier has flipped since it appeared in the 16th century, when it meant fine, clever, excellent or strong. A rum-bit, for example, was a clever rogue; a rum-mizzler an expert thief; a rum-ken a popular inn or brothel and a rum-topping a rich headdress.

[82] Foreshadowing. At the sight of the long leg, Lord Peter began hoping that Mr. Scoot might have been an accomplice.

[83] When Lord Peter tells her she'll have to organize a fundraising bazaar for the church roof.

CHAPTER V

M R. PARKER WAS A BACHELOR, and occupied a Georgian but inconvenient flat at No. 12 Great Ormond Street,[1] for which he paid a pound a week. His exertions in the cause of civilization were rewarded, not by the gift of diamond rings from empresses or munificent cheques from grateful Prime Ministers, but by a modest, though sufficient, salary, drawn from the pockets of the British taxpayer. He awoke, after a long day of arduous and inconclusive labour, to the smell of burnt porridge. Through his bedroom window, hygienically open top and bottom,[2] a raw fog was rolling slowly in, and the sight of a pair of winter pants, flung hastily over a chair the previous night, fretted him with a sense of the sordid absurdity of the human form. The telephone bell rang, and he crawled wretchedly out of bed and into the sitting-room, where Mrs. Munns, who did for him by the day,

---

[1] Inspector Parker lives on a short street in the Bloomsbury district. No. 12 exists as part of a series of brick buildings that appear suitable for rent at a pound a week in Parker's time. Buildings from the Georgian era were typically subdivided into apartments and rented out, and Parker might have found himself in one of those oddly divided "inconvenient" flats.

The *Georgian style* was popular between 1714 and 1830 and was named for the four King Georges who ruled during that period. Elements of the style include a simple 1- or 2-story symmetrical box frame built of brick or stone, with multi-paned windows, chimneys on both ends and a cornice — the horizontal projection that crowns the building — embellished with decorative moldings. Thomas Jefferson's Monticello is a superior example of the Georgian style.

[2] Public health officials advocated getting plenty of fresh air, to the point of sleeping with the windows open in all seasons.

was laying the table, sneezing as she went.

Mr. Bunter was speaking.

"His lordship says he'd be very glad, sir, if you could make it convenient to step round to breakfast."

If the odour of kidneys[3] and bacon had been wafted along the wire, Mr. Parker could not have experienced a more vivid sense of consolation.

"Tell his lordship I'll be with him in half an hour," he said, thankfully, and plunging into the bathroom, which was also the kitchen, he informed Mrs. Munns, who was just making tea from a kettle which had gone off the boil, that he should be out to breakfast.

"You can take the porridge home for the family," he added, viciously, and flung off his dressing-gown[4] with such determination that Mrs. Munns could only scuttle away with a snort.[5]

A 19 'bus deposited him in Piccadilly only fifteen minutes later than his rather sanguine[6] impulse had prompted him to suggest, and Mr. Bunter served him with glorious food, incomparable coffee, and the Daily Mail[7] before a blazing fire of wood and coal. A distant voice singing the "et iterum venturus est"[8] from Bach's

---

[3] Kidneys from lambs, pigs or oxen are considered part of a proper English breakfast.

[4] A robe designed to be worn over sleepwear.

[5] Porridge is oats or similar grains, boiled in milk or water and served in a bowl. Parker's reaction to Mrs. Munns' breakfast can be attributed to her possible lack of skill in fixing porridge combined with the prospect of eating sheep organs and bacon with Lord Peter.

[6] Optimistic. He had expected the bus to travel the two miles Lord Peter's flat in 30 minutes, and it took him 45 minutes.

[7] There are numerous newspapers in Britain, each aimed at a demographic or political belief. Hence, you can tell something about a person by the newspaper he favors. Founded in 1896, *The Daily Mail* was designed for the newly educated lower-middle class. It was not only the first newspaper to sell a million copies a day, it also printed articles for women, which still make up a majority of its readership.

[8] "And He shall come again," from Bach's Mass in B minor. The rest of the line, by the way, is "with glory to judge both the quick [living] and the dead." It is drawn from the Nicene Creed, the profession of faith used in Christian liturgy.

Mass in B minor proclaimed that for the owner of the flat cleanliness and godliness met at least once a day, and presently Lord Peter roamed in, moist and verbena-scented,[9] in a bathrobe

---

The version Sayers might have been most familiar with would have been this one from the 1662 Book of Common Prayer:

I believe in one God the Father Almighty,
Maker of heaven and earth,
And of all things visible and invisible:

And in one Lord Jesus Christ, the only-begotten Son of God,
Begotten of his Father before all worlds,
God of God, Light of Light,
Very God of very God,
Begotten, not made,
Being of one substance with the Father,
By whom all things were made;
Who for us men, and for our salvation came down from heaven,
And was incarnate by the Holy Ghost of the Virgin Mary,
And was made man,
And was crucified also for us under Pontius Pilate.
He suffered and was buried,
And the third day he rose again according to the Scriptures,
And ascended into heaven,
And sitteth on the right hand of the Father.
And he shall come again with glory to judge both the quick [living] and the
dead:
Whose kingdom shall have no end.

And I believe in the Holy Ghost,
The Lord and giver of life,
Who proceedeth from the Father and the Son,
Who with the Father and the Son together is worshipped and glorified,
Who spake by the Prophets.
And I believe one Catholick and Apostolick Church.
I acknowledge one Baptism for the remission of sins.
And I look for the Resurrection of the dead,
And the life of the world to come.
Amen.

[9] A perfume derived from a flowering plant that gives off a sweet musky aroma. Lord Peter's views on the use of scent by men changed during his life. While inspecting a man's rooms in "Clouds of Witness," he finds a bottle of "Baiser du Soir" (Evening Kiss) and comments "very nice too. New to me. Must draw

cheerfully patterned with unnaturally variegated peacocks.[10]

"Mornin', old dear," said that gentleman; "beast of a day, ain't it? Very good of you to trundle out in it, but I had a letter I wanted you to see, and I hadn't the energy to come round to your place. Bunter and I've been makin' a night of it."

"What's the letter?" asked Parker.

"Never talk business with your mouth full," said Lord Peter, reprovingly; "have some Oxford marmalade[11]—and then I'll show you my Dante; they brought it round last night. What ought I to read this morning, Bunter?"

"Lord Erith's collection is going to be sold, my lord. There is a column about it in the Morning Post.[12] I think your lordship should look at this review of Sir Julian Freke's new book on 'The Physiological Bases of the Conscience' in the Times Literary Supplement.[13] Then there is a very singular little burglary in the Chronicle,[14] my lord, and an attack on titled families in the Herald—rather ill-written, if I may say so, but not without

---

Bunter's attention to it." After he's married, in "Busman's Honeymoon," however, he says, "I disapprove on principle of perfumes for men."

[10] Variegated means discrete markings of different colors. It must have been a stunning bathrobe.

[11] A brand of marmalade created by the wife of Frank Cooper, who founded a company in 1874 under his name in Oxford to market it. In 1903, he established his factory near the Oxford railway station on Park End Street, and Frank Cooper's Oxford Marmalade became popular with the university's dons and students. It is still sold today.

[12] A conservative London newspaper. In 1920, it ran a series of articles based on the "Protocols of the Elders of Zion," a notorious anti-Semitic forgery purporting to detail a Jewish conspiracy to rule the world. The next year, The Times revealed that the book was a fraud, but "Protocols" is still published today as fact, especially in Arabic countries.

[13] A weekly literary review founded in 1902 as a supplement to The Times. It became an independent publication in 1914. Its writers have included T.S. Eliot, Henry James, Virginia Woolf, Philip Larkin and Martin Amis.

[14] A possible reference to the *Evening Chronicle*, a regional newspaper published in Newcastle, located on the River Tyne (hence you'll sometimes see it called "Newcastle upon Tyne") about 50 miles from the Scottish border. Its presence on Lord Peter's breakfast table reflects his interest in news, no matter how far from London.

unconscious humour which your lordship will appreciate."[15]

"All right, give me that and the burglary," said his lordship.

"I have looked over the other papers," pursued Mr. Bunter, indicating a formidable pile, "and marked your lordship's after-breakfast reading."

"Oh, pray don't allude to it," said Lord Peter, "you take my appetite away."

There was silence, but for the crunching of toast and the crackling of paper.

"I see they adjourned the inquest,"[16] said Parker presently.

"Nothing else to do," said Lord Peter, "but Lady Levy arrived last night, and will have to go and fail to identify the body this morning for Sugg's benefit."

"Time, too,"[17] said Mr. Parker shortly.

Silence fell again.

"I don't think much of your burglary, Bunter," said Lord Peter. "Competent, of course, but no imagination. I want imagination in a criminal. Where's the Morning Post?"

After a further silence, Lord Peter said: "You might send for the catalogue, Bunter, that Apollonios Rhodios[18] might be worth looking at.[19] No, I'm damned if I'm going to stodge through that review, but you can stick the book on the library list if you like. His book on Crime was entertainin' enough as far as it went, but

---

[15] *The Daily Herald*, a newspaper published 1912-1964, when it was relaunched as The Sun tabloid. Its leftish orientation makes it an ideal source for an article attacking the aristocracy. Its presence also shows Lord Peter's newspaper reading to be extensive — he has Bunter culling the three newspapers mentioned, as well as the "formidable pile" of other papers, irrespective of their politics.

[16] After a suspicious death, the coroner holds a hearing in which a jury examines the evidence and declares, if possible, the cause of death. The coroner suspended this inquest until Lady Levy could try to attempt to identify the body.

[17] "About time," he's saying.

[18] [Sayers' footnote] Apollonios Rhodios. Lorenzobodi Alopa. Firenze. 1496. (4to.) The excitement attendant on the solution of the Battersea Mystery did not prevent Lord Peter from securing this rare work before his departure for Corsica.

[19] A librarian at the Library of Alexandria. In the 3rd century BCE, he wrote the epic poem "Argonautica" about Jason and the Argonauts' quest for the Golden Fleece. The edition Lord Peter contemplates bidding on is the first printed edition of the work.

the fellow's got a bee in his bonnet. Thinks God's a secretion of the liver—all right once in a way, but there's no need to keep on about it. There's nothing you can't prove if your outlook is only sufficiently limited. Look at Sugg."

"I beg your pardon," said Parker, "I wasn't attending. Argentines are steadying a little, I see."

"Milligan," said Lord Peter.

"Oil's in a bad way. Levy's made a difference there. That funny little boom in Peruvians that came on just before he disappeared has died away again. I wonder if he was concerned in it. D'you know at all?"

"I'll find out," said Lord Peter, "what was it?"

"Oh, an absolutely dud enterprise that hadn't been heard of for years. It suddenly took a little lease of life last week. I happened to notice it because my mother got let in for a couple of hundred shares a long time ago. It never paid a dividend. Now it's petered out again."[20]

Wimsey pushed his plate aside and lit a pipe.

"Having finished, I don't mind doing some work," he said. "How did you get on yesterday?"

"I didn't," replied Parker. "I sleuthed up and down those flats in my own bodily shape and two different disguises. I was a gas-meter man[21] and a collector for a Home for Lost Doggies, and I didn't get a thing to go on, except a servant in the top flat[22] at the Battersea Bridge Road end of the row who said she thought she'd heard a bump on the roof one night. Asked which night, she couldn't rightly say. Asked if it was Monday night, she thought it very likely. Asked if it mightn't have been in that high wind on

---

[20] Parker is referring to a "pump and dump" scam, in which a group of stockholders spread rumors about a company to artificially boost its stock price, at which time they sell their shares and reap a profit.

[21] Homes were equipped with a meter that measured how much gas was used for cooking, lights and heating. Some operated on the pay-as-you-go method and worked only when a coin was dropped into the slot. The meter man would come in to check out problems, collect the coins or to inspect or replace the meter.

[22] Live-in servants were commonly given the attic room on the top floor. These were generally cramped, odd-sized rooms, and, because they were in the highest part of a poorly insulated house, oven-hot in summers and freezing in winters.

Saturday night that blew my chimney-pot[23] off, she couldn't say but what it might have been. Asked if she was sure it was on the roof and not inside the flat, said to be sure they did find a picture tumbled down next morning. Very suggestive girl. I saw your friends, Mr. and Mrs. Appledore, who received me coldly, but could make no definite complaint about Thipps except that his mother dropped her h's,[24] and that he once called on them uninvited, armed with a pamphlet about anti-vivisection.[25] The Indian Colonel on the first floor was loud, but unexpectedly friendly. He gave me Indian curry for supper and some very good whisky, but he's a sort of hermit, and all he could tell me was that he couldn't stand Mrs. Appledore."

"Did you get nothing at the house?"

"Only Levy's private diary. I brought it away with me. Here it is. It doesn't tell one much, though. It's full of entries like: 'Tom and Annie to dinner'; and 'My dear wife's birthday; gave her an old opal ring'; 'Mr. Arbuthnot dropped in to tea; he wants to marry Rachel, but I should like someone steadier for my treasure.' Still, I thought it would show who came to the house and so on. He evidently wrote it up at night. There's no entry for Monday."

"I expect it'll be useful," said Lord Peter, turning over the pages. "Poor old buffer. I say, I m not so certain now he was done away with."

He detailed to Mr. Parker his day's work.

"Arbuthnot?" said Parker, "is that the Arbuthnot of the diary?"

"I suppose so. I hunted him up because I knew he was fond of fooling round the Stock Exchange. As for Milligan, he looks all right, but I believe he's pretty ruthless in business and you never can tell. Then there's the red-haired secretary—lightnin' calculator man with a face like a fish, keeps on sayin' nuthin'—got the Tar-

---

[23] A column placed on top of the chimney to inexpensively extend its length and improve its draft.

[24] An indicator of a lower-class person, who pronounces house as 'ouse, or he as 'e. A person 'ypersensitive about class might go so far as to pronounce h's where it isn't needed, such as in hour, heir and honest.

[25] An opponent of cutting or operating on a living animal for physiological or pathological purposes. Dropping in uninvited was also a breach of etiquette and another reason for Mrs. Appledore to purse her lips at the Thippses.

baby in his family tree, I should think.[26] Milligan's got a jolly good motive for, at any rate, suspendin' Levy for a few days. Then there's the new man."

"What new man?"

"Ah, that's the letter I mentioned to you. Where did I put it? here we are. Good parchment paper, printed address of solicitor's office in Salisbury, and postmark to correspond. Very precisely written with a fine nib[27] by an elderly business man of old-fashioned habits."

Parker took the letter and read:

CRIMPLESHAM AND WICKS,
Solicitors[28]
MILFORD HILL SALISBURY,[29]
17 November, 192—.

Sir:

With reference to your advertisement to-day in the personal column of The Times, I am disposed to believe that the eyeglasses and chain in question may be those I lost on the L. B. & S. C. Electric Railway[30] while visiting London last Monday. I left Victoria by the 5:45 train, and did not notice my loss till I arrived at Balham.[31] This

---

[26] A reference to "The Wonderful Tar Baby Story" by Southern writer Joel Chandler Harris (1845-1908). Br'er Fox traps Br'er Rabbit by building a doll out of a lump of tar and dressing it in clothes. Br'er Rabbit encounters the Tar-Baby and talks to it, and when it keeps "sayin' nuthin'," attacks it and gets stuck. He escapes by pleading with Br'er Fox to do anything with him but not fling him in the brier-patch. Fox does so, and Br'er Rabbit escapes.

[27] The business end of a fountain pen where the ink meets the paper. A fine nib is narrow and the width of the line varies depending on the amount of pressure used.

[28] Along with barristers, one of two classes of lawyers in England. The solicitor — also known as an attorney — is a general practitioner, allowed to draw up contracts and conduct litigation. He also instructs the barrister, a specialist in certain branches of the law and who is allowed to appear in most major courts and speak on the client's behalf.

[29] A road in Salisbury, a city about 90 miles west of London.

[30] The London Brighton and South Coast Railway. Founded in 1846, it connected London with the south coast from Portsmouth to Hastings.

[31] Mr. Crimplesham was traveling a local line from Victoria Station near St. James's Park (south of Green Park, within a mile of Lord Peter's home), across

indication and the optician's specification of the glasses, which I enclose, should suffice at once as an identification and a guarantee of my bona fides.[32] If the glasses should prove to be mine, I should be greatly obliged to you if you would kindly forward them to me by registered post, as the chain was a present from my daughter, and is one of my dearest possessions.

Thanking you in advance for this kindness, and regretting the trouble to which I shall be putting you, I am

Yours very truly,

THOS. CRIMPLESHAM.

Lord Peter Wimsey,
   110, Piccadilly, W.
(Encl.)

"Dear me," said Parker, "this is what you might call unexpected."

"Either it is some extraordinary misunderstanding," said Lord Peter, "or Mr. Crimplesham is a very bold and cunning villain. Or possibly, of course, they are the wrong glasses. We may as well get a ruling on that point at once. I suppose the glasses are at the Yard. I wish you'd just ring 'em up and ask 'em to send round an optician's description of them at once—and you might ask at the same time whether it's a very common prescription."

"Right you are," said Parker, and took the receiver off its hook.

"And now," said his friend, when the message was delivered, "just come into the library for a minute."

On the library table, Lord Peter had spread out a series of bromide prints,[33] some dry, some damp, and some but half-washed.

"These little ones are the originals of the photos we've been

---

the Thames, to Balham Station south of Clapham Common. The line passes along the east side of Battersea Park, near Sir Julian's home and hospital.

[32] Latin for "in good faith," it is a synonym for credentials or identity.

[33] A photographic paper coated with pure silver bromide emulsion.

taking," said Lord Peter, "and these big ones are enlargements all made to precisely the same scale. This one here is the footmark on the linoleum; we'll put that by itself at present. Now these finger-prints can be divided into five lots. I've numbered 'em on the prints—see?—and made a list:

"A. The finger-prints of Levy himself, off his little bedside book and his hairbrush—this and this—you can't mistake the little scar on the thumb.

"B. The smudges made by the gloved fingers of the man who slept in Levy's room on Monday night. They show clearly on the water-bottle and on the boots—superimposed on Levy's. They are very distinct on the boots—surprisingly so for gloved hands, and I deduce that the gloves were rubber ones and had recently been in water.

"Here's another interestin' point. Levy walked in the rain on Monday night, as we know, and these dark marks are mud-splashes. You see they lie over Levy's finger-prints in every case. Now see: on this left boot we find the stranger's thumb-mark over the mud on the leather above the heel. That's a funny place to find a thumb-mark on a boot, isn't it? That is, if Levy took off his own boots. But it's the place where you'd expect to see it if somebody forcibly removed his boots for him. Again, most of the stranger's finger-marks come over the mud-marks, but here is one splash of mud which comes on top of them again. Which makes me infer that the stranger came back to Park Lane, wearing Levy's boots, in a cab, carriage or car, but that at some point or other he walked a little way—just enough to tread in a puddle and get a splash on the boots. What do you say?"

"Very pretty," said Parker. "A bit intricate, though, and the marks are not all that I could wish a finger-print to be."

"Well, I won't lay too much stress on it. But it fits in with our previous ideas. Now let's turn to:

"C. The prints obligingly left by my own particular villain on the further edge of Thipps's bath, where you spotted them, and I ought to be scourged[34] for not having spotted them. The left hand,

---

[34] Whipped or lashed, usually on the back, either as punishment or self-mortification for religious purposes.

you notice, the base of the palm and the fingers, but not the tips, looking as though he had steadied himself on the edge of the bath while leaning down to adjust something at the bottom, the pince-nez perhaps. Gloved, you see, but showing no ridge or seam of any kind—I say rubber, you say rubber. That's that. Now see here:

"D and E come off a visiting-card[35] of mine. There's this thing at the corner, marked F, but that you can disregard; in the original document it's a sticky mark left by the thumb of the youth who took it from me, after first removing a piece of chewing-gum from his teeth with his finger to tell me that Mr. Milligan might or might not be disengaged. D and E are the thumb-marks of Mr. Milligan and his red-haired secretary. I'm not clear which is which, but I saw the youth with the chewing-gum hand the card to the secretary, and when I got into the inner shrine I saw John P. Milligan standing with it in his hand, so it's one or the other, and for the moment it's immaterial to our purpose which is which. I boned[36] the card from the table when I left.

"Well, now, Parker, here's what's been keeping Bunter and me up till the small hours. I've measured and measured every way backwards and forwards till my head's spinnin', and I've stared till I'm nearly blind, but I'm hanged if I can make my mind up. Question 1. Is C identical with B? Question 2. Is D or E identical with B? There's nothing to go on but the size and shape, of course, and the marks are so faint—what do you think?"

Parker shook his head doubtfully.

"I think E might almost be put out of the question," he said, "it seems such an excessively long and narrow thumb. But I think there is a decided resemblance between the span of B on the water-bottle and C on the bath. And I don't see any reason why D shouldn't be the same as B, only there's so little to judge from."

"Your untutored judgment and my measurements have brought

---

[35] A small card presented at a home or business as a way of introducing oneself to strangers among the social class that employed servants. Admittance would not normally be granted upon a first visit, but agreeing to a future visit would be indicated by leaving a card at the first person's home. Also known as a calling card, nowadays it has evolved into business cards.

[36] Slang for steal, first used in the late 17th century.

us both to the same conclusion—if you can call it a conclusion," said Lord Peter, bitterly.

"Another thing," said Parker. "Why on earth should we try to connect B with C? The fact that you and I happen to be friends doesn't make it necessary to conclude that the two cases we happen to be interested in have any organic connection with one another. Why should they? The only person who thinks they have is Sugg, and he's nothing to go by. It would be different if there were any truth in the suggestion that the man in the bath was Levy, but we know for a certainty he wasn't. It's ridiculous to suppose that the same man was employed in committing two totally distinct crimes on the same night, one in Battersea and the other in Park Lane."

"I know," said Wimsey, "though of course we mustn't forget that Levy was in Battersea at the time, and now we know he didn't return home at twelve as was supposed, we've no reason to think he ever left Battersea at all."

"True. But there are other places in Battersea besides Thipps's bathroom. And he wasn't in Thipps's bathroom. In fact, come to think of it, that's the one place in the universe where we know definitely that he wasn't. So what's Thipps's bath got to do with it?"

"I don't know," said Lord Peter. "Well, perhaps we shall get something better to go on today."

He leaned back in his chair and smoked thoughtfully for some time over the papers which Bunter had marked for him.

"They've got you out in the limelight,"[37] he said. "Thank Heaven, Sugg hates me too much to give me any publicity. What a dull Agony Column![38] 'Darling Pipsey—Come back soon to your

---

[37] A form of stage lighting in which quicklime is ignited. It was first used in theatres and concert halls in 1837 until it was replaced by electric lighting. When someone's the object of intense media curiosity, we still say that they're "in the limelight."

[38] A newspaper column consisting of personal notices submitted by the public. Sherlock Holmes used the agony column frequently to place messages or secure information, such as this one in "The Sign of Four":

"Lost.--Whereas Mordecai Smith, boatman, and his son, Jim, left Smith's Wharf at or about three o'clock last Tuesday morning in the steam launch Aurora, black with two red stripes, funnel black with a white band, the sum of five pounds will

distracted Popsey'—and the usual young man in need of financial assistance, and the usual injunction to 'Remember thy Creator in the days of thy youth.'[39] Hullo! there's the bell. Oh, it's our answer from Scotland Yard."

The note from Scotland Yard enclosed an optician's specification identical with that sent by Mr. Crimplesham, and added that it was an unusual one, owing to the peculiar strength of the lenses and the marked difference between the sight of the two eyes.

"That's good enough," said Parker.

"Yes," said Wimsey. "Then Possibility No. 3 is knocked on the head. There remain Possibility No. 1: Accident or Misunderstanding, and No. 2: Deliberate Villainy, of a remarkably bold and calculating kind—of a kind, in fact, characteristic of the author or authors of our two problems. Following the methods inculcated at that University of which I have the honour to be a member, we will now examine severally the various suggestions afforded by Possibility No. 2. This Possibility may be again subdivided into two or more Hypotheses. On Hypothesis 1 (strongly advocated by my distinguished colleague Professor Snupshed),[40] the criminal, whom we may designate as X, is not identical with Crimplesham, but is using the name of Crimplesham as his shield, or ægis.[41] This hypothesis may be further subdivided into two alternatives. Alternative A: Crimplesham is an innocent and unconscious accomplice, and X is in his employment. X writes in Crimplesham's name on Crimplesham's office-paper and obtains that the object in question, i.e., the eyeglasses, be despatched to Crimplesham's address. He is in a position to intercept the parcel before it reaches Crimplesham. The presumption is that X is Crimplesham's charwoman, office-boy, clerk, secretary or porter.

---

be paid to any one who can give information to Mrs. Smith, at Smith's Wharf, or at 221b Baker Street, as to the whereabouts of the said Mordecai Smith and the launch Aurora."

[39] *Injunction.* Order or admonition. *Remember thy Creator.* From Ecclesiastes 12:1: "Remember now thy Creator in the days of thy youth, while the evil days come not, nor the years draw nigh, when thou shalt say, I have no pleasure in them."

[40] Sayers is parodying a style of academic debate frequently heard in universities.

[41] Protection.

This offers a wide field of investigation. The method of enquiry will be to interview Crimplesham and discover whether he sent the letter, and if not, who has access to his correspondence. Alternative B: Crimplesham is under X's influence or in his power, and has been induced to write the letter by (a) bribery, (b) misrepresentation or (c) threats. X may in that case be a persuasive relation or friend, or else a creditor, blackmailer or assassin; Crimplesham, on the other hand, is obviously venal or a fool. The method of enquiry in this case, I would tentatively suggest, is again to interview Crimplesham, put the facts of the case strongly before him, and assure him in the most intimidating terms that he is liable to a prolonged term of penal servitude as an accessory after the fact in the crime of murder— Ah-hem! Trusting, gentlemen, that you have followed me thus far, we will pass to the consideration of Hypothesis No. 2, to which I personally incline, and according to which X is identical with Crimplesham.

"In this case, Crimplesham, who is, in the words of an English classic, a man-of-infinite-resource-and-sagacity,[42] correctly deduces that, of all people, the last whom we shall expect to find answering our advertisement is the criminal himself. Accordingly, he plays a bold game of bluff. He invents an occasion on which the glasses may very easily have been lost or stolen, and applies for them. If confronted, nobody will be more astonished than he to learn where they were found. He will produce witnesses to prove that he left Victoria at 5:45 and emerged from the train at Balham at the scheduled time, and sat up all Monday night playing chess with a respectable gentleman well known in Balham. In this case, the method of enquiry will be to pump the respectable gentleman in Balham, and if he should happen to be a single gentleman with a deaf housekeeper, it may be no easy matter to impugn the alibi, since, outside detective romances, few ticket-collectors and 'bus-conductors keep an exact remembrance of all the passengers passing between Balham and London on any and every evening of the week.

"Finally, gentlemen, I will frankly point out the weak point of all these hypotheses, namely: that none of them offers any

---

[42] How the small fish described the shipwrecked mariner in the story "How the Whale Got His Throat," in "Just So Stories" by Rudyard Kipling (1865-1936).

explanation as to why the incriminating article was left so conspicuously on the body in the first instance."

Mr. Parker had listened with commendable patience to this academic exposition.

"Might not X," he suggested, "be an enemy of Crimplesham's, who designed to throw suspicion upon him?"

"He might. In that case he should be easy to discover, since he obviously lives in close proximity to Crimplesham and his glasses, and Crimplesham in fear of his life will then be a valuable ally for the prosecution."

"How about the first possibility of all, misunderstanding or accident?"

"Well! Well, for purposes of discussion, nothing, because it really doesn't afford any data for discussion."

"In any case," said Parker, "the obvious course appears to be to go to Salisbury."

"That seems indicated," said Lord Peter.

"Very well," said the detective, "is it to be you or me or both of us?"

"It is to be me," said Lord Peter, "and that for two reasons. First, because, if (by Possibility No. 2, Hypothesis 1, Alternative A) Crimplesham is an innocent cat's-paw,[43] the person who put in the advertisement is the proper person to hand over the property. Secondly, because, if we are to adopt Hypothesis 2, we must not overlook the sinister possibility that Crimplesham-X is laying a careful trap to rid himself of the person who so unwarily advertised in the daily press his interest in the solution of the Battersea Park mystery."

"That appears to me to be an argument for our both going," objected the detective.

"Far from it," said Lord Peter. "Why play into the hands of Crimplesham-X by delivering over to him the only two men in London with the evidence, such as it is, and shall I say the wits, to

---

[43] Getting someone else to unwittingly do your dirty work. The phrase was inspired by a fable by French poet Jean de La Fontaine (1621-1695), in which a monkey convinces a cat to pull chestnuts for him from a hot fire, burning his paw in the process.

connect him with the Battersea body?"

"But if we told the Yard where we were going, and we both got nobbled,"[44] said Mr. Parker, "it would afford strong presumptive evidence of Crimplesham's guilt, and anyhow, if he didn't get hanged for murdering the man in the bath he'd at least get hanged for murdering us."

"Well," said Lord Peter, "if he only murdered me you could still hang him—what's the good of wasting a sound, marriageable young male like yourself? Besides, how about old Levy? If you're incapacitated, do you think anybody else is going to find him?"

"But we could frighten Crimplesham by threatening him with the Yard."

"Well, dash it all, if it comes to that, I can frighten him by threatening him with you, which, seeing you hold what evidence there is, is much more to the point. And, then, suppose it's a wild-goose chase[45] after all, you'll have wasted time when you might have been getting on with the case. There are several things that need doing."

"Well," said Parker, silenced but reluctant, "why can't I go, in that case?"

"Bosh!" said Lord Peter. "I am retained (by old Mrs. Thipps, for whom I entertain the greatest respect) to deal with this case, and it's only by courtesy I allow you to have anything to do with it."

Mr. Parker groaned.

"Will you at least take Bunter?" he said.

"In deference to your feelings," replied Lord Peter, "I will take Bunter, though he could be far more usefully employed taking photographs or overhauling my wardrobe. When is there a good train to Salisbury, Bunter?"

"There is an excellent train at 10:50, my lord."

"Kindly make arrangements to catch it," said Lord Peter, throwing off his bathrobe and trailing away with it into his bedroom. "And Parker—if you have nothing else to do you might get hold of Levy's secretary and look into that little matter of the

---

[44] Hit on the head.

[45] A useless pursuit, as anyone who has tried to catch a goose that didn't want to be caught can tell you.

Peruvian oil."

Lord Peter took with him, for light reading in the train, Sir Reuben Levy's diary. It was a simple, and in the light of recent facts, rather a pathetic document. The terrible fighter of the Stock Exchange, who could with one nod set the surly bear dancing, or bring the savage bull to feed out of his hand,[46] whose breath devastated whole districts with famine or swept financial potentates from their seats, was revealed in private life as kindly, domestic, innocently proud of himself and his belongings, confiding, generous and a little dull. His own small economies were duly chronicled side by side with extravagant presents to his wife and daughter. Small incidents of household routine appeared, such as: "Man came to mend the conservatory[47] roof," or "The new butler (Simpson) has arrived, recommended by the Goldbergs. I think he will be satisfactory." All visitors and entertainments were duly entered, from a very magnificent lunch to Lord Dewsbury, the Minister for Foreign Affairs, and Dr. Jabez K. Wort, the American plenipotentiary,[48] through a series of diplomatic dinners to eminent financiers, down to intimate family gatherings of persons designated by Christian names or nicknames. About May there came a mention of Lady Levy's nerves, and further reference was made to the subject in subsequent months. In September it was stated that "Freke came to see my dear wife and advised complete rest and change of scene. She thinks of going abroad with Rachel." The name of the famous nerve-specialist occurred as a diner or luncher about once a month, and it came into Lord Peter's mind that Freke would be a good person to consult about Levy himself. "People sometimes tell things to the doctor," he murmured to

---

[46] Descriptions of the two states of the stock market. In a bull market, stock prices are rising. In a bear market, they are falling. The terms have changed since they first appeared in "Every Man His Own Broker," published in 1785 by Thomas Mortimer. In it, he describes two types of investors: bulls who are optimists who buy stocks on margin (i.e., on borrowed money) to sell later at a higher price; and bears who buy temporarily depressed stock to resell quickly when the price rebounds.

[47] A greenhouse-like room where plants are displayed.

[48] A diplomat sent on a mission who has been given the authority to make decisions on his country's behalf.

himself. "And, by Jove! if Levy was simply going round to see Freke on Monday night, that rather disposes of the Battersea incident, doesn't it?" He made a note to look up Sir Julian and turned on further. On September 18th, Lady Levy and her daughter had left for the south of France. Then suddenly, under the date October 5th, Lord Peter found what he was looking for: "Goldberg, Skriner and Milligan to dinner."

There was the evidence that Milligan had been in that house. There had been a formal entertainment—a meeting as of two duelists shaking hands before the fight. Skriner was a well-known picture-dealer; Lord Peter imagined an after-dinner excursion upstairs to see the two Corots[49] in the drawing-room, and the portrait of the eldest Levy girl, who had died at the age of sixteen. It was by Augustus John,[50] and hung in the bedroom. The name of the red-haired secretary was nowhere mentioned, unless the initial S., occurring in another entry, referred to him. Throughout September and October, Anderson (of Wyndham's) had been a frequent visitor.

Lord Peter shook his head over the diary, and turned to the consideration of the Battersea Park mystery. Whereas in the Levy affair it was easy enough to supply a motive for the crime, if crime it were, and the difficulty was to discover the method of its carrying out and the whereabouts of the victim, in the other case the chief obstacle to enquiry was the entire absence of any imaginable motive. It was odd that, although the papers had carried news of the affair from one end of the country to the other and a description of the body had been sent to every police station in the country, nobody had as yet come forward to identify the mysterious occupant of Mr. Thipps's bath. It was true that the description, which mentioned the clean-shaven chin, elegantly cut hair and the pince-nez, was rather misleading but on the other hand, the police had managed to discover the number of molars missing, and the height, complexion and other data were correctly

---

[49] Jean-Baptiste-Camille Corot (1796-1875), a French painter who used a Neo-Classical painting style to depict peasants in beautiful landscapes.
[50] A painter (1878-1961) noted for his portraiture, particularly of T.E. Lawrence, George Bernard Shaw and Dylan Thomas.

enough stated, as also the date at which death had presumably occurred. It seemed, however, as though the man had melted out of society without leaving a gap or so much as a ripple. Assigning a motive for the murder of a person without relations or antecedents or even clothes is like trying to visualize the fourth dimension— admirable exercise for the imagination, but arduous and inconclusive. Even if the day's interview should disclose black spots in the past or present of Mr. Crimplesham, how were they to be brought into connection with a person apparently without a past, and whose present was confined to the narrow limits of a bath and a police mortuary?

"Bunter," said Lord Peter, "I beg that in the future you will restrain me from starting two hares at once.[51] These cases are gettin' to be a strain on my constitution. One hare has nowhere to run from, and the other has nowhere to run to. It's a kind of mental D.T.,[52] Bunter. When this is over I shall turn pussyfoot, forswear the police news, and take to an emollient diet of the works of the late Charles Garvice."[53]

---

[51] A reference to the proverb, "He who hunts two hares leaves one and loses the other." A similar sentiment was expressed in Shakespeare's "Hamlet," when King Claudius reflects that "like a man to double business bound / I stand in pause where I shall first begin, / And both neglect."

[52] Delirium tremens, Latin for a "shaking frenzy" caused by a withdrawal from alcohol.

[53] *Pussyfoot.* William E. "Pussyfoot" Johnson, an American prohibitionist. As a U.S. special agent in the Indian Territory (and when it became a state, Oklahoma), he earned his nickname for his cat-like raids on gambling saloons, bars and brothels, earning more than 4,400 convictions during his three years in the service. He toured the U.S. and Europe extensively on behalf of the Anti-Saloon League. During his 1919 temperance campaign in Britain, medical students caught him and paraded him through London on a stretcher before police rescued him, but not before he lost the sight in an eye from a flying object. Abstinence advocates became known as "pussyfooters."

Emollient diet. Soft and soothing.

Charles Garvice. The James Patterson of his time, Garvice (1850-1920) sold more than seven million copies of his adventure and romance novels, all of them forgotten today.

It was its comparative proximity to Milford Hill that induced Lord Peter to lunch at the Minster Hotel[54] rather than at the White Hart[55] or some other more picturesquely situated hostel.[56] It was not a lunch calculated to cheer his mind; as in all Cathedral cities, the atmosphere of the Close[57] pervades every nook and corner of Salisbury, and no food in that city but seems faintly flavoured with prayer-books. As he sat sadly consuming that impassive pale substance known to the English as "cheese" unqualified (for there are cheeses which go openly by their names, as Stilton, Camembert, Gruyère, Wensleydale or Gorgonzola, but "cheese" is cheese and everywhere the same),[58] he enquired of the waiter the whereabouts of Mr. Crimplesham's office.

The waiter directed him to a house rather further up the street on the opposite side, adding, "But anybody'll tell you, sir; Mr. Crimplesham's very well known hereabouts."

"He's a good solicitor, I suppose?" said Lord Peter.

"Oh, yes, sir," said the waiter, "you couldn't do better than trust to Mr. Crimplesham, sir. There's folk say he's old-fashioned, but I'd rather have my little bits of business done by Mr. Crimplesham than by one of these fly-away young men. Not but what Mr. Crimplesham'll be retiring soon, sir, I don't doubt, for he must be close on eighty, sir, if he's a day, but then there's young Mr. Wicks

---

[54] A website that chronicles pubs and inns with literary connections identifies Lord Peter's choice for lunch as the Cathedral Hotel, a suitable restaurant for the middle-class Sayers — who boarded at Salisbury's Godolphin School before she entered Oxford — but far below the quality Lord Peter would expect.

[55] The four-star rated hotel on St. John Street, in its 17th century building, would have been far more suitable for a person of Lord Peter's social class.

[56] A hotel. Sometimes, it's a building owned by a charity or group that offers long-term accommodations to a particular clientele, such as students or nurses.

[57] A cathedral is a church that is designated as the headquarters of the diocese and ruled by a bishop. The city it is in is called a cathedral city. The close is the area near the cathedral, usually a green space surrounded by buildings, where can be found the homes of the bishop and other clergy, offices, schools and chapels. The close near Salisbury Cathedral, for example, consists of nearly 30 buildings and ample lawns.

[58] English cuisine is generally not held in high regard, except for its cheeses. George Orwell wrote a defense of English cooking in 1945, in which he called Stilton "the best cheese of its type in the world, with Wensleydale not far behind."

to carry on the business, and he's a very nice, steady-like young gentleman."

"Is Mr. Crimplesham really as old as that?" said Lord Peter. "Dear me! He must be very active for his years. A friend of mine was doing business with him in town last week."

"Wonderful active, sir," agreed the waiter, "and with his game leg, too, you'd be surprised. But there, sir, I often think, when a man's once past a certain age, the older he grows the tougher he gets, and women the same or more so."

"Very likely," said Lord Peter, calling up and dismissing the mental picture of a gentleman of eighty with a game leg carrying a dead body over the roof of a Battersea flat at midnight. "'He's tough, sir, tough, is old Joey Bagstock, tough and devilish sly,' " he added, thoughtlessly.[59]

"Indeed, sir?" said the waiter. "I couldn't say, I'm sure."

"I beg your pardon," said Lord Peter, "I was quoting poetry. Very silly of me. I got the habit at my mother's knee and I can't break myself of it."

"No, sir," said the waiter, pocketing a liberal tip. "Thank you very much, sir. You'll find the house easy. Just afore you come to Penny-farthing Street,[60] sir, about two turnings off, on the right hand side opposite."

"Afraid that disposes of Crimplesham-X," said Lord Peter. "I'm rather sorry; he was a fine sinister figure as I had pictured him. Still, his may yet be the brain behind the hands—the aged spider sitting invisible in the centre of the vibrating web,[61] you

---

[59] Lord Peter wasn't quoting a poem, but from Charles Dickens' "Dombey and Son." In Chapter 10, Major Joseph Bagstock, a retired army major, erupts in anger to Miss Tox's rejection of his marriage proposal:

"'Would you, Ma'am, would you!' said the Major, straining with vindictiveness, and swelling every already swollen vein in his head. 'Would you give Joey B. the go-by, Ma'am? Not yet, ma'am, not yet! Damme, not yet, Sir. Joe is awake, Ma'am. Bagstock is alive, Sir. J. B. knows a move or two, Ma'am. Josh has his weather-eye open, Sir. You'll find him tough, Ma'am. Tough, Sir, tough is Joseph. Tough, and de-vilish sly!'"

[60] This street exists in Salisbury. According to legend, it was named for the master masons building the cathedral, who went on strike for this daily wage.

[61] A reference to Professor Moriarty from the Sherlock Holmes story "The Final Problem":

know, Bunter."

"Yes, my lord," said Bunter. They were walking up the street together.

"There is the office over the way," pursued Lord Peter. "I think, Bunter, you might step into this little shop and purchase a sporting paper,[62] and if I do not emerge from the villain's lair—say within three-quarters of an hour, you may take such steps as your perspicuity[63] may suggest."

Mr. Bunter turned into the shop as desired, and Lord Peter walked across and rang the lawyer's bell with decision.

"The truth, the whole truth and nothing but the truth[64] is my long suit here, I fancy," he murmured, and when the door was opened by a clerk he delivered over his card with an unflinching air.

He was ushered immediately into a confidential-looking office, obviously furnished in the early years of Queen Victoria's reign, and never altered since. A lean, frail-looking old gentleman rose briskly from his chair as he entered and limped forward to meet him.

"My dear sir," exclaimed the lawyer, "how extremely good of you to come in person! Indeed, I am ashamed to have given you so much trouble. I trust you were passing this way, and that my glasses have not put you to any great inconvenience. Pray take a seat, Lord Peter." He peered gratefully at the young man over a pince-nez obviously the fellow of that now adorning a dossier in Scotland Yard.

Lord Peter sat down. The lawyer sat down. Lord Peter picked up a glass paper-weight from the desk and weighed it thoughtfully in his hand. Subconsciously he noted what an admirable set of finger-prints he was leaving upon it. He replaced it with precision on the exact centre of a pile of letters.

"He is the Napoleon of crime, Watson... He has a brain of the first order. He sits motionless, like a spider in the centre of its web, but that web has a thousand radiations, and he knows well every quiver of each of them."

[62] A newspaper that covers sports.

[63] Understanding of the situation.

[64] The tradition of taking oaths in legal proceedings is at least as old as the Romans. The phrase "the truth, the whole truth and nothing but the truth" has been traced back in English trials as far back as the 13th century.

"It's quite all right," said Lord Peter. "I was here on business. Very happy to be of service to you. Very awkward to lose one's glasses, Mr. Crimplesham."

"Yes," said the lawyer, "I assure you I feel quite lost without them. I have this pair, but they do not fit my nose so well— besides, that chain has a great sentimental value for me. I was terribly distressed on arriving at Balham to find that I had lost them. I made enquiries of the railway, but to no purpose. I feared they had been stolen. There were such crowds at Victoria, and the carriage was packed with people all the way to Balham. Did you come across them in the train?"

"Well, no," said Lord Peter, "I found them in rather an unexpected place. Do you mind telling me if you recognized any of your fellow-travellers on that occasion?"

The lawyer stared at him.

"Not a soul," he answered. "Why do you ask?"

"Well," said Lord Peter, "I thought perhaps the—the person with whom I found them might have taken them for a joke."

The lawyer looked puzzled.

"Did the person claim to be an acquaintance of mine?" he enquired. "I know practically nobody in London, except the friend with whom I was staying in Balham, Dr. Philpots, and I should be very greatly surprised at his practising a jest upon me. He knew very well how distressed I was at the loss of the glasses. My business was to attend a meeting of shareholders in Medlicott's Bank, but the other gentlemen present were all personally unknown to me, and I cannot think that any of them would take so great a liberty. In any case," he added, "as the glasses are here, I will not enquire too closely into the manner of their restoration. I am deeply obliged to you for your trouble."

Lord Peter hesitated.

"Pray forgive my seeming inquisitiveness," he said, "but I must ask you another question. It sounds rather melodramatic, I'm afraid, but it's this. Are you aware that you have any enemy—anyone, I mean, who would profit by your—er—decease or disgrace?"

Mr. Crimplesham sat frozen into stony surprise and disapproval.

"May I ask the meaning of this extraordinary question?" he enquired stiffly.

"Well," said Lord Peter, "the circumstances are a little unusual.

You may recollect that my advertisement was addressed to the jeweller who sold the chain."

"That surprised me at the time," said Mr. Crimplesham, "but I begin to think your advertisement and your behaviour are all of a piece."

"They are," said Lord Peter. "As a matter of fact I did not expect the owner of the glasses to answer my advertisement. Mr. Crimplesham, you have no doubt read what the papers have to say about the Battersea Park mystery. Your glasses are the pair that was found on the body, and they are now in the possession of the police at Scotland Yard, as you may see by this." He placed the specification of the glasses and the official note before Crimplesham.

"Good God!" exclaimed the lawyer. He glanced at the paper, and then looked narrowly at Lord Peter.

"Are you yourself connected with the police?" he enquired.

"Not officially," said Lord Peter. "I am investigating the matter privately, in the interests of one of the parties."

Mr. Crimplesham rose to his feet.

"My good man," he said, "this is a very impudent attempt, but blackmail is an indictable[65] offence, and I advise you to leave my office before you commit yourself." He rang the bell.

"I was afraid you'd take it like that," said Lord Peter. "It looks as though this ought to have been my friend Detective Parker's job, after all." He laid Parker's card on the table beside the specification, and added: "If you should wish to see me again, Mr. Crimplesham, before to-morrow morning, you will find me at the Minster Hotel."

Mr. Crimplesham disdained to reply further than to direct the clerk who entered to "show this person out."

In the entrance Lord Peter brushed against a tall young man who was just coming in, and who stared at him with surprised recognition. His face, however, aroused no memories in Lord Peter's mind, and that baffled nobleman, calling out Bunter from the newspaper shop, departed to his hotel to get a trunk-call through to Parker.

---

[65] An accusation by a grand jury that could lead to a criminal charge.

Meanwhile, in the office, the meditations of the indignant Mr. Crimplesham were interrupted by the entrance of his junior partner.

"I say," said the latter gentleman, "has somebody done something really wicked at last? What ever brings such a distinguished amateur of crime on our sober doorstep?"

"I have been the victim of a vulgar attempt at blackmail," said the lawyer; "an individual passing himself off as Lord Peter Wimsey—"

"But that is Lord Peter Wimsey," said Mr. Wicks, "there's no mistaking him. I saw him give evidence in the Attenbury emerald case.[66] He's a big little pot in his way, you know, and goes fishing with the head of Scotland Yard."

"Oh, dear," said Mr. Crimplesham.

Fate arranged that the nerves of Mr. Crimplesham should be tried that afternoon. When, escorted by Mr. Wicks, he arrived at the Minster Hotel, he was informed by the porter that Lord Peter Wimsey had strolled out, mentioning that he thought of attending Evensong.[67] "But his man is here, sir," he added, "if you like to leave a message."

Mr. Wicks thought that on the whole it would be well to leave a message. Mr. Bunter, on enquiry, was found to be sitting by the telephone, waiting for a trunk-call.[68] As Mr. Wicks addressed him the bell rang, and Mr. Bunter, politely excusing himself, took down the receiver.

"Hullo!" he said. "Is that Mr. Parker? Oh, thanks! Exchange! Exchange! Sorry, can you put me through to Scotland Yard? Excuse me, gentlemen, keeping you waiting.—Exchange! all right— Scotland Yard—Hullo! Is that Scotland Yard?—Is Detective Parker round there?—Can I speak to him?—I shall have done in a moment, gentlemen.—Hullo! is that you, Mr. Parker? Lord Peter would be much obliged if you could find it convenient to step down to Salisbury, sir. Oh, no, sir, he's in excellent health, sir—just stepped round to hear Evensong, sir—oh, no, I think to-morrow morning would do excellently, sir, thank you, sir."

---

[66] Lord Peter's first investigation, told in the 2011 novel by Jill Paton Walsh.

[67] The evening prayer service in the Anglican Church.

[68] A long-distance call.

CHAPTER VI

I T WAS, IN FACT, INCONVENIENT for Mr. Parker to leave London. He had had to go and see Lady Levy towards the end of the morning, and subsequently his plans for the day had been thrown out of gear and his movements delayed by the discovery that the adjourned inquest of Mr. Thipps's unknown visitor was to be held that afternoon, since nothing very definite seemed forthcoming from Inspector Sugg's enquiries. Jury and witnesses had been convened accordingly for three o'clock. Mr. Parker might altogether have missed the event, had he not run against Sugg that morning at the Yard and extracted the information from him as one would a reluctant tooth. Inspector Sugg, indeed, considered Mr. Parker rather interfering; moreover, he was hand-in-glove with Lord Peter Wimsey, and Inspector Sugg had no words for the interferingness of Lord Peter. He could not, however, when directly questioned, deny that there was to be an inquest that afternoon, nor could he prevent Mr. Parker from enjoying the inalienable right of any interested British citizen to be present. At a little before three, therefore, Mr. Parker was in his place, and amusing himself with watching the efforts of those persons who arrived after the room was packed to insinuate, bribe or bully themselves into a position of vantage. The coroner, a medical man of precise habits and unimaginative aspect, arrived punctually, and looking peevishly round at the crowded assembly, directed all the windows to be opened, thus letting in a stream of drizzling fog upon the heads of the unfortunates on that side of the room. This caused a commotion and some expressions of disapproval, checked sternly by the coroner, who said that with the influenza about again an unventilated room was a deathtrap; that anybody who chose to object to open windows had the obvious remedy of leaving the court, and further, that if any disturbance was made he would clear the court. He then took a Formamint lozenge,[1] and proceeded, after the usual preliminaries, to call up fourteen good and lawful persons and swear them diligently to enquire and a true presentment[2] make of all matters touching the death of the gentleman with the pince-nez and to give a true verdict according to the evidence, so help them God. When an expostulation[3] by a woman juror—an elderly lady in spectacles who kept a sweetshop,[4] and appeared to wish she was back there—had been summarily quashed by the coroner, the jury departed to view the body. Mr. Parker gazed round again and identified the unhappy Mr. Thipps and the girl Gladys led into an adjoining room under the grim guard of the police. They were soon followed by a gaunt old lady in a bonnet and mantle. With her, in a wonderful fur coat and a motor bonnet[5] of fascinating construction, came the Dowager Duchess of Denver, her quick, dark eyes darting hither and thither about the crowd. The next moment they had lighted on Mr. Parker, who had several times visited the Dower House, and she nodded to him, and spoke to a policeman. Before long, a way opened magically through the press, and Mr. Parker found himself accommodated with a front seat just behind the Duchess, who greeted him charmingly, and said: "What's happened to poor Peter?" Parker began to explain, and the coroner glanced irritably in their direction. Somebody went up and whispered in his ear, at which he coughed, and took another Formamint.

"We came up by car," said the Duchess—"so tiresome—such bad roads between Denver and Gunbury St. Walters—and there were people coming to lunch—I had to put them off—I couldn't let the old lady go alone, could I? By the way, such an odd thing's

---

[1] An over-the-counter drug used to treat sore throats.
[2] A legal term meaning a formal statement that notice has been taken of a criminal offense.
[3] Demand strongly and with reason.
[4] Candy store.
[5] A hat worn by women to protect their hair while riding in open-top cars.

happened about the Church Restoration Fund—the Vicar—oh, dear, here are these people coming back again;[6] well, I'll tell you afterwards—do look at that woman looking shocked, and the girl in tweeds trying to look as if she sat on undraped gentlemen every day of her life—I don't mean that—corpses of course—but one finds oneself being so Elizabethan nowadays—what an awful little man the coroner is, isn't he? He's looking daggers at me—do you think he'll dare to clear me out of the court or commit me for what-you-may-call-it?"[7]

The first part of the evidence was not of great interest to Mr. Parker. The wretched Mr. Thipps, who had caught cold in gaol,[8] deposed in an unhappy croak to having discovered the body when he went in to take his bath at eight o'clock. He had arrived at St. Pancras at ten o'clock. He sent the girl for brandy. He had never seen the deceased before. He had no idea how he came there.

Yes, he had been in Manchester the day before. He had arrived at St. Pancras at ten o'clock. He had cloak-roomed his bag. At this point Mr. Thipps became very red, unhappy and confused, and glanced nervously about the court.

"Now, Mr. Thipps," said the Coroner, briskly, "we must have your movements quite clear. You must appreciate the importance of the matter. You have chosen to give evidence, which you need not have done, but having done so, you will find it best to be perfectly explicit."

"Yes," said Mr. Thipps faintly.

"Have you cautioned this witness,[9] officer?" inquired the Coroner, turning sharply to Inspector Sugg.

The Inspector replied that he had told Mr. Thipps that anything he said might be used again' him at his trial. Mr. Thipps became ashy, and said in a bleating voice that he 'adn't—hadn't meant to do anything that wasn't right.

---

[6] After viewing the body. Inquests were typically held soon after the body is discovered but before it is released to the family.

[7] Perhaps a charge of committing a breach of the peace.

[8] Jail.

[9] Read his rights under the law. In England and Wales, this includes the right to silence and to choose whether to give evidence during any proceeding.

This remark produced a mild sensation, and the Coroner became even more acidulated[10] in manner than before.

"Is anybody representing Mr. Thipps?" he asked, irritably. "No? Did you not explain to him that he could—that he ought to be represented? You did not? Really, Inspector! Did you not know, Mr. Thipps, that you had a right to be legally represented?"

Mr. Thipps clung to a chair-back for support, and said "No" in a voice barely audible.

"It is incredible," said the Coroner, "that so-called educated people should be so ignorant of the legal procedure of their own country. This places us in a very awkward position. I doubt, Inspector, whether I should permit the prisoner—Mr. Thipps—to give evidence at all. It is a delicate position."

The perspiration stood on Mr. Thipps's forehead.

"Save us from our friends,"[11] whispered the Duchess to Parker. "If that cough-drop-devouring creature had openly instructed those fourteen people—and what unfinished-looking faces they have—so characteristic, I always think, of the lower middle-class, rather like sheep, or calves' head (boiled, I mean), to bring in wilful murder against the poor little man, he couldn't have made himself plainer."

"He can't let him incriminate himself, you know," said Parker.

"Stuff!" said the Duchess. "How could the man incriminate himself when he never did anything in his life? You men never think of anything but your red tape."

Meanwhile Mr. Thipps, wiping his brow with a handkerchief, had summoned up courage. He stood up with a kind of weak dignity, like a small white rabbit brought to bay.

"I would rather tell you," he said, "though it's reelly very unpleasant for a man in my position. But I reelly couldn't have it thought for a moment that I'd committed this dreadful crime. I assure you, gentlemen, I couldn't bear that. No. I'd rather tell you the truth, though I'm afraid it places me in rather a—well, I'll tell

---

[10] To be caustic.

[11] An old proverb, first recorded with altered wording in 1477. Queen Elizabeth I said in 1585 that "there is an Italian proverb which saith, From my enemy let me defend myself; but from a pretensed friend, good Lord deliver me."

you."

"You fully understand the gravity of making such a statement, Mr. Thipps," said the Coroner.

"Quite," said Mr. Thipps. "It's all right—I—might I have a drink of water?"

"Take your time," said the Coroner, at the same time robbing his remark of all conviction by an impatient glance at his watch.

"Thank you, sir," said Mr. Thipps. "Well, then, it's true I got to St. Pancras at ten. But there was a man in the carriage with me. He'd got in at Leicester.[12] I didn't recognize him at first, but he turned out to be an old schoolfellow of mine."

"What was this gentleman's name?" enquired the Coroner, his pencil poised.

Mr. Thipps shrank together visibly.

"I'm afraid I can't tell you that," he said. "You see—that is, you will see—it would get him into trouble, and I couldn't do that—no, I reelly couldn't do that, not if my life depended on it. No!" he added, as the ominous pertinence of the last phrase smote upon him, "I'm sure I couldn't do that."

"Well, well," said the Coroner.

The Duchess leaned over to Parker again. "I'm beginning quite to admire the little man," she said.

Mr. Thipps resumed.

"When we got to St. Pancras I was going home, but my friend said no. We hadn't met for a long time and we ought to—to make a night of it, was his expression. I fear I was weak, and let him overpersuade me to accompany him to one of his haunts. I use the word advisedly," said Mr. Thipps, "and I assure you, sir, that if I had known beforehand where we were going I never would have set foot in the place.

"I cloak-roomed my bag, for he did not like the notion of our being encumbered with it, and we got into a taxicab and drove to the corner of Tottenham Court Road and Oxford Street.[13] We then walked a little way, and turned into a side street (I do not recollect

---

[12] A city (pop. 1921: 234,143) in central England, about 100 miles north of London. Pronounced "lester."

[13] At St. Giles's Circus, near London's West End and Soho.

which) where there was an open door, with the light shining out. There was a man at a counter, and my friend bought some tickets, and I heard the man at the counter say something to him about 'Your friend,' meaning me, and my friend said, 'Oh, yes, he's been here before, haven't you, Alf?' (which was what they called me at school), though I assure you, sir"—here Mr. Thipps grew very earnest—"I never had, and nothing in the world should induce me to go to such a place again.

"Well, we went down into a room underneath, where there were drinks, and my friend had several, and made me take one or two—though I am an abstemious[14] man as a rule—and he talked to some other men and girls who were there—a very vulgar set of people, I thought them, though I wouldn't say but what some of the young ladies were nice-looking enough. One of them sat on my friend's knee and called him a slow old thing, and told him to come on—so we went into another room, where there were a lot of people dancing all these up-to-date dances.[15] My friend went and danced, and I sat on a sofa. One of the young ladies came up to me and said, didn't I dance, and I said 'No,' so she said wouldn't I stand her a drink then. 'You'll stand us a drink then, darling,' that was what she said, and I said, 'Wasn't it after hours?'[16] and she said that didn't matter. So I ordered the drink—a gin and bitters it was—for I didn't like not to, the young lady seemed to expect it of me and I felt it wouldn't be gentlemanly to refuse when she asked. But it went against my conscience—such a young girl as she was—and she put her arm round my neck afterwards and kissed me just like as if she was paying for the drink—and it reelly went to my 'eart," said Mr. Thipps, a little ambiguously, but with

---

[14] Showing restraint in eating and drinking.

[15] The era after World War I saw an explosion in the popularity of new types of music, such as jazz, and women moving from the tight corsets and long skirts to dresses that allowed greater freedom of movement. Dances, too, followed suit, with waltzes and foxtrots being replaced by the tango, imported from Argentina as a by-product of its economic boom, and the Charleston.

[16] At the beginning of World War I, to keep factory workers from turning up drunk and harming the war effort, a law was passed restricting the hours at pubs to noon-2:30 p.m. and 6:30-9:30 p.m. The rules were strictly enforced with police raids like the one from which Mr. Thipps escaped.

uncommon emphasis.

Here somebody at the back said, "Cheer-oh!" and a sound was heard as of the noisy smacking of lips.

"Remove the person who made that improper noise," said the Coroner, with great indignation. "Go on, please, Mr. Thipps."

"Well," said Mr. Thipps, "about half past twelve, as I should reckon, things began to get a bit lively, and I was looking for my friend to say good-night, not wishing to stay longer, as you will understand, when I saw him with one of the young ladies, and they seemed to be getting on altogether too well, if you follow me, my friend pulling the ribbons off her shoulder and the young lady laughing—and so on," said Mr. Thipps, hurriedly, "so I thought I'd just slip quietly out, when I heard a scuffle and a shout—and before I knew what was happening there were half a dozen policemen in, and the lights went out, and everybody stampeding and shouting—quite horrid, it was. I was knocked down in the rush, and hit my head a nasty knock on a chair—that was where I got that bruise they asked me about—and I was dreadfully afraid I'd never get away and it would all come out, and perhaps my photograph in the papers, when someone caught hold of me—I think it was the young lady I'd given the gin and bitters to—and she said, 'This way,' and pushed me along a passage and out at the back somewhere. So I ran through some streets, and found myself in Goodge Street,[17] and there I got a taxi and came home. I saw the account of the raid afterwards in the papers, and saw my friend had escaped, and so, as it wasn't the sort of thing I wanted made public and I didn't want to get him into difficulties, I just said nothing. But that's the truth."

"Well, Mr. Thipps," said the Coroner, "we shall be able to substantiate a certain amount of this story. Your friend's name—"

"No," said Mr. Thipps, stoutly, "not on any account."

"Very good," said the Coroner. "Now, can you tell us what time you did get in?"

"About half past one, I should think. Though reelly, I was so upset—"

---

[17] A street in Fitzrovia, near Tottenham Court Road and Oxford Street. See frontispiece map for location.

"Quite so. Did you go straight to bed?"

"Yes, I took my sandwich and glass of milk first. I thought it might settle my inside, so to speak," added the witness, apologetically, "not being accustomed to alcohol so late at night and on an empty stomach, as you may say."

"Quite so. Nobody sat up for you?"

"Nobody."

"How long did you take getting to bed first and last?"

Mr. Thipps thought it might have been half an hour.

"Did you visit the bathroom before turning in?"

"No."

"And you heard nothing in the night?"

"No. I fell fast asleep. I was rather agitated, so I took a little dose[18] to make me sleep, and what with being so tired and the milk and the dose, I just tumbled right off and didn't wake till Gladys called me."

Further questioning elicited little from Mr. Thipps. Yes, the bathroom window had been open when he went in in the morning, he was sure of that, and he had spoken very sharply to the girl about it. He was ready to answer any questions; he would be only too 'appy—happy to have this dreadful affair sifted to the bottom.

Gladys Horrocks stated that she had been in Mr. Thipps's employment about three months. Her previous employers would speak to her character. It was her duty to make the round of the flat at night, when she had seen Mrs. Thipps to bed at ten. Yes, she remembered doing so on Monday evening. She had looked into all the rooms. Did she recollect shutting the bathroom window that night? Well, no, she couldn't swear to it, not in particular, but when Mr. Thipps called her into the bathroom in the morning it certainly was open. She had not been into the bathroom before Mr. Thipps went in. Well, yes, it had happened that she had left that window open before, when anyone had been 'aving a bath in the evening and 'ad left the blind down. Mrs. Thipps 'ad 'ad a bath on Monday evening, Mondays was one of her regular bath nights. She was very much afraid she 'adn't shut the window on Monday

---

[18] A drug to aid in falling asleep, possibly containing barbiturates.

night, though she wished her 'ead 'ad been cut off afore she'd been so forgetful.

Here the witness burst into tears and was given some water, while the Coroner refreshed himself with a third lozenge.

Recovering, witness stated that she had certainly looked into all the rooms before going to bed. No, it was quite impossible for a body to be 'idden in the flat without her seeing of it. She 'ad been in the kitchen all evening, and there wasn't 'ardly room to keep the best dinner service there, let alone a body. Old Mrs. Thipps sat in the drawing-room.[19] Yes, she was sure she'd been into the dining-room. How? Because she put Mr. Thipps's milk and sandwiches there ready for him. There had been nothing in there,—that she could swear to. Nor yet in her own bedroom, nor in the 'all. Had she searched the bedroom cupboard and the box-room? Well, no, not to say searched; she wasn't used to searchin' people's 'ouses for skelintons every night. So that a man might have concealed himself in the box-room or a wardrobe? She supposed he might.

In reply to a woman juror—well, yes, she was walking out[20] with a young man. Williams was his name, Bill Williams—well, yes, William Williams, if they insisted. He was a glazier by profession.[21] Well, yes, he 'ad been in the flat sometimes. Well, she supposed you might say he was acquainted with the flat. Had she ever—no, she 'adn't, and if she'd thought such a question was going to be put to a respectable girl she wouldn't 'ave offered to give evidence. The vicar of St. Mary's would speak to her character and to Mr. Williams's. Last time Mr. Williams was at the flat was a fortnight ago.

Well, no, it wasn't exactly the last time she 'ad seen Mr. Williams. Well, yes, the last time was Monday—well, yes, Monday night. Well, if she must tell the truth, she must. Yes, the officer had cautioned her, but there wasn't any 'arm in it, and it was better to lose her place than to be 'ung, though it was a cruel

---

[19] A room used for entertaining visitors. The name is derived from "withdrawing room," a place where the homeowner and guest can go for greater privacy than the more public rooms.
[20] Courting.
[21] A tradesman who sets window panes.

shame a girl couldn't 'ave a bit of fun without a nasty corpse comin' in through the window to get 'er into difficulties. After she 'ad put Mrs. Thipps to bed, she 'ad slipped out to go to the Plumbers' and Glaziers' Ball at the "Black Faced Ram." Mr. Williams 'ad met 'er and brought 'er back. 'E could testify to where she'd been and that there wasn't no 'arm in it. She'd left before the end of the ball. It might 'ave been two o'clock when she got back. She'd got the keys of the flat from Mrs. Thipps's drawer when Mrs. Thipps wasn't looking. She 'ad asked leave to go, but couldn't get it, along of Mr. Thipps bein' away that night. She was bitterly sorry she 'ad be'aved so, and she was sure she'd been punished for it. She had 'eard nothing suspicious when she came in. She had gone straight to bed without looking round the flat. She wished she were dead.

No, Mr. and Mrs. Thipps didn't 'ardly ever 'ave any visitors; they kep' themselves very retired. She had found the outside door bolted that morning as usual. She wouldn't never believe any 'arm of Mr. Thipps. Thank you, Miss Horrocks. Call Georgiana Thipps, and the Coroner thought we had better light the gas.

The examination of Mrs. Thipps provided more entertainment than enlightenment, affording as it did an excellent example of the game called "cross questions and crooked answers."[22] After fifteen minutes' suffering, both in voice and temper, the Coroner abandoned the struggle, leaving the lady with the last word.

"You needn't try to bully me, young man," said that octogenarian with spirit, "settin' there spoilin' your stomach with them nasty jujubes."[23]

At this point a young man arose in court and demanded to give evidence. Having explained that he was William Williams, glazier, he was sworn, and corroborated the evidence of Gladys Horrocks in the matter of her presence at the "Black Faced Ram" on the

---

[22] A children's game in which players sit in a circle and one person starts by asking his neighbor a question and remembering the answer. The second person then asks his neighbor a different question and pairs that answer with the question he was asked. When everyone has done this, each person announces their question and answer. Merriment ensues.

[23] A type of candy generally sucked instead of chewed. Depending on the formula, it can be as soft as gummy candy or hard as a rock.

Monday night. They had returned to the flat rather before two, he thought, but certainly later than 1:30. He was sorry that he had persuaded Miss Horrocks to come out with him when she didn't ought. He had observed nothing of a suspicious nature in Prince of Wales Road at either visit.

Inspector Sugg gave evidence of having been called in at about half past eight on Monday morning. He had considered the girl's manner to be suspicious and had arrested her. On later information, leading him to suspect that the deceased might have been murdered that night, he had arrested Mr. Thipps. He had found no trace of breaking into the flat. There were marks on the bathroom window-sill which pointed to somebody having got in that way. There were no ladder marks or foot-marks in the yard; the yard was paved with asphalt. He had examined the roof, but found nothing on the roof. In his opinion the body had been brought into the flat previously and concealed till the evening by someone who had then gone out during the night by the bathroom window, with the connivance[24] of the girl. In that case, why should not the girl have let the person out by the door? Well, it might have been so. Had he found traces of a body or a man or both having been hidden in the flat? He found nothing to show that they might not have been so concealed. What was the evidence that led him to suppose that the death had occurred that night?

At this point Inspector Sugg appeared uneasy, and endeavoured to retire upon his professional dignity. On being pressed, however, he admitted that the evidence in question had come to nothing.

One of the jurors: Was it the case that any finger-marks had been left by the criminal?

Some marks had been found on the bath, but the criminal had worn gloves.

The Coroner: Do you draw any conclusion from this fact as to the experience of the criminal?

Inspector Sugg: Looks as if he was an old hand, sir.

The Juror: Is that very consistent with the charge against Alfred

---

[24] Someone who passively assists in wrongdoing.

Thipps, Inspector?

The Inspector was silent.

The Coroner: In the light of the evidence which you have just heard, do you still press the charge against Alfred Thipps and Gladys Horrocks?

Inspector Sugg: I consider the whole set-out highly suspicious. Thipps's story isn't corroborated, and as for the girl Horrocks, how do we know this Williams ain't in it as well?

William Williams: Now, you drop that. I can bring a 'undred witnesses—

The Coroner: Silence, if you please. I am surprised, Inspector, that you should make this suggestion in that manner. It is highly improper. By the way, can you tell us whether a police raid was actually carried out on the Monday night on any Night Club in the neighbourhood of St. Giles's Circus?[25]

Inspector Sugg (sulkily): I believe there was something of the sort.

The Coroner: You will, no doubt, enquire into the matter. I seem to recollect having seen some mention of it in the newspapers. Thank you, Inspector, that will do.

Several witnesses having appeared and testified to the characters of Mr. Thipps and Gladys Horrocks, the Coroner stated his intention of proceeding to the medical evidence.

"Sir Julian Freke."

There was considerable stir in the court as the great specialist walked up to give evidence. He was not only a distinguished man, but a striking figure, with his wide shoulders, upright carriage and leonine head. His manner as he kissed the Book presented to him with the usual deprecatory mumble by the Coroner's officer, was that of a St. Paul condescending to humour the timid mumbo-jumbo of superstitious Corinthians.[26]

---

[25] The intersection of Oxford Street, New Oxford Street, Charing Cross Road and Tottenham Court Road in London's West End, where Soho, Covent Garden, Bloomsbury and Fizrovia meet. It was known during the 17th and 18th centuries as "the Rookery," when it was a center for crime and immorality as depicted by William Hogarth in his engraving "Gin Lane."

[26] Natives of Corinth in Greece. The apostle Paul wrote two letters to the Corinthians on various religious and moral issues, especially erroneously held

"So handsome, I always think," whispered the Duchess to Mr. Parker, "just exactly like William Morris,[27] with that bush of hair and beard and those exciting eyes looking out of it—so splendid, these dear men always devoted to something or other—not but what I think socialism is a mistake—of course it works with all those nice people, so good and happy in art linen[28] and the weather always perfect—Morris, I mean, you know—but so difficult in real life. Science is different—I'm sure if I had nerves I should go to Sir Julian just to look at him—eyes like that give one something to think about, and that's what most of these people want, only I never had any—nerves, I mean. Don't you think so?"

"You are Sir Julian Freke," said the Coroner, "and live at St. Luke's House, Prince of Wales Road, Battersea, where you exercise a general direction over the surgical side of St. Luke's Hospital?"

Sir Julian assented briefly to this definition of his personality.

"You were the first medical man to see the deceased?"

"I was."

"And you have since conducted an examination in collaboration with Dr. Grimbold of Scotland Yard?"

"I have."

"You are in agreement as to the cause of death?"

"Generally speaking, yes."

"Will you communicate your impressions to the jury?"

"I was engaged in research work in the dissecting room at St. Luke's Hospital at about nine o'clock on Monday morning, when I was informed that Inspector Sugg wished to see me. He told me that the dead body of a man had been discovered under mysterious circumstances at 59 Queen Caroline Mansions. He asked me whether it could be supposed to be a joke perpetrated by any of the

---

views on Christian doctrine. They have been preserved in the Bible as Corinthians I and II.

[27] An artist, writer and textile designer (1834-1896) who was part of the Pre-Raphaelite Brotherhood and the Arts and Crafts movement. The books he published through his Kelmscott Press are considered masterpieces of design. He also wrote, spoke and organized extensively on behalf of socialism.

[28] A plain, fine-weaved fabric used for embroidery.

medical students at the hospital. I was able to assure him, by an examination of the hospital's books, that there was no subject missing from the dissecting room."

"Who would be in charge of such bodies?"

"William Watts, the dissecting-room attendant."

"Is William Watts present?" enquired the Coroner of the officer.

William Watts was present, and could be called if the Coroner thought it necessary.

"I suppose no dead body would be delivered to the hospital without your knowledge, Sir Julian?"

"Certainly not."

"Thank you. Will you proceed with your statement?"

"Inspector Sugg then asked me whether I would send a medical man round to view the body. I said that I would go myself."

"Why did you do that?"

"I confess to my share of ordinary human curiosity, Mr. Coroner."

Laughter from a medical student at the back of the room.

"On arriving at the flat I found the deceased lying on his back in the bath. I examined him, and came to the conclusion that death had been caused by a blow on the back of the neck, dislocating the fourth and fifth cervical vertebræ, bruising the spinal cord and producing internal hæmorrhage[29] and partial paralysis of the brain. I judged the deceased to have been dead at least twelve hours, possibly more. I observed no other sign of violence of any kind upon the body. Deceased was a strong, well-nourished man of about fifty to fifty-five years of age."

"In your opinion, could the blow have been self-inflicted?"

"Certainly not. It had been made with a heavy, blunt instrument from behind, with great force and considerable judgment. It is quite impossible that it was self-inflicted."

"Could it have been the result of an accident?"

"That is possible, of course."

"If, for example, the deceased had been looking out of window,

---

[29] Bleeding.

and the sash had shut violently down upon him?"

"No; in that case there would have been signs of strangulation and a bruise upon the throat as well."

"But deceased might have been killed through a heavy weight accidentally falling upon him?"

"He might."

"Was death instantaneous, in your opinion?"

"It is difficult to say. Such a blow might very well cause death instantaneously, or the patient might linger in a partially paralyzed condition for some time. In the present case I should be disposed to think that deceased might have lingered for some hours. I base my decision upon the condition of the brain revealed at the autopsy. I may say, however, that Dr. Grimbold and I are not in complete agreement on the point."

"I understand that a suggestion has been made as to the identification of the deceased. You are not in a position to identify him?"

"Certainly not. I never saw him before. The suggestion to which you refer is a preposterous one, and ought never to have been made. I was not aware until this morning that it had been made; had it been made to me earlier I should have known how to deal with it, and I should like to express my strong disapproval of the unnecessary shock and distress inflicted upon a lady with whom I have the honour to be acquainted."[30]

The Coroner: It was not my fault, Sir Julian; I had nothing to do with it; I agree with you that it was unfortunate you were not consulted.

The reporters scribbled busily, and the court asked each other what was meant, while the jury tried to look as if they knew already.

"In the matter of the eyeglasses found upon the body, Sir Julian. Do these give any indication to a medical man?"

"They are somewhat unusual lenses; an oculist[31] would be able

---

[30] Lady Levy, of course. None of this is brought up at the inquest, which is why the "court asked each other what was meant, while the jury tried to look as if they knew already."

[31] Eye doctor.

to speak more definitely, but I will say for myself that I should have expected them to belong to an older man than the deceased."

"Speaking as a physician, who has had many opportunities of observing the human body, did you gather anything from the appearance of the deceased as to his personal habits?"

"I should say that he was a man in easy circumstances, but who had only recently come into money. His teeth are in a bad state, and his hands show signs of recent manual labor."

"An Australian colonist, for instance, who had made money?"[32]

"Something of that sort; of course, I could not say positively."

"Of course not. Thank you, Sir Julian."

Dr. Grimbold, called, corroborated[33] his distinguished colleague in every particular, except that, in his opinion, death had not occurred for several days after the blow. It was with the greatest hesitancy that he ventured to differ from Sir Julian Freke, and he might be wrong. It was difficult to tell in any case, and when he saw the body, deceased had been dead at least twenty-four hours, in his opinion.

Inspector Sugg, recalled. Would he tell the jury what steps had been taken to identify the deceased?

A description had been sent to every police station and had been inserted in all the newspapers. In view of the suggestion made by Sir Julian Freke, had inquiries been made at all the seaports? They had. And with no results? With no results at all. No one had come forward to identify the body? Plenty of people had come forward; but nobody had succeeded in identifying it. Had any effort been made to follow up the clue afforded by the eyeglasses? Inspector Sugg submitted that, having regard to the interests of justice, he would beg to be excused from answering that question. Might the jury see the eyeglasses? The eyeglasses were handed to the jury.

William Watts, called, confirmed the evidence of Sir Julian

---

[32] England had settled Australia with willing colonists and unwilling convicts sentenced to be "transported." Usually, prisoners were given terms of seven years, after which they were pardoned and given parcels of land to farm.

[33] Supported.

THE COMPLETE, ANNOTATED WHOSE BODY?

Freke with regard to dissecting-room[34] subjects. He explained the system by which they were entered. They usually were supplied by the workhouses and free hospitals. They were under his sole charge. The young gentlemen could not possibly get the keys. Had Sir Julian Freke, or any of the house surgeons, the keys? No, not even Sir Julian Freke. The keys had remained in his possession on Monday night? They had. And, in any case, the enquiry was irrelevant, as there was no body missing, nor ever had been. That was the case.

The Coroner then addressed the jury, reminding them with some asperity[35] that they were not there to gossip about who the deceased could or could not have been, but to give their opinion as to the cause of death. He reminded them that they should consider whether, according to the medical evidence, death could have been accidental or self-inflicted or whether it was deliberate murder, or homicide. If they considered the evidence on this point insufficient, they could return an open verdict. In any case, their verdict could not prejudice any person; if they brought it in "murder," all the whole evidence would have to be gone through again before the magistrate. He then dismissed them, with the unspoken adjuration[36] to be quick about it.

Sir Julian Freke, after giving his evidence, had caught the eye of the Duchess, and now came over and greeted her.

"I haven't seen you for an age," said that lady. "How are you?"

"Hard at work," said the specialist. "Just got my new book out. This kind of thing wastes time. Have you seen Lady Levy yet?"

"No, poor dear," said the Duchess. "I only came up this morning, for this. Mrs. Thipps is staying with me—one of Peter's eccentricities, you know. Poor Christine! I must run round and see her. This is Mr. Parker," she added, "who is investigating that case."

"Oh," said Sir Julian, and paused. "Do you know," he said in a low voice to Parker, "I am very glad to meet you. Have you seen

---

[34] A room at a medical school where bodies are cut open for instructional purposes.
[35] Severity.
[36] Earnest advice.

Lady Levy yet?"

"I saw her this morning."

"Did she ask you to go on with the inquiry?"

"Yes," said Parker; "she thinks," he added, "that Sir Reuben may be detained in the hands of some financial rival or that perhaps some scoundrels are holding him to ransom."

"And is that your opinion?" asked Sir Julian.

"I think it very likely," said Parker, frankly.

Sir Julian hesitated again.

"I wish you would walk back with me when this is over," he said.

"I should be delighted," said Parker.

At this moment the jury returned and took their places, and there was a little rustle and hush. The Coroner addressed the foreman and enquired if they were agreed upon their verdict.

"We are agreed, Mr. Coroner, that deceased died of the effects of a blow upon the spine, but how that injury was inflicted we consider that there is not sufficient evidence to show."

Mr. Parker and Sir Julian Freke walked up the road together.

"I had absolutely no idea until I saw Lady Levy this morning," said the doctor, "that there was any idea of connecting this matter with the disappearance of Sir Reuben. The suggestion was perfectly monstrous, and could only have grown up in the mind of that ridiculous police officer. If I had had any idea what was in his mind I could have disabused him and avoided all this."

"I did my best to do so," said Parker, "as soon as I was called in to the Levy case—"

"Who called you in, if I may ask?" enquired Sir Julian.

"Well, the household first of all, and then Sir Reuben's uncle, Mr. Levy of Portman Square,[37] wrote to me to go on with the investigation."

"And now Lady Levy has confirmed those instructions?"

"Certainly," said Parker in some surprise.

---

[37] A square in the Westminster section of London. The location of Mr. Levy's residence so close to the centers of power — Westminster includes Buckingham Palace and Whitehall — suggests that he is a man of considerable wealth and influence.

Sir Julian was silent for a little time.

"I'm afraid I was the first person to put the idea into Sugg's head," said Parker, rather penitently.[38] "When Sir Reuben disappeared, my first step, almost, was to hunt up all the street accidents and suicides and so on that had turned up during the day, and I went down to see this Battersea Park body as a matter of routine. Of course, I saw that the thing was ridiculous as soon as I got there, but Sugg froze on to the idea—and it's true there was a good deal of resemblance between the dead man and the portraits I've seen of Sir Reuben."

"A strong superficial[39] likeness," said Sir Julian. "The upper part of the face is a not uncommon type, and as Sir Reuben wore a heavy beard and there was no opportunity of comparing the mouths and chins, I can understand the idea occurring to anybody. But only to be dismissed at once. I am sorry," he added, "as the whole matter has been painful to Lady Levy. You may know, Mr. Parker, that I am an old, though I should not call myself an intimate, friend of the Levys."

"I understood something of the sort."

"Yes. When I was a young man I—in short, Mr. Parker, I hoped once to marry Lady Levy." (Mr. Parker gave the usual sympathetic groan.) "I have never married, as you know," pursued Sir Julian. "We have remained good friends. I have always done what I could to spare her pain."

"Believe me, Sir Julian," said Parker, "that I sympathize very much with you and with Lady Levy, and that I did all I could to disabuse Inspector Sugg of this notion. Unhappily, the coincidence of Sir Reuben's being seen that evening in the Battersea Park Road—"

"Ah, yes," said Sir Julian. "Dear me, here we are at home. Perhaps you would come in for a moment, Mr. Parker, and have tea or a whisky-and-soda or something."

Parker promptly accepted this invitation, feeling that there were other things to be said.

The two men stepped into a square, finely furnished hall with a

---

[38] An expression of humble regret.
[39] Seen on the surface.

fireplace on the same side as the door, and a staircase opposite. The dining-room door stood open on their right, and as Sir Julian rang the bell a man-servant appeared at the far end of the hall.

"What will you take?" asked the doctor.

"After that dreadfully cold place," said Parker, "what I really want is gallons of hot tea, if you, as a nerve specialist, can bear the thought of it."

"Provided you allow of a judicious blend of China[40] with it," replied Sir Julian in the same tone, "I have no objection to make. Tea in the library at once," he added to the servant, and led the way upstairs.

"I don't use the downstairs rooms much, except the dining-room," he explained, as he ushered his guest into a small but cheerful library on the first floor.[41] "This room leads out of my bedroom and is more convenient. I only live part of my time here, but it's very handy for my research work at the hospital. That's what I do there, mostly. It's a fatal thing for a theorist, Mr. Parker, to let the practical work get behindhand.[42] Dissection is the basis of all good theory and all correct diagnosis. One must keep one's hand and eye in training. This place is far more important to me than Harley Street, and some day I shall abandon my consulting practice altogether and settle down here to cut up my subjects and write my books in peace. So many things in this life are a waste of time, Mr. Parker."

Mr. Parker assented to this.

"Very often," said Sir Julian, "the only time I get for any research work—necessitating as it does the keenest observation and the faculties at their acutest[43]—has to be at night, after a long day's work and by artificial light, which, magnificent as the lighting of the dissecting room here is, is always more trying to the eyes than daylight. Doubtless your own work has to be carried on under even more trying conditions."

---

[40] A reference to tea from that country.

[41] The floor above street level. What Americans call the first floor in their country is called in England the ground floor.

[42] Behind schedule.

[43] Keenest.

"Yes, sometimes," said Parker; "but then you see," he added, "the conditions are, so to speak, part of the work."

"Quite so, quite so," said Sir Julian; "you mean that the burglar, for example, does not demonstrate his methods in the light of day, or plant the perfect footmark in the middle of a damp patch of sand for you to analyze."

"Not as a rule," said the detective, "but I have no doubt many of your diseases work quite as insidiously as any burglar."

"They do, they do," said Sir Julian, laughing, "and it is my pride, as it is yours, to track them down for the good of society. The neuroses, you know, are particularly clever criminals—they break out into as many disguises as—"

"As Leon Kestrel, the Master-Mummer,"[44] suggested Parker, who read railway-stall detective stories on the principle of the 'busman's holiday.[45]

"No doubt," said Sir Julian, who did not, "and they cover up their tracks wonderfully. But when you can really investigate, Mr. Parker, and break up the dead, or for preference the living body with the scalpel, you always find the footmarks—the little trail of ruin or disorder left by madness or disease or drink or any other similar pest. But the difficulty is to trace them back, merely by observing the surface symptoms—the hysteria, crime, religion, fear, shyness, conscience, or whatever it may be; just as you observe a theft or a murder and look for the footsteps of the criminal, so I observe a fit of hysterics or an outburst of piety and hunt for the little mechanical irritation which has produced it."

"You regard all these things as physical?"

"Undoubtedly. I am not ignorant of the rise of another school of

---

[44] A recurring villain in the Sexton Blake stories. Known as the "Master Mummer" — that is, an actor — Kestrel was a master of disguise. Sayers was fond of the Sexton Blake stories and created Lord Peter to use as a supporting character in an unfinished attempt at one. In a lecture, she called the series "the nearest approach to a national folk-lore, conceived as the centre for a cycle of loosely connected romances in the Arthurian manner."

[45] A day off in which one does the same thing one is taking a vacation from. The phrase was inspired by the drivers of horse-drawn omnibuses, who were so concerned for their horses' well-being that, on their days off, they would ride their 'buses to ensure they were being treated properly.

thought, Mr. Parker, but its exponents are mostly charlatans or self-deceivers. 'Sie haben sich so weit darin eingeheimnisst'[46] that, like Sludge the Medium,[47] they are beginning to believe their own nonsense. I should like to have the exploring of some of their brains, Mr. Parker; I would show you the little faults and landslips[48] in the cells—the misfiring and short-circuiting of the nerves, which produce these notions and these books. At least," he added, gazing somberly at his guest, "at least, if I could not quite show you to-day, I shall be able to do so to-morrow—or in a year's time—or before I die."

He sat for some minutes gazing into the fire, while the red light played upon his tawny beard and struck out answering gleams from his compelling eyes.

Parker drank tea in silence, watching him. On the whole, however, he remained but little interested in the causes of nervous phenomena, and his mind strayed to Lord Peter, coping with the redoubtable[49] Crimplesham down in Salisbury. Lord Peter had wanted him to come: that meant, either that Crimplesham was proving recalcitrant or that a clue wanted following. But Bunter had said that to-morrow would do, and it was just as well. After all the Battersea affair was not Parker's case; he had already wasted valuable time attending an inconclusive inquest, and he really ought to get on with his legitimate work. There was still Levy's secretary to see and the little matter of the Peruvian Oil to be looked into. He looked at his watch.

"I am very much afraid—if you will excuse me—" he murmured.

Sir Julian came back with a start to the consideration of actuality.

"Your work calls you?" he said smiling. "Well, I can understand that. I won't keep you. But I wanted to say something

---

[46] "They have been eating too much of their own cooking" is the direct translation, attributed to a letter from Johann Wolfgang von Goethe (1749-1832).
[47] A reference to the Robert Browning poem, "Mr. Sludge, 'The Medium,' " in which a fraudulent spiritualist, caught rigging a séance, justifies his deceit.
[48] A landslide.
[49] Eminent.

to you in connection with your present inquiry—only I hardly know—I hardly like—"

Parker sat down again, and banished every indication of hurry from his face and attitude.

"I shall be very grateful for any help you can give me," he said.

"I'm afraid it's more in the nature of hindrance," said Sir Julian, with a short laugh. "It's a case of destroying a clue for you, and a breach of professional confidence[50] on my side. But since—accidentally—a certain amount has come out, perhaps the whole had better do so."

Mr. Parker made the encouraging noise which, among laymen, supplies the place of the priest's insinuating, "Yes, my son?"

"Sir Reuben Levy's visit on Monday night was to me," said Sir Julian.

"Yes?" said Mr. Parker, without expression.

"He found cause for certain grave suspicions concerning his health," said Sir Julian, slowly, as though weighing how much he could in honour disclose to a stranger. "He came to me, in preference to his own medical man, as he was particularly anxious that the matter should be kept from his wife. As I told you, he knew me fairly well, and Lady Levy had consulted me about a nervous disorder in the summer."

"Did he make an appointment with you?" asked Parker.

"I beg your pardon," said the other, absently.

"Did he make an appointment?"

"An appointment? Oh, no! He turned up suddenly in the evening after dinner when I wasn't expecting him. I took him up here and examined him, and he left me somewhere about ten o'clock, I should think."

"May I ask what was the result of your examination?"

"Why do you want to know?"

"It might illuminate—well, conjecture as to his subsequent conduct," said Parker, cautiously. This story seemed to have little coherence with the rest of the business, and he wondered whether coincidence was alone responsible for Sir Reuben's disappearance

---

[50] By law, doctors are protected against being compelled to testify in court about their discussions with a patient.

on the same night that he visited the doctor.

"I see," said Sir Julian. "Yes. Well, I will tell you in confidence that I saw grave grounds of suspicion, but as yet, no absolute certainty of mischief."

"Thank you. Sir Reuben left you at ten o'clock?"

"Then or thereabouts. I did not at first mention the matter as it was so very much Sir Reuben's wish to keep his visit to me secret, and there was no question of accident in the street or anything of that kind, since he reached home safely at midnight."

"Quite so," said Parker.

"It would have been, and is, a breach of confidence," said Sir Julian, "and I only tell you now because Sir Reuben was accidentally seen, and because I would rather tell you in private than have you ferreting round here and questioning my servants, Mr. Parker. You will excuse my frankness."

"Certainly," said Parker. "I hold no brief for the pleasantness of my profession, Sir Julian. I am very much obliged to you for telling me this. I might otherwise have wasted valuable time following up a false trail."

"I am sure I need not ask you, in your turn, to respect this confidence," said the doctor. "To publish the matter abroad could only harm Sir Reuben and pain his wife, besides placing me in no favourable light with my patients."

"I promise to keep the thing to myself," said Parker, "except of course," he added hastily, "that I must inform my colleague."

"You have a colleague in the case?"

"I have."

"What sort of person is he?"

"He will be perfectly discreet, Sir Julian."

"Is he a police officer?"

"You need not be afraid of your confidence getting into the records at Scotland Yard."

"I see that you know how to be discreet, Mr. Parker."

"We also have our professional etiquette, Sir Julian."

On returning to Great Ormond Street, Mr. Parker found a wire awaiting him, which said: "Do not trouble to come. All well. Returning to-morrow. Wimsey."

CHAPTER VII

ON RETURNING TO THE FLAT just before lunch-time on the following morning, after a few confirmatory researches in Balham and the neighbourhood of Victoria Station, Lord Peter was greeted at the door by Mr. Bunter (who had gone straight home from Waterloo) with a telephone message and a severe and nursemaid-like eye.

"Lady Swaffham rang up, my lord, and said she hoped your lordship had not forgotten you were lunching with her."

"I have forgotten, Bunter, and I mean to forget. I trust you told her I had succumbed to lethargic encephalitis[1] suddenly, no flowers by request."

"Lady Swaffham said, my lord, she was counting on you. She met the Duchess of Denver yesterday—"

"If my sister-in-law's there I won't go, that's flat," said Lord Peter.

"I beg your pardon, my lord, the elder Duchess."

"What's she doing in town?"

"I imagine she came up for the inquest, my lord."

"Oh, yes—we missed that, Bunter."

"Yes, my lord. Her Grace is lunching with Lady Swaffham."

"Bunter, I can't. I can't, really. Say I'm in bed with whooping cough, and ask my mother to come round after lunch."

---

[1] At about the same time as the worldwide Spanish influenza pandemic, there was another one between 1915 and 1926 of encephalitis, more commonly known as "sleepy sickness" because the lethargic victims would fall into a catatonic state.

"Very well, my lord. Mrs. Tommy Frayle will be at Lady Swaffham's, my lord, and Mr. Milligan—"

"Mr. Who?"

"Mr. John P. Milligan, my lord, and—"

"Good God, Bunter, why didn't you say so before? Have I time to get there before he does? All right. I'm off. With a taxi I can just—"

"Not in those trousers, my lord," said Mr. Bunter, blocking the way to the door with deferential firmness.

"Oh, Bunter," pleaded his lordship, "do let me—just this once. You don't know how important it is."

"Not on any account, my lord. It would be as much as my place is worth."

"The trousers are all right, Bunter."

"Not for Lady Swaffham's, my lord. Besides, your lordship forgets the man that ran against you with a milk can at Salisbury."

And Mr. Bunter laid an accusing finger on a slight stain of grease showing across the light cloth.

"I wish to God I'd never let you grow into a privileged family retainer, Bunter," said Lord Peter, bitterly, dashing his walking-stick into the umbrella-stand. "You've no conception of the mistakes my mother may be making."

Mr. Bunter smiled grimly and led his victim away.

When an immaculate Lord Peter was ushered, rather late for lunch, into Lady Swaffham's drawing-room, the Dowager Duchess of Denver was seated on a sofa, plunged in intimate conversation with Mr. John P. Milligan of Chicago.

"I'm vurry pleased[2] to meet you, Duchess," had been that financier's opening remark, "to thank you for your exceedingly kind invitation. I assure you it's a compliment I deeply appreciate."

The Duchess beamed at him, while conducting a rapid rally of all her intellectual forces.

"Do come and sit down and talk to me, Mr. Milligan," she said. "I do so love talking to you great business men—let me see, is it a

---

[2] Sayers was attempting to reproduce the flat intonations of an American accent.

railway king you are or something about puss-in-the-corner[3]—at least, I don't mean that exactly, but that game one used to play with cards, all about wheat and oats, and there was a bull and a bear, too—or was it a horse?—no, a bear, because I remember one always had to try and get rid of it and it used to get so dreadfully crumpled and torn, poor thing, always being handed about, one got to recognize it, and then one had to buy a new pack[4]—so foolish it must seem to you, knowing the real thing, and dreadfully noisy, but really excellent for breaking the ice with rather stiff people who didn't know each other—I'm quite sorry it's gone out."

Mr. Milligan sat down.

"Well, now," he said, "I guess it's as interesting for us business men to meet British aristocrats as it is for Britishers to meet American railway kings, Duchess. And I guess I'll make as many mistakes talking your kind of talk as you would make if you were tryin' to run a corner in wheat in Chicago. Fancy now, I called that fine lad of yours Lord Wimsey the other day, and he thought I'd mistaken him for his brother. That made me feel rather green."

This was an unhoped-for lead. The Duchess walked warily.

"Dear boy," she said, "I am so glad you met him, Mr. Milligan. Both my sons are a great comfort to me, you know, though, of course, Gerald is more conventional—just the right kind of person for the House of Lords,[5] you know, and a splendid farmer. I can't see Peter down at Denver half so well, though he is always going to all the right things in town, and very amusing sometimes, poor boy."

"I was very much gratified by Lord Peter's suggestion,"

---

[3] A children's game for five players, in which four players take their places at the corners of a square (marked out in a field or room) while the fifth — the "puss" — stands in the middle. The players in the corner attempt to swap places while the puss tries to get there first.

[4] The card game is Pit, invented in 1903. Players are dealt cards with commodities on them such as corn, barley and cotton. Players call out the number of cards they wish to trade, which other players can accept or decline. Acquiring all nine cards in one commodity ends the round. The Bull card is a wild card that can complete any set, and a Bear card not only must be discarded before a player can declare victory, but whoever holds it at the end of the round is penalized points.

[5] The upper house of parliament whose seats are held by hereditary peers.

pursued Mr. Milligan, "for which I understand you are responsible, and I'll surely be very pleased to come any day you like, though I think you're flattering me too much."

"Ah, well," said the Duchess, "I don't know if you're the best judge of that, Mr. Milligan. Not that I know anything about business myself," she added. "I'm rather old-fashioned for these days, you know, and I can't pretend to do more than know a nice man when I see him; for the other things I rely on my son."

The accent of this speech was so flattering that Mr. Milligan purred almost audibly, and said:

"Well, Duchess, I guess that's where a lady with a real, beautiful, old-fashioned soul has the advantage of these modern young blatherskites[6]—there aren't many men who wouldn't be nice—to her, and even then, if they aren't rock-bottom she can see through them."

"But that leaves me where I was," thought the Duchess. "I believe," she said aloud, "that I ought to be thanking you in the name of the vicar of Duke's Denver for a very munificent[7] cheque which reached him yesterday for the Church Restoration Fund. He was so delighted and astonished, poor dear man."

"Oh, that's nothing," said Mr. Milligan, "we haven't any fine old crusted buildings like yours over on our side, so it's a privilege to be allowed to drop a little kerosene into the worm-holes[8] when we hear of one in the old country suffering from senile decay. So when your lad told me about Duke's Denver I took the liberty to subscribe without waiting for the Bazaar."

"I'm sure it was very kind of you," said the Duchess. "You are coming to the Bazaar, then?" she continued, gazing into his face appealingly.

---

[6] A blustering, talkative fellow, combined from *blather*, from the Old Norse *blathra* for chatter, plus the Scots dialect word *skite*, from the Old Norse *skjóta* for to shoot, as in to move quickly. By the way, skite can also mean diarrhea, as in "That beer gave me the skitters last night," so calling someone a skitter in Scotland could put you in deep skit. Not necessarily in Australia and New Zealand, however. There, it only means a boaster or braggart.
[7] Generous.
[8] Infestations of termites, powder-post beetles and other wood-eating insects were treated by pouring kerosene into the wormholes to kill the eggs.

"Sure thing," said Mr. Milligan, with great promptness. "Lord Peter said you'd let me know for sure about the date, but we can always make time for a little bit of good work anyway. Of course I'm hoping to be able to avail myself of your kind invitation to stop, but if I'm rushed, I'll manage anyhow to pop over and speak my piece and pop back again."

"I hope so very much," said the Duchess. "I must see what can be done about the date—of course, I can't promise—"

"No, no," said Mr. Milligan heartily. "I know what these things are to fix up. And then there's not only me—there's Nat Rothschild and Cadbury, and all the other names your son mentioned, to be consulted."

The Duchess turned pale at the thought that any one of these illustrious persons might some time turn up in somebody's drawing-room, but by this time she had dug herself in comfortably, and was even beginning to find her range.[9]

"I can't say how grateful we are to you," she said, "it will be such a treat. Do tell me what you think of saying."

"Well—" began Mr. Milligan.

Suddenly everybody was standing up and a penitent voice was heard to say:

"Really, most awfully sorry, y'know—hope you'll forgive me, Lady Swaffham, what? Dear lady, could I possibly forget an invitation from you? Fact is, I had to go an' see a man down in Salisbury—absolutely true, 'pon my word, and the fellow wouldn't let me get away. I'm simply grovellin' before you, Lady Swaffham. Shall I go an' eat my lunch in the corner?"

Lady Swaffham gracefully forgave the culprit.

"Your dear mother is here," she said.

"How do, Mother?" said Lord Peter, uneasily.

"How are you, dear?" replied the Duchess. "You really oughtn't to have turned up just yet. Mr. Milligan was just going to tell me what a thrilling speech he's preparing for the Bazaar, when you came and interrupted us."

Conversation at lunch turned, not unnaturally, on the Battersea

---

[9] Terms associated with a batsman's behavior in cricket. Nowadays, we'd probably call it "entering the zone."

inquest, the Duchess giving a vivid impersonation of Mrs. Thipps being interrogated by the Coroner.

" 'Did you hear anything unusual in the night?' says the little man, leaning forward and screaming at her, and so crimson in the face and his ears sticking out so—just like a cherubim in that poem of Tennyson's—or is a cherub blue?—perhaps it's seraphim I mean[10]—anyway, you know what I mean, all eyes, with little wings on its head. And dear old Mrs. Thipps saying, 'Of course I have, any time these eighty years,' and such a sensation in court till they found out she thought he'd said, 'Do you sleep without a light?' and everybody laughing, and then the Coroner said quite loudly, 'Damn the woman,' and she heard that, I can't think why, and said: 'Don't you get swearing, young man, sitting there in the presence of Providence, as you may say. I don't know what young people are coming to nowadays'—and he's sixty if he's a day, you know," said the Duchess.

By a natural transition, Mrs. Tommy Frayle referred to the man who was hanged for murdering three brides in a bath.[11]

"I always thought that was so ingenious," she said, gazing soulfully at Lord Peter, "and do you know, as it happened, Tommy had just made me insure my life, and I got so frightened, I gave up my morning bath and took to having it in the afternoon when he was in the House—I mean, when he was not in the house—not at home, I mean."

"Dear lady," said Lord Peter, reproachfully, "I have a distinct recollection that all those brides were thoroughly unattractive. But it was an uncommonly ingenious plan—the first time of askin'— only he shouldn't have repeated himself."

"One demands a little originality in these days, even from murderers," said Lady Swaffham. "Like dramatists, you know—so much easier in Shakespeare's time, wasn't it? Always the same girl

---

[10] There is no mention in Tennyson of cherubim — a type of high-ranking angel — or seraphim — a fiery, usually serpent-like celestial being — so the Duchess' meaning remains unclear.

[11] George Joseph Smith (1872-1915) was the notorious "Brides in the Bath" murderer executed for murdering three women he had married for their money. See the essay "George Joseph Smith: Many Brides, One Tub, No Waiting."

dressed up as a man, and even that borrowed from Boccaccio or Dante or somebody.[12] I'm sure if I'd been a Shakespeare hero, the very minute I saw a slim-legged young page-boy I'd have said: 'Ods-bodikins![13] There's that girl again!' "

"That's just what happened, as a matter of fact," said Lord Peter. "You see, Lady Swaffham, if ever you want to commit a murder, the thing you've got to do is to prevent people from associatin' their ideas. Most people don't associate anythin'—their ideas just roll about like so many dry peas on a tray, makin' a lot of noise and goin' nowhere, but once you begin lettin' 'em string their peas into a necklace, it's goin' to be strong enough to hang you, what?"

"Dear me!" said Mrs. Tommy Frayle, with a little scream, "what a blessing it is none of my friends have any ideas at all!"

"Y'see," said Lord Peter, balancing a piece of duck on his fork and frowning, "it's only in Sherlock Holmes and stories like that, that people think things out logically. Or'nar'ly, if somebody tells you somethin' out of the way, you just say, 'By Jove!'[14] or 'How sad!' an' leave it at that, an' half the time you forget about it, 'nless somethin' turns up afterwards to drive it home. F'r instance, Lady Swaffham, I told you when I came in that I'd been down to Salisbury, 'n' that's true, only I don't suppose it impressed you much; 'n' I don't suppose it'd impress you much if you read in the paper to-morrow of a tragic discovery of a dead lawyer down in Salisbury, but if I went to Salisbury again next week 'n' there was a Salisbury doctor found dead the day after, you might begin to think I was a bird of ill omen for Salisbury residents; and if I went there again the week after, 'n' you heard next day that the see of

---

[12] Shakespeare used cross-dressing in about 20 percent of his plays, and it is central to "The Merchant of Venice," "As You Like It" and "Twelfth Night." While Dante didn't use cross-dressing, Giovanni Boccaccio retold the story of Iole, who convinced her lover, Hercules, to wear women's clothing and perform women's work.

[13] A variation of the oath "by God's body," altered to avoid blasphemy or breaking the commandment to take the Lord's name in vain.

[14] Derived from the Latinized version of the Greek god Zeus. Used as a substitute for God, as a way of cursing without committing blasphemy similar to 'Odsbodikins, above.

Salisbury had fallen vacant[15] suddenly, you might begin to wonder what took me to Salisbury, an' why I'd never mentioned before that I had friends down there, don't you see, an' you might think of goin' down to Salisbury yourself, an' askin' all kinds of people if they'd happened to see a young man in plum-coloured socks hangin' round the Bishop's Palace."[16]

"I daresay I should," said Lady Swaffham.

"Quite. An' if you found that the lawyer and the doctor had once upon a time been in business at Poggleton-on-the-Marsh when the Bishop had been vicar there, you'd begin to remember you'd once heard of me payin' a visit to Poggleton-on-the-Marsh a long time ago, an' you'd begin to look up the parish registers there an' discover I'd been married under an assumed name by the vicar to the widow of a wealthy farmer, who'd died suddenly of peritonitis,[17] as certified by the doctor, after the lawyer'd made a will leavin' me all her money, and then you'd begin to think I might have very good reasons for gettin' rid of such promisin' blackmailers as the lawyer, the doctor an' the bishop. Only, if I hadn't started an association in your mind by gettin' rid of 'em all in the same place, you'd never have thought of goin' to Poggleton-on-the-Marsh,[18] 'n' you wouldn't even have remembered I'd ever been there."

"Were you ever there, Lord Peter?" enquired Mrs. Tommy, anxiously.

"I don't think so," said Lord Peter, "the name threads no beads in my mind. But it might, any day, you know."

"But if you were investigating a crime," said Lady Swaffham, "you'd have to begin by the usual things, I suppose—finding out

---

[15] Originally, the see was the throne of the bishop. Over time, it came to refer to the area under the bishop's control.

[16] A large building in the center of the Salisbury Close near the cathedral. Begun in 1225, additions have been made to it throughout the years. In 1947, the then-bishop chose to live in the South Canonry — a separate building at the south end of the close — and turned the palace over to the cathedral school, which uses it today.

[17] An inflammation of the peritoneum, the membrane that lines the abdominal cavity.

[18] A fictional village.

what the person had been doing, and who'd been to call, and looking for a motive, wouldn't you?"

"Oh, yes," said Lord Peter, "but most of us have such dozens of motives for murderin' all sorts of inoffensive people. There's lots of people I'd like to murder, wouldn't you?"

"Heaps," said Lady Swaffham. "There's that dreadful—perhaps I'd better not say it, though, for fear you should remember it later on."

"Well, I wouldn't if I were you," said Peter, amiably. "You never know. It'd be beastly awkward if the person died suddenly to-morrow."

"The difficulty with this Battersea case, I guess," said Mr. Milligan, "is that nobody seems to have any associations with the gentleman in the bath."

"So hard on poor Inspector Sugg," said the Duchess. "I quite felt for the man, having to stand up there and answer a lot of questions when he had nothing at all to say."

Lord Peter applied himself to the duck, having got a little behindhand. Presently he heard somebody ask the Duchess if she had seen Lady Levy.

"She is in great distress," said the woman who had spoken, a Mrs. Freemantle, "though she clings to the hope that he will turn up. I suppose you knew him, Mr. Milligan—know him, I should say, for I hope he's still alive somewhere."

Mrs. Freemantle was the wife of an eminent railway director, and celebrated for her ignorance of the world of finance. Her faux pas[19] in this connection enlivened the tea parties of city men's wives.

"Well, I've dined with him," said Mr. Milligan, good-naturedly. "I think he and I've done our best to ruin each other, Mrs. Freemantle. If this were the States," he added, "I'd be much inclined to suspect myself of having put Sir Reuben in a safe place. But we can't do business that way in your old country; no, ma'am."

"It must be exciting work doing business in America," said

---

[19] A social blunder, from the French for false step.

Lord Peter.

"It is," said Mr. Milligan. "I guess my brothers are having a good time there now. I'll be joining them again before long, as soon as I've fixed up a little bit of work for them on this side."

"Well, you mustn't go till after my bazaar," said the Duchess.

Lord Peter spent the afternoon in a vain hunt for Mr. Parker. He ran him down eventually after dinner in Great Ormond Street.

Parker was sitting in an elderly but affectionate armchair, with his feet on the mantelpiece, relaxing his mind with a modern commentary on the Epistle to the Galatians.[20] He received Lord Peter with quiet pleasure, though without rapturous enthusiasm, and mixed him a whisky-and-soda. Peter took up the book his friend had laid down and glanced over the pages.

"All these men work with a bias in their minds, one way or other," he said; "they find what they are looking for."

"Oh, they do," agreed the detective, "but one learns to discount that almost automatically, you know. When I was at college, I was all on the other side—Conybeare and Robertson and Drews[21] and

---

[20] In an early draft, Lord Peter recognized that the body in the bath was not Sir Reuben because he was not circumcised. The indelicate clue was removed at the publisher's insistence, but Sayers left this hint behind. Paul's epistle to the Galatians concerned the question of whether Christians needed to be circumcised according to Jewish law, with Paul thumping heavily on the no side. Galatians 5:2: "Behold, I Paul say unto you, that if ye be circumcised, Christ shall profit you nothing."

[21] Parker was referring to the debate over the nature of Jesus Christ. There are the orthodox Christians who see Christ as both a man and the Son of God; there's the Christ-as-myth advocates who say he was created by the early Christian community; and somewhere in between are those who attempt to reconstruct the life and times of Jesus using historical methods.

The three names refer to:

* *Frederick Cornwallis Conybeare* (1856-1924), a professor of theology at Oxford whose "The Origins of Christianity" attacked orthodox Christianity, criticized the Jesus-myth theory and supported attempts to reconstruct the life of Jesus.

* *John Mackinnon Robertson* (1856-1933), a journalist, secularist and advocate of the Jesus myth theory.

* *Arthur Drews* (1865-1935), a German philosopher and writer, also a leading advocate of Jesus as myth. His "The Christ Myth" (1909) argued that everything about Jesus' life had a mythical character.

those people, you know, till I found they were all so busy looking for a burglar whom nobody had ever seen, that they couldn't recognize the footprints of the household, so to speak. Then I spent two years learning to be cautious."

"Hum," said Lord Peter, "theology must be good exercise for the brain then, for you're easily the most cautious devil I know. But I say, do go on reading—it's a shame for me to come and root you up in your off-time like this."

"It's all right, old man," said Parker.

The two men sat silent for a little, and then Lord Peter said:

"D'you like your job?"

The detective considered the question, and replied:

"Yes—yes, I do. I know it to be useful, and I am fitted to it. I do it quite well—not with inspiration, perhaps, but sufficiently well to take a pride in it. It is full of variety and it forces one to keep up to the mark and not get slack. And there's a future to it. Yes, I like it. Why?"

"Oh, nothing," said Peter. "It's a hobby to me, you see. I took it up when the bottom of things was rather knocked out for me, because it was so damned exciting, and the worst of it is, I enjoy it—up to a point. If it was all on paper I'd enjoy every bit of it. I love the beginning of a job—when one doesn't know any of the people and it's just exciting and amusing. But if it comes to really running down a live person and getting him hanged, or even quodded, poor devil, there don't seem as if there was any excuse for me buttin' in, since I don't have to make my livin' by it. And I feel as if I oughtn't ever to find it amusin'. But I do."

Parker gave this speech his careful attention.

"I see what you mean," he said.

"There's old Milligan, f'r instance," said Lord Peter. "On paper, nothin' would be funnier than to catch old Milligan out. But he's rather a decent old bird to talk to. Mother likes him. He's taken a fancy to me. It's awfully entertainin' goin' and pumpin' him with stuff about a bazaar for church expenses, but when he's so jolly pleased about it and that, I feel a worm. S'pose old Milligan has cut Levy's throat and plugged him into the Thames. It ain't my business."

"It's as much yours as anybody's," said Parker; "it's no better to do it for money than to do it for nothing."

"Yes, it is," said Peter stubbornly. "Havin' to live is the only excuse there is for doin' that kind of thing."

"Well, but look here!" said Parker. "If Milligan has cut poor old Levy's throat for no reason except to make himself richer, I don't see why he should buy himself off by giving £1,000 to Duke's Denver church roof, or why he should be forgiven just because he's childishly vain, or childishly snobbish."

"That's a nasty one," said Lord Peter.

"Well, if you like, even because he has taken a fancy to you."

"No, but—"

"Look here, Wimsey—do you think he has murdered Levy?"

"Well, he may have."

"But do you think he has?"

"I don't want to think so."

"Because he has taken a fancy to you?"

"Well, that biases me, of course—"

"I daresay it's quite a legitimate bias. You don't think a callous murderer would be likely to take a fancy to you?"

"Well—besides, I've taken rather a fancy to him."

"I daresay that's quite legitimate, too. You've observed him and made a subconscious deduction from your observations, and the result is, you don't think he did it. Well, why not? You're entitled to take that into account."

"But perhaps I'm wrong and he did do it."

"Then why let your vainglorious[22] conceit in your own power of estimating character stand in the way of unmasking the singularly cold-blooded murder of an innocent and lovable man?"

"I know—but I don't feel I'm playing the game somehow."

"Look here, Peter," said the other with some earnestness, "suppose you get this playing-fields-of-Eton complex[23] out of your system once and for all. There doesn't seem to be much doubt that

[22] Marked by an excessive amount of pride in one's accomplishments.
[23] From a saying attributed to Arthur Wellesley, 1st Duke of Wellington (1769-1852) that the battle of Waterloo was won on the playing fields of Eton. While it serves to reinforce the public school notion that discipline and stout-heartedness in the face of adversity could be learned through organized games and sports, it's doubtful that the commander of the allied forces at the battle said it. He despised his time at Eton, and besides, the school then did not have playing fields.

something unpleasant has happened to Sir Reuben Levy. Call it murder, to strengthen the argument. If Sir Reuben has been murdered, is it a game? and is it fair to treat it as a game?"

"That's what I'm ashamed of, really," said Lord Peter. "It is a game to me, to begin with, and I go on cheerfully, and then I suddenly see that somebody is going to be hurt, and I want to get out of it."

"Yes, yes, I know," said the detective, "but that's because you're thinking about your attitude. You want to be consistent, you want to look pretty, you want to swagger debonairly[24] through a comedy of puppets or else to stalk magnificently through a tragedy of human sorrows and things. But that's childish. If you've any duty to society in the way of finding out the truth about murders, you must do it in any attitude that comes handy. You want to be elegant and detached? That's all right, if you find the truth out that way, but it hasn't any value in itself, you know. You want to look dignified and consistent—what's that got to do with it? You want to hunt down a murderer for the sport of the thing and then shake hands with him and say, 'Well played—hard luck—you shall have your revenge to-morrow!' Well, you can't do it like that. Life's not a football[25] match. You want to be a sportsman. You can't be a sportsman. You're a responsible person."

"I don't think you ought to read so much theology," said Lord Peter. "It has a brutalizing influence."

He got up and paced about the room, looking idly over the bookshelves. Then he sat down again, filled and lit his pipe, and said:

"Well, I'd better tell you about the ferocious and hardened Crimplesham."

He detailed his visit to Salisbury. Once assured of his bona fides, Mr. Crimplesham had given him the fullest details of his visit to town.

"And I've substantiated it all," groaned Lord Peter, "and unless he's corrupted half Balham, there's no doubt he spent the night

---

[24] To act with overbearing self-confidence, but with a touch of lighthearted urbanity, a different balance even for Lord Peter.

[25] Soccer.

there. And the afternoon was really spent with the bank people. And half the residents of Salisbury seem to have seen him off on Monday before lunch. And nobody but his own family or young Wicks seems to have anything to gain by his death. And even if young Wicks wanted to make away with him, it's rather far-fetched to go and murder an unknown man in Thipps's place in order to stick Crimplesham's eyeglasses on his nose."

"Where was young Wicks on Monday?" asked Parker.

"At a dance given by the Precentor,"[26] said Lord Peter, wildly. "David—his name is David—dancing before the ark of the Lord[27] in the face of the whole Cathedral Close."

There was a pause.

"Tell me about the inquest," said Wimsey.

Parker obliged with a summary of the evidence.

"Do you believe the body could have been concealed in the flat after all?" he asked. "I know we looked, but I suppose we might have missed something."

"We might. But Sugg looked as well."

"Sugg!"

"You do Sugg an injustice," said Lord Peter; "if there had been any signs of Thipps's complicity in the crime, Sugg would have found them."

"Why?"

"Why? Because he was looking for them. He's like your commentators on Galatians. He thinks that either Thipps, or Gladys Horrocks, or Gladys Horrocks's young man did it. Therefore he found marks on the window sill where Gladys Horrocks's young man might have come in or handed something in to Gladys Horrocks. He didn't find any signs on the roof,

---

[26] A cleric who directs the choral services at a church or cathedral.

[27] A reference to 1 Chronicles 15:29: "And it came to pass, as the ark of the covenant of the Lord came to the city of David, that Michal, the daughter of Saul looking out at a window saw king David dancing and playing: and she despised him in her heart." A similar reference can be found in II Samuel 6:13-14: "And it was so, that when they that bare the ark of the Lord had gone six paces, he sacrificed oxen and fatlings.
And David danced before the Lord with all his might; and David was girded with a linen ephod [an embroidered outer vestment worn by Jewish priests]."

because he wasn't looking for them."

"But he went over the roof before me."

"Yes, but only in order to prove that there were no marks there. He reasons like this: Gladys Horrocks's young man is a glazier. Glaziers come on ladders. Glaziers have ready access to ladders. Therefore Gladys Horrocks's young man had ready access to a ladder. Therefore Gladys Horrocks's young man came on a ladder. Therefore there will be marks on the window sill and none on the roof. Therefore he finds marks on the window sill but none on the roof. He finds no marks on the ground, but he thinks he would have found them if the yard didn't happen to be paved with asphalt. Similarly, he thinks Mr. Thipps may have concealed the body in the box-room or elsewhere. Therefore you may be sure he searched the box-room and all the other places for signs of occupation. If they had been there he would have found them, because he was looking for them. Therefore, if he didn't find them it's because they weren't there."

"All right," said Parker, "stop talking. I believe you."

He went on to detail the medical evidence.

"By the way," said Lord Peter, "to skip across for a moment to the other case, has it occurred to you that perhaps Levy was going out to see Freke on Monday night?"

"He was; he did," said Parker, rather unexpectedly, and proceeded to recount his interview with the nerve-specialist.

"Humph!" said Lord Peter. "I say, Parker, these are funny cases, ain't they? Every line of enquiry seems to peter out. It's awfully exciting up to a point, you know, and then nothing comes of it. It's like rivers getting lost in the sand."

"Yes," said Parker. "And there's another one I lost this morning."

"What's that?"

"Oh, I was pumping Levy's secretary about his business. I couldn't get much that seemed important except further details about the Argentine and so on. Then I thought I'd just ask 'round in the City about those Peruvian Oil shares, but Levy hadn't even heard of them, so far as I could make out. I routed out the brokers, and found a lot of mystery and concealment, as one always does, you know, when somebody's been rigging the market, and at last I found one name at the back of it. But it wasn't Levy's."

"No? Whose was it?"

"Oddly enough, Freke's. It seems mysterious. He bought a lot of shares last week, in a secret kind of way, a few of them in his own name, and then quietly sold 'em out on Tuesday at a small profit—a few hundreds, not worth going to all that trouble about, you wouldn't think."

"Shouldn't have thought he ever went in for that kind of gamble."

"He doesn't as a rule. That's the funny part of it."

"Well, you never know," said Lord Peter; "people do these things, just to prove to themselves or somebody else that they could make a fortune that way if they liked. I've done it myself in a small way."

He knocked out his pipe[28] and rose to go.

"I say, old man," he said suddenly, as Parker was letting him out, "does it occur to you that Freke's story doesn't fit in awfully well with what Anderson said about the old boy having been so jolly at dinner on Monday night? Would you be, if you thought you'd got anything of that sort?"

"No, I shouldn't," said Parker; "but," he added with his habitual caution, "some men will jest in the dentist's waiting-room. You, for one."

"Well, that's true," said Lord Peter, and went downstairs.

---

[28] Disposed of the ashes in the bowl by tapping his pipe in the ashtray.

CHAPTER VIII

LORD PETER REACHED HOME ABOUT midnight, feeling extraordinarily wakeful and alert. Something was jigging and worrying in his brain; it felt like a hive of bees, stirred up by a stick. He felt as though he were looking at a complicated riddle, of which he had once been told the answer but had forgotten it and was always on the point of remembering.

"Somewhere," said Lord Peter to himself, "somewhere I've got the key to these two things. I know I've got it, only I can't remember what it is. Somebody said it. Perhaps I said it. I can't remember where, but I know I've got it. Go to bed, Bunter, I shall sit up a little. I'll just slip on a dressing-gown."

Before the fire he sat down with his pipe in his mouth and his jazz-coloured peacocks gathered about him. He traced out this line and that line of investigation—rivers running into the sand. They ran out from the thought of Levy, last seen at ten o'clock in Prince of Wales Road. They ran back from the picture of the grotesque dead man in Mr. Thipps's bathroom—they ran over the roof, and were lost—lost in the sand. Rivers running into the sand—rivers running underground, very far down—

Where Alph,[1] the sacred river, ran

---

[1] The fictional river mentioned in the third line of "Kubla Khan" by Samuel Taylor Coleridge (1772-1834), composed in 1797 and considered one of his greatest poems. The first two lines run: "In Xanadu did Kubla Khan / A stately pleasure-dome decree."

Through caverns measureless to man
Down to a sunless sea.

By leaning his head down, it seemed to Lord Peter that he could hear them, very faintly, lipping and gurgling somewhere in the darkness. But where? He felt quite sure that somebody had told him once, only he had forgotten.

He roused himself, threw a log on the fire, and picked up a book which the indefatigable Bunter, carrying on his daily fatigues amid the excitements of special duty, had brought from the Times Book Club.[2] It happened to be Sir Julian Freke's "Physiological Bases of the Conscience," which he had seen reviewed two days before.

"This ought to send one to sleep," said Lord Peter; "if I can't leave these problems to my subconscious I'll be as limp as a rag to-morrow."

He opened the book slowly, and glanced carelessly through the preface.

"I wonder if that's true about Levy being ill," he thought, putting the book down; "it doesn't seem likely. And yet— Dash it all, I'll take my mind off it."

He read on resolutely for a little.

"I don't suppose Mother's kept up with the Levys much," was the next importunate train of thought. "Dad always hated self-made people and wouldn't have 'em at Denver. And old Gerald keeps up the tradition. I wonder if she knew Freke well in those days. She seems to get on with Milligan. I trust Mother's judgment a good deal. She was a brick[3] about that bazaar business. I ought to

---

[2] A program set up by the London Times newspaper in 1905 in which books were available for rent, then resold later at a lower price. It was an instantly popular program, and booksellers resenting the competition sued the newspaper, but lost in court.

[3] A kind, reliable person. The phrase was inspired by a story the historian and biographer Plutarch (c. 46-120) tells about King Lycurgus of Sparta, who didn't believe in building walls around the city. When the ambassador from Epirus asked why, he received his answer the next morning, when he was awoken and taken to a field outside the city. There, he saw the army of Sparta drawn up in battle formation. "There are the walls of Sparta," King Lycurgus told him, "and every man is a brick."

have warned her. She said something once—"

He pursued an elusive memory for some minutes, till it vanished altogether with a mocking flicker of the tail. He returned to his reading.

Presently another thought crossed his mind, aroused by a photograph of some experiment in surgery.

"If the evidence of Freke and that man Watts hadn't been so positive," he said to himself, "I should be inclined to look into the matter of those shreds of lint on the chimney."

He considered this, shook his head and read with determination.

Mind and matter were one thing, that was the theme of the physiologist.[4] Matter could erupt, as it were, into ideas. You could carve passions in the brain with a knife. You could get rid of imagination with drugs and cure an outworn convention like a disease. "The knowledge of good and evil is an observed phenomenon,[5] attendant upon a certain condition of the brain-cells, which is removable." That was one phrase; and again:

"Conscience in man may, in fact, be compared to the sting of a hive-bee, which, so far from conducing to the welfare of its possessor, cannot function, even in a single instance, without occasioning its death. The survival-value in each case is thus purely social; and if humanity ever passes from its present phase of social development into that of a higher individualism, as some of our philosophers have ventured to speculate, we may suppose that this interesting mental phenomenon may gradually cease to appear; just as the nerves and muscles which once controlled the movements of our ears and scalps have, in all save a few backward individuals, become atrophied and of interest only to the physiologist."

"By Jove!" thought Lord Peter, idly, "that's an ideal doctrine for the criminal. A man who believed that would never—"

And then it happened—the thing he had been half-unconsciously expecting. It happened suddenly, surely, as unmistakably as sunrise. He remembered—not one thing, nor another thing, nor a logical succession of things, but everything—the whole thing, perfect, complete, in all its dimensions as it were

---

[4] One who studies the science of living systems.
[5] Meaning that it can be seen with the human eye.

and instantaneously; as if he stood outside the world and saw it suspended in infinitely dimensional space. He no longer needed to reason about it, or even to think about it. He knew it.

There is a game in which one is presented with a jumble of letters and is required to make a word out of them, as thus:

COSSSSRI

The slow way of solving the problem is to try out all the permutations and combinations in turn, throwing away impossible conjunctions of letters, as:

SSSIRC

or

SCSRSO

Another way is to stare at the inco-ordinate[6] elements until, by no logical process that the conscious mind can detect, or under some adventitious external stimulus, the combination

SCISSORS

presents itself with calm certainty. After that, one does not even need to arrange the letters in order. The thing is done.

Even so, the scattered elements of two grotesque conundrums, flung higgledy-piggledy[7] into Lord Peter's mind, resolved themselves, unquestioned henceforward. A bump on the roof of the end house—Levy in a welter of cold rain talking to a prostitute in the Battersea Park Road—a single ruddy hair—lint bandages[8]—Inspector Sugg calling the great surgeon from the dissecting-room of the hospital—Lady Levy with a nervous attack—the smell of carbolic soap[9]—the Duchess's voice—"not really an engagement, only a sort of understanding with her father"—shares in Peruvian Oil—the dark skin and curved, fleshy profile of the man in the

---

[6] Lacking coordination.

[7] In confusion, or topsy-turvy.

[8] Rolled bandages weaved from lint.

[9] A mildly disinfectant soap containing carbolic acid and one of the most common disinfectants in homes and hospitals at the time. Its powerful smell could evoke memories of childhood much like Proust's madeleines.

bath—Dr. Grimbold giving evidence, "In my opinion, death did not occur for several days after the blow"—india-rubber gloves—even, faintly, the voice of Mr. Appledore, "He called on me, sir, with an anti-vivisectionist pamphlet"—all these things and many others rang together and made one sound, they swung together like bells in a steeple, with the deep tenor booming through the clamour:

"The knowledge of good and evil is a phenomenon of the brain, and is removable, removable, removable. The knowledge of good and evil is removable."

Lord Peter Wimsey was not a young man who habitually took himself very seriously, but this time he was frankly appalled. "It's impossible," said his reason, feebly; "credo quia impossibile,"[10] said his interior certainty with impervious self-satisfaction. "All right," said conscience, instantly allying itself with blind faith, "what are you going to do about it?"

Lord Peter got up and paced the room: "Good Lord!" he said. "Good Lord!" He took down "Who's Who" from the little shelf over the telephone, and sought comfort in its pages.

FREKE, Sir Julian. Kt. er. 1916; G. C. V. O. er. 1919; K.C.V.O. 1917; K.C.B. 1918; M.D., F.R.C.P., F.R.C.S., Dr. en Méd. Paris; D. Sci. Cantab.; Knight of Grace of the Order of S. John of Jerusalem; Consulting Surgeon of St. Luke's Hospital, Battersea. b. Gryllingham, 16 March 1872, only son, of Edward Curzon Freke Esq. of Gryll Court, Gryllingham. Educ. Harrow and Trinity Coll. Cambridge; Col. A.M.S.; late Member of the Advisory Board of the Army Medical Service. Publications: Some Notes on the Pathological Aspects of Genius, 1892; Statistical Contributions to the Study of Infantile Paralysis in England and Wales, 1894; Functional Disturbances of the Nervous System, 1899; Cerebro-Spinal Diseases, 1904; The

---

[10] Latin for "I believe it because it is impossible," from "De Carne Christi" by Tertullian (c. 160-c. 230). Tertullian was attacking the belief, expressed in Docetism, that Jesus did not have a physical body, but was a pure spirit and, therefore, could not physically die. Journalist and critic H.L. Mencken (1880-1956) had fun at Tertullian's expense when he quipped, "Tertullian is credited with the motto 'Credo quia absurdum' — 'I believe because it is impossible.' Needless to say, he began life as a lawyer."

Borderland of Insanity, 1906; An Examination into the
Treatment of Pauper Lunacy in the United Kingdom, 1906;
Modern Developments in Psycho-Therapy: A Criticism, 1910;
Criminal Lunacy, 1914; The Application of Psycho-Therapy to
the Treatment of Shell-Shock, 1917; An Answer to Professor
Freud, with a Description of Some Experiments Carried Out at
the Base Hospital at Amiens, 1919; Structural Modifications
Accompanying the More Important Neuroses, 1920. Clubs:
White's; Oxford and Cambridge; Alpine, etc. Recreations:
Chess, Mountaineering, Fishing. Address: 82, Harley Street and
St. Luke's House, Prince of Wales Road, Battersea Park, S.W.
11.[11]

He flung the book away. "Confirmation!" he groaned. "As if I
needed it!"

He sat down again and buried his face in his hands. He
remembered quite suddenly how, years ago, he had stood before the

---

[11] These summarize the honors earned by Sir Julian, listed in order of royal
precedence (that is, of importance in the class hierarchy):

   * *Kt.* means knight (*cr.* means created)

   * *G.C.V.O.*: Knight Grand Cross, a grade of the Royal Victorian Order (the
abbreviation means Grand Cross Victorian Order). The order was established in
1896 and is bestowed by the monarch for distinguished personal service to the
monarch, her family or her viceroy.

   * *K.C.V.O.*: Knight Commander, a grade from the same order, but one step
down from the G.C.V.O. in precedence.

   * *K.C.B.*: Knight Commander of the Order of the Bath. This is the second of
three classes in this order, above a Companion but below the Knight Grand Cross.

   * *M.D.*: Doctor of Medicine.

   * *F.R.C.P.* (Fellowship of the Royal College of Physicians) and *F.R.C.S.*
(Fellowship of the Royal College of Surgeons) represent membership in the two
groups required to practice medicine and perform surgery in the United Kingdom.

   * *Harrow* is a school for boys in northwest London established under
Elizabeth I in 1572. *Trinity* is a college at Oxford University.

   * *Cambridge.* Cambridge University.

   * *Col. A.M.S.* Colonel, Army Medical School.

   * *Amiens.* A city in northern France.

   * *White's; Oxford and Cambridge; Alpine. White's* and *Oxford and
Cambridge* are two gentlemen's clubs in London. *Alpine* is the Alpine Club,
founded in 1857 and probably the world's first mountaineering group.

breakfast table at Denver Castle—a small, peaky boy in blue knickers,[12] with a thunderously beating heart. The family had not come down; there was a great silver urn with a spirit lamp[13] under it, and an elaborate coffee-pot boiling in a glass dome. He had twitched the corner of the tablecloth—twitched it harder, and the urn moved ponderously forward and all the teaspoons rattled. He seized the tablecloth in a firm grip and pulled his hardest—he could feel now the delicate and awful thrill as the urn and the coffee machine and the whole of a Sèvres[14] breakfast service had crashed down in one stupendous ruin—he remembered the horrified face of the butler, and the screams of a lady guest.

A log broke across and sank into a fluff of white ash. A belated motor-lorry[15] rumbled past the window.

Mr. Bunter, sleeping the sleep of the true and faithful servant, was aroused in the small hours by a hoarse whisper, "Bunter!"

"Yes, my lord," said Bunter, sitting up and switching on the light.

"Put that light out, damn you!" said the voice. "Listen—over there—listen—can't you hear it?"

"It's nothing, my lord," said Mr. Bunter, hastily getting out of bed and catching hold of his master; "it's all right, you get to bed quick and I'll fetch you a drop of bromide.[16] Why, you're all shivering—you've been sitting up too late."

"Hush! no, no—it's the water," said Lord Peter with chattering teeth, "it's up to their waists down there, poor devils. But listen! can't you hear it? Tap, tap, tap—they're mining us—but I don't know where—I can't hear—I can't. Listen, you! There it is again—we must find it—we must stop it . . . Listen! Oh, my God! I can't hear—I can't hear anything for the noise of the guns. Can't they stop the guns?"[17]

---

[12] *Peaky.* Pale or wan.
Knickers. A shortened form of knickerbockers, a style of baggy-kneed trousers worn by boys at the time.

[13] A small portable burner that uses alcohol or methylated spirits as a fuel.

[14] High-quality porcelain made in the Sèvres area of Paris since 1756.

[15] A vehicle designed to move cargo, now called a truck or lorry.

[16] Different from the bromide print mentioned above, this compound was used as a sedative. A bromide subsequently came to mean a cliché.

[17] Lord Peter is having a nervous breakdown and imaging that he is in the trenches again. During World War I, soldiers on both sides would dig tunnels through no-

"Oh, dear!" said Mr. Bunter to himself. "No, no—it's all right, Major—don't you worry."

"But I hear it," protested Peter.

"So do I," said Mr. Bunter stoutly; "very good hearing, too, my lord. That's our own sappers at work in the communication trench. Don't you fret about that, sir."

Lord Peter grasped his wrist with a feverish hand.

"Our own sappers,"[18] he said; "sure of that?"

"Certain of it," said Mr. Bunter, cheerfully.

"They'll bring down the tower,"[19] said Lord Peter.

"To be sure they will," said Mr. Bunter, "and very nice, too. You just come and lay down a bit, sir—they've come to take over this section."

"You're sure it's safe to leave it?" said Lord Peter.

"Safe as houses,[20] sir," said Mr. Bunter, tucking his master's arm under his and walking him off to his bedroom.

Lord Peter allowed himself to be dosed and put to bed without further resistance. Mr. Bunter, looking singularly un-Bunterlike in striped pyjamas, with his stiff black hair ruffled about his head, sat grimly watching the younger man's sharp cheekbones and the purple stains under his eyes.

"Thought we'd had the last of these attacks," he said. "Been overdoin' of himself. Asleep?" He peered at him anxiously. An affectionate note crept into his voice. "Bloody little fool!" said Sergeant Bunter.

---

man's-land to set off explosives in coordination with an attack. The tactic was first used during the Civil War during the 1864 siege of Petersburg, Va., when Union soldiers turned a victory into defeat by failing to charge through the crater, allowing the Confederates to recover from the shock and slaughter them.

[18] An engineer that specialized in construction and demolitions. Trench warfare developed to an extraordinary degree during World War I, featuring multiple parallel lines with different functions. There was the front-line trench with dug-outs providing shelter from artillery attacks. Behind that was dug the support and reserve trenches containing more troops, with all linked by communication trenches.

[19] An observation tower, used to track the movement of military units.

[20] Another way of saying "as certain as."

CHAPTER IX

M R. PARKER, SUMMONED THE NEXT morning to 110 Piccadilly, arrived to find the Dowager Duchess in possession. She greeted him charmingly.

"I am going to take this silly boy down to Denver for the week-end," she said, indicating Peter, who was writing and only acknowledged his friend's entrance with a brief nod. "He's been doing too much—running about to Salisbury and places and up till all hours of the night—you really shouldn't encourage him, Mr. Parker, it's very naughty of you—waking poor Bunter up in the middle of the night with scares about Germans, as if that wasn't all over years ago, and he hasn't had an attack for ages, but there! Nerves are such funny things, and Peter always did have nightmares when he was quite a little boy—though very often of course it was only a little pill he wanted; but he was so dreadfully bad in 1918, you know, and I suppose we can't expect to forget all about a great war in a year or two,[1] and, really, I ought to be very thankful with both my boys safe. Still, I think a little peace and quiet at Denver won't do him any harm."

"Sorry you've been having a bad turn, old man," said Parker, vaguely sympathetic; "you're looking a bit seedy."

---

[1] This helps us to date the book. It must be after 1920 since Thomas Crimplesham's letter from Salisbury regarding his missing pince-nez is dated 192-. Since "Clouds" is set a year after the events in "Whose Body?" and gives Wimsey's age as 33, we can conclude that this book take place in November 1922.

DOROTHY L. SAYERS

"Charles," said Lord Peter, in a voice entirely void of expression, "I am going away for a couple of days because I can be no use to you in London. What has got to be done for the moment can be much better done by you than by me. I want you to take this"—he folded up his writing and placed it in an envelope—"to Scotland Yard immediately and get it sent out to all the workhouses,[2] infirmaries, police stations, Y.M.C.A.s[3] and so on in London. It is a description of Thipps's corpse as he was before he was shaved and cleaned up. I want to know whether any man answering to that description has been taken in anywhere, alive or dead, during the last fortnight. You will see Sir Andrew Mackenzie[4] personally, and get the paper sent out at once, by his authority; you will tell him that you have solved the problems of the Levy murder and the Battersea mystery"—Mr. Parker made an astonished noise to which his friend paid no attention—"and you will ask him to have men in readiness with a warrant to arrest a very dangerous and important criminal at any moment on your information. When the replies to this paper come in, you will search for any mention of St. Luke's Hospital, or of any person connected with St. Luke's Hospital, and you will send for me at once.

"Meanwhile you will scrape acquaintance[5]—I don't care how—with one of the students at St. Luke's. Don't march in there blowing about murders and police warrants, or you may find yourself in Queer Street.[6] I shall come up to town as soon as I hear

[2] An institution where the poor, elderly and infirm were cared for at public expense. Those who could work were given jobs, usually involving menial, repetitive tasks. The Poor Law Amendment Act of 1834 discouraged the use of charities to help the poor and made workhouse life intentionally harsh in the belief that poverty was a result of laziness and shirking.
[3] Young Men's Christian Association. The organization rents rooms for transient men.
[4] Although not explicitly identified, we know that Lord Peter goes fly-fishing with the head of Scotland Yard, so this is probably he. During 1922, the time the book is set, the commissioner was actually Brigadier-General Sir William Horwood.
[5] Meet and befriend.
[6] In a difficulty.

151

from you, and I shall expect to find a nice ingenuous Sawbones[7] here to meet me." He grinned faintly.

"D'you mean you've got to the bottom of this thing?" asked Parker.

"Yes. I may be wrong. I hope I am, but I know I'm not."

"You won't tell me?"

"D'you know," said Peter, "honestly I'd rather not. I say I may be wrong—and I'd feel as if I'd libelled the Archbishop of Canterbury."[8]

"Well, tell me—is it one mystery or two?"

"One."

"You talked of the Levy murder. Is Levy dead?"

"God—yes!" said Peter, with a strong shudder.

The Duchess looked up from where she was reading the Tatler.[9]

"Peter," she said, "is that your ague[10] coming on again? Whatever you two are chattering about, you'd better stop it at once if it excites you. Besides, it's about time to be off."

"All right, Mother," said Peter. He turned to Bunter, standing respectfully in the door with an overcoat and suitcase. "You understand what you have to do, don't you?" he said.

"Perfectly, thank you, my lord. The car is just arriving, your Grace."

"With Mrs. Thipps inside it," said the Duchess. "She'll be delighted to see you again, Peter. You remind her so of Mr. Thipps. Good-morning, Bunter."

"Good-morning, your Grace."

Parker accompanied them downstairs.

When they had gone he looked blankly at the paper in his hand—then, remembering that it was Saturday and there was need for haste, he hailed a taxi.

"Scotland Yard!" he cried.

---

[7] Slang for a doctor.

[8] The Archbishop of Canterbury is the leader of the Anglican Church, headquartered in the city of Canterbury, about 60 miles east of London.

[9] A weekly magazine that chronicles the lives and lifestyle of the upper classes. It is now published monthly.

[10] A fever marked by chills and sweating.

Tuesday morning saw Lord Peter and a man in a velveteen[11] jacket swishing merrily through seven acres of turnip-tops, streaked yellow with early frosts. A little way ahead, a sinuous undercurrent of excitement among the leaves proclaimed the unseen yet ever-near presence of one of the Duke of Denver's setter[12] pups. Presently a partridge flew up with a noise like a police rattle,[13] and Lord Peter accounted for it[14] very creditably for a man who, a few nights before, had been listening to imaginary German sappers. The setter bounded foolishly through the turnips, and fetched back the dead bird.

"Good dog," said Lord Peter.

Encouraged by this, the dog gave a sudden ridiculous gambol[15] and barked, its ear tossed inside out over its head.

"Heel," said the man in velveteen, violently. The animal sidled up, ashamed.

"Fool of a dog, that," said the man in velveteen; "can't keep quiet. Too nervous, my lord. One of old Black Lass's pups."

"Dear me," said Peter, "is the old dog still going?"

"No, my lord; we had to put her away in the spring."

Peter nodded. He always proclaimed that he hated the country and was thankful to have nothing to do with the family estates, but this morning he enjoyed the crisp air and the wet leaves washing darkly over his polished boots. At Denver things moved in an orderly way; no one died sudden and violent deaths except aged setters—and partridges, to be sure. He sniffed up the autumn smell with appreciation. There was a letter in his pocket which had come by the morning post, but he did not intend to read it just yet. Parker had not wired; there was no hurry.

---

[11] A cotton cloth made to imitate velvet.

[12] Setters are dogs used for hunting game. Typical breeds include English, Irish, Black Welsh and Gordon.

[13] A noisemaker consisting of a box with a metal flange attached to a geared stick. A policeman on patrol needing assistance would whirl the box around the stick, creating a loud clacking sound, used to attract the attention of policemen within hearing. Rattles were used by the Metropolitan Police Service until the 1880s when they were replaced by whistles. They can still be seen at soccer games.

[14] Shot it.

[15] To playfully skip about.

He read it in the smoking-room[16] after lunch. His brother was there, dozing over the Times—a good, clean Englishman, sturdy and conventional, rather like Henry VIII in his youth; Gerald, sixteenth Duke of Denver. The Duke considered his cadet[17] rather degenerate, and not quite good form; he disliked his taste for police-court news.

The letter was from Mr. Bunter.

> 110, Piccadilly,
> W.I.

MY LORD:

I write (Mr. Bunter had been carefully educated and knew that nothing is more vulgar than a careful avoidance of beginning a letter with the first person singular) as your lordship directed, to inform you of the result of my investigations.

I experienced no difficulty in becoming acquainted with Sir Julian Freke's man-servant. He belongs to the same club as the Hon. Frederick Arbuthnot's man, who is a friend of mine, and was very willing to introduce me. He took me to the club yesterday (Sunday) evening, and we dined with the man, whose name is John Cummings, and afterwards I invited Cummings to drinks and a cigar in the flat. Your lordship will excuse me doing this, knowing that it is not my habit, but it has always been my experience that the best way to gain a man's confidence is to let him suppose that one takes advantage of one's employer.

("I always suspected Bunter of being a student of human nature," commented Lord Peter.)

I gave him the best old port ("The deuce you did," said Lord Peter), having heard you and Mr. Arbuthnot talk over it. ("Hum!"

---

[16] A room set aside in a home or club for that purpose. Smoking rooms were generally for men only, which served the dual purpose of keeping the smell away from the rest of the place, and giving men an excuse to gather away from the ladies.

[17] Younger brother or son.

said Lord Peter.)

Its effects were quite equal to my expectations as regards the principal matter in hand, but I very much regret to state that the man had so little understanding of what was offered to him that he smoked a cigar with it (one of your lordship's Villar Villars). You will understand that I made no comment on this at the time, but your lordship will sympathize with my feelings. May I take this opportunity of expressing my grateful appreciation of your lordship's excellent taste in food, drink and dress? It is, if I may say so, more than a pleasure—it is an education, to valet and buttle[18] your lordship.

Lord Peter bowed his head gravely.

"What on earth are you doing, Peter, sittin' there noddin' an' grinnin' like a what-you-may-call-it?" demanded the Duke, coming suddenly out of a snooze. "Someone writin' pretty things to you, what?"

"Charming things," said Lord Peter.

The Duke eyed him doubtfully.

"Hope to goodness you don't go and marry a chorus beauty,"[19] he muttered inwardly, and returned to the Times.

Over dinner I had set myself to discover Cummings's tastes, and found them to run in the direction of the music-hall stage. During his first glass I drew him out in this direction, your lordship having kindly given me opportunities of seeing every performance in London, and I spoke more freely than I should consider becoming in the ordinary way in order to make myself pleasant to him. I may say that his views on women and the stage were such as I should have expected from a man who would smoke with your lordship's port.

With the second glass I introduced the subject of your lordship's enquiries. In order to save time I will write our

[18] To perform the duties of a butler.
[19] A performer in a chorus line of a theatrical show. Marrying a "chlorine" (a slang term derived from the chemical used to bleach hair a startling blonde) was a common trope in fiction and the movies. A few years after "Whose Body?" was published, the duke's concern was made real when Lord Anthony Ashley-Cooper scandalized society by marrying Edith Sylvia Hawkes, an actress who danced in the chorus line as a Cochran Dancer, an English version of the Ziegfeld Follies.

conversation in the form of a dialogue, as nearly as possible as it actually took place.

Cummings: You seem to get many opportunities of seeing a bit of life, Mr. Bunter.

Bunter: One can always make opportunities if one knows how.

Cummings: Ah, it's very easy for you to talk, Mr. Bunter. You're not married, for one thing.

Bunter: I know better than that, Mr. Cummings.

Cummings: So do I—now, when it's too late. (He sighed heavily, and I filled up his glass.)

Bunter: Does Mrs. Cummings live with you at Battersea?

Cummings: Yes; her and me we do for my governor. Such a life! Not but what there's a char[20] comes in by the day. But what's a char? I can tell you it's dull all by ourselves in that d—d[21] Battersea suburb.

Bunter: Not very convenient for the Halls,[22] of course.

Cummings: I believe you. It's all right for you, here in Piccadilly, right on the spot as you might say. And I daresay your governor's often out all night, eh?

Bunter: Oh, frequently, Mr. Cummings.

Cummings: And I daresay you take the opportunity to slip off yourself every so often, eh?

Bunter: Well, what do you think, Mr. Cummings?

Cummings: That's it; there you are! But what's a man to do with a nagging fool of a wife and a blasted scientific doctor for a governor, as sits up all night cutting up dead bodies and experimenting with frogs?

Bunter: Surely he goes out sometimes.

Cummings: Not often. And always back before twelve. And the way he goes on if he rings the bell and you ain't there. I give you my word, Mr. Bunter.

Bunter: Temper?

---

[20] Charwoman or cleaning lady.

[21] Damned.

[22] The Battersea area was not known for its nightlife. To enjoy one of London's music halls, one must travel north to Oxford Road — where Mr. Thipps found unexpected and uncomfortable fun — or the West End.

Cummings: No-o-o—but looking through you, nasty-like, as if you was on that operating table of his and he was going to cut you up. Nothing a man could rightly complain of, you understand, Mr. Bunter, just nasty looks. Not but what I will say he's very correct. Apologizes if he's been inconsiderate. But what's the good of that when he's been and gone and lost you your nights rest?

Bunter: How does he do that? Keeps you up late, you mean?

Cummings: Not him; far from it. House locked up and household to bed at half past ten. That's his little rule. Not but what I'm glad enough to go as a rule, it's that dreary. Still, when I do go to bed I like to go to sleep.

Bunter: What does he do? Walk about the house?

Cummings: Doesn't he? All night. And in and out of the private door to the hospital.

Bunter: You don't mean to say, Mr. Cummings, a great specialist like Sir Julian Freke does night work at the hospital?

Cummings: No, no; he does his own work—research work, as you may say. Cuts people up. They say he's very clever. Could take you or me to pieces like a clock, Mr. Bunter, and put us together again.

Bunter: Do you sleep in the basement, then, to hear him so plain?

Cummings: No; our bedroom's at the top. But, Lord! what's that? He'll bang the door so you can hear him all over the house.

Bunter: Ah, many's the time I've had to speak to Lord Peter about that. And talking all night. And baths.

Cummings: Baths? You may well say that, Mr. Bunter. Baths? Me and my wife sleep next to the cistern-room.[23] Noise fit to wake the dead. All hours. When d'you think he chose to have a bath, no later than last Monday night, Mr. Bunter?

Bunter: I've known them to do it at two in the morning, Mr. Cummings.

---

[23] A room containing a tank, filled with water, usually found in the top floor or attic of a house. The cistern uses gravity to distribute water throughout the house. Water is heavy, so the size of the tank, usually made of wood and lined with metal, would depend on the amount of structural support built into the floor under it.

Cummings: Have you, now? Well, this was at three. Three o'clock in the morning we was waked up. I give you my word.

Bunter: You don't say so, Mr. Cummings.

Cummings: He cuts up diseases, you see, Mr. Bunter, and then he don't like to go to bed till he's washed the bacilluses[24] off, if you understand me. Very natural, too, I daresay. But what I say is, the middle of the night's no time for a gentleman to be occupying his mind with diseases.

Bunter: These great men have their own way of doing things.

Cummings: Well, all I can say is, it isn't my way.

(I could believe that, your lordship. Cummings has no signs of greatness about him, and his trousers are not what I would wish to see in a man of his profession.)

Bunter: Is he habitually as late as that, Mr. Cummings?

Cummings: Well, no, Mr. Bunter, I will say, not as a general rule. He apologized, too, in the morning, and said he would have the cistern seen to—and very necessary, in my opinion, for the air gets into the pipes, and the groaning and screeching as goes on is something awful. Just like Niagara,[25] if you follow me, Mr. Bunter, I give you my word.

Bunter: Well, that's as it should be, Mr. Cummings. One can put up with a great deal from a gentleman that has the manners to apologize. And, of course, sometimes they can't help themselves. A visitor will come in unexpectedly and keep them late, perhaps.

Cummings: That's true enough, Mr. Bunter. Now I come to think of it, there was a gentleman come in on Monday evening. Not that he came late, but he stayed about an hour, and may have put Sir Julian behindhand.

Bunter: Very likely. Let me give you some more port, Mr. Cummings. Or a little of Lord Peter's old brandy.

Cummings: A little of the brandy, thank you, Mr. Bunter. I suppose you have the run of the cellar here. (He winked at me.)

"Trust me for that," I said, and I fetched him the Napoleon.[26] I

---

[24] A type of disease-producing bacteria.

[25] Niagara Falls, located on the U.S.-Canadian border outside Buffalo, N.Y.

[26] Originally meant to describe any brandy laid down during Napoleon's reign (1804-1814 and 1815), by Lord Peter's time it was probably more commonly

assure your lordship it went to my heart to pour it out for a man like that. However, seeing we had got on the right tack, I felt it wouldn't be wasted.

"I'm sure I wish it was always gentlemen that come here at night," I said. (Your lordship will excuse me, I am sure, making such a suggestion.)

("Good God," said Lord Peter, "I wish Bunter was less thorough in his methods.")

Cummings: Oh, he's that sort, his lordship, is he? (He chuckled and poked me. I suppress a portion of his conversation here, which could not fail to be as offensive to your lordship as it was to myself. He went on:) No, it's none of that with Sir Julian. Very few visitors at night, and always gentlemen. And going early as a rule, like the one I mentioned.

Bunter: Just as well. There's nothing I find more wearisome, Mr. Cummings, than sitting up to see visitors out.

Cummings: Oh, I didn't see this one out. Sir Julian let him out himself at ten o'clock or thereabouts. I heard the gentleman shout "Good-night" and off he goes.

Bunter: Does Sir Julian always do that?

Cummings: Well, that depends. If he sees visitors downstairs, he lets them out himself; if he sees them upstairs in the library, he rings for me.

Bunter: This was a downstairs visitor, then?

Cummings: Oh, yes. Sir Julian opened the door to him, I remember. He happened to be working in the hall. Though now I come to think of it, they went up to the library afterwards. That's funny. I know they did, because I happened to go up to the hall with coals, and I heard them upstairs. Besides, Sir Julian rang for me in the library a few minutes later. Still, anyway, we heard him go at ten, or it may have been a bit before. He hadn't only stayed about three-quarters of an hour. However, as I was saying, there was Sir Julian banging in and out of the private door all night, and a bath at three in the morning, and up again for breakfast at eight— it beats me. If I had all his money, curse me if I'd go poking about

___

used for any long-aged brandy. Now, it is a grade assigned by France's Bureau National Interprofessionnel du Cognac.

with dead men in the middle of the night. If it was a nice live girl, now, Mr. Bunter—

I need not repeat any more of his conversation, as it became unpleasant and incoherent, and I could not bring him back to the events of Monday night. I was unable to get rid of him till three. He cried on my neck, and said I was the bird, and you were the governor for him. He said that Sir Julian would be greatly annoyed with him for coming home so late, but Sunday night was his night out and if anything was said about it he would give notice. I think he will be ill-advised to do so, as I feel he is not a man I could conscientiously recommend if I were in Sir Julian Freke's place. I noticed that his boot-heels were slightly worn down.

I should wish to add, as a tribute to the great merits of your lordship's cellar, that, although I was obliged to drink a somewhat large quantity both of the Cockburn '68[27] and the 1800 Napoleon I feel no headache or other ill effects this morning.

Trusting that your lordship is deriving real benefit from the country air, and that the little information I have been able to obtain will prove satisfactory, I remain,

With respectful duty to all the family, their ladyships,

Obediently yours,

MERVYN BUNTER.

"Y'know," said Lord Peter thoughtfully to himself, "I sometimes think Mervyn Bunter's pullin' my leg. What is it, Soames?"

"A telegram, my lord."

"Parker," said Lord Peter, opening it. It said:

"Description recognized Chelsea Workhouse.[28] Unknown vagrant injured street accident Wednesday week. Died workhouse Monday. Delivered St. Luke's same evening by order Freke. Much puzzled. Parker."

"Hurray!" said Lord Peter, suddenly sparkling. "I'm glad I've

---

[27] Cockburn is a port produced by a house established in 1815.

[28] Chelsea is an area, once a county borough, in central London north of the Thames. Located west of the Battersea area and southwest from Lord Peter's home on Piccadilly, it was the home of writers and painters such as T.S. Eliot, Dante Gabriel Rossetti, James McNeill Whistler, and John Singer Sargent.

puzzled Parker. Gives me confidence in myself. Makes me feel like Sherlock Holmes. 'Perfectly simple, Watson.' Dash it all, though! this is a beastly business. Still, it's puzzled Parker."

"What's the matter?" asked the Duke, getting up and yawning.

"Marching orders," said Peter, "back to town. Many thanks for your hospitality, old bird—I'm feelin' no end better. Ready to tackle Professor Moriarty[29] or Leon Kestrel[30] or any of 'em."

"I do wish you'd keep out of the police courts," grumbled the Duke. "It makes it so dashed awkward for me, havin' a brother makin' himself conspicuous."

"Sorry, Gerald," said the other, "I know I'm a beastly blot on the 'scutcheon."[31]

"Why can't you marry and settle down and live quietly, doin' something useful?" said the Duke unappeased.

"Because that was a wash-out as you perfectly well know," said Peter; "besides," he added cheerfully, "I'm bein' no end useful. You may come to want me yourself, you never know. When anybody comes blackmailin' you, Gerald, or your first deserted wife turns up unexpectedly from the West Indies, you'll realize the pull of havin' a private detective in the family. 'Delicate private business arranged with tact and discretion. Investigations undertaken. Divorce evidence a specialty. Every guarantee!' Come, now."

"Ass!" said Lord Denver, throwing the newspaper violently into his armchair. "When do you want the car?"

"Almost at once. I say, Jerry, I'm taking Mother up with me."

"Why should she be mixed up in it?"

"Well, I want her help."

---

[29] Sherlock Holmes' greatest enemy, called by him the "Napoleon of Crime."

[30] A recurring villain in the Sexton Blake stories. Known as the "Master Mummer" — that is, an actor — Kestrel was a master of disguise. Sayers was fond of the stories and created Lord Peter as a character in an unfinished attempt at one. In a lecture, she called the series "the nearest approach to a national folklore, conceived as the centre for a cycle of loosely connected romances in the Arthurian manner."

[31] The escutcheon is the surface, typically shield-shaped, on which a family's armorial bearings are displayed. Ironically, Gerald himself will blot the family's 'scutcheon when he is tried for murder in "Clouds of Witness."

"I call it most unsuitable," said the Duke.

The Dowager Duchess, however, made no objection.

"I used to know her quite well," she said, "when she was Christine Ford. Why, dear?"

"Because," said Lord Peter, "there's a terrible piece of news to be broken to her about her husband."

"Is he dead, dear?"

"Yes; and she will have to come and identify him."

"Poor Christine."

"Under very revolting circumstances, Mother."

"I'll come with you, dear."

"Thank you, Mother, you're a brick. D'you mind gettin' your things on straight away and comin' up with me? I'll tell you about it in the car."

CHAPTER X

MR. PARKER, A FAITHFUL THOUGH doubting Thomas,[1] had duly secured his medical student: a large young man like an overgrown puppy, with innocent eyes and a freckled face. He sat on the Chesterfield before Lord Peter's library fire, bewildered in equal measure by his errand, his surroundings and the drink which he was absorbing. His palate, though untutored, was naturally a good one, and he realized that even to call this liquid a drink—the term ordinarily used by him to designate cheap whisky, post-war beer or a dubious glass of claret[2] in a Soho restaurant—was a sacrilege; this was something outside normal experience: a genie in a bottle.

The man called Parker, whom he had happened to run across the evening before in the public-house at the corner of Prince of Wales Road, seemed to be a good sort. He had insisted on bringing him round to see this friend of his, who lived splendidly in Piccadilly. Parker was quite understandable; he put him down as a government servant, or perhaps something in the City. The friend was embarrassing; he was a lord, to begin with, and his clothes were a kind of rebuke[3] to the world at large. He talked the most

---

[1] A skeptic who refuses to believe what he sees. Named for the apostle Thomas, who, according to the Gospel of John, saw Jesus after his death and demanded to feel his wounds before being convinced that he is alive.
[2] A red wine from the Bordeaux region of France.
[3] To sharply criticize.

fatuous[4] nonsense, certainly, but in a disconcerting way. He didn't dig into a joke and get all the fun out of it; he made it in passing, so to speak, and skipped away to something else before your retort was ready. He had a truly terrible manservant—the sort you read about in books—who froze the marrow in your bones with silent criticism. Parker appeared to bear up under the strain, and this made you think more highly of Parker; he must be more habituated to the surroundings of the great than you would think to look at him. You wondered what the carpet had cost on which Parker was carelessly spilling cigar ash; your father was an upholsterer—Mr. Piggott, of Piggott & Piggott, Liverpool—and you knew enough about carpets to know that you couldn't even guess at the price of this one. When you moved your head on the bulging silk cushion in the corner of the sofa, it made you wish you shaved more often and more carefully. The sofa was a monster—but even so, it hardly seemed big enough to contain you. This Lord Peter was not very tall—in fact, he was rather a small man, but he didn't look undersized. He looked right; he made you feel that to be six-foot-three was rather vulgarly assertive; you felt like Mother's new drawing-room curtains—all over great, big blobs. But everybody was very decent to you, and nobody said anything you couldn't understand, or sneered at you. There were some frightfully deep-looking books on the shelves all round, and you had looked into a great folio Dante which was lying on the table, but your hosts were talking quite ordinarily and rationally about the sort of books you read yourself—clinking good love stories and detective stories. You had read a lot of those, and could give an opinion, and they listened to what you had to say, though Lord Peter had a funny way of talking about books, too, as if the author had confided in him beforehand, and told him how the story was put together, and which bit was written first. It reminded you of the way old Freke took a body to pieces.

"Thing I object to in detective stories," said Mr. Piggott, "is the way fellows remember every bloomin' thing that's happened to 'em within the last six months. They're always ready with their

---

[4] Complacently foolish.

time of day and was it rainin' or not, and what were they doin' on such an' such a day. Reel it all off like a page of poetry. But one ain't like that in real life, d'you think so, Lord Peter?" Lord Peter smiled, and young Piggott, instantly embarrassed, appealed to his earlier acquaintance. "You know what I mean, Parker. Come now. One day's so like another, I'm sure I couldn't remember—well, I might remember yesterday, p'r'aps, but I couldn't be certain about what I was doin' last week if I was to be shot for it."

"No," said Parker, "and evidence given in police statements sounds just as impossible. But they don't really get it like that, you know. I mean, a man doesn't just say, 'Last Friday I went out at ten o'clock a.m. to buy a mutton chop.[5] As I was turning into Mortimer Street I noticed a girl of about twenty-two with black hair and brown eyes, wearing a green jumper,[6] check skirt, Panama hat and black shoes riding a Royal Sunbeam Cycle[7] at about ten miles an hour turning the corner by the Church of St. Simon and St. Jude[8] on the wrong side of the road riding towards the market place!' It amounts to that, of course, but it's really wormed out of him by a series of questions."

"And in short stories," said Lord Peter, "it has to be put in statement form, because the real conversation would be so long and twaddly[9] and tedious, and nobody would have the patience to read it. Writers have to consider their readers, if any, y'see."

"Yes," said Mr. Piggott, "but I bet you most people would find it jolly difficult to remember, even if you asked 'em things. I should—of course, I know I'm a bit of a fool, but then, most people are, ain't they? You know what I mean. Witnesses ain't detectives, they're just average idiots like you and me."

"Quite so," said Lord Peter, smiling as the force of the last phrase sank into its unhappy perpetrator; "you mean, if I were to ask you in a general way what you were doin'—say, a week ago to-day, you wouldn't be able to tell me a thing about it offhand."

---

[5] A cut of meat from a mature sheep.
[6] Slang for sweater.
[7] A brand of bicycle.
[8] A Roman Catholic church in the Streatham Hill section of south London.
[9] A variation of twaddle, or silly, idle talk.

"No—I'm sure I shouldn't." He considered. "No. I was in at the Hospital as usual, I suppose, and, being Tuesday, there'd be a lecture on something or the other—dashed if I know what—and in the evening I went out with Tommy Pringle—no, that must have been Monday—or was it Wednesday? I tell you, I couldn't swear to anything."

"You do yourself an injustice," said Lord Peter gravely. "I'm sure, for instance, you recollect what work you were doing in the dissecting-room on that day, for example."

"Lord, no! not for certain. I mean, I daresay it might come back to me if I thought for a long time, but I wouldn't swear to it in a court of law."

"I'll bet you half a crown to sixpence,"[10] said Lord Peter, "that you'll remember within five minutes."

"I'm sure I can't."

"We'll see. Do you keep a notebook of the work you do when you dissect? Drawings or anything?"

"Oh, yes."

"Think of that. What's the last thing you did in it?"

"That's easy, because I only did it this morning. It was leg muscles."

"Yes. Who was the subject?"

"An old woman of sorts; died of pneumonia."

"Yes. Turn back the pages of your drawing-book in your mind. What came before that?"

"Oh, some animals—still legs; I'm doing motor muscles at present. Yes. That was old Cunningham's demonstration on comparative anatomy. I did rather a good thing of a hare's legs and a frog's, and rudimentary legs on a snake."

"Yes. Which day does Mr. Cunningham lecture?"

"Friday."

"Friday; yes. Turn back again. What comes before that?"

Mr. Piggott shook his head.

"Do your drawings of legs begin on the right-hand page or the

---

[10] Lord Peter is offering 5-to-1 odds. A half crown is one-eighth of a pound. Since a pound in 1920 is worth roughly £21, or $70, in 2010, he's putting up £2.63 against 52 pence (or $8.75 to $1.75).

left-hand page? Can you see the first drawing?"

"Yes—yes—I can see the date written at the top. It's a section of a frog's hind leg, on the right-hand page."

"Yes. Think of the open book in your mind's eye. What is opposite to it?"

This demanded some mental concentration.

"Something round—coloured—oh, yes—it's a hand."

"Yes. You went on from the muscles of the hand and arm to leg- and foot-muscles?"

"Yes; that's right. I've got a set of drawings of arms."

"Yes. Did you make those on the Thursday?"

"No; I'm never in the dissecting-room on Thursday."

"On Wednesday, perhaps?"

"Yes; I must have made them on Wednesday. Yes; I did. I went in there after we'd seen those tetanus[11] patients in the morning. I did them on Wednesday afternoon. I know I went back because I wanted to finish 'em. I worked rather hard—for me. That's why I remember."

"Yes; you went back to finish them. When had you begun them, then?"

"Why, the day before."

"The day before. That was Tuesday, wasn't it?"

"I've lost count—yes, the day before Wednesday—yes, Tuesday."

"Yes. Were they a man's arms or a woman's arms?"

"Oh, a man's arms."

"Yes; last Tuesday, a week ago to-day, you were dissecting a man's arms in the dissecting-room. Sixpence, please."

"By Jove!"

"Wait a moment. You know a lot more about it than that. You've no idea how much you know. You know what kind of man he was."

"Oh, I never saw him complete, you know. I got there a bit late that day, I remember. I'd asked for an arm specially, because I was rather weak in arms, and Watts—that's the attendant—had

---

[11] An infectious disease that causes spasms of the voluntary muscles such as the jaw, causing lockjaw.

promised to save me one."

"Yes. You have arrived late and found your arm waiting for you. You are dissecting it—taking your scissors and slitting up the skin and pinning it back. Was it very young, fair skin?"

"Oh, no—no. Ordinary skin, I think—with dark hairs on it—yes, that was it."

"Yes. A lean, stringy arm, perhaps, with no extra fat anywhere?"

"Oh, no—I was rather annoyed about that. I wanted a good, muscular arm, but it was rather poorly developed and the fat got in my way."

"Yes; a sedentary[12] man who didn't do much manual work."

"That's right."

"Yes. You dissected the hand, for instance, and made a drawing of it. You would have noticed any hard calluses."[13]

"Oh, there was nothing of that sort."

"No. But should you say it was a young man's arm? Firm young flesh and limber joints?"

"No—no."

"No. Old and stringy, perhaps."

"No. Middle-aged—with rheumatism. I mean, there was a chalky deposit in the joints, and the fingers were a bit swollen."

"Yes. A man about fifty."

"About that."

"Yes. There were other students at work on the same body."

"Oh, yes."

"Yes. And they made all the usual sort of jokes about it."

"I expect so—oh, yes!"

"You can remember some of them. Who is your local funny man, so to speak?"

"Tommy Pringle."

"What was Tommy Pringle doing?"

"Can't remember."

"Whereabouts was Tommy Pringle working?"

"Over by the instrument-cupboard—by sink C."

"Yes. Get a picture of Tommy Pringle in your mind's eye."

---

[12] Not physically active.

[13] A thickening or roughening of the skin, in this case from manual labor.

Piggott began to laugh.

"I remember now. Tommy Pringle said the old Sheeny—"[14]

"Why did he call him a Sheeny?"

"I don't know. But I know he did."

"Perhaps he looked like it. Did you see his head?"

"No."

"Who had the head?"

"I don't know—oh, yes, I do, though. Old Freke bagged the head himself, and little Bouncible Binns was very cross about it, because he'd been promised a head to do with old Scrooger."

"I see; what was Sir Julian doing with the head?"

"He called us up and gave us a jaw on spinal hæmorrhage and nervous lesions."[15]

"Yes. Well, go back to Tommy Pringle."

Tommy Pringle's joke was repeated, not without some embarrassment.[16]

"Quite so. Was that all?"

"No. The chap who was working with Tommy said that sort of thing came from overfeeding."

"I deduce that Tommy Pringle's partner was interested in the alimentary canal."

"Yes; and Tommy said, if he'd thought they'd feed you like that he'd go to the workhouse himself."

"Then the man was a pauper from the workhouse."

"Well, he must have been, I suppose."

"Are workhouse paupers usually fat and well-fed?"

---

[14] An insulting term for Jews. Its origin is unknown, but one theory says it comes from the German word *schön* for "beautiful," used by Jewish merchants to describe the goods they offered for sale.

[15] Sayers' love for Grand Guignol — the French theater (1897-1962) that specialized in naturalistic horror shows — surfaces here, with Sir Julian lecturing his medical students about the discharge of blood (*hæmorrhage*) from the spine and the injury (*lesions*) to the nervous system that he inflicted. It's also indicative of Sir Julian's cold nature that he could calmly teach a lesson using the body of his recently killed rival.

[16] Since Sir Julian had disfigured the head to make it unrecognizable, it could be that Tommy Pringle had spotted Sir Reuben's uncircumcised penis, a leftover clue that Sayers had to remove.

"Well, no—come to think of it, not as a rule."

"In fact, it struck Tommy Pringle and his friend that this was something a little out of the way in a workhouse subject?"

"Yes."

"And if the alimentary canal[17] was so entertaining to these gentlemen, I imagine the subject had come by his death shortly after a full meal."

"Yes—oh, yes—he'd have had to, wouldn't he?"

"Well, I don't know," said Lord Peter. "That's in your department, you know. That would be your inference, from what they said."

"Oh, yes. Undoubtedly."

"Yes, you wouldn't, for example, expect them to make that observation if the patient had been ill for a long time and fed on slops."

"Of course not."

"Well, you see, you really know a lot about it. On Tuesday week you were dissecting the arm muscles of a rheumatic middle-aged Jew, of sedentary habits, who had died shortly after eating a heavy meal, of some injury producing spinal hæmorrhage and nervous lesions, and so forth, and who was presumed to come from the workhouse."

"Yes."

"And you could swear to those facts, if need were?"

"Well, if you put it that way, I suppose I could."

"Of course you could."

Mr. Piggott sat for some moments in contemplation.

"I say," he said at last, "I did know all that, didn't I?"

"Oh, yes—you knew it all right—like Socrates's slave."[18]

"Who's he?"

"A person in a book I used to read as a boy."

"Oh—does he come in 'The Last Days of Pompeii'?"[19]

"No—another book—I daresay you escaped it. It's rather dull."

---

[17] The tubular passage that runs from mouth to anus that digests and absorbs food and eliminates waste.

[18] In Plato's "Meno," Socrates proves to Meno that his ignorant house slave can deduce a principle of geometry without being taught how.

[19] A novel published in 1834 by Edward Bulwer-Lytton (1803-1873).

"I never read much except Henty and Fenimore Cooper[20] at school.... But—have I got rather an extra good memory, then?"

"You have a better memory than you credit yourself with."

"Then why can't I remember all the medical stuff? It all goes out of my head like a sieve."[21]

"Well, why can't you?" said Lord Peter, standing on the hearthrug[22] and smiling down at his guest.

"Well," said the young man, "the chaps who examine one don't ask the same sort of questions you do."

"No?"

"No—they leave you to remember all by yourself. And it's beastly hard. Nothing to catch hold of, don't you know? But, I say—how did you know about Tommy Pringle being the funny man and—"

"I didn't, till you told me."

"No; I know. But how did you know he'd be there if you did ask? I mean to say—I say," said Mr. Piggott, who was becoming mellowed by influences themselves not unconnected with the alimentary canal—"I say, are you rather clever, or am I rather stupid?"

"No, no," said Lord Peter, "it's me. I'm always askin' such stupid questions, everybody thinks I must mean somethin' by 'em."

This was too involved for Mr. Piggott.

"Never mind," said Parker, soothingly, "he's always like that. You mustn't take any notice. He can't help it. It's premature senile decay, often observed in the families of hereditary legislators. Go away, Wimsey, and play us the 'Beggar's Opera,'[23] or something."

"That's good enough, isn't it?" said Lord Peter, when the happy Mr. Piggott had been despatched home after a really delightful evening.

---

[20] *George Alfred Henty* (1832-1902) wrote children's adventure novels set in different historical eras and adult novels such as "With Clive in India" and "Wulf the Saxon." American novelist *James Fenimore Cooper* (1789-1851) was an American novelist best known for "The Last of the Mohicans."

[21] A device with mesh or perforations through which material is filtered.

[22] A small rug placed in front of the fireplace.

[23] John Gay's 1728 mock opera, later adapted by Kurt Weill and Bertolt Brecht as "The Threepenny Opera." A song from it, "Mack the Knife," became a pop hit in 1960 by Bobby Darin (1936-1973).

"I'm afraid so," said Parker. "But it seems almost incredible."

"There's nothing incredible in human nature," said Lord Peter; "at least, in educated human nature. Have you got that exhumation order?"

"I shall have it to-morrow. I thought of fixing up with the workhouse people for to-morrow afternoon. I shall have to go and see them first."

"Right you are; I'll let my mother know."

"I begin to feel like you, Wimsey, I don't like this job."

"I like it a deal better than I did."

"You are really certain we're not making a mistake?"

Lord Peter had strolled across to the window. The curtain was not perfectly drawn, and he stood gazing out through the gap into lighted Piccadilly. At this he turned round:

"If we are," he said, "we shall know to-morrow, and no harm will have been done. But I rather think you will receive a certain amount of confirmation on your way home. Look here, Parker, d'you know, if I were you I'd spend the night here. There's a spare bedroom; I can easily put you up."

Parker stared at him.

"Do you mean—I'm likely to be attacked?"

"I think it very likely indeed."

"Is there anybody in the street?"

"Not now; there was half an hour ago."

"When Piggott left?"

"Yes."

"I say—I hope the boy is in no danger."

"That's what I went down to see. I don't think so. Fact is, I don't suppose anybody would imagine we'd exactly made a confidant of Piggott. But I think you and I are in danger. You'll stay?"

"I'm damned if I will, Wimsey; why should I run away?"

"Bosh!" said Peter, "you'd run away all right if you believed me, and why not? You don't believe me. In fact, you're still not certain I'm on the right tack.[24] Go in peace, but don't say I didn't

---

[24] A nautical term describing the path a sailing ship takes in relation to the direction of the wind. If the wind is coming from the ship's right side, it is on a starboard tack; if it's from the left side, the ship is on the port tack. Tacking is

warn you."

"I won't; I'll dictate a message with my dying breath to say I was convinced."

"Well, don't walk—take a taxi."

"Very well, I'll do that."

"And don't let anybody else get into it."

"No."

It was a raw, unpleasant night. A taxi deposited a load of people returning from the theatre at the block of flats next door, and Parker secured it for himself. He was just giving the address to the driver, when a man came hastily running up from a side street. He was in evening dress[25] and an overcoat.[26] He rushed up, signalling frantically.

"Sir—sir!—dear me! why, it's Mr. Parker! How fortunate! If you would be so kind—summoned from the club—a sick friend— can't find a taxi—everybody going home from the theatre—if I might share your cab—you are returning to Bloomsbury? I want Russell Square[27]—if I might presume—a matter of life and death."

He spoke in hurried gasps, as though he had been running violently and far. Parker promptly stepped out of the taxi.

"Delighted to be of service to you, Sir Julian," he said; "take my taxi. I am going down to Craven Street myself, but I'm in no hurry. Pray make use of the cab."

"It's extremely kind of you," said the surgeon. "I am ashamed—"

"That's all right," said Parker, cheerily. "I can wait." He assisted Freke into the taxi. "What number? 24 Russell Square, driver, and look sharp."

---

when a ship moves from the port tack to starboard, or vice versa. A ship on the right — that is, correct — tack is taking advantage of the wind direction to move as fast as possible.

[25] Formal wear worn by a man to events such as balls, the opera or banquets. It usually consists of a white tie, black tailcoat, waistcoat or vest, stiff-winged collar, black trousers with two stripes of satin down the outer side of the leg, black silk stockings and black pumps. Silk top hat optional.

[26] A long coat intended as the outermost garment.

[27] A large garden square in Bloomsbury, a few blocks west of Parker's flat at 12 Great Ormond Street.

The taxi drove off. Parker remounted the stairs and rang Lord Peter's bell.

"Thanks, old man," he said. "I'll stop the night, after all."

"Come in," said Wimsey.

"Did you see that?" asked Parker.

"I saw something. What happened exactly?"

Parker told his story. "Frankly," he said, "I've been thinking you a bit mad, but now I'm not quite so sure of it."

Peter laughed.

"Blessed are they that have not seen and yet have believed.[28] Bunter, Mr. Parker will stay the night."

"Look here, Wimsey, let's have another look at this business. Where's that letter?"

Lord Peter produced Bunter's essay in dialog. Parker studied it for a short time in silence.

"You know, Wimsey, I'm as full of objections to this idea as an egg is of meat."[29]

"So'm I, old son. That's why I want to dig up our Chelsea pauper. But trot out your objections."

"Well—"

"Well, look here, I don't pretend to be able to fill in all the blanks myself. But here we have two mysterious occurrences in one night, and a complete chain connecting the one with another through one particular person. It's beastly, but it's not unthinkable."

"Yes, I know all that. But there are one or two quite definite stumbling-blocks."

"Yes, I know. But, see here. On the one hand, Levy disappeared after being last seen looking for Prince of Wales Road at nine o'clock. At eight next morning a dead man, not unlike him in

---

[28] From John 20:29, when apostle Thomas said he will not believe that Jesus had risen, "Except I shall see in his hands the print of the nails, and put my finger into the print of the nails, and thrust my hand into his side." Jesus appeared before him and said, "because thou hast seen me, thou hast believed: blessed are they that have not seen, and yet have believed."

[29] Meaning a lot. An earlier version can be found in "Gammer Gurton's Needle," a comic play from c.1553: "An egg is not so full of meat as she is full of lies." A more notable version is in "Romeo and Juliet": "Thy head is as full of quarrels as an egg is of meat."

general outline, is discovered in a bath in Queen Caroline Mansions. Levy, by Freke's own admission, was going to see Freke. By information received from Chelsea workhouse a dead man, answering to the description of the Battersea corpse in its natural state, was delivered that same day to Freke. We have Levy with a past, and no future, as it were; an unknown vagrant with a future (in the cemetery) and no past, and Freke stands between their future and their past."

"That looks all right—"

"Yes. Now, further: Freke has a motive for getting rid of Levy—an old jealousy."

"Very old—and not much of a motive."

"People have been known to do that sort of thing.[30] You're thinking that people don't keep up old jealousies for twenty years or so. Perhaps not. Not just primitive, brute jealousy. That means a word and a blow. But the thing that rankles[31] is hurt vanity. That sticks. Humiliation. And we've all got a sore spot we don't like to have touched. I've got it. You've got it. Some blighter said hell knew no fury like a woman scorned.[32] Stickin' it on to women, poor devils. Sex is every man's loco[33] spot—you needn't fidget, you know it's true—he'll take a disappointment, but not a humiliation. I knew a man once who'd been turned down—not too charitably—by a girl he was engaged to. He spoke quite decently

---

[30] [Sayers' footnote] Lord Peter was not without authority for his opinion: "With respect to the alleged motive, it is of great importance to see whether there was a motive for committing such a crime, or whether there was not, or whether there is an improbability of its having been committed so strong as not to be overpowered by positive evidence. But *if there be any motive which can be assigned, I am bound to tell you that the inadequacy of that motive is of little importance.* We know, from the experience of criminal courts, that atrocious crimes of this sort have been committed from very slight motives; *not merely from malice and revenge,* but to gain a small pecuniary advantage, and to drive off for a time pressing difficulties."—L. C. J. Campbell, summing up in Reg. v. Palmer,[30] Shorthand Report, p. 308 C. C. C., May, 1856, Sess. Pa. 5. (Italics mine. D.L.S.)

[31] Deep anger or bitterness.

[32] A paraphrase from "The Mourning Bride" a play by William Congreve (1670-1729). He wrote: "Heaven has no rage like love to hatred turned, nor hell a fury like a woman scorned."

[33] Crazy.

about her. I asked what had become of her. 'Oh,' he said, 'she married the other fellow.' And then burst out—couldn't help himself. 'Lord, yes!' he cried. 'I think of it—jilted[34] for a Scotchman!' I don't know why he didn't like Scots, but that was what got him on the raw. Look at Freke. I've read his books. His attacks on his antagonists are savage. And he's a scientist. Yet he can't bear opposition, even in his work, which is where any first-class man is most sane and open-minded. Do you think he's a man to take a beating from any man on a side-issue? On a man's most sensitive side-issue? People are opinionated about side-issues, you know. I see red if anybody questions my judgment about a book. And Levy—who was nobody twenty years ago—romps in and carries off Freke's girl from under his nose. It isn't the girl Freke would bother about—it's having his aristocratic nose put out of joint by a little Jewish nobody.

"There's another thing. Freke's got another side-issue. He likes crime. In that criminology book of his he gloats over a hardened murderer. I've read it, and I've seen the admiration simply glaring out between the lines whenever he writes about a callous and successful criminal. He reserves his contempt for the victims or the penitents or the men who lose their heads and get found out. His heroes are Edmond de la Pommerais,[35] who persuaded his mistress into becoming an accessory to her own murder, and George Joseph Smith of Brides-in-a-bath fame, who could make passionate love to his wife in the night and carry out his plot to murder her in the morning.[36] After all, he thinks conscience is a sort of vermiform[37] appendix. Chop it out and you'll feel all the better. Freke isn't troubled by the usual conscientious deterrent. Witness his own hand in his books. Now again. The man who went to Levy's house in his place knew the house: Freke knew the house; he was a red-haired

---

[34] Rejected unfeelingly by a lover.

[35] A homeopathic doctor who was executed by guillotine for murder in 1864. See the essay "Edmond de la Pommerais: Deceived Into Murder."

[36] Smith (1872-1915) was executed for murdering three women he had married for their money. See the essay "George Joseph Smith: Many Brides, One Bath, No Waiting."

[37] From the Latin for worm-shaped. It is sometimes attached to the word appendix to describe its appearance.

man, smaller than Levy, but not much smaller, since he could wear his clothes without appearing ludicrous: you have seen Freke—you know his height—about five-foot-eleven, I suppose, and his auburn[38] mane; he probably wore surgical gloves: Freke is a surgeon; he was a methodical[39] and daring man: surgeons are obliged to be both daring and methodical. Now take the other side. The man who got hold of the Battersea corpse had to have access to dead bodies. Freke obviously had access to dead bodies. He had to be cool and quick and callous about handling a dead body. Surgeons are all that. He had to be a strong man to carry the body across the roofs and dump it in at Thipps's window. Freke is a powerful man and a member of the Alpine Club.[40] He probably wore surgical gloves and he let the body down from the roof with a surgical bandage. This points to a surgeon again. He undoubtedly lived in the neighbourhood. Freke lives next door. The girl you interviewed heard a bump on the roof of the end house. That is the house next to Freke's. Every time we look at Freke, he leads somewhere, whereas Milligan and Thipps and Crimplesham and all the other people we've honoured with our suspicion simply led nowhere."

"Yes; but it's not quite so simple as you make out. What was Levy doing in that surreptitious way at Freke's on Monday night?"

"Well, you have Freke's explanation."

"Rot, Wimsey. You said yourself it wouldn't do."

"Excellent. It won't do. Therefore Freke was lying. Why should he lie about it, unless he had some object in hiding the truth?"

"Well, but why mention it at all?"

"Because Levy, contrary to all expectation, had been seen at the corner of the road. That was a nasty accident for Freke. He thought it best to be beforehand with an explanation—of sorts. He reckoned, of course, on nobody's ever connecting Levy with Battersea Park."

"Well, then, we come back to the first question: Why did Levy go there?"

---

[38] Reddish.

[39] Performs tasks in order.

[40] A club for mountain climbers, founded in 1857 and probably the world's first mountaineering group.

"I don't know, but he was got there somehow. Why did Freke buy all those Peruvian Oil shares?"

"I don't know," said Parker in his turn.

"Anyway," went on Wimsey, "Freke expected him, and made arrangement to let him in himself, so that Cummings shouldn't see who the caller was."

"But the caller left again at ten."

"Oh, Charles! I did not expect this of you. This is the purest Suggery! Who saw him go? Somebody said 'Good-night' and walked away down the street. And you believe it was Levy because Freke didn't go out of his way to explain that it wasn't."

"D'you mean that Freke walked cheerfully out of the house to Park Lane, and left Levy behind—dead or alive—for Cummings to find?"

"We have Cummings's word that he did nothing of the sort. A few minutes after the steps walked away from the house, Freke rang the library bell and told Cummings to shut up for the night."

"Then—"

"Well—there's a side door to the house, I suppose—in fact, you know there is—Cummings said so—through the hospital."

"Yes—well, where was Levy?"

"Levy went up into the library and never came down. You've been in Freke's library. Where would you have put him?"

"In my bedroom next door."

"Then that's where he did put him."

"But suppose the man went in to turn down the bed?"

"Beds are turned down by the housekeeper, earlier than ten o'clock."

"Yes... But Cummings heard Freke about the house all night."

"He heard him go in and out two or three times. He'd expect him to do that, anyway."

"Do you mean to say Freke got all that job finished before three in the morning?"

"Why not?"

"Quick work."

"Well, call it quick work. Besides, why three? Cummings never saw him again till he called him for eight o'clock breakfast."

"But he was having a bath at three."

"I don't say he didn't get back from Park Lane before three.

But I don't suppose Cummings went and looked through the bathroom keyhole to see if he was in the bath."

Parker considered again.

"How about Crimplesham's pince-nez?" he asked.

"That is a bit mysterious," said Lord Peter.

"And why Thipps's bathroom?"

"Why, indeed? Pure accident, perhaps—or pure devilry."

"Do you think all this elaborate scheme could have been put together in a night, Wimsey?"

"Far from it. It was conceived as soon as that man who bore a superficial resemblance to Levy came into the workhouse. He had several days."

"I see."

"Freke gave himself away at the inquest. He and Grimbold disagreed about the length of the man's illness. If a small man (comparatively speaking) like Grimbold presumes to disagree with a man like Freke, it's because he is sure of his ground."

"Then—if your theory is sound—Freke made a mistake."

"Yes. A very slight one. He was guarding, with unnecessary caution, against starting a train of thought in the mind of anybody—say, the workhouse doctor. Up till then he'd been reckoning on the fact that people don't think a second time about anything (a body, say) that's once been accounted for."

"What made him lose his head?"

"A chain of unforeseen accidents. Levy's having been recognized—my mother's son having foolishly advertised in the Times his connection with the Battersea end of the mystery— Detective Parker (whose photograph has been a little prominent in the illustrated press[41] lately) seen sitting next door to the Duchess of Denver at the inquest. His aim in life was to prevent the two ends of the problem from linking up. And there were two of the links, literally side by side. Many criminals are wrecked by over-caution."

Parker was silent.

---

[41] Tabloid newspapers, which emphasized photographs and stories full of gossip, scandal and sex.

CHAPTER XI

"A REGULAR PEA-SOUPER,[1] BY JOVE," said Lord Peter.

Parker grunted, and struggled irritably into an overcoat.

"It affords me, if I may say so, the greatest satisfaction," continued the noble lord, "that in a collaboration like ours all the uninteresting and disagreeable routine work is done by you."

Parker grunted again.

"Do you anticipate any difficulty about the warrant?" enquired Lord Peter.

Parker grunted a third time.

"I suppose you've seen to it that all this business is kept quiet?"

"Of course."

"You've muzzled the workhouse people?"

"Of course."

"And the police?"

---

[1] Thick London fog, although really a foul mixture of water vapor, smoke and soot, encouraged by the pervasive use of coal for heat and power. The fog weakened lungs and caused fatal traffic collisions. R. Russell in "London Fogs" (1880) described it as "brown, reddish-yellow, or greenish, darkens more than a white fog, has a smoky, or sulphurous smell, is often somewhat dryer than a country fog, and produces, when thick, a choking sensation. Instead of diminishing while the sun rises higher, it often increases in density, and some of the most lowering London fogs occur about midday or late in the afternoon. Sometimes the brown masses rise and interpose a thick curtain at a considerable elevation between earth and sky. A white cloth spread out on the ground rapidly turns dirty, and particles of soot attach themselves to every exposed object." By the 1920s, when traffic lights and electric billboards were installed, the lights of Piccadilly Circus must have gleamed under a thick blanket of English industrial fog.

"Yes."

"Because, if you haven't, there'll probably be nobody to arrest."

"My dear Wimsey, do you think I'm a fool?"

"I had no such hope."

Parker grunted finally and departed.

Lord Peter settled down to a perusal of his Dante. It afforded him no solace. Lord Peter was hampered in his career as a private detective by a public-school education. Despite Parker's admonitions, he was not always able to discount it. His mind had been warped in its young growth by "Raffles"[2] and "Sherlock Holmes," or the sentiments for which they stand. He belonged to a family which had never shot a fox.[3]

"I am an amateur," said Lord Peter.

Nevertheless, while communing with Dante, he made up his mind.

In the afternoon he found himself in Harley Street. Sir Julian Freke might be consulted about one's nerves from two till four on Tuesdays and Fridays. Lord Peter rang the bell.

"Have you an appointment, sir?" enquired the man who opened the door.

"No," said Lord Peter, "but will you give Sir Julian my card? I think it possible he may see me without one."

He sat down in the beautiful room in which Sir Julian's patients awaited his healing counsel. It was full of people. Two or three fashionably dressed women were discussing shops and servants together, and teasing a toy griffon.[4] A big, worried-looking man by himself in a corner looked at his watch twenty times a minute. Lord Peter knew him by sight. It was Wintrington, a millionaire, who had tried to kill himself a few months ago. He controlled the finances of five countries, but he could not control his nerves. The

---

[2] The gentleman thief-hero of fiction whose stories are entertaining to read today. Raffles' creator, E.W. Hornung (1866-1921), was a brother-in-law of Arthur Conan Doyle (1859-1930). A publisher had suggested they collaborate on a book that would pit Sherlock Holmes against Raffles, but nothing came of it.

[3] When fox-hunting, you let the dogs chase the fox and tear it apart. That is sporting. To kill him yourself is considered bad form.

[4] A small dog that's a mix of a Brussels griffon and an English toy spaniel.

finances of five countries were in Sir Julian Freke's capable hands. By the fireplace sat a soldierly-looking young man, of about Lord Peter's own age. His face was prematurely lined and worn; he sat bolt upright, his restless eyes darting in the direction of every slightest sound. On the sofa was an elderly woman of modest appearance, with a young girl. The girl seemed listless and wretched; the woman's look showed deep affection, and anxiety tempered with a timid hope. Close beside Lord Peter was another, younger woman, with a little girl, and Lord Peter noticed in both of them the broad cheekbones and beautiful, grey, slanting eyes of the Slav.[5] The child, moving restlessly about, trod on Lord Peter's patent-leather toe,[6] and the mother admonished her in French before turning to apologize to Lord Peter.

"Mais je vous en prie, madame," said the young man, "it is nothing."[7]

"She is nervous, pauvre petite," said the young woman.

"You are seeking advice for her?"

"Yes. He is wonderful, the doctor. Figure to yourself, monsieur, she cannot forget, poor child, the things she has seen." She leaned nearer, so that the child might not hear. "We have escaped—from starving Russia—six months ago. I dare not tell you—she has such quick ears, and then, the cries, the tremblings, the convulsions— they all begin again. We were skeletons when we arrived—mon Dieu!—but that is better now. See, she is thin, but she is not starved. She would be fatter but for the nerves that keep her from eating. We who are older, we forget—enfin, on apprend à ne pas y penser[8]—but these children! When one is young, monsieur, tout ça impressionne trop."[9]

Lord Peter, escaping from the thraldom of British good form, expressed himself in that language in which sympathy is not condemned to mutism.

"But she is much better, much better," said the mother, proudly,

---

[5] Slavic people from central and eastern Europe.
[6] Leather given a glossy finish that is suitable for formal wear.
[7] "But I beg you, madame."
[8] "Finally, we learn not to think about it."
[9] "Our memories are too strong to forget."

"the great doctor, he does marvels."

"C'est un homme précieux,"[10] said Lord Peter.

"Ah, monsieur, c'est un saint qui opère des miracles! Nous prions pour lui, Natasha et moi, tous les jours. N'est-ce pas, chérie? And consider, monsieur, that he does it all, ce grand homme, cet homme illustre, for nothing at all. When we come here, we have not even the clothes upon our backs—we are ruined, famished. Et avec ça que nous sommes de bonne famille—mais hélas! monsieur, en Russie, comme vous savez, ça ne vous vaut que des insultes—des atrocités. Enfin! the great Sir Julian sees us, he says—'Madame, your little girl is very interesting to me. Say no more. I cure her for nothing—pour ses beaux yeux,' a-t-il ajouté en riant. Ah, monsieur, c'est un saint, un véritable saint! and Natasha is much, much better."[11]

"Madame, je vous en félicite."[12]

"And you, monsieur? You are young, well, strong—you also suffer? It is still the war, perhaps?"

"A little remains of shell-shock,"[13] said Lord Peter.

"Ah, yes. So many good, brave, young men—"

"Sir Julian can spare you a few minutes, my lord, if you will come in now," said the servant.

Lord Peter bowed to his neighbour, and walked across the waiting-room. As the door of the consulting-room closed behind him, he remembered having once gone, disguised, into the staff-room of a German officer. He experienced the same feeling—the

---

[10] "He is a precious man," is the direct translation, meaning that Sir Julian is a valuable man.

[11] This is what she says in general: "Sir, he is a saint who can perform miracles. We pray for him, Natasha and I. Don't we, darling? And consider, monsieur, that he does it all, this great man, this illustrious man, for nothing. When we came here, we had not even the clothes upon our backs — we were ruined, famished. And we, from a good family. But alas, sir, in Russia, that gets you not only insults, but atrocities. Finally, the great Sir Julian sees us, he says — Madame, your little girl is very interesting to me. Say no more. I will cure her for nothing — for her beautiful eyes,' he said with a laugh. Ah, monsieur, he is a saint, a true saint! And Natasha is much better."

[12] "I congratulate you."

[13] Psychological damage from battle. It is also known as battle fatigue, or post-traumatic stress syndrome.

feeling of being caught in a trap, and a mingling of bravado and shame.

He had seen Sir Julian Freke several times from a distance, but never close. Now, while carefully and quite truthfully detailing the circumstances of his recent nervous attack, he considered the man before him. A man taller than himself, with immense breadth of shoulder, and wonderful hands. A face beautiful, impassioned and inhuman; fanatical, compelling eyes, bright blue amid the ruddy bush of hair and beard. They were not the cool and kindly eyes of the family doctor, they were the brooding eyes of the inspired scientist, and they searched one through.

"Well," thought Lord Peter, "I shan't have to be explicit, anyhow."

"Yes," said Sir Julian, "yes. You had been working too hard. Puzzling your mind. Yes. More than that, perhaps—troubling your mind, shall we say?"

"I found myself faced with a very alarming contingency."

"Yes. Unexpectedly, perhaps."

"Very unexpected indeed."

"Yes. Following on a period of mental and physical strain."

"Well—perhaps. Nothing out of the way."

"Yes. The unexpected contingency was—personal to yourself?"

"It demanded an immediate decision as to my own actions yes, in that sense it was certainly personal."

"Quite so. You would have to assume some responsibility, no doubt."

"A very grave responsibility."

"Affecting others besides yourself?"

"Affecting one other person vitally, and a very great number indirectly."

"Yes. The time was night. You were sitting in the dark?"

"Not at first. I think I put the light out afterwards."

"Quite so—that action would naturally suggest itself to you. Were you warm?"

"I think the fire had died down. My man tells me that my teeth were chattering when I went in to him."

"Yes. You live in Piccadilly?"

"Yes."

"Heavy traffic sometimes goes past during the night, I expect."

"Oh, frequently."

"Just so. Now this decision you refer to—you had taken that decision."

"Yes."

"Your mind was made up?"

"Oh, yes."

"You had decided to take the action, whatever it was."

"Yes."

"Yes. It involved perhaps a period of inaction."

"Of comparative inaction—yes."

"Of suspense, shall we say?"

"Yes—of suspense, certainly."

"Possibly of some danger?"

"I don't know that that was in my mind at the time."

"No—it was a case in which you could not possibly consider yourself."

"If you like to put it that way."

"Quite so. Yes. You had these attacks frequently in 1918?"

"Yes—I was very ill for some months."

"Quite. Since then they have recurred less frequently?"

"Much less frequently."

"Yes—when did the last occur?"

"About nine months ago."

"Under what circumstances?"

"I was being worried by certain family matters. It was a question of deciding about some investments, and I was largely responsible."

"Yes. You were interested last year, I think in some police case?"

"Yes—in the recovery of Lord Attenbury's emerald necklace."

"That involved some severe mental exercise?"

"I suppose so. But I enjoyed it very much."

"Yes. Was the exertion of solving the problem attended by any bad results physically?"

"None."

"No. You were interested, but not distressed.''

"Exactly."

"Yes. You have been engaged in other investigations of the kind?"

"Yes. Little ones."

"With bad results for your health?"

"Not a bit of it. On the contrary. I took up these cases as a sort of distraction. I had a bad knock just after the war, which didn't make matters any better for me, don't you know."

"Ah! you are not married?"

"No."

"No. Will you allow me to make an examination? Just come a little nearer to the light. I want to see your eyes. Whose advice have you had till now?"

"Sir James Hodges'."

"Ah! yes—he was a sad loss to the medical profession. A really great man—a true scientist. Yes. Thank you. Now I should like to try you with this little invention."

"What's it do?"

"Well—it tells me about your nervous reactions. Will you sit here?"

The examination that followed was purely medical. When it was concluded, Sir Julian said:

"Now, Lord Peter, I'll tell you about yourself in quite untechnical language—"

"Thanks," said Peter, "that's kind of you. I'm an awful fool about long words."

"Yes. Are you fond of private theatricals, Lord Peter?"

"Not particularly," said Peter, genuinely surprised. "Awful bore as a rule. Why?"

"I thought you might be," said the specialist, drily. "Well, now. You know quite well that the strain you put on your nerves during the war has left its mark on you. It has left what I may call old wounds in your brain. Sensations received by your nerve-endings sent messages to your brain, and produced minute physical changes there—changes we are only beginning to be able to detect, even with our most delicate instruments. These changes in their turn set up sensations; or I should say, more accurately, that sensations are the names we give to these changes of tissue when we perceive them: we call them horror, fear, sense of responsibility and so on."

"Yes, I follow you."

"Very well. Now, if you stimulate those damaged places in

your brain again, you run the risk of opening up the old wounds. I mean, that if you get nerve-sensations of any kind producing the reactions which we call horror, fear, and sense of responsibility, they may go on to make disturbance right along the old channel, and produce in their turn physical changes which you will call by the names you were accustomed to associate with them—dread of German mines, responsibility for the lives of your men, strained attention and the inability to distinguish small sounds through the overpowering noise of guns."

"I see."

"This effect would be increased by extraneous circumstances producing other familiar physical sensations—night, cold or the rattling of heavy traffic, for instance."

"Yes."

"Yes. The old wounds are nearly healed, but not quite. The ordinary exercise of your mental faculties has no bad effect. It is only when you excite the injured part of your brain."

"Yes, I see."

"Yes. You must avoid these occasions. You must learn to be irresponsible, Lord Peter."

"My friends say I'm only too irresponsible already."

"Very likely. A sensitive nervous temperament often appears so, owing to its mental nimbleness."

"Oh!"

"Yes. This particular responsibility you were speaking of still rests upon you?"

"Yes, it does."

"You have not yet completed the course of action on which you have decided?"

"Not yet."

"You feel bound to carry it through?"

"Oh, yes—I can't back out of it now."

"No. You are expecting further strain?"

"A certain amount."

"Do you expect it to last much longer?"

"Very little longer now."

"Ah! Your nerves are not all they should be."

"No?"

"No. Nothing to be alarmed about, but you must exercise care while undergoing this strain, and afterwards you should take a complete rest. How about a voyage in the Mediterranean or the South Seas or somewhere?"

"Thanks. I'll think about it."

"Meanwhile, to carry you over the immediate trouble I will give you something to strengthen your nerves. It will do you no permanent good, you understand, but it will tide you over the bad time. And I will give you a prescription."

"Thank you."

Sir Julian got up and went into a small surgery leading out of the consulting-room. Lord Peter watched him moving about— boiling something and writing. Presently he returned with a paper and a hypodermic syringe.

"Here is the prescription. And now, if you will just roll up your sleeve, I will deal with the necessity of the immediate moment."

Lord Peter obediently rolled up his sleeve. Sir Julian Freke selected a portion of his forearm and anointed it with iodine.[14]

"What's that you're goin' to stick into me. Bugs?"[15]

The surgeon laughed.

"Not exactly," he said. He pinched up a portion of flesh between his finger and thumb. "You've had this kind of thing before, I expect."

"Oh, yes," said Lord Peter. He watched the cool fingers, fascinated, and the steady approach of the needle. "Yes—I've had it before—and, d'you know—I don't care frightfully about it."

He had brought up his right hand, and it closed over the surgeon's wrist like a vise.

The silence was like a shock. The blue eyes did not waver; they burned down steadily upon the heavy white lids below them. Then these slowly lifted; the grey eyes met the blue—coldly, steadily— and held them.

When lovers embrace, there seems no sound in the world but their own breathing. So the two men breathed face to face.

"As you like, of course, Lord Peter," said Sir Julian, courteously.

---

[14] A chemical used as a disinfectant.

[15] Germs.

"Afraid I'm rather a silly ass," said Lord Peter, "but I never could abide these little gadgets. I had one once that went wrong and gave me a rotten bad time. They make me a bit nervous."

"In that case," replied Sir Julian, "it would certainly be better not to have the injection. It might rouse up just those sensations which we are desirous of avoiding. You will take the prescription, then, and do what you can to lessen the immediate strain as far as possible."

"Oh, yes—I'll take it easy, thanks," said Lord Peter. He rolled his sleeve down neatly. "I'm much obliged to you. If I have any further trouble I'll look in again."

"Do—do—" said Sir Julian. cheerfully. "Only make an appointment another time. I'm rather rushed these days. I hope your mother is quite well. I saw her the other day at that Battersea inquest. You should have been there. It would have interested you."

CHAPTER XII

T HE VILE, RAW FOG TORE your throat and ravaged your eyes.
You could not see your feet. You stumbled in your walk over
poor men's graves.

The feel of Parker's old trench-coat beneath your fingers
was comforting. You had felt it in worse places. You clung on now
for fear you should get separated. The dim people moving in front
of you were like Brocken spectres.[1]

"Take care, gentlemen," said a toneless voice out of the yellow
darkness, "there's an open grave just hereabouts."

You bore away to the right, and floundered in a mass of freshly
turned clay.

"Hold up, old man," said Parker.

"Where is Lady Levy?"

"In the mortuary; the Duchess of Denver is with her. Your
mother is wonderful, Peter."

"Isn't she?" said Lord Peter.

A dim blue light carried by somebody ahead wavered and stood
still.

"Here you are," said a voice.

Two Dantesque shapes with pitchforks loomed up.

---

[1] An optical illusion caused when an observer sees his shadow cast on a distant
surface, such as a cloud if the observer is on a mountainside. This creates a ghost-
like shadow that can appear to move quickly due to variations in the cloud's
density. Brocken, where the phenomenon was discovered, is a peak in Germany's
Harz Mountains.

"Have you finished?" asked somebody.

"Nearly done, sir." The demons fell to work again with the pitchforks—no, spades.

Somebody sneezed. Parker located the sneezer and introduced him.

"Mr. Levett represents the Home Secretary.[2] Lord Peter Wimsey. We are sorry to drag you out on such a day, Mr. Levett."

"It's all in the day's work," said Mr. Levett, hoarsely. He was muffled to the eyes.

The sound of the spades for many minutes. An iron noise of tools thrown down. Demons stooping and straining.

A black-bearded spectre at your elbow. Introduced. The Master of the Workhouse.[3]

"A very painful matter, Lord Peter. You will forgive me for hoping you and Mr. Parker may be mistaken."

"I should like to be able to hope so too."

Something heaving, straining, coming up out of the ground.

"Steady, men. This way. Can you see? Be careful of the graves—they lie pretty thick hereabouts. Are you ready?"

"Right you are, sir. You go on with the lantern. We can follow you."

Lumbering footsteps. Catch hold of Parker's trench-coat again. "That you, old man? Oh, I beg your pardon, Mr. Levett—thought you were Parker."

"Hullo, Wimsey—here you are."

More graves. A headstone shouldered crookedly aslant. A trip and jerk over the edge of the rough grass. The squeal of gravel under your feet.

"This way, gentlemen, mind the step."

The mortuary. Raw red brick and sizzling gas-jets. Two women in black, and Dr. Grimbold. The coffin laid on the table with a heavy thump.

---

[2] The minister in charge of the Home Office, responsible for national security, policing, immigration and other internal affairs. It's one of the four Great Offices of State, the others being the prime minister, chancellor of the exchequer (e.g., treasurer) and foreign secretary.

[3] The man in charge of the Chelsea Workhouse.

"'Ave you got that there screw-driver, Bill? Thank 'ee. Be keerful wi' the chisel now. Not much substance to these 'ere boards, sir."

Several long creaks. A sob. The Duchess's voice, kind but peremptory.[4]

"Hush, Christine. You mustn't cry."

A mutter of voices. The lurching departure of the Dante demons—good, decent demons in corduroy.

Dr. Grimbold's voice—cool and detached as if in the consulting-room.

"Now—have you got that lamp, Mr. Wingate? Thank you. Yes, here on the table, please. Be careful not to catch your elbow in the flex,[5] Mr. Levett. It would be better, I think, if you came on this side. Yes—yes—thank you. That's excellent."

The sudden brilliant circle of an electric lamp over the table. Dr. Grimbold's beard and spectacles. Mr. Levett blowing his nose. Parker bending close. The Master of the Workhouse peering over him. The rest of the room in the enhanced dimness of the gas-jets and the fog.

A low murmur of voices. All heads bent over the work.

Dr. Grimbold again—beyond the circle of the lamplight.

"We don't want to distress you unnecessarily, Lady Levy. If you will just tell us what to look for—the—? Yes, yes, certainly—and—yes—stopped with gold? Yes—the lower jaw, the last but one on the right? Yes—no teeth missing—no—yes? What kind of a mole? Yes—just over the left breast? Oh, I beg your pardon, just under—yes—appendicitis?[6] Yes—a long one—yes—in the middle? Yes, I quite understand—a scar on the arm? Yes, I don't know if we shall be able to find that—yes—any little constitutional weakness that might—? Oh, yes—arthritis—yes—thank you, Lady Levy—that's very clear. Don't come unless I ask you to. Now, Wingate."

A pause. A murmur. "Pulled out? After death, you think—well,

---

[4] A command intended to cut short a response.

[5] An electric cord.

[6] An inflammation of the appendix. They were searching for the characteristic scar caused by the operation to remove the organ.

so do I. Where is Dr. Colegrove? You attended this man in the workhouse? Yes. Do you recollect—? No? You're quite certain about that? Yes—we mustn't make a mistake, you know. Yes, but there are reasons why Sir Julian can't be present; I'm asking you, Dr. Colegrove. Well, you're certain—that's all I want to know. Just bring the light closer, Mr. Wingate, if you please. These miserable shells let the damp in so quickly. Ah! what do you make of this? Yes—yes—well, that's rather unmistakable, isn't it? Who did the head? Oh, Freke—of course. I was going to say they did good work at St. Luke's. Beautiful, isn't it, Dr. Colegrove? A wonderful surgeon—I saw him when he was at Guy's.[7] Oh, no, gave it up years ago. Nothing like keeping your hand in. Ah—yes, undoubtedly that's it. Have you a towel handy, sir? Thank you. Over the head, if you please—I think we might have another here. Now, Lady Levy—I am going to ask you to look at a scar, and see if you recognize it. I'm sure you are going to help us by being very firm. Take your time—you won't see anything more than you absolutely must."

"Lucy, don't leave me."

"No, dear."

A space cleared at the table. The lamplight on the Duchess's white hair.

"Oh, yes—oh, yes! No, no—I couldn't be mistaken. There's that funny little kink in it. I've seen it hundreds of times. Oh, Lucy—Reuben!"

"Only a moment more, Lady Levy. The mole—"

"I—I think so—oh, yes, that is the very place."

"Yes. And the scar—was it three-cornered, just above the elbow?"

"Yes, oh, yes."

"Is this it?"

"Yes—yes—"

"I must ask you definitely, Lady Levy. Do you, from these three marks identify the body as that of your husband?"

---

[7] A noted teaching hospital founded in 1721 by Thomas Guy (1644-1724), funded with the proceeds from the fortune he made in the South Sea Bubble, a ballooning stock speculation that ended up causing financial ruin for many.

"Oh! I must, mustn't I? Nobody else could have them just the same in just those places? It is my husband. It is Reuben. Oh—"

"Thank you, Lady Levy. You have been very brave and very helpful."

"But—I don't understand yet. How did he come here? Who did this dreadful thing?"

"Hush, dear," said the Duchess, "the man is going to be punished."

"Oh, but—how cruel! Poor Reuben! Who could have wanted to hurt him? Can I see his face?"

"No, dear," said the Duchess. "That isn't possible. Come away—you mustn't distress the doctors and people."

"No—no—they've all been so kind. Oh, Lucy!"

'We'll go home, dear. You don't want us any more, Dr. Grimbold?"

'No, Duchess, thank you. We are very grateful to you and to Lady Levy for coming."

There was a pause, while the two women went out, Parker, collected and helpful, escorting them to their waiting car. Then Dr. Grimbold again:

"I think Lord Peter Wimsey ought to see—the correctness of his deductions—Lord Peter—very painful—you may wish to see—yes, I was uneasy at the inquest—yes—Lady Levy—remarkably clear evidence—yes—most shocking case—ah, here's Mr. Parker—you and Lord Peter Wimsey entirely justified—do I really understand—? Really? I can hardly believe it—so distinguished a man—as you say, when a great brain turns to crime—yes—look here! Marvellous work—marvellous—somewhat obscured by this time, of course—but the most beautiful sections[8]—here, you see, the left hemisphere—and here—through the corpus striatum[9]—here again—the very track of the damage done by the blow—wonderful—

---

[8] Cuts. He's admiring Sir Julian's ability to make incisions at the operating or dissection tables.

[9] A part of the brain consisting of the caudate nucleus and lentiform nucleus. The brain is subdivided into clusters of neurons called a nucleus. The caudate and lentiform nuclei are found deep in the brain. That Dr. Grimbold could see damage there from Sir Julian's killing blow indicates how strong it was.

guessed it—saw the effect of the blow as he struck it, you know—ah, I should like to see his brain, Mr. Parker—and to think that—heavens, Lord Peter, you don't know what a blow you have struck at the whole profession—the whole civilized world! Oh, my dear sir! Can you ask me? My lips are sealed of course—all our lips are sealed."

The way back through the burial ground. Fog again, and the squeal of wet gravel.

"Are your men ready, Charles?"

"They have gone. I sent them off when I saw Lady Levy to the car."

"Who is with them?"

"Sugg."

"Sugg?"

"Yes—poor devil. They've had him up on the mat at headquarters for bungling the case. All that evidence of Thipps's about the night club was corroborated, you know. That girl he gave the gin-and-bitters[10] to was caught, and came and identified him, and they decided their case wasn't good enough, and let Thipps and the Horrocks girl go. Then they told Sugg he had overstepped his duty and ought to have been more careful. So he ought, but he can't help being a fool. I was sorry for him. It may do him some good to be in at the death. After all, Peter, you and I had special advantages."

"Yes. Well, it doesn't matter. Whoever goes won't get there in time. Sugg's as good as another."

But Sugg—an experience rare in his career—was in time.

Parker and Lord Peter were at 110 Piccadilly. Lord Peter was playing Bach and Parker was reading Origen[11] when Sugg was announced.

"We've got our man, sir," said he.

---

[10] Bitters are an alcoholic flavoring used in cocktails. It is also an accurate description of its taste. One variety, Angostura bitters, is made from a tree bark found in South America. It can also be made from a variety of bitter herbs.
[11] Parker is a true theology student if he is reading Origen Adamantius (c.185-254), who promoted the spread of Christianity through extensive commentaries on many of the books in the Bible. His dedication led him to castrate himself so he could tutor women without suspicion.

"Good God!" said Peter. "Alive?"

"We were just in time, my lord. We rang the bell and marched straight up past his man to the library. He was sitting there doing some writing. When we came in, he made a grab for his hypodermic,[12] but we were too quick for him, my lord. We didn't mean to let him slip through our hands, having got so far. We searched him thoroughly and marched him off."

"He is actually in gaol, then?"

"Oh, yes—safe enough—with two warders to see he doesn't make away with himself."

"You surprise me, Inspector. Have a drink."

"Thank you, my lord. I may say that I'm very grateful to you— this case was turning out a pretty bad egg for me. If I was rude to your lordship—"

"Oh, it's all right, Inspector," said Lord Peter, hastily. "I don't see how you could possibly have worked it out. I had the good luck to know something about it from other sources."

"That's what Freke says." Already the great surgeon was a common criminal in the inspector's eyes—a mere surname. "He was writing a full confession when we got hold of him, addressed to your lordship. The police will have to have it, of course, but seeing it's written for you, I brought it along for you to see first. Here it is."

He handed Lord Peter a bulky document.

"Thanks," said Peter. "Like to hear it, Charles?"

"Rather."

Accordingly Lord Peter read it aloud.

---

[12] A needle with a plunger at one end of a tube, used for injections.

CHAPTER XIII

D EAR LORD PETER—WHEN I WAS a young man I used to play chess with an old friend of my father's. He was a very bad, and a very slow, player, and he could never see when a checkmate was inevitable, but insisted on playing every move out. I never had any patience with that kind of attitude, and I will freely admit now that the game is yours. I must either stay at home and be hanged or escape abroad and live in an idle and insecure obscurity. I prefer to acknowledge defeat.

If you have read my book on "Criminal Lunacy," you will remember that I wrote: "In the majority of cases, the criminal betrays himself by some abnormality attendant upon this pathological condition of the nervous tissues. His mental instability shows itself in various forms: an overweening vanity, leading him to brag of his achievement; a disproportionate sense of the importance of the offence, resulting from the hallucination of religion, and driving him to confession; egomania, producing the sense of horror or conviction of sin, and driving him to headlong flight without covering his tracks; a reckless confidence, resulting in the neglect of the most ordinary precautions, as in the case of Henry Wainwright, who left a boy in charge of the murdered woman's remains while he went to call a cab,[1] or on the other hand, a nervous distrust of

---

[1] In 1875, Wainwright was executed for killing and dismembering his mistress. Sayers might have drawn two names from the case. To explain his mistress' disappearance, Wainwright had spread the story that she had run off with an Edward Frieake. The victim's name, Harriet Lane, might have inspired the name

apperceptions in the past, causing him to revisit the scene of the crime to assure himself that all traces have been as safely removed as his own judgment knows them to be. I will not hesitate to assert that a perfectly sane man, not intimidated by religious or other delusions, could always render himself perfectly secure from detection, provided, that is, that the crime were sufficiently premeditated and that he were not pressed for time or thrown out in his calculations by purely fortuitous coincidence.

You know as well as I do, how far I have made this assertion good in practice. The two accidents which betrayed me, I could not by any possibility have foreseen. The first was the chance recognition of Levy by the girl in the Battersea Park Road, which suggested a connection between the two problems. The second was that Thipps should have arranged to go down to Denver on the Tuesday morning, thus enabling your mother to get word of the matter through to you before the body was removed by the police and to suggest a motive for the murder out of what she knew of my previous personal history. If I had been able to destroy these two accidentally forged links of circumstance, I will venture to say that you would never have so much as suspected me, still less obtained sufficient evidence to convict.

Of all human emotions, except perhaps those of hunger and fear, the sexual appetite produces the most violent and, under some circumstances, the most persistent reactions; I think, however, I am right in saying that at the time when I wrote my book, my original sensual impulse to kill Sir Reuben Levy had already become profoundly modified by my habits of thought. To the animal lust to slay and the primitive human desire for revenge, there was added the rational intention of substantiating my own theories for the satisfaction of myself and the world. If all had turned out as I had planned, I should have deposited a sealed account of my experiment with the Bank of England,[2] instructing my executors to publish it after my death. Now that accident has spoiled the completeness of my demonstration, I entrust the account to you,

---

of Lord Peter's future wife, Harriet Vane. See the essay "Henry Wainwright: Hard To Find Good Help."

[2] The nation's central bank, established in 1694.

whom it cannot fail to interest, with the request that you will make it known among scientific men, in justice to my professional reputation.

The really essential factors of success in any undertaking are money and opportunity, and as a rule, the man who can make the first can make the second. During my early career, though I was fairly well-off, I had not absolute command of circumstance. Accordingly I devoted myself to my profession, and contented myself with keeping up a friendly connection with Reuben Levy and his family. This enabled me to remain in touch with his fortunes and interests, so that, when the moment for action should arrive, I might know what weapons to use.

Meanwhile, I carefully studied criminology in fiction and fact—my work on "Criminal Lunacy" was a side-product of this activity—and saw how, in every murder, the real crux of the problem was the disposal of the body. As a doctor, the means of death were always ready to my hand, and I was not likely to make any error in that connection. Nor was I likely to betray myself on account of any illusory sense of wrongdoing. The sole difficulty would be that of destroying all connection between my personality and that of the corpse. You will remember that Michael Finsbury, in Stevenson's entertaining romance,[3] observes: "What hangs people is the unfortunate circumstance of guilt." It became clear to me that the mere leaving about of a superfluous corpse could convict nobody, provided that nobody was guilty in connection with that particular corpse. Thus the idea of substituting the one body for the other was early arrived at, though it was not till I obtained the practical direction of St. Luke's Hospital that I found myself perfectly unfettered in the choice and handling of dead bodies. From this period on, I kept a careful watch on all the material brought in for dissection.

---

[3] A reference to "The Wrong Box," a novel Robert Louis Stevenson (1850-1894) co-wrote with his stepson, Lloyd Osbourne, about two brothers who are the last surviving members of a tontine. A tontine is an agreement by a group of people to pool their money in an investment, with each member receiving a share of the annual dividend. As investors die, the dividend is reallocated among the survivors, with the sole survivor receiving the entire amount.

My opportunity did not present itself until the week before Sir Reuben's disappearance, when the medical officer at the Chelsea workhouse sent word to me that an unknown vagrant had been injured that morning by the fall of a piece of scaffolding, and was exhibiting some very interesting nervous and cerebral reactions. I went round and saw the case, and was immediately struck by the man's strong superficial resemblance to Sir Reuben. He had been heavily struck on the back of the neck, dislocating the fourth and fifth cervical vertebræ[4] and heavily bruising the spinal cord. It seemed highly unlikely that he could ever recover, either mentally or physically, and in any case there appeared to me to be no object in indefinitely prolonging so unprofitable an existence. He had obviously been able to support life until recently, as he was fairly well nourished, but the state of his feet and clothing showed that he was unemployed, and under present conditions he was likely to remain so. I decided that he would suit my purpose very well, and immediately put in train certain transactions in the City which I had already sketched out in my own mind. In the meantime, the reactions mentioned by the workhouse doctor were interesting, and I made careful studies of them, and arranged for the delivery of the body to the hospital when I should have completed my preparations.

On the Thursday and Friday of that week I made private arrangements with various brokers to buy the stock of certain Peruvian oil-fields, which had gone down almost to waste-paper. This part of my experiment did not cost me very much, but I contrived to arouse considerable curiosity, and even a mild excitement. At this point I was of course careful not to let my name appear. The incidence of Saturday and Sunday gave me some anxiety lest my man should after all die before I was ready for him, but by the use of saline injections I contrived to keep him alive and, late on Sunday night, he even manifested disquieting symptoms of at any rate a partial recovery.

On Monday morning the market in Peruvians opened briskly. Rumours had evidently got about that somebody knew something, and this day I was not the only buyer in the market. I bought a

---

[4] The top section of the spinal cord that connects to the skull. The fourth and fifth vertebrae are found in the neck.

couple of hundred more shares in my own name, and left the matter to take care of itself. At lunch time I made my arrangements to run into Levy accidentally at the corner of the Mansion House.[5] He expressed (as I expected) his surprise at seeing me in that part of London. I simulated some embarrassment and suggested that we should lunch together. I dragged him to a place a bit off the usual beat, and there ordered a good wine and drank of it as much as he might suppose sufficient to induce a confidential mood. I asked him how things were going on 'Change. He said, "Oh, all right," but appeared a little doubtful, and asked me whether I did anything in that way. I said I had a little flutter occasionally, and that, as a matter of fact, I'd been put on to rather a good thing. I glanced round apprehensively at this point, and shifted my chair nearer to his.

"I suppose you don't know anything about Peruvian Oil, do you?" he said.

I started and looked round again, and leaning across to him, said, dropping my voice:

"Well, I do, as a matter of fact, but I don't want it to get about. I stand to make a good bit on it."

"But I thought the thing was hollow," he said; "it hasn't paid a dividend[6] for umpteen years."

"No," I said, "it hasn't, but it's going to. I've got inside information." He looked a bit unconvinced, and I emptied off my glass, and edged right up to his ear.

"Look here," I said, "I'm not giving this away to everyone, but I don't mind doing you and Christine a good turn. You know, I've always kept a soft place in my heart for her, ever since the old days. You got in ahead of me that time, and now it's up to me to heap coals of fire on you both."[7]

I was a little excited by this time, and he thought I was drunk.

"It's very kind of you, old man," he said, "but I'm a cautious bird, you know, always was. I'd like a bit of proof."

And he shrugged up his shoulders and looked like a

---

[5] The Lord Mayor of London's official home, located in the financial district.
[6] A share of the profits, divided among the shareholders.
[7] From Romans 12:20: "Therefore if thine enemy hunger, feed him; if he thirst, give him drink: for in so doing thou shalt heap coals of fire on his head."

pawnbroker.[8]

"I'll give it to you," I said, "but it isn't safe here. Come round to my place to-night after dinner, and I'll show you the report."

"How d'you get hold of it?" said he.

"I'll tell you to-night," said I. "Come round after dinner—any time after nine, say."

"To Harley Street?" he asked, and I saw that he meant coming.

"No," I said, "to Battersea—Prince of Wales Road; I've got some work to do at the hospital. And look here," I said, "don't you let on to a soul that you're coming. I bought a couple of hundred shares to-day, in my own name, and people are sure to get wind of it. If we're known to be about together, someone'll twig something. In fact, it's anything but safe talking about it in this place."

"All right," he said, "I won't say a word to anybody. I'll turn up about nine o'clock. You're sure it's a sound thing?"

"It can't go wrong," I assured him. And I meant it.

We parted after that, and I went round to the workhouse. My man had died at about eleven o'clock. I had seen him just after breakfast, and was not surprised. I completed the usual formalities with the workhouse authorities, and arranged for his delivery at the hospital about seven o'clock.

In the afternoon, as it was not one of my days to be in Harley Street, I looked up an old friend who lives close to Hyde Park, and found that he was just off to Brighton[9] on some business or other. I had tea with him, and saw him off by the 5:35 from Victoria. On issuing from the barrier it occurred to me to purchase an evening paper, and I thoughtlessly turned my steps to the bookstall. The usual crowds were rushing to catch suburban trains home, and on moving away I found myself involved in a contrary stream of travellers coming up out of the Underground, or bolting from all sides for the 5:45 to Battersea Park and Wandsworth Common.[10] I

---

[8] Sir Julian couldn't help but indulge in a little anti-Semitism by portraying Sir Reuben in an occupation stereotypically associated with Jews.

[9] A coastal town south of London.

[10] An area in the Borough of Wandsworth south of the Thames and west of the Battersea area. A common is an open area traditionally available for use by everyone in the village for hunting, gathering firewood or walking. In England,

disengaged myself after some buffeting and went home in a taxi; and it was not till I was safely seated there that I discovered somebody's gold-rimmed pince-nez involved in the astrakhan collar[11] of my overcoat. The time from 6:15 to seven I spent concocting something to look like a bogus report for Sir Reuben.

At seven I went through to the hospital, and found the workhouse van just delivering my subject at the side door. I had him taken straight up to the theatre, and told the attendant, William Watts, that I intended to work there that night. I told him I would prepare the body myself—the injection of a preservative would have been a most regrettable complication. I sent him about his business, and then went home and had dinner. I told my man that I should be working in the hospital that evening, and that he could go to bed at 10:30 as usual, as I could not tell whether I should be late or not. He is used to my erratic ways. I only keep two servants in the Battersea house—the man-servant and his wife, who cooks for me. The rougher domestic work is done by a charwoman, who sleeps out. The servants' bedroom is at the top of the house, overlooking Prince of Wales Road.

As soon as I had dined I established myself in the hall with some papers. My man had cleared dinner by a quarter past eight, and I told him to give me the siphon and tantalus;[12] and sent him downstairs. Levy rang the bell at twenty minutes past nine, and I opened the door to him myself. My man appeared at the other end of the hall, but I called to him that it was all right, and he went away. Levy wore an overcoat with evening dress and carried an umbrella. "Why, how wet you are!" I said. "How did you come?" "By 'bus," he said, "and the fool of a conductor forgot to put me down at the end of the road. It's pouring cats and dogs and pitch-

---

many commons were converted to private ownership, with only the name left behind.

[11] A wide collar in which the wool lining is turned out. Astrakhan is a port on Russia's Volga River where lambs with loose curls, ideal for coats, were bred.

[12] A siphon is a pressurized bottle used to create carbonated water. A tantalus is a carrying case for bottles. The case could be designed so that the handle locked down the tops of the bottles, making them secure for transporting and also impervious to tampering by servants tempted to sneak a tot and fill it back up with water.

dark—I couldn't see where I was." I was glad he hadn't taken a taxi, but I had rather reckoned on his not doing so. "Your little economies will be the death of you one of these days," I said. I was right there, but I hadn't reckoned on their being the death of me as well. I say again, I could not have foreseen it.

I sat him down by the fire, and gave him a whisky. He was in high spirits about some deal in Argentines he was bringing off the next day. We talked money for about a quarter of an hour and then he said:

"Well, how about this Peruvian mare's-nest[13] of yours?"

"It's no mare's-nest," I said; "come and have a look at it."

I took him upstairs into the library, and switched on the centre light and the reading lamp on the writing table. I gave him a chair at the table with his back to the fire, and fetched the papers I had been faking, out of the safe. He took them, and began to read them, poking over them in his short-sighted way, while I mended the fire. As soon as I saw his head in a favourable position I struck him heavily with the poker, just over the fourth cervical. It was delicate work calculating the exact force necessary to kill him without breaking the skin, but my professional experience was useful to me. He gave one loud gasp, and tumbled forward on to the table quite noiselessly. I put the poker back, and examined him. His neck was broken, and he was quite dead. I carried him into my bedroom and undressed him. It was about ten minutes to ten when I had finished. I put him away under my bed, which had been turned down for the night, and cleared up the papers in the library. Then I went downstairs, took Levy's umbrella, and let myself out at the hall door, shouting "Good-night" loudly enough to be heard in the basement if the servants should be listening. I walked briskly away down the street, went in by the hospital side door, and returned to the house noiselessly by way of the private passage. It would have been awkward if anybody had seen me then, but I leaned over the back stairs and heard the cook and her husband still talking in the kitchen. I slipped back into the hall, replaced the umbrella in the stand, cleared up my papers there, went up into the library and rang

---

[13] An illusion. The earliest phrase found is "to find a mare's nest," suggested by the fact that mares — female horses — do not make nests.

the bell. When the man appeared I told him to lock up everything except the private door to the hospital. I waited in the library until he had done so, and about 10:30 I heard both servants go up to bed. I waited a quarter of an hour longer and then went through to the dissecting-room. I wheeled one of the stretcher-tables through the passage to the house door, and then went to fetch Levy. It was a nuisance having to get him downstairs, but I had not liked to make away with him in any of the ground-floor rooms, in case my servant should take a fancy to poke his head in during the few minutes that I was out of the house, or while locking up. Besides, that was a flea-bite to what I should have to do later. I put Levy on the table, wheeled him across to the hospital and substituted him for my interesting pauper. I was sorry to have to abandon the idea of getting a look at the latter's brain, but I could not afford to incur suspicion. It was still rather early, so I knocked down a few minutes getting Levy ready for dissection. Then I put my pauper on the table and trundled him over to the house. It was now five past eleven, and I thought I might conclude that the servants were in bed. I carried the body into my bedroom. He was rather heavy, but less so than Levy, and my Alpine experience had taught me how to handle bodies. It is as much a matter of knack as of strength, and I am, in any case, a powerful man for my height. I put the body into the bed—not that I expected anyone to look in during my absence, but if they should they might just as well see me apparently asleep in bed. I drew the clothes a little over his head, stripped, and put on Levy's clothes, which were fortunately a little big for me everywhere, not forgetting to take his spectacles, watch and other oddments. At a little before half past eleven I was in the road looking for a cab. People were just beginning to come home from the theatre, and I easily secured one at the corner of Prince of Wales Road. I told the man to drive me to Hyde Park Corner. There I got out, tipped him well, and asked him to pick me up again at the same place in an hour's time. He assented with an understanding grin, and I walked on up Park Lane. I had my own clothes with me in a suitcase, and carried my own overcoat and Levy's umbrella. When I got to No. 9 there were lights in some of the top windows. I was very nearly too early, owing to the old man's having sent the servants to the theatre. I waited about for a few minutes, and heard it strike the quarter past midnight. The lights were extinguished shortly after, and I let myself in with Levy's key.

It had been my original intention, when I thought over this plan of murder, to let Levy disappear from the study or the dining-room, leaving only a heap of clothes on the hearth-rug. The accident of my having been able to secure Lady Levy's absence from London, however, made possible a solution more misleading, though less pleasantly fantastic. I turned on the hall light, hung up Levy's wet overcoat and placed his umbrella in the stand. I walked up noisily and heavily to the bedroom and turned off the light by the duplicate switch on the landing. I knew the house well enough, of course. There was no chance of my running into the man-servant. Old Levy was a simple old man, who liked doing things for himself. He gave his valet little work, and never required any attendance at night. In the bedroom I took off Levy's gloves and put on a surgical pair, so as to leave no telltale finger-prints. As I wished to convey the impression that Levy had gone to bed in the usual way, I simply went to bed. The surest and simplest method of making a thing appear to have been done is to do it. A bed that has been rumpled about with one's hands, for instance, never looks like a bed that has been slept in. I dared not use Levy's brush, of course, as my hair is not of his colour, but I did everything else. I supposed that a thoughtful old man like Levy would put his boots handy for his valet, and I ought to have deduced that he would fold up his clothes. That was a mistake, but not an important one. Remembering that well-thought-out little work of Mr. Bentley's,[14] I had examined Levy's mouth for false teeth, but he had none. I did not forget, however, to wet his toothbrush.

At one o'clock I got up and dressed in my own clothes by the light of my own pocket torch. I dared not turn on the bedroom lights, as there were light blinds to the windows. I put on my own boots and an old pair of galoshes outside the door. There was a thick Turkey carpet on the stairs and hall-floor, and I was not

---

[14] A reference to "Trent's Last Case" by Edmund Clerihew Bentley (1875-1956), which had an enormous effect on the development of Lord Peter. Sayers borrowed Philip Trent's mannerisms as well as the idea of a detective-hero who exists as a personality, not simply a cardboard-thin cipher designed to move along the plot. Sayers admitted in a letter to Bentley that "I am always ashamed to admit how much my poor Peter owes to Trent, besides his habit of quotation."

afraid of leaving marks. I hesitated whether to chance the banging of the front door, but decided it would be safer to take the latchkey. (It is now in the Thames. I dropped it over Battersea Bridge the next day.) I slipped quietly down, and listened for a few minutes with my ear to the letter-box. I heard a constable tramp past. As soon as his steps had died away in the distance I stepped out, and pulled the door gingerly to. It closed almost soundlessly, and I walked away to pick up my cab. I had an overcoat of much the same pattern as Levy's, and had taken the precaution to pack an opera hat in my suitcase. I hoped the man would not notice that I had no umbrella this time. Fortunately the rain had diminished for the moment to a sort of drizzle, and if he noticed anything he made no observation. I told him to stop at 50 Overstrand Mansions,[15] and I paid him off there, and stood under the porch till he had driven away. Then I hurried round to my own side door and let myself in. It was about a quarter to two, and the harder part of my task still lay before me.

My first step was so to alter the appearance of my subject as to eliminate any immediate suggestion either of Levy or of the workhouse vagrant. A fairly superficial alteration was all I considered necessary, since there was not likely to be any hue-and-cry after the pauper. He was fairly accounted for, and his deputy was at hand to represent him. Nor, if Levy was after all traced to my house, would it be difficult to show that the body in evidence was, as a matter of fact, not his. A clean shave and a little hair-oiling and manicuring seemed sufficient to suggest a distinct personality for my silent accomplice. His hands had been well washed in hospital, and though calloused, were not grimy. I was not able to do the work as thoroughly as I should have liked, because time was getting on. I was not sure how long it would take me to dispose of him, and, moreover, I feared the onset of rigor mortis,[16] which would make my task more difficult. When I had him barbered to my satisfaction, I fetched a strong sheet and a couple of wide roller bandages, and

---

[15] The name of a block of apartments on Prince of Wales Drive, across the street from Battersea Park.

[16] The stiffening of the body after death. A rigid body would be tougher to move, particularly if you plan on conveying it across roofs and into a bathtub.

fastened him up carefully, padding him with cotton wool wherever the bandages might chafe or leave a bruise.

Now came the really ticklish part of the business. I had already decided in my own mind that the only way of conveying him from the house was by the roof. To go through the garden at the back in this soft wet weather was to leave a ruinous trail behind us. To carry a dead man down a suburban street in the middle of the night seemed outside the range of practical politics. On the roof, on the other hand, the rain, which would have betrayed me on the ground, would stand my friend.

To reach the roof, it was necessary to carry my burden to the top of the house, past my servants' room, and hoist him out through the trapdoor in the box-room[17] roof. Had it merely been a question of going quietly up there myself, I should have had no fear of waking the servants, but to do so burdened by a heavy body was more difficult. It would be possible, provided that the man and his wife were soundly asleep, but if not, the lumbering tread on the narrow stair and the noise of opening the trapdoor would be only too plainly audible. I tiptoed delicately up the stair and listened at their door. To my disgust I heard the man give a grunt and mutter something as he moved in his bed.

I looked at my watch. My preparations had taken nearly an hour, first and last, and I dared not be too late on the roof. I determined to take a bold step and, as it were, bluff out an alibi. I went without precaution against noise into the bathroom, turned on the hot and cold water taps to the full and pulled out the plug.

My household has often had occasion to complain of my habit of using the bath at irregular night hours. Not only does the rush of water into the cistern[18] disturb any sleepers on the Prince of Wales Road side of the house, but my cistern is afflicted with peculiarly loud gurglings and thumpings, while frequently the pipes emit a loud groaning sound. To my delight, on this particular occasion, the cistern was in excellent form, honking, whistling and booming like a railway terminus. I gave the noise five minutes' start, and when I

---

[17] A box room is used to store boxes, trunks and other items. Roof traps are hatches that allow access to the roof from inside the house.
[18] A small tank used to supply water for drinking and bathing.

calculated that the sleepers would have finished cursing me and put their heads under the clothes to shut out the din, I reduced the flow of water to a small stream and left the bathroom, taking good care to leave the light burning and lock the door after me. Then I picked up my pauper[19] and carried him upstairs as lightly as possible.

The box-room is a small attic on the side of the landing opposite to the servants' bedroom and the cistern-room. It has a trapdoor, reached by a short, wooden ladder. I set this up, hoisted up my pauper and climbed up after him. The water was still racing into the cistern, which was making a noise as though it were trying to digest an iron chain, and with the reduced flow in the bathroom the groaning of the pipes had risen almost to a hoot. I was not afraid of anybody hearing other noises. I pulled the ladder through on to the roof after me.

Between my house and the last house in Queen Caroline Mansions there is a space of only a few feet. Indeed, when the Mansions were put up, I believe there was some trouble about ancient lights, but I suppose the parties compromised somehow. Anyhow, my seven-foot ladder reached well across. I tied the body firmly to the ladder, and pushed it over till the far end was resting on the parapet of the opposite house. Then I took a short run across the cistern-room and the box-room roof, and landed easily on the other side, the parapet being happily both low and narrow.

The rest was simple. I carried my pauper along the flat roofs, intending to leave him, like the hunchback in the story, on someone's staircase or down a chimney. I had got about half way along when I suddenly thought, "Why, this must be about little Thipps's place," and I remembered his silly face, and his silly chatter about vivisection. It occurred to me pleasantly how delightful it would be to deposit my parcel with him and see what he made of it. I lay down and peered over the parapet at the back. It was pitch-dark and pouring with rain again by this time, and I risked using my torch. That was the only incautious thing I did, and the odds against being seen from the houses opposite were long enough. One second's flash showed me what I had hardly

[19] Poor.

dared to hope—an open window just below me.

I knew those flats well enough to be sure it was either the bathroom or the kitchen. I made a noose in a third bandage that I had brought with me, and made it fast under the arms of the corpse. I twisted it into a double rope, and secured the end to the iron stanchion of a chimney-stack. Then I dangled our friend over. I went down after him myself with the aid of a drain-pipe and was soon hauling him in by Thipps's bathroom window.

By that time I had got a little conceited with myself, and spared a few minutes to lay him out prettily and make him shipshape. A sudden inspiration suggested that I should give him the pair of pince-nez which I had happened to pick up at Victoria. I came across them in my pocket while I was looking for a penknife to loosen a knot, and I saw what distinction they would lend his appearance, besides making it more misleading. I fixed them on him, effaced all traces of my presence as far as possible, and departed as I had come, going easily up between the drain-pipe and the rope.

I walked quietly back, re-crossed my crevasse and carried in my ladder and sheet. My discreet accomplice greeted me with a reassuring gurgle and thump. I didn't make a sound on the stairs. Seeing that I had now been having a bath for about three-quarters of an hour, I turned the water off, and enabled my deserving domestics to get a little sleep. I also felt it was time I had a little myself.

First, however, I had to go over to the hospital and make all safe there. I took off Levy's head, and started to open up the face. In twenty minutes his own wife could not have recognized him. I returned, leaving my wet galoshes[20] and mackintosh[21] by the garden door. My trousers I dried by the gas stove in my bedroom, and brushed away all traces of mud and brick-dust. My pauper's beard I burned in the library.

I got a good two hours' sleep from five to seven, when my man called me as usual. I apologized for having kept the water running so long and so late, and added that I thought I would have the

---

[20] Rubber boots slipped over shoes to keep them from getting wet.

[21] A raincoat made from rubberized fabric, invented by Charles Macintosh in 1823.

cistern seen to.

I was interested to note that I was rather extra hungry at breakfast, showing that my night's work had caused a certain wear-and-tear of tissue. I went over afterwards to continue my dissection. During the morning a peculiarly thickheaded police inspector came to inquire whether a body had escaped from the hospital. I had him brought to me where I was, and had the pleasure of showing him the work I was doing on Sir Reuben Levy's head. Afterwards I went round with him to Thipps's and was able to satisfy myself that my pauper looked very convincing.

As soon as the Stock Exchange opened I telephoned my various brokers, and by exercising a little care, was able to sell out the greater part of my Peruvian stock on a rising market. Towards the end of the day, however, buyers became rather unsettled as a result of Levy's death, and in the end I did not make more than a few hundreds by the transaction.

Trusting I have now made clear to you any point which you may have found obscure, and with congratulations on the good fortune and perspicacity which have enabled you to defeat me, I remain, with kind remembrances to your mother,

Yours very truly,
JULIAN FREKE.

Post-Scriptum:[22] My will is made, leaving my money to St. Luke's Hospital, and bequeathing my body to the same institution for dissection. I feel sure that my brain will be of interest to the scientific world. As I shall die by my own hand, I imagine that there may be a little difficulty about this. Will you do me the favour, if you can, of seeing the persons concerned in the inquest, and obtaining that the brain is not damaged by an unskillful practitioner at the post-mortem, and that the body is disposed of according to my wish?

By the way, it may be of interest to you to know that I appreciated your motive in calling this afternoon. It conveyed a

---

[22] Indicating an addition to a letter, from the Latin for written after. Frequently shortened to P.S.

warning, and I am acting upon it. In spite of the disastrous consequences to myself, I was pleased to realize that you had not underestimated my nerve and intelligence, and refused the injection. Had you submitted to it, you would, of course, never have reached home alive. No trace would have been left in your body of the injection, which consisted of a harmless preparation of strychnine,[23] mixed with an almost unknown poison, for which there is at present no recognized test, a concentrated solution of sn—

At this point the manuscript broke off.

"Well, that's all clear enough," said Parker.

"Isn't it queer?" said Lord Peter. "All that coolness, all those brains—and then he couldn't resist writing a confession to show how clever he was, even to keep his head out of the noose."

"And a very good thing for us," said Inspector Sugg, "but Lord bless you, sir, these criminals are all alike."

"Freke's epitaph,"[24] said Parker, when the Inspector had departed. "What next, Peter?"

"I shall now give a dinner party," said Lord Peter, "to Mr. John P. Milligan and his secretary and to Messrs. Crimplesham and Wicks. I feel they deserve it for not having murdered Levy."

"Well, don't forget the Thippses," said Mr. Parker.

"On no account," said Lord Peter, "would I deprive myself of the pleasure of Mrs. Thipps's company. Bunter!"

"My lord?"

"The Napoleon brandy."

THE END

---

[23] A fast-acting poison that causes muscular convulsions and death through asphyxia or exhaustion. Sayers' "almost unknown poison" doesn't exist.

[24] A message found on a gravestone.

THE WORLD
OF
WHOSE BODY?

"Whose Body?" cover, Avon paperback, 1948.

Argentine Banks

Argentina plays a large but shadowy role in "Whose Body?" Since 1900, the South American country loomed large in the imagination and bank books of Britain and Europe. Investors were making money helping the country to industrialize, the tango was sweeping the dance halls, and the phrase "as rich as an Argentine" became common.

The reason why leads us into the dismal science of economics. At the risk of putting everyone to sleep, I'll cover the highlights to show that the world simply didn't wake up one day and decide to fall in love with Argentina.

What happened is that Argentina set itself up to attract overseas investments. It succeeded, and as the country developed (and helped the investors turn a profit), it drew more investments. As the country got richer, so did the investors.

Then, catastrophe struck, but we'll get to that in a moment. In the meantime, here's the nickel tour of Argentina history during what is commonly called the "Belle Époque" period, which lasted from 1900 to 1914, when the outbreak of war in Europe changed the game.

Until 1900, the Argentine economy was in the doldrums. The country had great natural resources, but not enough money to develop (and profit) from them. The first railroad was built in 1857, and as the lines grew, more areas were able to ship their produce – beef, wool and grain especially – to the coast for export.

Then, in 1899, the country joined the gold standard, pegging the value of its currency to the precious metal (2.27 paper pesos per gold peso if you must know). It also established two institutions to handle gold redemption and currency stability, the

Caja de Conversión (the currency board) and the Banco de la Nación. The CC was responsible for maintaining the gold standard and convertibility of currency externally, while the Banco engaged in normal commercial banking operations as the state's bank. Most importantly, the country made sure that the currency board was preserved from political interference.

This is an important point. Freed from politics and linked to a stable precious metal made the country attractive to investors. Investment money started coming in. More rail lines were built, more goods were exported. The country also underwent an immigration boom, especially from Spain and Italy. By 1914, nearly 30 percent of Argentina came from somewhere else. Even today, 60 percent of Argentina's population – about 25 million – can trace their ancestry to Spain or Italy.

Argentina grew wealthy. Between 1900 and 1912, it doubled the number of railroad miles to more than 20,000. It also managed to hold a significant chuck of the world's gold supply: 3.7 percent of the world's monetary gold and 5.7 percent of the gold held in central banks and treasuries. The largest Argentine companies, the railroads, were listed on the London Stock Exchange. The investments in the railroads helped finance the country's development, particularly the port city of Buenos Aires and most industries. Argentina, in turn, was given access to capital at low interest rates.

Per capital income rose to astonishing heights: 50 percent higher than Italy, five times higher in neighboring Brazil. Argentina went on a building spree, and it used European architecture as its model. Argentines, as flush with money as the Japanese were in the 1980s, went on a buying spree in Europe, bringing with them the exotic, sensual dance, the tango.

Then World War I upended the table. Investors cashed in, selling their securities around the world. Nations went on a borrowing binge to pay for the war. They issued more money than they could cover by their gold reserves. They cut loose their currencies from stable gold, letting their values rise and fall, and Argentina had to follow. Trade fell off.

As a result, businesses in Argentina starting going bankrupt. Banks lost between 20 percent and 45 percent of their deposits (by comparison, during the worst of the Great Depression in the U.S., bank deposits fell by 39.5 percent). Their stock prices collapsed dramatically. For example, the Banco de Galicia dropped from a high of 160 in 1911 to 48 three years later.

Argentina's Belle Époque era was over.

Detail from "The Terrace Café, Mar del Plata, Argentina"
by Eugenio Alvarez Dumont, 1912.

ADOLF BECK

SEEING IS NOT BELIEVING

It sounds like the beginning of an Alfred Hitchcock movie. A man on the street is accosted by a woman he has never seen before and accused of stealing her jewelry. He summons a policeman, only to find himself arrested and put on trial.

But instead of the Cary Grant fleeing the police and working to clear his name, this story is about Adolf Beck, who suffered a more terrifying and tragic fate than anything the master of suspense dreamed up.

On a November day in 1895, an unmarried language teacher walking down Victoria Street meets a nicely dressed man with smooth, aristocratic manners. He tips his hat and addresses her as Lady Everton. Ottilie

Adolf Beck, top, and Wilhelm Meyer.

Meissonnier corrects him, and as they chat she picks up hints that he is very rich and very well connected. He is a cousin of Lord Salisbury, the prime minister. He owns an estate in Lincolnshire and a yacht. Although she isn't Lady Everton, the man is clearly attracted to Ottilie and she, in return, is certainly drawn to him.

The next day, they meet for a cup of tea. Over the crumpets, he invites her to the Riviera on his yacht. The subject of her wardrobe is raised, and he writes her a check for £40 to buy new clothes. When he offers to give her jewelry, Ottilie is so carried away by her good fortune – or at least the prospect of a good time – that she hands over two wrist watches and her rings so he could properly size her gifts. He also borrows £2.

Her dream of seeing the French coast from the desk of a rich man's yacht lasts until that afternoon, when a bank clerk informs her that the check is worthless.

Ottilie fumes and regrets, until fate seemingly took a hand. Several weeks later, walking again down Victoria Street – and the novelist in me wonders if she did so hoping to find His Lordship – she spies Lord Salisbury's "cousin." She confronts him, demanding her jewelry back. Startled, he denies ever meeting the woman and calls a policeman to pry her off him.

For Adolf Beck, this is where his life took a sudden turn for the worst. Because the police at Scotland Yard have been wanting to get their hands on Lord Salisbury's mythical cousin. For some time, a man known as John Smith had been pulling this scam under the names Lord Wilton and Lord Willoughby. They order an identity parade, and Beck is put in line with men who don't look at all like him. Not surprisingly, Ottilie picks him out. His handwriting is compared with Smith's, and the expert announced that the samples didn't match. The police ignored that on the assumption that the criminal Beck would know to disguise his handwriting.

The absurdities pile up at Beck's trial. A policeman identified Beck as Smith based on their last meeting 20 years ago. The presiding judge, who had sentenced Smith then, said he recognized Beck as well. Beck is convicted and sentenced to 7 years in prison. He is even given Smith's prison number.

As Beck served his sentence, his solicitor petitioned the Home Office to re-examine the case. He pointed to a report from the prison doctor saying that Beck wasn't circumcised. Smith was. In the face of a magically regenerating foreskin, the Home Office concluded that Beck was not Smith, but not that he had been subjected to an unfair trial. They did, however, give him his own prison number.

Meanwhile, a Daily Mail journalist, George R. Sims, who had known Beck since 1885, took up the case. His articles swayed public opinion, but it was not enough. Beck was paroled after five years for good behavior in 1901, but in the eyes of the law, he was a criminal. The best he could do was attempt to resume a normal life.

Until his nightmare returned. Three years later, Paulina Scott, a servant, told police that a grey-haired distinguished-looking man had met her on the street, flattered her, and stolen her jewelry. The police inspector remembered the Beck case and took her to a restaurant that he frequented. Scott could not say if Beck was the man.

The inspector set up a trap. As Beck left his flat, Scott accosted him, saying he was the thief. He denied it. She said an officer was waiting to arrest him. Beck fled. To the police, this was the proof they needed, and he was arrested.

Another trial, and this time five women testified against him, and he was found guilty. But this time, the judge had some doubts about the case. He delayed sentencing.

Ten days later, in a coincidence only a novelist could come up with, the real John Smith was arrested while trying to pawn several women's rings. He was Wilhelm Meyer, a Viennese doctor who had fallen on hard times. Many of the women who had identified Beck on the stand agreed that it was actually Meyer who had sweet-talked them.

Looking at the police photographs, it's easy to see why they could have been mistaken. Although there are differences between the two men – Meyer looks heavier – both were close enough otherwise to be brothers.

After an investigation, the Home Office was criticized for not reopening the case even after it found that Beck and Smith were not the same man. The judge in the first trial was also found at fault for his conduct. Several reforms were instituted, including the establishment of the Court of Criminal Appeal, charged specifically with ruling on the facts on the case, and not just how the law was applied .

Beck was given a pardon by the King Edward VII and £5,000 in compensation, but it wasn't enough. He spent it all and died in poverty in 1909.

COMMERCIAL CODES

SECRECY ON THE CHEAP

When business tycoon John P. Milligan dictated coded cables to his secretary in Chapter 4, he was using cutting-edge technology that united the British Empire. The first successful transatlantic telegraph cable was laid down in 1865, and, by 1870, another cable succeeded in reaching India. Design, construction and installation of the cable cost enormous sums of money, and Britain had the entrepreneurs with the capital and the will to see the project through. This, in turn, gave the British government enormous advantages in transmitting intelligence and information to its far-flung territories.

The price of a telegram was determined by the number of words sent, usually with a flat fee for the first 10 or 50 words. Customers were advised to save money by omitting needless words, truncating addresses and never using punctuation (which counted as a word). Businesses used codes, either developed in-house or bought to not only save money, but keep messages secret from the telegraph operators.

One book, "Unicode," published in 1889, lists detailed codes under a variety of subjects that truncated as much as a dozen words into one:

* Appointments: "Wish to see you particularly. Shall be here until –" (Afforem)

* Births: "Confined yesterday, twins, one alive, a boy, mother well" (Animor)

* Cheques: "Cheque returned unpaid, send cash by return of post" (Argyritis)

* Deaths: "Baby died today, particulars by letter" (Capedo)

* Dining: Will dine with you on Monday (Colossus); Will dine

with you on Tuesday (Columba); Will dine with you on
Wednesday (Colurnus); Will dine with you on Thursday
(Coluthea); Will dine with you on Friday (Comatus); Will dine
with you on Saturday (Comicus); Will dine with you on Sunday
(Comitium).

* Health: Amputation is considered necessary (Dionysia); Has
changed for the worse, but doctor gives hope (Dipsas); Operation
has been performed successfully (Draucus); Telegraph health of
yourself, am very anxious (Femella).

* Hotels: "Reserve one single bedroom, one double bedroom,
one double-bedded room, and a sitting-room, shall arrive on – "
(Folium)

* Marriages: "Marriage postponed in consequence of – "
(Natalis)

* Military: "Furlough to all officers on leave has been
cancelled, and they are ordered to rejoin at once" (Nossem)

* Money: No money, send at once £250. (Obfero).

* Racing: "Lay the odds to £5,000 against – " (Plumbo)

* Railway traveling: "Leaving by train arriving at London
Bridge at – " (Secretio)

* Train: Have missed train, impossible to be with you to-night
(Scirroma); Leaving by train arriving at Charing Cross Station at –
(Scytala); Leaving by train arriving at St. Pancras at – (Sedecula);
Leaving by train, send carriage to meet me at – (Segrego).

* Unicode: To decipher this message refer to the Unicode
(Unicode).

UNICODE USERS.

The following is a List of important firms and establishments to whom messages in
the "Unicode" may be sent by any persons at any time without necessity for
previous arrangement. Their registered telegraphic address is also given.

NAME OF FIRM.	REGISTERED TELEGRAPHIC ADDRESS.
Addams-Williams, R., 16, Commercial Street, Newport, Monmouth (and at Crickhowell)	Addams-Williams, Newport, Mon.
Alabaster, Passmore & Sons, Fann Street, Aldersgate Street, London	Alamores, London.
Allan Brothers & Co., Allan Royal Mail Line, 103, Leadenhall Street, London	Allanline, London.
"Anchor" Line (see Henderson Brothers).	
Anglo-American Brush Electric Light Corporation, Limited, Belvedere Road, London	Magneto, London.
Anglo-American Rope and Oakum Company, 12, Hopwood Street, Liverpool	Oakum, Liverpool.
Army and Navy Co-operative Society, Limited, 117, Victoria Street, London	Army, London.
Arnold, E. J., 3, Briggate, Leeds	Arnold, Leeds.
Artistic Stationery Co., Limited, Plough Court, Fetter Lane, London	Artistic, London.

ENGLISH ANTI-SEMITISM

OR, WHY CAN'T THE JEWS BE MORE LIKE US?

Part of the problem with English anti-Semitism is in identifying it. The English pride themselves on a sense of humor that emphasizes irony, sarcasm and taking the piss out of everyone, regardless of race, creed and national origin. When soccer fans chant, as they did a few years back, "I'd rather be a Paki than a Jew ... I've got a foreskin, haven't you, fucking Jew" and "Gas a Jew, Jew, Jew, put him in the oven, cook him through," are they hating Jews or indulging in offensive behavior for its own sake? When Monty Python's Eric Idle has Sir Robin singing in "Spamalot" that "we won't succeed on Broadway / if we don't have any Jews," is he anti-Semitic or merely using a shopworn trope to make a joke?

The Jewish history of England has shifted between uneasy tolerance to enthusiastic pogroms. Jews have been living in England since Roman times. They surface in the records around the time of William the Conqueror. Although they never numbered more than 6,000, living in scattered communities but mostly in London, they were subjected to the usual restrictions and blood libels Jews faced elsewhere, interrupted with the occasional massacre and expulsion from various cities. Other times, they were tolerated, largely because they contributed beyond their numbers to society, particularly as moneylenders to royalty. They were well-positioned for the task because Christians were forbidden to charge interest on loans and Jews were not.

Eventually, this ability to make money led to trouble. In the 12th century, Jewish financier Aaron of Lincoln amassed a fortune by making loans on land, commodities, and to build abbeys and monasteries. When he died in 1186, King Henry II acquired his fortune and loans under a law mandating that the property of usurers go to the crown.

One wonders if the king had realized just how far Aaron's empire extended. When the books were opened, it was found that Aaron was the second-wealthiest man in England, apart from Henry (who was also in debt to Aaron).

Henry shipped Aaron's treasure to France to pay for his war against Philip Augustus. The ship sank, but Henry still had the loans, totaling about £15,000. The amount was so large that a separate department within the exchequer was created to handle the payments.

In 1190, a fire broke out in York, and a debtor of Aaron, Richard de Malbis, used it to incite a mob into attacking the home of Aaron's former land agent. The widow and children were killed and the house set on fire. The rest of York's Jews took refuge in a wooden tower on a hill above the city. They were besieged for several days until the tower caught fire. Some died, but the rest, rather than fall into the hands of the mob, killed themselves. The survivors were promised their freedom if they surrendered. They did, and they were killed, too.

The Jews fared little better under Henry's successor, Richard, and future kings. Aaron's death had revealed how much money flowed through Jewish fingers, and thereafter the crown made sure it was a silent partner in their business transactions. In 1194, Richard declared that the king will keep track of all Jewish transactions using a chirography, a document that could be cut into pieces with a portion held by each party. Because the king could keep track of all transactions, he could efficiently tax them (Richard, no fool he, also allowed English courts to help Jews recover on defaulted loans, taking 10 percent of the proceeds).

This state of affairs was bad enough, but then the popes got involved. In 1198, Pope Innocent III urged all Christian princes to renounce usury. Then, he ruled that all Jews were doomed to perpetual servitude for killing Jesus. By 1218, English Jews were required to wear a badge of oblong white cloth. While it was intended to keep Jews or Muslims from having sex with Christians (or, to deprive Christians of an excuse to have sex with Jews), it also made them a target of hostility.

By 1290, the Jewish community had been bled so much they

contributed less to the royal treasury. King Edward I had developed other sources of revenue, and they were expelled. For the next 350 years, England would be, in the language of Nazi Germany, "Judenfrei."

We have Oliver Cromwell to thank for the official return of Jews to England. In the 1650s, a leader of the Dutch Jewish community asked Cromwell to readmit them. Cromwell couldn't think of a reason not to, so when he couldn't get a council formed to make it official, he simply declared that the ban would no longer be enforced.

Jewish families found homes in port cities and manufacturing towns such as Birmingham, Leeds and Manchester. London became the center of Jewish activity. Over time, there was a loosening of legal restrictions and a granting of rights. Synagogues were established in 1657. By 1698, England allowed Judaism to be practiced openly. An attempt in 1753 to grant citizenship to foreign-born Jews was dropped due to opposition, but the momentum was still moving toward emancipation.

The process accelerated during the Victorian period. Jews were admitted into the legal profession in 1833 and London elected its first Jewish mayor in 1855. Lionel Rothschild was elected to Parliament in 1847, but couldn't take his seat until 1858 because, understandably, he refused to swear an oath "on the true faith of a Christian." During the 1800s, Jews slowly gained more rights such as admission into colleges, Disraeli was appointed prime minister. By 1890, all religious and commercial restrictions were gone.

During the 1880s, there was a massive wave of immigration from Eastern Europe, particularly from Russia where Jews were persecuted. In the cities, they replaced the assimilated Jews who moved into the suburbs alongside their English counterparts. The increase in immigration coincided with an rise in fear from the importation of potentially dangerous ideas and political beliefs such as anarchism, socialism and Zionism. Inevitably, the link became forged in the public mind between foreigners who looked different, spoke a different language and who followed non-English customs, and the specter of revolution.

By 1914, there were about 250,000 Jews living in England. After World War I, several events raised and altered their profile.

In 1917, the British government issued the Balfour Declaration that supported a Jewish national home in Palestine. During the war, English forces with the help of Capt. T.E. Lawrence – more popularly known as Lawrence of Arabia – assisted the Arab Revolt against Ottoman Turkish rule and captured the southern portion of the empire in what is now Israel, the Gaza Strip, the West Bank and Jordan. In 1923, the League of Nations instituted the British Mandate for Palestine, formalizing British rule for the area "until such time as they are able to stand alone."

At about the same time, an English translation of "The Protocols of the Learned Elders of Zion" was published in Britain under the title "The Jewish Peril." Appearing in the Russian Empire as early as 1903, the anti-Semitic tract, claiming to be a document stolen from a secret Jewish organization, outlined a Jewish plan to dominate the world.

In reality, much of the "Protocols" was plagiarized from an 1864 French novel that attacked Napoleon III. Nevertheless, many groups through the years have found "Protocols" to be a useful tool. The White Russians used it to discredit Communism by blaming Jews for the Russian Revolution. In America, Henry Ford distributed a half-million copies. Sometimes, the references to Jews were

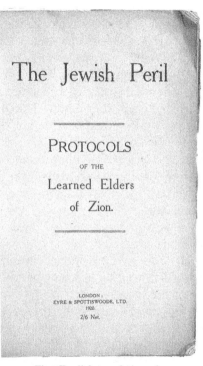

First English translation of "Protocols of the Learned Elders of Zion," 1920.

replaced with Bolsheviks and publicized as an expose of Communist goals. Today, "Protocols" is sold throughout the Middle East, where it has been endorsed by many Arabic governments and intellectuals.

In Sayers' time, anti-Semitism was no longer government policy, but it existed, as Harold Abrams says in "Chariots of Fire," "on the edge of a remark." There even seemed to be a boundary between acceptable and unacceptable forms of anti-Semitism. At Bloomsbury gatherings, Virginia Woolf would poke fun at the Jewishness of her husband, Leonard, although it should be noted she later regretted her snobbishness over marrying a Jew. When composer Arthur Benjamin won a scholarship at the Royal College of Music in London, his composition teacher remarked to him that "you Jews can't write long tunes."

We see this attitude reflected in "Whose Body?" when we contrast the attitudes of Sir Julian Freke and the Dowager Duchess. By losing the woman he loved to Sir Reuben Levy, Sir Julian had "his aristocratic nose put out of joint by a little Jewish nobody" and so he plots to murder him. This is bad. Throughout the novel, the Duchess says the most foolish things about Jews – "I'm sure some Jews are very good people, and personally I'd much rather they believed something, though of course it must be very inconvenient, what with not working on Saturdays and circumcising the poor little babies and everything depending on the new moon and that funny kind of meat they have with such a slang-sounding name, and never being able to have bacon for breakfast." – that is not even remarked upon. That seems acceptable.

Sayers' attitude toward Jews is a contentious issue among biographers. She personally knew and got along well with many Jews. This included John Cournos, her Russian-Jewish lover who broke her heart by opposing marriage, only to emigrate to America and marrying.

But Sayers held to the common belief that, as a people, Jewish loyalties tended to favor their religion over their nation. In one letter written during World War II, she listed the ways the British people saw how Jews acted among them – of Jews sending their money to America instead of risking it in England, avoiding fire-watching duty during bombing raids, breaking the law to secure an apartment then informing against the landlady – "but it all really boils down to the same thing: 'bad citizens.'" Their rejection of Jesus Christ as the Messiah merely confirmed in her mind that by setting themselves apart, they shouldn't object if their presence is resented. Perhaps the best that could be said of Sayers' beliefs is that she tried to do no harm with it.

OMNIBUS

ONE VEHICLE'S JOURNEY THROUGH LINGUISTICS

Alert readers of "Whose Body?" will see the word 'bus and wonder about that mark to the left of the b. The more insightful readers might even feel a flicker of curiosity about the rare sighting of the word's reverse apostrophe. Or, if you're blessed with astigmatism like me, assume it's a typo, or a bit of dirt. That is the vertiginous appendage left by a longer word that suffered a verbal appendectomy.

In the novel's second paragraph, Lord Peter's cab driver evades a No. 19 'bus. Later, police Inspector Parker hops on that same bus to accept a breakfast invitation at 110A Piccadilly, where he was served "glorious food, incomparable coffee, and the Daily Mail before a blazing fire of wood and coal." The self-made wealthy businessman, Sir Reuben Levy, still rode to work on the No. 96 'bus, and even took one to his fatal assignation with Sir Julian Freike, who observed to his romantic rival that his little economies would be the death of him.

A slightly longer form of the word appears when Inspector Parker delights in reading "railway-stall detective stories on the principle of the 'busman's holiday."

So 'bus is an example of evolution in language, the revival of the ancient Latin word omnibus, revived and applied, first, to a means of transportation never seen in Roman times, then amputated, staunched temporarily with the apostrophe, given new life with new definitions.

Omnibus began life as *omnis*, the Latin word for all. Attaching the *–ibus* suffix turned it into the dative plural word meaning "for all." In 1828, when an enterprising businessman put long coaches with seats on the streets of France and offered to carry anyone with a few francs, they were called a carriage for everyone, or a voiture omnibus.

As use of the vehicle spread, so did its name. A year after its introduction in France, a London newspaper announced that "the new vehicle, called the omnibus, commenced running this morning from Paddington to the City." Already, the practical British had dropped the voiture part, and within a few years would cut off the omni- part as well.

Over time, the useful word became applied to other things. In politics, an omnibus bill is legislation that collects miscellaneous proposals, an omnibus train stops at all the stations on its route, and an omnibus book is a collection of different pieces. In electronics, an omnibus bar carries power from a source, and computer technicians today talk earnestly about busses. When a NASA technician in the movie "Apollo 13" talks about an undervolt in "main bus B," he's using a descendant of a word that originated 170 years before, and caught in transition by Sayers' pen.

London General Omnibus Company vehicle, 1903.

WILLIAM PALMER

GAMBLING ON POISON

Dr. William Palmer's trial and execution in 1856 was a sensation, combining sex, gambling, debt, a creative murder method and the possibility of multiple killings. The publicity over the case was so extensive in Staffordshire that it poisoned the jury pool, and the trial had to be moved to London, a first in English judicial history. In his diary, the presiding judge called it "the most memorable judicial proceedings for the last fifty years, engaging the attention not only of his country but of all Europe."

Palmer can blame his widespread notoriety by being caught on the cusp of technological change. Before the Industrial Revolution, newspapers were expensive and served a diet of news aimed at businessmen and politicians. The growth of literate middle and working classes inspired newspapers for them. These papers were less expensive, selling usually for a penny, and focused more on crime and human-interest stories.

Into this maw was fed the Palmer case, and the public snapped it up. One newspaper's special illustrated issue sold more than 400,000 copies.

The arc of Palmer's story ran a decade, beginning in 1846, when he qualified as a doctor at St. Bartholomew's Hospital in London, and set up his practice in his hometown of Rugeley, Staffordshire, a landlocked county near the Welsh border. He married the next year and spent several years building his practice and his family. His wife bore him a son, William, who outlived his father, and four children who died in infancy.

Rural Staffordshire was known as a center of horse racing, and in this semi-shady world, where fortunes were raised and lost in convivial times of gambling, fixed races and celebrations, Palmer began to lose his way. He began gambling heavily and quickly ran up debts. Not content with losing money solely on betting, he bought racehorses. He spent his days neglecting his practice, attending the races and mingling with the touts, gamblers, riders and other denizens of the sporting life.

As pressure from his debtors grew, the people who associated with Palmer began dying. In 1849, his mother-in-law came to stay with the Palmers. She lasted a fortnight before dying unexpectedly, leaving her estate to her daughter and son-in-law. The next year, a racing acquaintance to whom Palmer owned £800 died. Between 1851 and 1854 came the turns of the four infants – although their deaths could be chalked up to high infant mortality of the

THE ONLY AUTHENTIC LIKENESS OF WILLIAM PALMER.

William Palmer, from "The Illustrated Life and Career of William Palmer."

times. The death of Palmer's wife in September 1854 could be more suspicious; she left behind an insurance policy for £13,000.

Despite the substantial sums, Palmer's expenses still outran his earnings. He turned to forging his mother's name to win loans totaling £13,500. He covered his risk by taking out an insurance policy for that amount on his brother, Walter.

But when Walter died 11 months later, the suspicious insurance company initiated an inquiry. Palmer tried to insure his groom for £10,000, but the appearance of two writs for payment drove Palmer to more desperate measures.

The next month, Palmer attended the races in Shrewsbury with John Parsons Cook, a solicitor who, like the doctor, had abandoned his profession for gambling on the horses.

Their day at the races was profitable for Cook, less so for Palmer, so Cook arranged a supper party to celebrate. That night, he began vomiting. Palmer took him back to Rugeley and put him up at the Talbot Arms Inn opposite the doctor's house. Palmer's solicitude extended to traveling to London to pick up Cook's winnings at Tattersall's – a sum of £1,000 – which he used to pay his debts. He also forged Cook's name to a check.

Meanwhile, Cook grew sicker until he died five days later, reportedly "bent in the shape of a bow, resting on head and heels." An old doctor called in pronounced death by apoplexy.

Cook's stepfather was not convinced. He arranged a post mortem, which Palmer attended. Antimony, a chemical element whose poisoning symptoms resembled strychnine, was found in Cook's organs. Palmer's behavior also aroused suspicions that he was trying to sabotage the tests. He jostled a person carrying the glass jar containing the stomach, intestines, and its contents. Later, it was discovered that someone had cut slits into their paper covers that could contaminate the samples. Palmer was among those who handled the jar, but denied vandalizing it.

Palmer was arrested and brought to London for his trial. One sensation was caused by Alfred Swaine Taylor, the leading toxicologist of his day, whose "Manual of Medical Jurisprudence" became the first standard work on the subject. On the stand, Taylor testified about the antimony found in the organs, but admitted, "I have never had under my observation the effects of strychnia on the human body; but I have written a book on the subject."

After a 12-day trial, Palmer was found guilty. At his hanging, he said, "I am innocent of poisoning Cook by strychnia," leaving open the question of what he did use.

Edmond De La Pommerais

From Deception To Murder

As in the cases of William Palmer, George Joseph Smith and Thomas Wainwright, the French doctor Edmond de la Pommerais found murder a shortcut both to fortune and the grave.

Pommerais was a homeopathic doctor who reinvented himself as a count and succeeded in 1861 in marrying Mademoiselle Dabizy, who stood to inherit her family's fortune. He also acquired several mistresses, including Séraphine de Pauw, who became a widow after Pommerais treated her husband.

Edmond de la Pommerais

Pommerais' first victim was his mother-in-law, who had objected to the marriage and retained a firm hold on her daughter's money. She died two months after the marriage and a few hours after dining with the doctor, certified the cause as Asiatic cholera. His wife inherited the estate, and for awhile his life was occupied with spending her money and gambling.

When the money ran out, he turned to his Séraphine, who was in debt as well, and suggested committing insurance fraud. He convinced her to let him take out a policy on her for 500,000 francs. She would fake a fall down the stairs and appear to be so close to death that the company would give her an annuity of 5,000 francs a year to avoid paying off on her death. Considering that in 1871, the average worker in Paris earned 1,500 francs a year, this was a substantial sum. As part of his plan, she agreed to write several letters to Pommerais after her "fall," describing her symptoms and praising him for his medical skills and charity.

She duly fell ill, and the insurance company's doctors examined her but couldn't agree on a diagnosis. She also received regular visits from her doctor – Pommerais, of course – who prescribed drugs for her to take.

When she died, Pommerais raised suspicions by quickly applying for a payout. Then, Séraphine's sister went to the police. Unbeknownst to Pommerais, Séraphine had told her about the insurance scheme.

Séraphine had been in the ground for only 13 days when she was exhumed and examined by Dr. Auguste Ambroise Tardieu, the pre-eminent forensic medical scientist. He couldn't find any proof of the usual poisons, such as arsenic and antimony. Séraphine's complaints of a racing heart led him to suspect digitalis, but no test existed to trace its presence.

Fortunately, the police had preserved the contents of her stomach, so Tardieu made an extract from it and fed it to a frog, while he gave another an extract of digitalis. Both died in the same manner.

At the trial, Pommerais' lawyer attacked Tardieu's evidence, but the combination of his testimony and that of Séraphine's sister, plus the large amount of digitalis in Pommerais' possession that he couldn't explain away, was enough for the jury. He was convicted and sentenced to be guillotined.

On June 9, 1864, an estimated 40,000 Parisians crowded the streets around the Square de la Petite Roquette to watch the execution. It was a scene worthy of Balzac: students from the Latin Quarter, the workingmen and idlers, women and children, hallooing, smoking and drinking. Spectators gazed down from the roof tiles.

American reporter George Alfred Townsend witnessed Pommerais' last moments:

At four minutes to six o'clock on Thursday morning, the wicket in the prison-gate swung open; the condemned appeared, with his hands tied behind his back, and his knees bound together. He walked with difficulty, so fettered; but other than the artificial restraints, there was no hesitation nor terror in his movements. His hair, which had been long, dark, and wavy, was severed close to his scalp; his beard had likewise been clipped, and the fine moustache and goatee, which had set off his most interesting face, no longer appeared to enhance his romantic, expressive physiognomy. Yet his black eyes and cleanly cut mouth, nostrils, and eyebrows, demonstrated that Count de la Pommerais was not a beauty dependent upon small accessories. There was a dignity even in his painful gait; the coarse prison-shirt, scissored low in the neck, exhibited the straight columnar throat and swelling chest; for the rest, he wore only a pair of black pantaloons and his own shapely boots.

As he emerged from the wicket, the chill morning air, laden with the dew of the truck gardens near at hand, blew across the open spaces of the suburbs, and smote him with a cold chill. He was plainly seen to tremble; but in an instant, as if by the mere force of his will, he stood motionless, and cast a first and only glance at the guillotine straight before him. It was the glance of a man who meets an enemy's eye, not shrinkingly, but half-defiant, as if even the bitter retribution could not abash his strong courage … he seemed to feel that forty thousand men and women, and young children were looking upon him to see how he dared to die, and that for a generation his bearing should go into fireside descriptions.

Then he moved on between the files of soldiers at his shuffling pace, and before him went the chaplain, swaying the crucifix, behind him the executioner of Versailles — a rough and bearded man — to assist in the final horror.

It was at this intense moment a most wonderful spectacle. As the prisoner had first appeared, a single great shout had shaken the multitude. It was the French word "Voila!" which means "Behold!" "See!" Then every spectator stood on tiptoe; the silence of death succeeded; all the close street was undulant with human emotion; a few house roofs near by were dizzy with folks who gazed down from the tiles; all the way up the heights of Pere la Chaise, among the pale chapels and monuments of the dead, the thousands of stirred beings swung and shook like so many drowned corpses floating on the sea. Every eye and mind turned to the little structure raised among the trees, on the space before La Roquette, and there they saw a dark, shaven, disrobed young man, going quietly toward his grave.

He mounted the steps deliberately, looking towards his feet; the priest held up the crucifix, and he felt it was there, but did not see it; his lips one moment touched the image of Christ, but he did not look up nor speak; then, as he gained the last step, the bascule or swingboard sprang up before him; the executioner gave him a single push, and he fell prone upon the plank, with his face downward; it gave way before him, bearing him into the space between the upright beams, and he lay horizontally beneath the knife, presenting the back of his neck to it. Thus resting, he could look into the pannier or basket, into whose sawdust lining his head was to drop in a moment.

And in that awful space, while all the people gazed with their fingers tingling, the legitimate Parisian executioner gave a jerk at the cord which held the fatal knife. With a quick, keen sound, the steel became detached; it fell hurtling through the grooves; it struck something with a dead, dumb thump; a jet of bright blood spurted into the light, and dyed the face of an attendant horribly red; and Count de la Pommerais's head lay in the sawdust of the pannier, while every vein in the lopped trunk trickled upon the scaffold-floor!

They threw a cloth upon the carcass and carried away the pannier; the guillotine disappeared beneath the surrounding heads; loud exclamations and acclaims burst from the multitude; the venders of trash and edibles resumed their cheerful cries, and a hearse dashed through the mass, carrying the warm body of the guillotined to the cemetery of Mt. Parnasse. In thirty minutes, newsboys were hawking the scene of the execution upon all the quays and bridges. In every cafe of Paris some witness was telling the incidents of the show to breathless listeners, and the crowds which stopped to see the funeral procession of the great Marshal Pelissier divided their attention between the warrior and the poisoner, — the latter obtaining the preponderance of fame.

The Daily Mirror

CERTIFIED CIRCULATION LARGER THAN ANY OTHER PICTURE PAPER IN THE WORLD

No. 3,647.   Registered at the G.P.O. as a Newspaper.   FRIDAY, JULY 2, 1915   One Halfpenny.

THE MURDERER IN "THE BRIDES IN THE BATH" CASE SENTENCED TO DEATH AT THE OLD BAILEY.

Miss Mundy, one of the brides whom Smith murdered.   Miss Pegler, the woman to whom Smith always returned.   Alice Reavil, one of the women whom Smith married.   Alice Burnham, another "wife" who died in her bath.

Newspaper announcing George Joseph Smith's conviction and sentencing, 1915.

GEORGE JOSEPH SMITH

THREE BRIDES, ONE BATH. NO WAITING

George Joseph Smith was a murderous bigamist with great game and a penchant for aliases. By the time he visited the hangman in 1915, he had matched and dispatched three women and married several more that he had left poorer and, hopefully, wiser.

Smith's career in matrimony began in 1898 when he married Caroline Thornhill under the name Oliver George Love. He ran a bread shop at the time, and when it went bankrupt, put his wife to work as a maidservant, stealing her employers' jewelry. When she was caught, Smith fled, and Caroline took the fall, spending a year in prison. But she got her revenge when she encountered Love/Smith by chance. She called the police, testified against him, and he was sentenced to two years.

From 1908 to 1914, Smith married at least seven women. Most of the time, he simply took whatever cash and bonds was at hand and fled. But in August 1910, under the name Henry Williams, he married Annie "Bessie" Mundy. At 33, she was already a spinster and presumably grateful for being rescued from that state. Unfortunately,

Smith loved her £2,500 in savings more. When he discovered it was held in a trust for her, he grabbed £150 in spare cash instead and fled. In a charming touch, he left behind a letter accusing her of infecting him with a venereal disease.

Then fate took an interest in Bessie. Two years later, she encountered Smith by chance at the seaside resort of Weston-super-Mare. He explained that he had abandoned her because he learned he had contracted venereal disease. Rather than infect her, he chose to leave. He had regretted his rash act ever since and had devoted himself to looking for her. Now they were reunited, he told her, they would live together for the rest of their days.

Bessie believed him. They settled in Herne Bay, a seaside town in Kent, southeast England. Happy again, Bessie signed a new will in Smith's favor, meaning that he'd inherit the trust if she died. They visited an ironmonger and bought a tin bath. He took Bessie to a doctor, saying she had had an epileptic fit. She complained only of headaches, for which medication was prescribed, but the groundwork had been laid for Smith's next step.

Less than a week later, he called the doctor again. Bessie was in the tub, dead, a cake of soap in her hand. The doctor concluded drowning by epilepsy, Smith buried his wife in a pauper's grave, pocketed the £2,500 and returned the tub.

Next year, Smith began courting 25-year-old Alice Burnham. When her father asked Smith for information about his family, he wrote in reply "my mother was a Buss horse, my father a Cab driver, my sister a Roughrider over the Arctic regions, my brothers were all gallant sailors on a steam-roller."

Despite getting up her father's nose – or perhaps because of it? – Alice married Smith. This time, he insured her life for £500, and they moved to Blackpool where they rented a house. With a bath.

This marriage lasted longer – six weeks – before she was found dead in the bath. The inquest ruled "death by misadventure." Smith took the money and fled, with the suspicious landlady shouting "Crippen" – the name of the notorious wife-murderer – at his back.

Incredibly, he did it again the next year. This time, as John Lloyd, he selected Margaret Elizabeth Lofty, a clergyman's daughter. They were married in Bath, and the next day traveled to London and took lodgings in the Highgate area. That afternoon, she visited her solicitor and signed a will in her husband's favor.

That night, the landlady heard unusual splashing in the bath, followed by music. Smith was in the parlor, playing "Nearer My God to Thee" on the harmonium. There was silence for awhile, then "Lloyd" popped in. He had stepped out to buy tomatoes for dinner. Has she come out of the tub? She hadn't. Another "death by misadventure."

Only this time, Margaret's death was covered by the London papers and read by both the "Crippen"-shouting landlady and Alice Burnham's father. He told police, and Smith was arrested.

While prosecutors had Smith bang to rights for bigamy, proving he killed Bessie Mundy and Alice Burnham was more difficult. Enter Bernard Spilsbury, the brilliant pathologist for the Home Office. Five years before, his forensic evidence had helped convict Dr. Hawley Crippen in the murder of his wife. This time, he was charged with determining how the women died.

It was a difficult task. An examination of the bodies and the medical records showed no signs of struggle. They were not drugged and they did not suffer a stroke or heart attack. In Bessie Mundy's case, Spilsbury compared the bathtub's five-foot length with five-foot-six Bessie. There was no way she could have drowned from an epileptic seizure.

When the newspapers picked up the story about the "brides in the bath," the police chief of Herne Bay remembered a similar death in his jurisdiction. He sent a letter to Spilsbury, and police confirmed that the "Henry Williams" of Herne Bay was the same man as the George Smith of Blackpool and "John Lloyd" of Highgate. Now, police had three murders to solve.

The problem was, how did Smith do it? Spilsbury came up with a theory. He and Detective Inspector Arthur Neil experimented on female divers similar in size as the victims, using the same tubs the women drowned in. Pushing them down resulted in water splashing everywhere, including on the attacker.

Then, Spilsbury yanked on the woman's feet. Caught by surprise, she slid underwater. Water was forced up her nose and into her lungs, and she passed out. It took doctors a half-hour to revive her.

The jury took less than a half-hour to convict Smith of the murder of Bessie Williams, with the deaths of Alice Smith and Margaret Lloyd used to buttress the prosecution's case. On August 13, 1915, he was hanged at Maidstone Prison.

Henry Wainwright

Hard To Find Good Help

In a world of innocent bystanders who stand by and do nothing, Henry Wainwright had the bad fortune to find the one man who wouldn't leave well enough alone.

Wainwright ran a brush-making business on Whitechapel Road, but sales were down and he had to sell the building. But before he did, he had to do something about the awful smell that had been hanging in the air around it for a year.

On Sept. 11, 1875, he met Alfred Stokes, his former employee, on the sidewalk outside the business. He had asked him to help carry a few parcels in return for some tools Wainwright no longer needed. Wainwright's brother, Thomas, owned an unused building across the Thames, and he had agreed to let Henry store a few things there until he could get back on his feet.

Wainwright let Stokes into the building and showed him two heavy parcels wrapped in oil cloth. Stokes picked them up and found they were heavy and awkward to handle. As they set off down the street, he began complaining about the nasty smell emanating from them. Wainwright stopped them, told Stokes to guard the bundles, and walked down the street in search of a cab.

While Wainwright was away, Stokes opened one of the parcels. Staring back at him was the head of a decomposed woman laying on a severed arm. Stokes rewrapped the package and said nothing as Wainwright returned with the cab.

As Stokes loaded the bundles inside, Wainwright coolly smoked a cigar and chatted with a woman friend who had stepped out of a tavern. He talked her into the cab and said goodbye to Stokes. The cab driver whipped up his horses, and the wagon rolled off for London Bridge.

Stokes took off in pursuit. He encountered two policemen and gasped out his incredible story. They didn't believe him. He resumed his pursuit as the cab crossed the bridge and turned down Borough High Street.

The winded Stokes feared he would have to abandon the chase, but the cab stopped. As Wainwright carried the bundles into the building, Stokes found two policemen who were more willing to investigate. They stopped Wainwright, opened a bundle and, after declining Wainwright's bribe of £200, arrested him.

The victim was Miss Harriet Lane, who had been Wainwright's mistress for two years and murder victim for one. She knew him as Percy King, when he had set her up in lodgings. Their relationship was good at first, and she bore him two children.

Then, business fell off at his brush-making business. He burned down one of his buildings for the insurance, but the company was suspicious and denied the claim. He had to cut Harriet's allowance. She complained bitterly, then threatened to go to his wife.

So, in June 1874, Wainwright severed the relationship. He took her to his business, shot her three times, slit her throat, and buried her beneath the floor. Since he also sold cleaning supplies, he took out of stock 50 pounds of chloride of lime and threw that into Harriet's grave to speed decomposition.

But Wainwright's knowledge of chemistry was on a par with his business skills. Not all lime act the same. Quicklime aids decomposition; chloride of lime retards it.

In the days after Harriet's disappearance, her father and a friend who was caring for Harriet's children grew worried. Wainwright told them that she had eloped to the Continent with Edward Frieake. In October, Mrs. Wilmore received a telegram from Frieake telling her, "We are just off to Paris and intend to have a jolly spree." Everyone found this disturbing, but reassuring, except for the real Edward Frieake, who knew Harriet and was upset that someone was using his name. Wainwright reassured him that this was an entirely different Frieake, and he was right. The eloping Frieake was actually Henry's brother, Thomas, who had not only posted the phony letters from the Continent, but had even planted the idea of Harriet eloping with another man by visiting her disguised as Frieake.

This came out at Henry's trial, in one of those human moments that testimony in a homicide case preserves. Harriet's landlady

Wainwright's execution, depicted in "The Illustrated Police News."

testified that Frieake/Thomas Wainwright was visiting Harriet when they sent her to the pub for champagne. She returned with the bottle and three glasses, hoping to cage a drink and was put out when they ignored the hint. She got her revenge at the trial, as the counsel for the defense noted in his closing speech that "whether or not she thought the rising generation less polite than in her younger days, the disappointment was one likely to impress the matter upon her memory."

Another measure of the brothers' relationship came out at the trial. When Henry needed to move the late Harriet, he had Thomas buy some tools, a cleaver and a garden spade, which he used to cut Harriet up into 10 pieces for easier moving. The trial transcript noted that Thomas charged his brother five shillings for tools that cost him three, a 66 percent markup.

Readers of the trial record may be surprised to see the name of W.S. Gilbert surface as a barrister for the defense. But the librettist half of Gilbert and Sullivan had nothing to do with the case. He was busy working on "Broken Hearts," a drama in blank verse, when he was called for jury duty. Rather than attend, he got a friend to assign him to the Wainwright case for two days, long enough so he could be excused.

"Broken Hearts" debuted on Dec. 7, but Wainwright never got to see it. Four days before Christmas, he mounted the scaffold, sneered, "Come to see a man die, have you, you curs?" and was hanged. His brother got seven years. Stokes received £30 and public contributions raised £1,200 for Harriett's children.

THE WORLD
OF
DOROTHY
L. SAYERS

INVENTING LORD PETER

IN THE BEGINNING

In "Gaudy Night," one of Harriet Vane's Oxford contemporaries discussing the belief that everyone has a "proper job" – the problem being how to determine what that job is – advised that "we can only know what things are of overmastering importance when they have overmastered us."

Newly minted author
Dorothy L. Sayers.

This statement could sum up the career of Dorothy L. Sayers. After leaving Oxford, she tried several professions – teacher, academic, manager of a school, advertising – but she found her passion in translating classical works and chronicling the adventures of Lord Peter Death Bredon Wimsey.

Sayers found her way to Lord Peter through her love of crime stories, particularly those about Sexton Blake. The adventures of "the poor man's Sherlock Holmes" were chronicled by a stable of hired writers in the same way that the Stratemeyer syndicate published the Hardy Boys and Nancy Drew stories.

Working at a school in the Normandy area of France in 1919-20, Sayers spent her spare time reading crime stories. When she came down with mumps and had to spend three weeks in isolation, she begged her friend Muriel Jaeger – to whom she would later dedicate "Whose Body?" – to mail her all the Sexton Blake books she could find. By mail, they amused themselves with mock-intellectual discussions of the stories' and their relationship to folk rituals and mythology.

About this time, Sayers was inspired to attempt a Sexton Blake story. A French politician is found dead in a flat lent to him by Lord Peter. In this draft, he is described as a "harmless sort of fellow." He is a war hero, a skilled horseback rider and a collector of first editions. One character described him as "fair-haired, big nose, aristocratic sort of man whose socks match his tie. No politics." He gets involved in the investigation, ferrets out an important clue and helps chase the villain in his private airplane, which seems a lot of action by a minor character. From the first, Lord Peter seems determined to edge himself to center stage.

Sayers did not try to get her Sexton Blake story published, but she tried Lord Peter in an unfinished play "The Mousehole: A Detective Fantasia in Three Flats." Lord Peter and his Piccadilly flat are retained, but this time the crime scene is an upstairs apartment where a couple are found dead. This version lasts only a few pages, but long enough to introduce Constable Sugg, his nemesis in "Whose Body?"

By this time, Sayers had left her job in France and resettled in London. Her prospects were not promising. She was 27, unmarried and had held three jobs in four years. Her publishing record consisted of two slim volumes of poetry. She seemed rudderless, but she was intelligent, well-educated, enormously confident and capable of hard work. Between applying unsuccessfully for jobs and doing freelance editing, she boned up on criminology in the British Museum's Reading Room.

Despite two unfinished attempts, Lord Peter seemed determined to hang around. On Jan 22, 1921, Sayers wrote to her mother that she had an idea for a detective story about a fat lady found dead in her bath – an echo of the "Brides in the Bath" murder case? – wearing nothing but her pince-nez.

For her detective-hero's name, Sayers chose Peter and combined it with the elegantly playful Death – pronounced to rhyme with "teeth." Bredon was possibly inspired by the A.E. Housman poem "On Bredon Hill." His last name is a play on whimsy – defined as a whim or caprice – and beautifully evokes his detecting behavior and habit of taking an interest in other people's business. His family's motto, after all, is "As my Whimsy takes me."

For Lord Peter's looks, Sayers drew on a memory from her first year Oxford. In 1913, she attended the graduation ceremony where the Newdigate prize for best student composition was given to Roy Ridley. Ridley had an aristocratic profile that resembled Dante, addressed friends as "old thing" and favored spats and a monocle.

He was also a heavy drinker, favoring what were known at Oxford as "Roy Ridley specials," sherry lacked with a dollop of gin, that he would drink throughout the day. A former pupil of his, Canadian author Robertson Davies, later wrote that "Ridley was the only clergyman I ever saw celebrate Holy Communion wearing a monocle." (Later, Ridley would lose his position and his wife over an affair with the master's secretary and end up a reviewer and examiner in Bristol.)

Maurice Roy Ridley at Oxford.

In a letter to a friend, Sayers wrote that she'd "fell head over ears in love with him on the spot" and that his full name — Maurice Roy Ridley — was "like the hero of a six-penny novelette."

(Sayers would later forget that Ridley inspired Wimsey. In 1935, she would meet Ridley, then chaplain of Balliol, and write in shock that she "had seen the perfect Peter Wimsey." Ridley's later claim that he inspired Wimsey would annoy Sayers.)

For Wimsey's personality, Sayers drew on two men: Eric Whelpton and Charles Crichton. Sayers had met Whelpton as a neighbor in London, and had fallen in love with him. Her attachment to him was firm enough that when he moved to Normandy to run an exchange bureau for French and English students, she followed to act as his secretary. He was well-dressed, educated, knew food and wine and came from an aristocratic family, complete with an ancient manor in Wales.

Another piece of the puzzle was supplied by Crichton, a co-worker at the school. He had attended Eton, served in the war as a cavalry officer and was familiar with London society. His valet, Bates, probably inspired Lord Peter's servant, Bunter. A former footman at a ducal house, he had enlisted in the war alongside Crichton and served as his batman. Although Crichton and Sayers disliked each other, they could not avoid each other's company, and at mealtimes, she listened to his stories about the high life familiar to Lord Peter, with its parties, balls and weekends at country houses.

Combining in a character a university education with aristocratic privileges was new in crime fiction. Lord Peter's rank as the brother of a duke meant he wasn't encumbered by the requirement to attend the House of Lords and maintain an estate, but high enough to lend him respectability and connections. His wealth – its source never explained – enabled him to buy anything he needed for his detecting activities, maintain his flat in Piccadilly and acquire rare books. His Oxford education gave Sayers an opportunity to display her learning.

Lord Peter's wealth also gave the impoverished Sayers a way to enjoy luxury by proxy. "At the time I was particularly hard up," she wrote, "and it gave me pleasure to spend his fortune for him. When I was dissatisfied with my single unfurnished room I took a luxurious flat for him in Piccadilly. When my cheap rug got a hole in it, I ordered him an Aubusson carpet. When I had no money to pay my bus fare I presented him with a Daimler double-six, upholstered in a style of sober magnificence, and when I felt dull I let him drive it. I can heartily recommend this inexpensive way of furnishing to all who are discontented with their incomes. It relieves the mind and does no harm to anybody."

Building detective stories also satisfied Sayers' love of order and form. In a letter to her onetime lover, John Cournos, she compared fiction to laying a mosaic, laying it down piece by piece, "apparently meaningless and detached – into its place, until one suddenly sees the thing." Her favorite method was to find the murder method and build her plot and characters around it.

By the summer of 1921, Sayers had finished her first novel. Lord Peter, at last, was born.

Timeline Of Lord Peter Wimsey's Cases

The Lord Peter stories are unique in the mystery genre in that Sayers' allowed the great detective to age and grow, from the shell-shocked bachelor nobleman of "Whose Body?" to the 52-year-old husband and father of "Talboys." The following is a chronology of Lord Peter's life and cases, derived from information stated in the stories and inferred from the clues.

This timeline assumes that the novels and short stories were published in chronological order unless told otherwise.

Thanks to Michael Rawdon for his groundbreaking work on the timeline.

1890
Peter Death Bredon Wimsey born at Duke's Denver, Norfolk. His birthday is never given.

1900
Harriet Vane born.

1903-8
Attends Eton.

1912
Graduates from Balliol College's School of Modern History with first-class honors.

1914-18
Serves as major in a rifle brigade and sees fighting in France. In one battle, an artillery shell buries him in his bunker. He is rescued by Bunter, his batman, but suffers from trauma.

1921

The Attenbury Emeralds. His first case, which takes place after the April strike by coal miners.

Summer: *The Vindictive Story of the Footsteps that Ran*

1922

Whose Body? Mr. Crimplesham's letter from Salisbury is dated November 192–, and the Dowager Duchess notes that no one can forget about a great war in a year or two. Since "Clouds" opens a year after the events in "Whose Body?" and gives Lord Peter's age as 33, that places the year as 1922.

1923

Clouds of Witness. The story opens in autumn with a 33-year-old Lord Peter coming home from a vacation after the events in "Whose Body?" which places this in October and November.

1924

"The Abominable History of the Man with the Copper Fingers" Most of the story is told in flashback in 1920, but the rest must occur about this time.

1925

April: *The Entertaining Episode of the Article in Question.* The story opens with Lord Peter and Bunter having spent three months in Italy: "Accordingly, it was with no surprise at all that the reliable Bunter, one April morning, received the announcement of an abrupt change of plan."

June: *The Fascinating Problem of Uncle Meleager's Will.* The story opens with "it was a beautiful June that year."

Summer: *The Fantastic Horror of the Cat in the Bag.* Philip Storey on the trans-Atlantic liner says he's off to meet his wife at the lakes: "Very pleasant there in summer."

Fall: *The Learned Adventure of the Dragon's Head.* The key is the age of Peter's nephew, the 10-year-old Viscount St. George (a.k.a., Young Jerry, Jerrykins or Pickled Gherkins). Since in "Gaudy Night," set in 1935, he is 21 or 22, that places this story in 1925, possibly in the fall since he's home from school due to an outbreak of measles.

1925-6

The Unprincipled Affair of the Practical Joker: No date is given, so the story takes place between the fall of 1925 and April of 1926.

1926

April: *Unnatural Death.* Chapter 2 begins with "The April night was clear and chilly, and a brisk wood fire burned in a welcoming manner on the hearth."

1926-7

The Bibulous Business of a Matter of Taste and *The Piscatorial Farce of the Stolen Stomach.*

1927

Aug. 1: *The Unsolved Puzzle of the Man with No Face.* The story opens during the rush at the end of the Bank Holiday weekend, which in 1927 was Saturday, July 30 to Monday, Aug. 1. This assumes that the victim, found dead while swimming, would find the waters of the English Channel too cold during the spring Bank Holiday on June 6.

1927

November-December: *The Unpleasantness at the Bellona*

Club begins on Nov. 11, Armistice Day.

1927

November: *The Undignified Melodrama of the Bone of Contention.* Lord Peter gives the policeman his card and asks him to look up "Chief Inspector Parker." Parker was promoted to that rank between "Bellona Club" and "Strong Poison," and in this story Lord Peter finds himself shivering in "a white November fog" that places the story in November of 1927.

1927-1929

The Adventurous Exploit of the Cave of Ali Baba. This story spans two years, from Lord Peter's "death" until his reappearance. Since his obituary mentioned that he died at 37 "the previous December," that puts the year as 1927.

1929

December: *Strong Poison.* Philip Boyes meets Harriet Vane in 1927, and she agrees to live with him in March 1928. They separate in February of 1929 and Boyes dies on June 23, 1929. Given a month between her first trial, which ends in a hung jury, and the second, combined with Miss Climpson's letter of Jan. 7, 1930, places her trial in December 1929. The judge's comment that Harriet is 29 places her birth year at 1900.

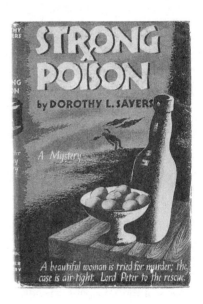

1930

The Nine Tailors. Lord Peter's car runs off the road on New Year's Eve, and Lady Henry's funeral occurs on Saturday, Jan. 4, which places it in 1930. This neatly dovetails with the events in "Strong Poison." In Chapter 15, unable to secure the evidence to free Harriet Vane, Lord Peter gives Miss Climpson the task of acquiring an old woman's will. That is on Dec. 30, 1929. While Miss Climpson is away, Lord Peter has to remain idle, and "to chronicle Lord Peter Wimsey's daily life during the ensuing week would be neither kind nor edifying. An enforced inactivity will produce irritable symptoms in the best of men" (Chapter 16).

On New Year's Eve, Lord Peter drives to Walbeach to visit friends, only to get his car stuck outside Fenchurch St. Paul. He participates in ringing in the New Year, gets his car repaired, and is back on the road on the afternoon of Jan. 1, giving him plenty of time to make it to Walbeach and back to receive Miss Climpson's celebratory letter of Jan. 7 ("Strong Poison," Chapter 19).

Also occurring this year: *The Image in the Mirror, The Incredible Elopement of Lord Peter Wimsey, The Five Red Herrings* and *The Queen's Square.*

1931

June 18: *Have His Carcase.* The chapter headings carry the month and date, and Harriet Vane refers to herself as "the Harriet Vane who was tried for murder two years ago" (Chapter 3). Also, the Christmas party story, *The Necklace of Pearls,* occurs this year.

1933

Murder Must Advertise. The victim dies in May, and this story begins a few weeks later and runs for a month. Followed by *In The Teeth of the Evidence.*

1934

Striding Folly.

1935

Gaudy Night. The Author's Note states that the book occurs in 1935, and Lord Peter is 45 (Chapter 2). The story occurs during the first half of the year. Harriet went travelling after the events in "Have His Carcase" (Chapter 4) and returned around June 1933 to write two novels and several stories based on her experiences, and that she and Peter had only sporadic meetings since then.

1935

Busman's Honeymoon occurs in the same year as "Gaudy Night." Lord Peter is 45 when he weds Harriet on Oct. 8.

1936

Thrones, Dominations. Begins in January and runs through late March. The author's note by Jill Paton Walsh gives dates for the births of Peter and Harriet's three sons: Bredon (Oct. 15, 1936), Roger (1938) and Paul (1941).

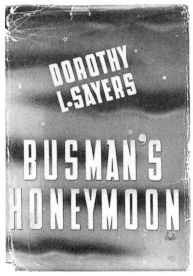

Oct. 15: *The Haunted Policeman* begins when Peter and Harriet's son Bredon is born. See the 1936 note regarding "Thrones, Dominations."

1940

Feb. 10: *A Presumption of Death.* Harriet writes Peter on Feb. 6 and mentions an air-raid rehearsal will take place Saturday after the dance at the village hall.

1942

Talboys. Peter is 52, Bredon is six and Roger is four. Paul would therefore be a year old.

1951

The Attenbury Emeralds. The crime takes place in 1921, and the story is narrated 30 years later, when Lord Peter is 60.

1952

The Late Scholar. Lord Peter is 61 when he is called to Oxford to resolve a scholarly dispute.

Timeline of Dorothy L. Sayers' Life

This chronology draws on Barbara Reynolds' excellent biography for most of its information. Events that occurred without a month or day attached are listed at the head of the appropriate year. All quotes are from Sayers' letters.

1893   *June 13:* Born Dorothy Leigh Sayers in Oxford, the only child of the Rev. Henry Sayers, chaplain of Christ Church Cathedral and headmaster of the choir school, and Helen Mary Leigh. On her father's side, ancestors came from Littlehampton, West Sussex; on her mother's from the Isle of Wight.

1897   Family moves to Bluntisham-cum-Earith, Cambridgeshire, where her father was rector.

1898   Meets Ivy Shrimpton, a cousin eight years older than Dorothy, who would later help raise Dorothy's child.

1899   Taught to read at four, Dorothy begins learning Latin at age six from her father. She also knows how to write in cursive and read newspaper articles.

1901-2   Dorothy and Ivy's friendship deepens. Ivy joins in playing imaginative games, writing stories and poems, and gives Dorothy books such as "Little Women" and "The Ingoldsby Legends."

1906-7   Dorothy reads "The Three Musketeers" in French, identifying with the hopeless romantic Athos. She engages her family in role-playing scenes from the book, and she acquires a musketeer costume, complete with wig and facial hair. She also reads John Milton, Alexander Pope, Samuel Butler, Moliere, and

Thomas Beddoes' "Death's Jest Book," from which she would later draw on for epigrams in "Have His Carcase."

1908   Dorothy plays four pieces on the violin at a village concert in Somersham.

1909   Enters Godolphin School in Salisbury. She takes violin and piano lessons, sings, and has several plays produced.

1911   *Spring:* Dorothy scores highest rank in Cambridge Higher Local Examination with distinctions in French and spoken German. At Godolphin, she contracts measles and double pneumonia and almost dies. She recovers under her mother's care well enough by October to play Shylock in a production of "The Merchant of Venice."

1912   Returns home, possibly from illness, and continues studies by mail.

March: Wins scholarship to Somerville College, Oxford. Godolphin commemorates achievement with plaque in the school hall.

October: Begins studying modern languages and medieval literature at Oxford. Joins Oxford Bach Choir. Forms the Mutual Admiration Society with fellow students, including Muriel "Jim" Jaeger, to read and critique each others works.

1913   Sees Maurice Roy Ridley, a recent Balliol College graduate, when he receives the Newdigate Prize for best composition in English verse. She "fell head over ears in love with him on the spot," and will base Lord Peter Wimsey on his likeness. In 1935, she will see him again when he is chaplain of Balliol and, forgetting her 1913 encounter, calls him "the perfect Peter Wimsey."

1914   *July 30-31:* Arrives with two friends in Le Havre, France, for a vacation. The next day, Germany declares war on Russia and invades Luxembourg. Train travel stopped as France

mobilizes for war. They return to the Sayers' family home at
Bluntisham on Aug. 25

1915   Decides against a career in academia: "I was really
meant to be sociable." Declines father's offer to stay at Oxford
another year and finishes with first-class honours. As was custom
at the time, she was not awarded a degree. Considers training as a
nurse and unsuccessfully applies for a job with the Board of Trade.
Accepts post as French teacher at a school in Hull.

December: The 1915 volume of "Oxford Poetry" appears with a
lay (12 poems) by Dorothy.

1916   Travels to Hull for teaching post. Amid frequent zeppelin
raids, Dorothy moves students away from learning by rote,
encourages them to put on plays in French and forms school choir.

August: At Cambridge, begins translating "Chanson de Roland"
into rhymed couplets, and returns to Hull for autumn term. Father
accepts a living as rector of Christchurch in what is now
Cambridgeshire, and offers to pay for Dorothy's education in
publishing with Basil Blackwell in Oxford. Dorothy accepts and
resigns teaching job as of Easter, 1917.

Dec. 28: Her first book of poetry, "Op. I," is published by
Blackwell Publishing, Oxford, in a limited edition of 350 copies.

1917   *May:* Moves to 17 Long Wall Street, Oxford, and begins
work at Basil Blackwell. After only two meetings, receives
marriage proposal from the Rev. Leonard Hodgson, later Regius
Professor of Divinity at Oxford and Canon of Christ Church. She
turns him down, and his persistence irritates her.

July: Operated on for appendicitis, and while recovering flirts with
the surgeon.

1918   *September:* Dorothy's second book, "Catholic Tales and
Christian Songs" is published by Blackwell.

1919   *January:* Moves to 5 Bath Place, Oxford. Catches German measles.

May: Leaves Blackwell's, finding office work tedious and the company moving away from publishing literature to textbooks. Works as a freelance editor, journalist and teacher. Falls in love with Capt. Eric Whelpton, who suffers from polio, misdiagnosed as epilepsy, that causes fainting fits and amnesia, a detail Dorothy would use in "The Unpleasantness at the Bellona Club."

Whelpton accepts post teaching English in Normandy, France. Dorothy seeks a job in France as well, and Whelpton hires her as his secretary, responsible for organizing exchanges of French and English students. She reads mysteries and mentions to Whelpton her idea of forming a syndicate with Oxford friends to write crime stories.

October: Elected member of Modern Language Association.

Near end of the year, Whelpton falls in love with a married woman in London and becomes bored with his job. Dorothy becomes jealous and comes down with mumps. Asks friend, Murial Jaeger, for Sexton Blake books to read while recuperating.

1920   Turns down Whelpton's offer to buy his share in the business.

June/August: Part of her translated "Tristan" appears in "Modern Languages," the journal of the Modern Language Association, and receives praise in an editorial.

September: Leaves job and moves to London, settling in an unfurnished room at a women's club, 36 St. George's Square, Pimlico. She lives on fees from freelance translating and a stipend from her father. Tries writing film scenarios and begins creating Lord Peter Wimsey.

October: Oxford changes its rules on degrees for women and holds first ceremony. Sayers receives a B.A., followed by a M.A.

Accepts temporary teaching job at Clapham High School. Moves to rooms at 44 Mecklenburg Square that she would give to Harriet Vane in "Gaudy Night." Spends Saturdays reading criminology books at British Museum.

1921   Plans detective story that would become "Whose Body?" and Grand Guignol play (unwritten). Collects material for Wilkie Collins biography, of which only a few chapters would be written.

Summer: Finishes "Whose Body?" at rectory in Christchurch.

November: Sends "Whose Body?" manuscript to be typed and begins "Clouds of Witness."

December: Moves to 24 Great James Street, St. Pancras, London, that would be her London home until her death.

1922   English publishers reject "Whose Body?"

March: Meets Sir Arthur Marshall, barrister and politician, and pumps him for information about the House of Lords and its legal proceedings for "Clouds of Witness." His information came from Lord Russell, who had been tried for bigamy. Applies for job as copywriter with advertising firm S.H. Benson's, accepts offer in June.

April: Signs with agent Andrew Dakers.

Summer: Falls in love with author John Cournos.

July: Boni and Liveright offers $250, no royalties, for U.S. rights to "Whose Body?" Relationship with Cournos falls apart over his desire to use contraceptives (she calls it "that taint of the rubber-shop"). He would leave England in October.

December: Sayers involved with Bill White, a motor car salesman who lives in the flat above Sayers.

1923   *May:* Becomes pregnant by White. He admits he's married, introduces Sayers to his wife, who agrees to see her through the pregnancy. Sayers decides not to tell her elderly parents to protect them. Arranges with cousin Ivy Shrimpton, making a living as a foster parent, to care for her infant. "Whose Body?" published by Boni and Liveright in the U.S.

October: "Whose Body?" published in England by T. Fisher Unwin.

November: Sayers takes leave of absence to give birth in secret. Moves to "mother's hospital" in Southbourne, Hampshire (now Dorset). Bill White's wife moves into Sayers' Great James Street flat to handle mail and care for the cat.

1924   *Jan. 3:* Gives birth to John Anthony Sayers. The doctor is the brother of Bill White's wife, who doesn't know about the affair.

Jan. 30: Gives John Anthony to Ivy Shrimpton to care for, which she does until he reaches maturity. Returns to work at S.H. Benson.

August: Learns John Cournos had married Helen Kestner Satterthwaite, who has two children and writes detective stories under pseudonym Sybil Norton. She writes him to express congratulations, opening correspondence in which they discuss their former relationship. Cournos would portray Sayers and their affair in his novel "The Devil Is an English Gentleman."

1925   Meets Oswald Atherton "Mac" Fleming, a Scottish journalist who suffers from shell-shock after a gas attack during the war.

1926   *February:* "Clouds of Witness" published by T. Fisher Unwin.

April 13: Marries "Mac" Fleming at Holborn Register Office, London. Benson launches Mustard Club advertising campaign, designed by Sayers, for Colman's mustard.

1927   *Sept. 16:* "Unnatural Death," the first of three novels sold to Ernest Benn, published.

1928   Sayers collaborates on a novel with Dr. Eustace Barton, who writes mystery stories under the pseudonym Robert Eustace. They will work on the book throughout the year and in 1930, publish "The Documents in the Case."

July: "The Unpleasantness at the Bellona Club" published by Ernest Benn.

August: Sayers acquires flat about her and begins renovations to provide Mac and her with more space.

September: First volume of "Great Short Stories of Detection, Mystery and Horror" published by Victor Gollancz.

Sept. 20: Rev. Henry Sayers, Dorothy's father, dies of pneumonia. She will portray him as the Rev. Theodore Venables, rector of Fenchurch St. Paul, in "The Nine Tailors."

October: Mac buys "Sunnyside," at house at 24 Newland Street, Withan, Essex for Helen Sayers and her sister, Mabel Leigh.

Nov. 12: "Lord Peter Views the Body," a collection of 12 short stories, published by Gollancz.

Mac leaves News of the World and freelances.

1929   *June:* Sayers and Mac visits Kirkcudbrightshire, Scotland. They will return frequently and Sayers will use this location as the basis for "Five Red Herrings."

July: Translation of "Tristan in Brittany" published by Benn.

July 27: Helen Sayers dies 10 months after her husband's death from an internal stoppage connected with a rupture of the bowel.

August: Successful negotiations with American publishers enable Sayers to leave Benson's at the end of the year.

1930 The Detection Club is formed by a group of mystery writers including Sayers, Agatha Christie, Austin Freeman, E.C. Bentley and Freeman Wills Croft.

February: Finishes "The Documents in the Case."

April: Manuscript of "Strong Poison" sent to Victor Gollancz in response to inquiry as to the title of her next Lord Peter novel.

September: "Strong Poison" published by Gollancz.

July 4: "The Documents in the Case" published by Gollancz.

August: Aunt Mabel Sayers dies suddenly while Sayers and Mac are in Scotland. Sayers invites her mother's sister, Maud Sayers, to stay with them to act as buffer with Mac.

1931 *Feb. 26:* "Five Red Herrings" published.

March: Works on "Have His Carcase" while arranging for hospital treatment of John Anthony's scarlet fever. Mac ill.

July: "Great Short Stories of Detection, Mystery and Horror, Second Series" published by Gollancz.

December: "The Floating Admiral," a collaboration with members of the Detection Club in which Sayers wrote the final chapter, is published by Hodder and Stoughton.

1932 Works on "My Edwardian Childhood," a memoir that she leaves unfinished.

February: Begins "The Nine Tailors." Research into the ringing of church bells proves longer than expected, and she writes "Murder Must Advertise" to meet her publishing deadline. Continues work on Collins biography, in which five chapters are written before it is abandoned.

April 11: "Have His Carcase" published by Gollancz.

1933   *Feb. 6:* "Murder Must Advertise" published by Gollancz.

May: "Hangman's Holiday" a collection of 12 short stories, four of them involving Lord Peter, published by Gollancz.

"Ask a Policeman" another collaboration with the Detection Club, published by Arthur Barker. Sayers also begins two years of weekly book reviews for the Sunday Times, which requires reading as much as two novels a day.

November: Visits Muriel St. Clare Byrne on a vacation to discuss separating from Mac. She decides against it.

1934   During the year, Sayers works on autobiographical novel "Cat o' Mary" under the pseudonym of Johanna Leigh, that is abandoned after 200 pages.

January: "The Nine Tailors" published by Gollancz.

June 13: Attends gaudy at Somerville College, which would inspire "Gaudy Night."

1935   "The Silent Passenger" a Lord Peter movie with a scenario written by Sayers, appears in a greatly altered form.

February: Works on "Busman's Honeymoon," a Lord Peter play with Muriel St. Clare Byrne.

March: Lectures at Oxford on "Aristotle and the Art of Detective Fiction." Meets Roy Ridley, recognizing him as Lord Peter's double (and forgetting that she was inspired by him in 1913).

September: Eleven-year-old John Anthony is told he has been "adopted" by Cousin Dorothy and Cousin Mac and his surname would be Fleming. He is asked not to reveal that his "mother" is

Dorothy L. Sayers, ostensibly to keep away fans.

Nov. 4: "Gaudy Night" published by Gollancz.

1936   "Papers Relating to the Family of Wimsey," a pamphlet of "historical" material about the family created for their amusement by Sayers and her friends, including heraldry expert Wilfrid Scott-Giles, privately printed. Begins "Thrones, Domination," the 13th Lord Peter novel, but abandons it after writing six chapters and outlining the plot. It would be finished by Jill Paton Walsh and published in 1998.

October: Asked by Margaret Babington, organizer of the Canterbury Festival, to write a play for next year's festival.

November: Rehearsals begin for "Busman's Honeymoon." The play opens on Dec. 16 at London's Comedy Theatre. Reviews are positive and it runs for nine months. In an article, she writes that Lord Peter has become "a permanent resident in the house of my mind."

1937   "Busman's Honeymoon" published by Gollancz.

June 12: "The Zeal of Thy House," a play about the architect who rebuilt the central portion of the cathedral after the fire of 1176, opens in Canterbury Cathedral. Sayers attends opening night with her friends. Mac stays home.

1938   BBC invites Sayers to write a nativity play for Children's Hour. She writes "He That Should Come," using everyday speech with no suggestion of reverence, that's broadcast on Christmas Day.

March: Strand magazine publishes "The Haunted Policeman," a short story about Lord Peter and the birth of his first son.

August: Visits Venice for three weeks. During the frequent rainstorms, passes time writing comic-romantic play set partly in Venice entitled "Love All." It will be produced in 1940.

1939 "In the Teeth of the Evidence," 17 short stories, including two involving Lord Peter, published by Gollancz.

"The Devil to Pay" about Doctor Faustus, opens at the Canterbury Festival. It is moved to London in August to His Majesty's Theatre, where it closes due in part to the German declaration of war on Sept. 3.

May: Sayers offers her services to the Director of Public Relations for the War Office. Her work on two secret pamphlets was halted in September after the ministry found her difficult to work with.

October: "The Idea of a Christian Society," a pamphlet based on three lectures given at Corpus Christi College, Cambridge, is published by Gollancz.

November: Writes first of 11 letters for the Spectator about Lord Peter's family and their response to the war on the home front. These will form the basis for Jill Paton Walsh's second Lord Peter novel, "Presumption of Death."

1940 *Feb. 5:* The director of religious broadcasting for the BBC asks Sayers to write a series of half-hour radio plays for children on the life of Christ.

April: The comic play "Love All" debuts at the Torch Theatre in Knightsbridge. It was not a success.

August: The movie "Busman's Honeymoon" ("Haunted Honeymoon" in the U.S.) released. Robert Montgomery played Lord Peter to Constance Cummings' Harriet and Sir Seymour Hicks' Bunter.

Nov. 5: Mails first play, "Kings in Judaea," in the "The Man Born to Be King" series to BBC producer. Despite praise from readers and promises of cooperation, the producer's assistant suggests changes, which Sayers rejects out of hand, refusing "to argue about my plays to a committee."

1941   *Jan. 8:* Presents paper on "The Church's Responsibility" at a conference in Malvern, discussing the role of the Anglican Church in the reconstruction of civilization after the war.

Feb. 2: The BBC asks her to prepare six ten-minute talks on the Nicene Creed, which would occupy her until July. Sayers also lectures across the country.

July: "The Mind of the Maker" published.

December: John Anthony wins scholarship to Balliol, Oxford, Lord Peter's college. He delays entering until 1945 by joining the Royal Air Force.

Dec. 10: At a press conference to publicize the "King" broadcasts, Sayers reads a section from "The Heirs to the Kingdom." Her interpretation of Matthew in a Cockney accent speaking modern English causes an uproar and sparks opposition from Christian groups. Sayers resists changing the text to appease pressure groups, and the BBC sends copies of the second and third plays to its Central Religious Advisory Committee for their approval, which they give.

Dec. 21: The first play in the series, "Kings in Judaea," is broadcast to near-universal praise.

1942   *Jan. 25:* The second play, "The King's Herald," is broadcast.

Writes "Talboys," her last Lord Peter short story, that would not be published until after her death.

1943   The scripts for "The Man Born to Be King" are published by Gollancz. The Archbishop of Canterbury offers Sayers a Doctor of Divinity degree which she turns down with thanks.

June: Turns down request to submit paper to religious conference, promising to give up speaking on religious subjects. She does not always succeed.

1944   *August:* During an air raid, takes a copy of Dante's "Inferno" into the shelter. Decides to translate the work, a task that will occupy the rest of her life.

1945   Sayers learns her German music mistress from the Godolphin School survived the war in Germany. Sends her food parcels and clothes until her death in 1948.

1946-1957   Occupied with lecturing on Dante and translating his works. She would finish "Hell" and "Purgatory" but die before finishing "Paradise." She also translates "Chanson de Roland."

1946   Writes "The Just Vengeance" for the Lichfield Cathedral festival.

1949   "The Comedy of Dante Alighieri the Florentine. Cantica I: Hell" published by Penguin Classics. "The Zeal of Thy House" revived in Canterbury. Sayers elected president of the Detection Club, a post she will hold until her death.

Oct. 24: Writes to a fellow mystery writer that she is so "sickened by importunity" to write another Lord Peter story that the thought of doing so "fills me with distaste."

1950   *June 9:* Mac dies at 68 of a cerebral hemorrhage at Sunnyside Cottage, Witham, Essex.

June: Visits S.H. Benson's to unveil a plaque commemorating the circular staircase used in "Murder Must Advertise."

1951   Writes "The Emperor Constantine" for the Colchester Festival and participates in designing props and costumes for its production.

March: Ivy Shrimpton dies at 70 of broncho-pneumonia and measles. She wills her estate to Sayers, who turns it over to

Anthony.

1955 "The Comedy of Dante Alighieri the Florentine. Cantica II: Purgatory" published by Penguin Classics.

March 25: Writes that the last thing she wishes to be known for was as a "writer of Christian Apologetics."

1957 *Dec. 17:* Dies suddenly from a stroke at Sunnyside Cottage, Witham, Essex. She is cremated and her ashes buried beneath the tower of St. Anne's Church, Soho, London, where she had been a churchwarden.

1962 "The Comedy of Dante Alighieri the Florentine. Cantica III: Paradise," finished by Barbara Reynolds, published by Penguin Classics.

1973 "Striding Folly," containing the last three Lord Peter short stories, the title story, "The Haunted Policeman," and "Talboys," published by New English Library.

1998 *Feb. 5:* "Thrones, Dominations" by Dorothy L. Sayers and Jill Paton Walsh, based on the novel abandoned in 1938, published by Hodder & Stoughton.

2002 *Nov. 7:* "A Presumption of Death" by Dorothy L. Sayers and Jill Paton Walsh, based on the Spectator's Lord Peter letters, published by Hodder & Stoughton.

2010 *Sept. 16:* "The Attenbury Emeralds" by Jill Paton Walsh published by Hodder & Stoughton.

2013 *Dec. 5:* "The Late Scholar by Jill Paton Walsh published by Hodder & Stoughton.

The Lord Peter Novels And Short Stories

THE NOVELS
Whose Body? (1923)
Clouds of Witness (1926)
Unnatural Death (published in the U.S. as The Dawson Pedigree) (1927)
The Unpleasantness at the Bellona Club (1928)
Strong Poison (1930)
Five Red Herrings (published in the U.S. as Suspicious Characters) (1931)
Have His Carcase (1932)
Murder Must Advertise (1933)
The Nine Tailors (1934)
Gaudy Night (1935)
Busman's Honeymoon (1937)

With Jill Paton Walsh
Thrones, Dominations (1998)
A Presumption of Death (2002)
The Attenbury Emeralds (2010)
The Late Scholar (2014)

THE SHORT STORIES
(Collected in Lord Peter)
The Abominable History of the Man With the Copper Fingers
The Entertaining Episode of the Article in Question
The Fascinating Problem of Uncle Meleager's Will
The Fantastic Horror of the Cat in the Bag
The Unprincipled Affair of the Practical Joker
The Undignified Melodrama of the Bone of Contention
The Vindictive Story of the Footsteps That Ran
The Bibulous Business of a Matter of Taste

The Learned Adventure of the Dragon's Head
The Piscatorial Farce of the Stolen Stomach
The Unsolved Puzzle of the Man with No Face
The Adventurous Exploit of the Cave of Ali Baba
The Image in the Mirror
The Incredible Elopement of Lord Peter Wimsey
The Queen's Square
The Necklace of Pearls
In the Teeth of the Evidence
Absolutely Elsewhere
Striding Folly
The Haunted Policeman
Talboys

Acknowledgments

When Harriet Vane is advised in "Gaudy Night" that we know when we have an overmastering passion for a subject when it has overmastered us, I recognized a bit of wisdom that has served me well through the years. The amusing irony is that my overmastering passion has been for the works of Dorothy L. Sayers, which inspired my annotations on my website at www.planetpeschel.com as well as this book. If I had known that this project was going to require an understanding of Greek philosophy, the works of Shakespeare, Robert Burns and John Donne, the rules of royal precedence, British society of the 1920s and a dozen other subjects, I would have paid more attention to my education.

But one can do only one's best, and this is mine. Fortunately, "The Complete, Annotated Whose Body?" was improved with the help of many hands, and to them I owe my thanks and gratitude.

To John Mark Ockerbloom and Mary Mark Ockerbloom, whose transcription of the first edition of "Whose Body?" was the basis for this edition.

To Dan Drake, who published the first annotation to the novel many years ago.

To Michael Rawdon, whose timeline of the Lord Peter stories inspired and formed the basis of my effort.

To the contributors to the Lord Peter Wimsey group at Yahoo for providing insightful commentary on the works.

To Barbara Reynolds, whose biography "Dorothy L. Sayers: Her Life and Soul" and editions of Sayers' letters are well worth reading and re-reading.

To the many contributors and fans of the Annotated Wimsey at www.planetpeschel.com, whose praise, advice and suggestions have kept the still unfinished project alive these many years.

Finally, to Teresa, my enabler and inspiration. My acushla.

Bill Peschel
Hershey, Pennsylvania
May 22, 2011

BIBLIOGRAPHY

General

Asimov, Isaac. *Asimov's Guide to Shakespeare.* New York: Avenel Books, 1978.

Brabazon, James. *Dorothy L. Sayers: A Biography.* New York: Charles Scribners' Sons, 1981.

Hone, Ralph E. *Dorothy L. Sayers: A Literary Biography.* Kent, Ohio: Kent State University Press, 1979.

"Pork Packer's Wisdom," *The New York Times,* Oct. 11, 1902. Accessed Dec. 27, 2010.

Rawdon, Michael, "Timeline of Lord Peter Wimsey," *Dorothy L. Sayers: The Lord Peter Wimsey Stories,* http://www.leftfield.org/~rawdon/books/mystery/sayers.html, accessed Oct. 19, 2010.

Reynolds, Barbara. *Dorothy L. Sayers: Her Life and Soul.* New York: St. Martin's Griffin. 1993.

Room, Adrian. *Brewer's Dictionary of Phrase and Fable,* 16th edition. New York: HarperResource, 1999.

Walsh, William Shepard. *Handy-book of Literary Curiosities.* New York: J.B. Lippincott Co., 1892.

Wikipedia

True-Crime Cases (Adolf Beck, Brides in the Bath, Edmond De La Pommerais, William Palmer)

Altick, Richard Daniel. *Victorian Studies in Scarlet: Murders and Manners in the Age of Victoria.* New York: W.W. Norton, 1970.

Burnaby, Evelyn Henry Villebois. *Memories of Famous Trials.* London: Sisley's Ltd., 1907.

Curtis, Lewis Perry. *Jack the Ripper and the London Press.* New Haven, Conn.: Yale University Press, 2001.

Gaute, J.H.H. and Robin Odell. *The Murderers' Who's Who.* New York: Pan Books, 1980.

Griffiths, Arthur. *Mysteries of Police and Crime: A General*

Survey of Wrongdoing and Its Pursuit. Cassell and Co., 1899.

Headsman. "1864: Doctor Edmond-Desire Couty de la Pommerais, poisoner," *Executed Today,* http://www.executedtoday. com/2009/06/09/1864-doctor-edmond-desire-couty-de-la-pommerais-poisoner/, accessed Oct. 19, 2010.

McClure's Magazine, Volume 39, "Marie Belloc Lowndes".

The Medical Times and Gazette, a Journal of Medical Science, Literature, Criticism, and News. London: J.&A. Churchill, 1881.

Nash, Jay Robert. *Great Pictorial History of World Crime: Murder.* New York: Scarecrow Press, 2004.

Ramsland, Katherine, "Auguste Ambroise Tardeau: Investigator's Methods Become the Standard for Future Forensic Scientists," *The Forensic Examiner,* http://www.theforensicexaminer.com/archive/fall08/1/, accessed Oct. 19, 2010.

Ramsland, Katherine, "Forensic Toxicology," *TruTv,* http://www. trutv.com/library/crime/criminal_mind/forensics/toxicology/9. html, accessed Oct. 19, 2010.

Symonds, Julian. *Pictorial History of Crime.* New York: Crown, 1966.

Wood, Walter, ed. *Survivor's Tales of Famous Crimes.* London: Cassell and Company, 1916.

Argentina

Paolera, Gerardo Della and Alan M. Taylor. *A New Economic History of Argentina, Volume 1.* Cambridge: Cambridge University Press, 2003.

Paolera, Gerardo Della and Alan M. Taylor. *Straining at the Anchor: The Argentine Currency Board and the Search for Macroeconomic Stability, 1880-1935.* Chicago: University of Chicago Press, 2001.

Taylor, Alan M., "Three Phases of Argentine Economic Growth: A Summary," *The Cliometric Society,* http://cliometrics.org/ conferences/ASSA/Jan_93/Alan_Taylor_Abstract/index.html, accessed Feb. 25, 2011.

Cable Codes

Unicode: The Universal Telegraphic Phrase-book. London:

Cassell & Co., Ltd., 1889. Available at Google Books, accessed Jan. 18, 2011.

Jews in England
"A Chronology of the Jews in Britain," *Jewish Virtual Library,* http://www.jewishvirtuallibrary.org/jsource/vjw/ukchron.htm, accessed Aug. 20, 2010.
Hitchens, Christopher, "The Toxin of Anti-Semitism Isn't a Threat Only to Jews," *Jerusalem Center for Public Affairs,* http://www.jcpa.org/dje/articles3/british.htm, accessed Oct. 12, 2010.
"Jewish History 1920-1929," *Jewish History,* http://www. jewishhistory.org.il/history.php, accessed Oct. 12, 2010.

Omnibus
Quinion, Michael. "The Odd History of Omnibus." *World Wide Words,* www.worldwidewords.org/articles/omnibus.htm, accessed Feb. 25, 2011.

About The Authors

One of the great mystery novelists of the 20th century,
DOROTHY L. SAYERS was born in Oxford in 1893 and was
one of the first women to be granted a degree by Oxford
University. She wrote more than a dozen Lord Peter novels and
short stories, and three more novels were written by Jill Paton
Walsh. Sayers was also noted for her Christian writings and plays
and her translation of Dante. She died in 1957.

BILL PESCHEL Bill Peschel is a former journalist who shares a
Pulitzer Prize with the staff of *The Patriot-News* in Harrisburg, Pa.
He also is a mystery fan who runs the Wimsey Annotations at
Planetpeschel.com. The author of *Writers Gone Wild* (Penguin), he
publishes the 223B Casebook Series of Sherlockian parodies and
pastiches and annotated editions of novels by Dorothy L. Sayers and
Agatha Christie. He lives with his family and animal menagerie in
Hershey, where the air really does smell like chocolate.

The Complete, Annotated Series

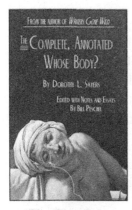

The Complete, Annotated Whose Body?
Dorothy L. Sayers

The Complete, Annotated Mysterious Affair at Styles
Agatha Christie

The Complete, Annotated Deluxe Secret Adversary
Agatha Christie

The 223B Casebook Series

Classic and newly discovered fanfiction written during Arthur Conan Doyle's life, with original art plus extensive historical notes.

The Early Punch Parodies of Sherlock Holmes
Parodies, book reviews, & cartoons. Includes parodies by R.C. Lehmann and P.G. Wodehouse. *281 pages.*

Victorian Parodies & Pastiches: 1888-1899
With stories by Conan Doyle, Robert Barr, Jack Butler Yeats, and James M. Barrie. *279 pages.*

Edwardian Parodies & Pastiches I: 1900-1904
With stories by Mark Twain, Finley Peter Dunn, John Kendrick Bangs, and P.G. Wodehouse. *390 pages.*

Edwardian Parodies & Pastiches II: 1905-1909
With stories by 'Banjo' Paterson, Max Beerbohm, Carolyn Wells, and Lincoln Steffens. *401 pages.*

Great War Parodies and Pastiches I: 1910-1914
With stories by O. Henry, Maurice Baring, and Stephen Leacock. *362 pages.*

Great War Parodies and Pastiches II: 1915-1919
With stories by Ring Lardner, Carolyn Wells, and a young George Orwell. *390 pages.*

Jazz Age Parodies and Pastiches I: 1920-1924
With stories by Dashiell Hammett, James Thurber, and Arthur Conan Doyle. *353 pages.*

Jazz Age Parodies and Pastiches II: 1925-1930
With stories by August Derleth, Frederic Dorr Steele, and Edgar Wallace. *373 pages.*

ALSO: The Best of the 223B Casebook, featuring the best stories from 1888 to 1930.

The Rugeley Poisoner Series

Meet the murderer who inspired Christie and Sayers

The Rugeley Poisoner Vol. 1
Edited by Bill Peschel

The Rugeley Poisoner Vol. 2
Edited by Bill Peschel

The Rugeley Poisoner Vol. 3
George Fletcher * Bill Peschel

The Illustrated Life and Career of William Palmer
(1856)

- Gossip about Palmer, racing scams, and London's fleshpots.
- More than 50 restored woodcuts.
- Excerpts from Palmer's love letters. *225 pages.*

The Times Report of the Trial of William Palmer
(1856)

- The *Times'* trial transcript edited, corrected, & annotated.
- More than 50 original woodcuts restored to better-than-new condition. *426 pages.*

The Life and Career of Dr. William Palmer of Rugeley
(1925)

- Written by a doctor who interviewed witnesses and jurors.
- Rare photos and art.
- Essays on Palmer's impact on culture, strychnine, and Rugeley. *227 pages.*

The trial in London's Old Bailey, from "The Times Report of the Trial of William Palmer."

The Casebook
of Twain and Holmes

Beloved Humorist. Best-Selling Author.
Consulting Detective.

Meet Mark Twain like you never knew him.

Now it can be told: Mark Twain knew Sherlock Holmes. And Dr. Watson. And Mycroft Holmes. And Irene Adler.

In these seven stories, Mark Twain seeks Holmes' to get out of paying blackmail over his dirty manuscript, nearly gets poisoned by arsenic, goes grave-robbing, and runs a boxing scam. But that's not the only trouble he finds in Holmes' world. He meets the young noble idiot Watson in Gold Rush San Francisco's Chinatown, explains why a young Mycroft Holmes kept him from telling everything about Tangier in "The Innocents Abroad," and as for Irene Adler and the duel in Heidelberg -- well, Sherlock wasn't the only man who underestimated her.

Bill Peschel, the Pulitzer-Prize winning editor, uncovers the Mark Twain the biographers missed. With his characteristic wit and verve, Twain late in life recounted these stories as part of his autobiography, then at the last minute scrawled BURN THESE on the box and gave them to his maid. More than a hundred years later, they turned up at a Carlisle, Pa., farm auction.

As he did with the annotated editions of Agatha Christie's novels, Peschel transcribed the manuscripts, added explanatory notes and contemporary art, but mostly got out of the way to let Twain tell his wild tales about Sherlock and company. You'll never look at Conan Doyles' stories the same.

The book contains seven short stories: four featuring Holmes, and one each featuring Watson, Mycroft Holmes, and Irene Adler. They were first published in the eight-volume 223B Casebook series featuring Sherlockian parodies and pastiches from Arthur Conan Doyle's lifetime.